Praise for Lynda Curnyn's previous novels

BOMBSHELL

"The hook is the laugh-out-loud humor mixed with just the right amount of Mae West *savoir faire* and iced with the Carrie Bradshaw insight we all know and love. This one is a page turner in the truest sense of the word."
—*Zink Magazine*

"Things like the right touch on personal issues, the allusion to a romantic happy ending and fully realized characters—such as Grace's wonderful adopted parents and her age-phobic boss 'Claud-zilla'—make *Bombshell* an endearing, enjoyable and uplifting read for women of all ages."
—*Romantic Times*

"This is the writer's third novel and it's her best yet. The heroine is sexy, beautiful, smart and likeable. The hero is lovable, lost and handsome. The story is rich with detail that gives you great insight into their characters. A grown-up chick lit story you will want to keep."
—*Rendezvous*

ENGAGING MEN

"Curnyn delivers another fun and frothy crowd-pleaser."
—*Booklist*

"This dose of chick lit features entertaining supporting characters and may inspire readers to think about what they really want out of relationships and life."
—*Romantic Times*

"*Engaging Men* is a truly funny and thoroughly enjoyable read."
—*Romance Reviews Today*

CONFESSIONS OF AN EX-GIRLFRIEND

"First-time novelist Curnyn pens an easy, breezy first novel that's part *Sex and the City* with more heart and part Bridget Jones with less booze."
  —*Publishers Weekly*

"A diverse cast of engaging, occasionally offbeat characters, the hilarious sayings attributed to them, and a fast-paced style facilitated by Emma's pithy sound-bite 'confessions' add to the fun in a lively Manhattan-set story..."
  —*Library Journal*

"Readers will eagerly turn the pages."
  —*Booklist*

Lynda Curnyn

Killer Summer

**RED
DRESS
INK**

First edition June 2005

KILLER SUMMER

A Red Dress Ink novel

ISBN 0-373-89522-4

www.RedDressInk.com

Printed in U.S.A.

For my brother, Brian

Acknowledgments

This book was born during one hot summer on Fire Island, and so I must thank my wonderful housemates, for barely batting an eye while I plotted in their midst.

First and foremost, my dear friend Linda Guidi, who convinced me that life is just better at the beach. Thank you for your inspiration, for sharing your knowledge of the leather industry and for the killer title!

My lovable hosts, Jane and Gregg Weisser, who opened their beautiful beach house to me, fed me gourmet meals and even let me walk their dog, Sophie. And outside of the house, the dog and the good eats, all resemblances to real life, purely coincidental.

For helping me keep my facts straight, I'm indebted to Bryan Mechutan, for giving me the scoop on the music business (and for the TLC). Andrew Rauchberg, whose considerable brain I picked regarding the life and times of a law student. Detective Lieutenant Jack Fitzpatrick, Commanding Officer of the Suffolk County Homicide Squad, for patiently answering my questions. Joe Scotto di Carlo, aka Uncle Joe, my favorite garmento, for brainstorming plot ideas about the garment industry. (Any mistakes are mine, of course.)

Many thanks to Sarah Mlynowski, who suggested I put a dead body in this story and who lugged my drafts on airplanes to read. Lisa Sklar, for listening to my ever-changing plot ideas and for lots of emotional support. Robert Clegg, for helping me hash out plot details. Anne Canadeo, for all sorts of writerly advice, but especially the use of earplugs.

My fabulous agent, Laura Dail, whose publishing savvy and outlook eased my transition to the full-time writer's life.

A huge thank-you (and a big hug) to my wonderful editor, Joan Marlow Golan, who went the extra mile to guide me on my first mystery. Thanks to Anna Cory-Watson, superb editorial assistant. Margaret O'Neill Marbury and everyone at Red Dress Ink for letting me push the boundaries of the genre with this book. And a special thanks to Pam Lawson, for her kind patience and for keeping the production gods at bay.

And as always, lots of love and thanks to my family, especially my mother, for endless support.

 Prologue

Maggie
What a way to spend a Saturday night.
Kismet, Fire Island, 10:00 p.m.

I'd always heard that when you die, your whole life flashes before your eyes.

In my case, it was a song. Janis Joplin. Good ol' Janis. She was always there when I needed her. Of course, "Freedom's Just Another Word for Nothing Left to Lose" has a whole new meaning once you're floating facedown in the tide.

The water was so cold. Even colder now that I had been left alone. But as I learned, just moments before I took my last breath, I've always been alone.

Who knew death would make an existentialist out of me?

Kind of ironic that my husband was once a lifeguard. That was when Tom was a teenager spending summers on the shores of North Carolina. He used to brag to everyone in earshot that he had saved seven lives over the course of two summers. Oh, Tom was everybody's hero. At one time, he was even mine.

But not now. Definitely not now.

Of course, I probably deserved to drown. I wasn't, after all, the best wife.

God, what a waste. My life. My marriage…

Even my death was a disappointment. Tom once told me that something like three thousand people a year die in drowning incidents. Well, la-di-da. Now I'm a fucking statistic.

I just wished I had some clothes on. I knew there was a reason I never skinny-dipped before. Too many opportunities for humiliation. This was worse than humiliating. It was downright pathetic.

I can just see the headlines now: LONELY MILLIONAIRE'S WIFE DROWNS DURING DRUNKEN FIFTY-YARD DASH. I wasn't even that drunk. Or swimming. But after ten years of marriage and more than my share of disappointment, I have discovered that nothing is ever what it seems.

# Prologue

Zoe
How I would have spent my summer vacation

There's nothing worse than being alone on the ferry to Fire Island on a Saturday night. Okay, there is something worse. Being on the ferry to Fire Island with two bags too many when you're really only going to get one day of beach time. If I even got that, I thought, looking out the window at the dark, overcast sky.

I wasn't even sure why I had bothered, though I did have some niggling thought that it had a lot to do with the three voice-mail messages I had received from my best friend, Sage.

"At least come out on Saturday morning," was the first. This in response to my message, declaring that I wouldn't be done with work until late Friday night. A rather pathetic declaration on my part, considering the financial compensation I was receiving for this particular job. I'm a documentary filmmaker—an award-winning documentary filmmaker, I might add. But before you get too impressed with me, note that the award was received four years ago for a piece on the homeless and that my current film was a digital short for dogsnatchers.com, paid for by a sixty-four-year-old widow who'd had her King Charles spaniel snatched in Washington Square Park. Not the kind of thing PBS will be airing any time soon. Still, it was a job, and since I hadn't had a job in about three months, I wasn't about to argue for beach time with the one person I had come across of late who was willing to bankroll me.

"You're not done yet?" was the second message from Sage. Sage is a sales rep for Edge Leather, which means she has the good fortune of being able to do a job she loves between the hours of 9:00 a.m. and 5:00 p.m. In fact, when I missed our last two beach weekends, she acted like I had committed a federal offense. I suppose she had every right to be offended, seeing as she did put up half the money for my share when I couldn't come up with the cash.

Okay, so maybe that was the real reason I was on this ferry. It was hard to say no to Sage, which was probably why I'd let her slap down the remaining deposit in the first place. At this point, I wasn't even sure I needed a day of beach time, much less a summer. After a Saturday spent explaining to Adelaide Gibson why I thought we should edit down the six hours of home footage she had given me featuring Fifi running in the park, Fifi lying on Adelaide's French provincial sofa, Fifi nipping playfully at Adelaide's designer pumps, I just wanted to go home and sleep through next Wednesday.

"You better be coming out tonight." That was the last message I'd received, about four this afternoon. I could only assume the reason I hadn't heard from Sage since was because she was either mad at me for blowing off two of the sixteen beach weekends she begged me to take on, or because she'd given up on me.

Or because she knew I wouldn't say no to Maggie, who had also left me a message this afternoon. "I've decided to make grilled spicy lamb with coriander sauce," she'd announced merrily to my voice-mail box, "and we have no coriander in the house!" Maggie Landon is probably the only person I've ever known who might find a lack of coriander in her beach house peculiar. I might not even have known her either, if it hadn't been for Sage, who managed to wangle us shares in her boss's beach house. No easy task, mind you, since Maggie and her husband, Tom, hadn't even opened up their house to shareholders until this summer. But for Sage, who had a way of seducing everyone over to her point of view, it was a no-brainer for her to land sixteen weekends in an oceanfront house for her, me and Nick, Nick being Sage's other best friend and beneficiary of her endless— and somewhat strenuous—generosity.

Truth be told, until I'd gotten that message from Maggie, asking me to pick up not only coriander, but a Vidalia onion and "a crisp, citrusy white" because she had also discovered, much to her horror, that she only had a chardonnay at the house, I was thinking about staying home. I had missed two of the three weekends of our share so far—what was one more? But apparently the market at Kismet, the hamlet on Fire Island where our house was located, didn't carry most of these items, and since, as Maggie went on to say, I was the only shareholder still on the mainland, she "surely hoped" it wouldn't be a problem for me to pick up a few things. So of course I went to the market for her, even though, as a vegetarian, I wouldn't even be able to partake in the main course. I had been forbidden by Sage to deny our happy hosts anything. Sage had only two conditions when we took these shares: that we have a good time, and that we not offend Tom and Maggie. As for offending her boss—well, I think I might have already done that tonight. As for having fun…

I wasn't even sure I knew how to do that anymore.

Don't get me wrong. I love the beach. Sage, Nick and I had practically grown up on it, the beach being one of the perks of our long-suffering Long Island youth. I'd left lazy summer days on the beach behind when I moved to Manhattan during college, but three summers ago Sage had joined the ranks of those urbanites who flee to the shore and had been badgering me to get on the bandwagon ever since. I hadn't been able to allow myself such an indulgence—not with my income. But I had come out as Sage's guest last summer, and during one brief shining moment, I had even bought into the dream while sitting on what was likely the very same ferry.

Except last time I wasn't alone. Wasn't sitting in the damp, half-empty bowels of the boat, breathing in a nauseating mix of sea and fuel. That evening I was with my then-boyfriend, Myles, on the top of the ferry with the wind in my hair, the sun setting and splitting the sky open into a spectrum of color that always induced a kind of silent wonder in me. Myles had felt it, too. I could tell by the way his fingers paused in the midst of the gentle circle he was making on my shoulder. Once the sun had dipped beneath the horizon, we both looked at one another and vowed to come back next summer. "Maybe we can even get our own house," he had said, a bit of a heady claim, since, at the time, our combined income didn't even come near the median household income required to support a Manhattan existence, much less a Manhattan-plus-beach-rental existence. But we had just turned the bend on our second year together and were still in that blissful state where everything seemed possible.

By February, when it came time to put down the first deposit, even a shared oceanfront room seemed too much for Myles. "I don't know, Zoe. Sixteen weekends is a big commitment," he'd said.

By April, the relationship I had once imagined would see me through the rest of my life was over.

Of course, backing out of the beach house was not an option for me at that point. "What are you gonna do in the city all summer by yourself?" Sage demanded. When I pointed out that I wouldn't exactly be alone, that surely some of the eight million people who lived on the island of Manhattan wouldn't be fleeing to the shore, she simply rolled her eyes at me. She knew as well as I did that out of those eight million people, there were only a handful I could truly claim as company. Actually, less than a handful. When Myles had dumped me, he'd taken with him the smattering of friends I had adopted as my own. Now I was left with Sage and Nick, Nick being more Sage's friend than mine, but who was counting?

"When was the last time we did anything together?" Sage said, and it was this last comment that had me slapping down the first five hundred bucks for a deposit, whether out of guilt at being one of those women who had ditched her friends in favor of her boyfriend, or because I believed what I needed most in the post-Myles phase was the solid bolstering of a summer spent with friends.

"Is this yours?"

I looked up to see an overly freckled, lanky teenager holding a somewhat bruised Vidalia onion. "Uh, yeah," I said, my gaze dropping to the shopping bag I'd placed on the floor beside my seat. It now gaped open, making me wonder what other vital ingredients I had lost. Not that it mattered. Because the other bit of ridiculousness was that I had missed the earlier ferry because I couldn't locate a jar of coriander in a timely manner. The first two stores I'd tried had sold out of the stuff. Who knew coriander was in such high demand? Though I did finally find a bottle at Gourmet Garage, I had missed my train and was out of the running for anything but the late ferry. Which meant that, despite all my efforts to please Maggie, I had failed miserably. I had left her a message, but whether she'd had to postpone her gourmet meal until ten when my ferry arrived, or whether she'd been forced to bag the whole thing and was sitting fuming at me over a badly cooked burger at one of the two restaurants in Kismet, was anyone's guess.

"Um, thanks," I said, taking the onion from the kid with a grateful smile, though what I had to be grateful for at the moment was beyond me.

"Where're you going?" he said, making me realize that this kid was not some eager do-gooder but none other than an employee of the Fire Island Ferry Company. At least that's what his T-shirt said.

"Kismet. Roundtrip." I hadn't even arrived yet and I couldn't wait to get home. He handed me a ticket and I forked over the $12.50 fare. That was another thing I hadn't remembered when I'd signed on for this share. Between the train, the ferry and the taxi between the two, the commute alone cost nearly thirty bucks. After I handed over my cash and watched the boy amble over to the few remaining passengers, I knew why I didn't remember how much this trip cost. Myles had paid that first time we'd come out.

I would despise Myles for walking away from me after I had suffered through law school with him if I didn't understand *why* he felt it necessary to walk away. He had recently turned thirty. His father had just died. I knew these were the kind of mind-altering events that might make a person do irrational things. I should know. My father hadn't died, but he'd left when I was ten and was as good as dead to me, because I hadn't seen him since. And I had rounded the corner on thirty a full two months before

Myles did. Yes, I'd felt the chill of age coming on, the clutch of anxiety that comes from not having lived up to my own expectations. Not that I felt a need to dump *him*.

Okay, so now I was angry. And even more nauseous as the ferry jumped over a wave that would have surely sent a spray on my face if I had been sitting on the top of the ferry in the setting sun like I had that time with Myles. But there was no sun—not even a star—and there was, of course, no Myles. I wasn't even sure there would be Sage, since my cell phone battery died on the train and I couldn't let her know I was on my way. Sage, who acted as if her whole happiness this weekend was dependent on my arrival, if those messages she'd left were any indication. Sage, who had likely hooked up with the bartender, or the guy she'd been flirting with who worked the docks, or any one of the other myriad men she had at her fingertips, and forgotten all about me. Sage, whose biggest worry in life was whether or not there was fresh lime for her tequila.

"Kismet," the scrawny fare collector bellowed, practically in my ear, now that he was done collecting fares from the few other idiots braving this late night ferry ride. "The first stop on this ferry will be Kismet!" I looked out the window, trying to figure out just how far from the dock we were, but all I could see was the darkness and what seemed liked endless water.

Yeah, Kismet.

Everyone gets what they deserve, I guess.

Including me.

2

Sage
Beach Blanket Boomerang

"It's not that I don't want to…"

I paused as I pulled on my jeans, giving Chad's hard-on a meaningful look. "Well, that's clear at least."

"C'mon, Sage, you know what I mean."

"I'm not sure I do," I replied, bending to search the floor for the tank I had tossed off in a frenzy of passion. Passion? That was a laugh. This kid wouldn't know real passion if it bit him in the ass. Maybe that was the problem, I thought, locating my tank top and yanking it over my head. He *was* a kid. Twenty-two, I think he said. I turned to the bed again, my eye roaming over his sulking yet adorable face, his well-muscled chest and perfect abs.

Had twenty-two looked that good when I was twenty-two? Clearly, I hadn't appreciated it enough back then.

It was a damn shame. I wasn't sure what was more of a shame— that he was so hot or that I had spent the past two weekends at the beach trying to seduce him only to get nowhere. At least I hadn't had to spring for dinner tonight—which was usually what happened when you went out with these young guys. Chad had gotten off work at seven, but the minute I saw him waiting for me at the dock, I was hungry for something else. So we had a couple of drinks at The Inn, a local bar, then headed back to the beach house he shared with his friends. His friends had conveniently not been around when we came through the door, practically tumbling over one another to get to the bedroom. And I was just three minutes away from getting that gorgeous piece of equipment of his inside me when suddenly he brings up the girlfriend. The *girlfriend*. He might have mentioned the girlfriend before he had me naked and panting on his bed.

"At least you had an orgasm," he offered.

I stared at him. This was obviously some strange side effect of living your formative years during the Clinton presidency. Apparently his little girlfriend wasn't an issue when he had his head between my legs. But the minute I maneuvered for more than oral sex, suddenly it's, "I can't. I have a girlfriend."

Blah, blah, blah.

Sliding my feet into my flip-flops, I said, "Sorry, Chad, but I'm more of a penetration kind of girl."

And because I didn't want to hear another word about it, or because the sight of that beautiful body was starting to make me feel wistful, I left.

Once I was outside, blanketed by the heat, I felt better, though I couldn't remember a hotter June night in my short history of Fire Island summers. Not that I was complaining. At least we were getting the most out of this summer share. Or I was anyway. I was betting that Zoe hadn't made the last ferry out tonight and was forfeiting yet another weekend at the beach in the name of work. I wondered why I had even bothered browbeating her into a share. Or Nick, for that matter. I guess I had some stupid idea that a summer out at the beach with my two best friends would be fun, though I was starting to think Zoe and Nick were like my little friend Chad. They didn't know a good thing when they had it. Zoe was probably still filming poodles, and Nick…if I knew Nick, he was probably down at The Inn or The Out, the only two bars in town, chatting up anyone who would listen about his latest get-rich-and-maintain-his-integrity scheme, a record label he was developing. But I wouldn't be surprised if he found investors here. Nick could be pretty charming. In high school he had convinced the football coach he could create software that might predict the most successful plays based on the stats of the players. Of course, he got caught smoking pot in the woods behind the school a week later, losing any support he had gained for the project. But that was classic Nick. He was brilliant enough to be the next Bill Gates, except he tended to use that B.S. in Business Administration of his for *b.s.* more than anything else.

It was starting to get on my nerves.

But then, I was on my last nerve tonight, even more so when I saw the lights of our beach house twinkling in the distance. God, it was a beautiful house. An oceanfront, sprawling three-bedroom ranch hovering high above the beach.

"Maggie's Dream." My boss, Tom, had named it for his wife. Though now that I thought about it, Maggie's Dream would have been a lot better sans Maggie.

There was a price to pay for an ocean view. And my price, I had discovered, was Maggie.

I had met them both at the beginning of last summer, at the beach, of course. Maggie seemed fine then—from a distance anyway. She was simply the smiling, semi-Stepford wife of Tom Landon. I adored Tom immediately. Maybe because we had so much in common—we both worked in the garment industry, though I was in retail at the time. Our acquaintance turned quickly into a business relationship when I bought some products from Tom's ladies' wear line, Luxe, to put in the store I managed. But The Bomb Boutique was a bit too downtown hip for me to carry more than a few well-styled pieces from Tom's line, and then it was mostly accessories—handbags and the odd belt. We became friends, though, so much so that I used to tease him about how he needed to add a little hipness to his line if he hoped to win over customers like The Bomb. As it turned out, I won Tom over. By the end of the summer, he approached me about a new venture he was working on, an urban leather outerwear line. And with the promise of a fat salary as the head sales rep for Edge, he lured me on board. It was the best decision I'd ever made. I loved my job. In fact, I lived for my job. Even had dreams of managing Edge myself some day.

Those dreams ended when Maggie came to work for Edge. Suddenly Ms. Stay-At-Home Wife wanted a career, and Tom—sweet, generous Tom—handed her mine on a silver platter.

Now I had to share a beach house with her. For sixteen weekends. Actually, counting this weekend it was only twelve now, since I'd already managed to survive four. Barely.

I started to walk again, feeling my irritation with Maggie rear its head once more, remembering the row she'd started with me tonight for blowing off the big dinner she was planning. As if, just because I was sharing a house with her this summer, I had to be her fucking buddy. Like I really felt like sitting around the table praising her lamb chops when I had a piece of prime booty waiting for me at the dock. She even went as far as saying that I wasn't a team player, implying that I was somehow threatening my job by ditching out on her dinner party.

Fucking prima donna.

If I'd only known she would be like this when I took this share, I might not have taken it. But I had put the money down back in February—a full month before Maggie had taken over the management of Edge and made my life a misery.

I shuddered as I reached the wooden walkway to the house, wondering if Maggie was still reigning like a queen over her stupid dinner party. The house did seem kind of quiet.

Fuck it. I wasn't going in there. Wasn't going to tolerate the satisfied smile on her face when I walked in after the all-too-brief date I had shrugged off her little party for. After all, it couldn't be any later than nine-thirty.

I headed for the beach, figuring a moonlit walk might do me good.

It was the weekend after all.

And I didn't have to answer to anyone.

Not tonight.

And if I had things my way…

Never again.

Nick
Women. You can't live with them and you can't...

"I'm having a few beers, for chrissakes, Bern. What's the big deal?" I said into my cell phone, wishing my reception, which was usually nonexistent at The Inn, would give out at this point. This conversation had already gone on way too long. As in six months too long. But this was what Bernadine and I had come to.

"So you're trying to tell me you're just sitting in a bar on a Saturday night all by yourself," she said, for the fifth time in as many minutes.

"It's Kismet, Bern. There's nothing else to do." I almost pointed out that she might have been here with me, if she hadn't up and moved to San Francisco six months earlier. But I really didn't want to start that argument again. This long-distance relationship stuff sucked big-time, especially when the woman in question got jealous if I so much as sneezed in the vicinity of another woman.

"And there's no one there with you?" she asked now.

I looked around at the crowd lining the bar and surrounding the pool table. "Well, there are lots of people here, Bern. But even if I was with someone, don't you think I might have blown my chances with her, considering that I've been on this phone arguing with you for the past fifteen minutes?"

"Fuck you, Nick."

Click.

Shit. That sure wasn't my reception going out.

"Another beer, dude?" asked the bartender as I put my cell phone down on the bar once more.

I picked up my beer bottle, which was down to the last quarter. The last quarter of my fourth beer and she still wasn't here. Okay, so I hadn't been completely honest with Bern. I was waiting for someone, and, yes, someone female, but it wasn't like that. At least, not on my end anyway. This was strictly business, but from the way things were going so far, it looked like I might have to fuck Maggie, if only to get the upper hand in this deal we were working on. Though at the moment, I had no hand to play. It was almost nine-thirty already. I'd been waiting for her nearly two hours. Actually, I'd moved on from waiting to just simply drinking. Maybe Maggie had gotten that spice or whatever she was missing for her meal and decided to stay home and cook after all. Which didn't make sense, seeing as Sage had already taken off and Tom had given up and gone over to a friend's house. He was pissed and I couldn't blame him. Surely she could have figured out something else to do with all those lamp chops besides whatever the hell was called for in that recipe she was making. But I could see Maggie was like a dog with a bone when it came to her dinner parties. She was pretty upset when she realized her dinner plan was not happening tonight. I thought I had managed to talk her out of cooking, even offered to buy her a burger at The Inn. She told me she just needed to clean up the aborted dinner she'd started. "I'll meet you at The Inn in half an hour," she'd said. Yeah, right. Time is money, babe. And since it was her money we were talking about, you'd think she'd be a little more punctual.

"Another beer, dude?"

"I'm thinking, man," I replied.

"Don't think too hard," the bartender said with a chuckle before he ambled away.

Yeah, yeah, buddy. Why don't you go blow a few more brain cells at the other end of the bar?

I looked at my near-empty beer. I shouldn't have another. And not just because I was outta cash. It was the principle of the thing, really. I'm not sure what principle exactly—but all I know is that I shouldn't be paying five bucks a pop for beer when I got a six-pack I paid nine bucks for at the house. Not that I felt like going back there. It was the kind of thing four beers on an empty stomach could do to a guy. I suddenly had the urge to party all night. Come to think of it, there were some pretty hot chicks over there by the pool table.

See what you've done now, Bern? You're driving me to other women.

Yeah, as if one woman wasn't enough trouble. I had the feeling that getting involved with Maggie—even on a business level—was going to be trouble, too, which was why I was hoping to talk to her tonight. But since she was the first person to show a real interest in my company—even suggested she was going to put her money where her mouth was—I had to treat the matter…delicately.

Still, I was grateful for Maggie's interest in my latest venture. In fact, when she first said she wanted to invest in the music label I'm starting up, I was pretty fucking pumped. Capital was the only thing I was lacking. I had a business plan, even had a band lined up for the launch, which was going to be huge with all the PR I was planning. Even Sage was excited about my ideas, and Sage didn't get excited about anything I did ever since I lost all that money in that pyramid scheme. The only thing she seemed to get excited about lately was this damn beach house. Had some grand idea that getting me and Zoe out here for the summer would be like high school all over again. Sage loved high school. Why wouldn't she? She was like the fucking mayor of Babylon High. She knew everyone. And since me and Zoe were her best friends, everyone knew us, too.

Fire Island was more like high school than I even imagined it would be. Sage also knew everyone on Fire Island, but then she had been coming out here three summers already. Tonight I'd had another little taste of high school when Sage ditched me to hang out with that dock boy. No one could get between Sage and her booty.

I didn't mind. What Sage didn't know was that my little investment in this share was paying off big, in ways I hadn't expected.

Yeah, I had hoped to find investors when I came out here. I'm not stupid. I knew there were not a few people out here that might have money to sink into a solid business investment such as Revelation Records. I just hadn't expected one of those people to be Maggie Landon. I didn't even know her, which is probably why our first weekend out here I started telling her about the label I was planning. Just making conversation, you know? Tom was out fishing, Zoe was taking a jog, Sage was down by the beach, working on that dock boy she was probably sleeping with right about now, and I was stuck in the house with Maggie, mostly because the sun was making me nauseous and I was hungry. I also knew that if Maggie wasn't on the beach, she was in the house cooking. She was like some kind of Martha Stewart on speed, the way she was always whipping something together. When Maggie cooked, she was usually looking for someone to sample the goods. And since it was lunchtime, and since I thought a nice beer in the cool house might be a good idea, I went inside.

Two beers later, I was chowing down on leftover filet mignon that Maggie had made sandwiches with on some crusty bread. I was feeling pretty good—so good in fact, I started telling her about my label, in case she had the idea that I was just some sandwich-mooching shareholder. I guess I didn't expect her to get so excited about it. At first, I thought she just wanted to fuck me. She had that greedy look women get sometimes when they've had too much wine, and she'd had three glasses of white to my two beers and it was only 3:00 p.m. Then she said she had a little money set aside she'd wanted to do something with, which wasn't hard to believe, considering she and Tom not only own the oceanfront spread we're staying in this summer, but a triplex on the Upper East Side. She started asking details, like what my promotional plans were and whatnot. So I told her, and she was getting more and more excited. Could have been that she'd cracked a second bottle of wine, but the next thing you know, she's talking dollars. As in the dollars she thought I might need to get started. *Her* dollars. It was almost too much to believe, but as it turned out, Maggie Landon had been a bona fide rock-and-roller at one time in her life. Over glass of wine number four, she told me that she'd followed the Dead around as a teenager. Not that I'm a Dead fan, but I wasn't about to argue her taste in music at that point. I guess I should have figured she had some interest in good old-fashioned rock and roll, considering she named her dog Janis Joplin. Not that I'm a fan of Janis either, but I'm capable of showing a little respect for talent—especially when Maggie seemed ready to open her prissy little pocketbook.

I hadn't told Sage about Maggie yet, mostly because I don't like to talk about things that I think are gonna happen until they happen. Now I was glad I hadn't, because something about the Maggie situation was funky. For one thing, she begged me not to tell Tom about our discussion. Which kinda weirded me out a little, 'cause I know she's attracted to me by the way she's always touching me. You should have seen the way she looked at me when she asked me to keep our plans a secret from Tom. Made me feel like she was asking for something else, you know what I'm saying? Of course, she said it was because it was her money and Tom didn't have a say over what she did with her money, which was weird, too, 'cause they're married and shit.

Now there's a good reason not to get married: women are fucking sneaky. Just like Bern. Who knew she had even applied for a job in San Francisco until suddenly she was moving out of our apartment. Of course, she wanted me to come. Like I got nothing better to do than follow her around. She knew I was trying to get Revelation off the ground.

At least Maggie understands my dreams a little bit. Maybe a little too much. That's why I need to talk to her before things get outta hand. She keeps referring to the business plan for Revelation in the plural. As in, "our" business plan.

Which kinda pisses me off, you know? Her money notwithstanding, this is *my* business plan. That's the thing about people with money. As soon as they offer to put a little down, they think they own you. And Maggie—well, let's just say she's more territorial than most. I started to explain my position after Tom left tonight, but she seemed a tad wound up. Actually, she looked a little pissed herself, even muttered something that suggested she might not be so willing to put up money for a venture she didn't have a voice in. Which was why I suggested perhaps we should discuss it further over drinks. I wasn't worried. I figured I could get her to see things from my point of view over a couple of cocktails. If there was one thing I could handle, it was chicks. All this required was a little Maggie-management. As soon as she got here, I would explain that I was going to be handling the business plan and that she would be more like a silent partner. As soon as she got here, I would set her straight.

If she ever got here.

"Dude, what's it gonna be? Another beer or what?"

I glared at him. This guy was a pest. Even if I had any money left, I wouldn't buy another beer here.

Maybe it was the reminder I was broke that had me standing up. "Nah, I'm outta here, man."

There was no use waiting any longer. Besides, I'm not really the type to wait around for anyone. Now that I had a few beers in me, it was time to talk business. And the first order of business was finding Maggie.

And letting her know just who was boss.

4

Zoe
No rest for the weary. Or the wicked, for that matter.

No one was waiting for me at the ferry. And why should anybody be waiting for me? I was technically supposed to be here ten ferries ago.

Not that that stopped me from having a pity party for myself as I lugged a wheelie suitcase, a shopping bag and a knapsack down the long dark roads to the house. I had definitely brought too much stuff, but somehow the thought of leaving Manhattan without at least two pairs of shoes, four pairs of shorts, two bathing suits, six books and my camera (I never left home without my camera) had been even more anxiety-producing than lugging it all here.

So with my wheelie firmly in one hand, the shopping bag in the other and my knapsack clamped to my back, I made my way slowly down the long path that would lead me to the beach and Maggie's Dream, though I was sure that by now I was Maggie's nightmare. I had discovered on opening weekend that Maggie didn't tolerate tardiness in her dinner guests. Even more so, I imagined, from the houseguest bringing the key ingredients.

Good thing I had been to the house once before, because the streets—or I should say trails?—through the tall grasses and brush that covered most of Fire Island were pretty dark. I could barely even see some of the houses, which were set back a distance from the road. And there wasn't a soul around. But that was Kismet for you. Since the nightlife wasn't exactly on a par with your usual Manhattan scene, most people stayed home after dark, getting soused behind closed doors, judging by the lights I saw coming from the windows of houses set deep in tall grasses that rustled ominously in the soft breeze.

Creepy. Maybe it was the thought of what might be lurking in the underbrush that sent me hurrying along, despite the fact that my shoulders had begun to ache from my pack and that my wheelie was bumping none too easily across the cracked pavement.

The only disadvantage to an oceanfront share was that it was generally the farthest walk from the ferry. But since Fire Island was only about a quarter mile wide, it wasn't usually an issue, unless, like me, you couldn't leave Manhattan at home when you came to Fire Island. But I got to Maggie's Dream eventually, though my right hand was raw from the handle of my heavy shopping bag, my wheelie was practically on its last wheel and I was on the verge of a permanent back disorder from my pack. Now I understood why Sage never brought more than a tote bag. But then, I guess if your clothes were as tiny as Sage's and all your other entertainment needs would likely be met by most of the male population, you really didn't need much.

I felt a shot of relief at the sight of the lights burning as I made my way up the walkway to the deck. But it was only momentary. I wasn't sure what state everyone would be in at this point. Hungry and dissatisfied? Hopefully Maggie had been able to whip something together to soothe the hungry crowd. She was supposed to be some kind of culinary whiz anyway. Yeah, they were probably all drunk by now and yucking it up, I thought, remembering the well-stocked bar that Tom had opened up to us on Memorial Day weekend and we partook in until we were all practically prone on the carpet in the living room. At least Nick and Maggie were likely yucking it up, I thought, remembering how they had sat out on the deck last time I was here while the rest of us played Scrabble inside. I remembered glancing out at them, wondering at the way they leaned in close to talk to one another.

Nick knew Maggie about as well as I did, which made me curious how they could possibly have so much to say to one another. Not that Tom seemed to mind, which was even weirder. He just sat there laying down letter tiles, teasing Sage mercilessly every time he racked up a triple word score.

When I finally made it to the screen door with all my baggage, I was surprised to discover that Tom was alone, except for Janis Joplin—the dog, that is—who let out the kind of howl that explained how she had gotten that name, and practically mowed me over in an attempt to get past me and out into greener—or in this case, sandier—pastures.

"Don't let the dog out!" Tom yelled by way of greeting.

"Sorry," I said, shutting the screen firmly behind me, which only caused Janis to start to whimper and paw at me, nearly unbalancing me. "Nice doggie," I said, dropping my shopping bag and wheelie, and sliding my pack off my back. I assumed if I wasn't supposed to offend the master of the house, I should be careful not to offend the master's dog.

Not that Tom noticed. "So you finally made it," he said. Since I wasn't sure from his bland tone whether he was being sarcastic or not, I glanced up at him once I had successfully brushed off Janis's advances. My eyes widened. Not only was Tom dressed in nothing more than a towel around his waist, his hair damp as if he had just come from the shower, but he was chopping garlic with what looked like a barely contained fury. I wasn't sure if it was the way he was wielding that knife that weirded me out, or the strangeness of seeing Tom in nothing more than a towel, which looked in danger of slipping every time he brought the knife down on another clove of garlic. Somehow the sight of his damp chest, covered in gray hair and a bit saggy with age—he was, after all, nearing fifty—made me uneasy. Kinda the way you feel uneasy the first time you catch your father running from the bedroom to the bathroom in nothing more than his skivvies, which was one of the few memories I actually had of my father. But that was the other thing about Fire Island. Living in close quarters with strangers often brought you an up close and personal view of them, whether you wanted one or not.

I would have slid away to the bedroom, except it looked like

Tom was in the midst of making that dinner I had heard so much about. And was none too happy about it. "Well, you didn't miss much," he said, peeling the skin away from a fresh garlic clove. "Maggie disappeared. Last I saw her, she said she was going to Fair Harbor Market to look for coriander. But that was almost three hours ago." He brought the knife down on the clove with a solid *whack*.

Oops.

"I come home a little while ago and find dinner half-made," he continued, shaking his head. "I don't know what gets into her."

"So, uh, dinner is still on?" I said hopefully, wondering how I could surreptitiously put the coriander on the counter without him realizing I was the cause of this culinary disaster.

He finally looked up at me, eyes roaming over me as if I had two heads. "It's ten o'clock. We can't eat now. I'm just trying to finish the sauce she started before she took off to God knows where." He sighed, as if the thought of the wasted meal deeply disturbed him. "I guess we'll eat this tomorrow. If Maggie ever gets back with the coriander," he continued. *Whack. Whack. Whack.*

Seeing my opening, I said, "Actually, I think I might have some coriander in one of these bags."

He looked up, knife paused in midair as he regarded me anew. I guess he didn't figure me for the type to be packing a jar of coriander. And with good reason. I didn't even know what coriander was until the grocer at Gourmet Garage kindly explained it to me. Locating the jar in the shopping bag, I placed it on the counter before him, transforming myself from the neglectful tardy dinner guest to the heroine of the piece.

For all of thirty seconds. "Oh, so you got Maggie's message? She wasn't sure you did."

"Uh, yeah. I, uh, got a later ferry than I expected." And since I figured I had already effectively destroyed my momentary heroic status, I decided to come completely clean, pulling out the wine and the Vidalia onion, which was looking a bit bruised. "I got these, too."

"Ah, well," he said, eyeing the onion. "I already used the Spanish onions we had in the fridge. I can't tell the difference anyway, but that's Maggie for you," he said with a roll of the eyes. "An onion's an onion, if you ask me."

"Yep, it's all the same to me," I said, in an attempt to bond with dear old Tom over our mutual ignorance of the varieties of onions.

Janis Joplin, who had been humming a low whine as I emptied the contents of my shopping bag, was now clawing at the screen door.

"Dammit, Janis!" Tom roared, returning to his former austere—and somehow more intimidating in that towel—stance.

Even Janis backed down, lowering to her stomach and whimpering, her eyes on me, pleading.

"I don't know what's gotten into that mutt," Tom muttered. "Must be a full moon tonight." *Whack. Whack. Whack.*

I didn't think there was any moon tonight, judging by all the darkness I had just ploughed through. But I wasn't about to argue. *Whack. Whack. Whack.*

"So, um, where is everyone…else, that is?" I asked, not wanting to invoke the name of Maggie again, seeing as Tom was none too pleased with her at the moment.

He lined up another garlic clove. "Sage had a date or something. And I'm not sure where Nick is." He frowned, and I wondered if he was remembering how cozy Nick and Maggie had gotten on Memorial Day weekend. God, maybe Nick and Maggie were… Oh, yuck. I wouldn't put it past Nick, though. He didn't seem to have many scruples when it came to his love life. And ever since Bernadine had moved to San Francisco, he seemed to have even less. *Whack. Whack. Whack.*

Janis let out a low moan.

"Shut up, you damn mutt!"

I nearly jumped out of my skin. "Um, maybe I should take her for a walk or something?" I said, realizing I had found my escape.

"Yeah, why don't you do that?" Tom replied, in a tone that implied that perhaps I should make myself useful for a change. *Whack. Whack. Whack.*

Grabbing my wheelie and my knapsack, I quickly shuffled my load down the long hall that led to the back bedroom, which Tom and Maggie had designated as my and Sage's sleeping quarters.

I unloaded my stuff in the middle of the room, then flicked

on the lamp on the nightstand between the two twin beds, shedding a dim light over the small room. The green room, as it was aptly referred to with its mint-green walls and matching mint-green curtains, looked like a little girl's bedroom with white furniture and ruffled bedspreads. But at the moment, it looked more like the inside of the dressing room at Victoria's Secret. Must have been some date, I thought, figuring the assortment of bikini tops, bras, postage-stamp-size skirts and slinky tops that littered both Sage's bed and mine was Sage's date-preparation debris. I briefly wondered who she might be out with—Sage had no small amount of admirers on Kismet—then figured it was likely the dock boy she'd been chatting up on the beach the last time I was here. I couldn't remember his name, but I wasn't sure it would matter in the long run. He was the kind of young, buff little boy that Sage usually aspired to. But who was I to judge? I hadn't had sex in two months. Almost three, I thought, remembering that July Fourth was coming up. Maybe it was the reminder that I had spent last July Fourth weekend with Myles that had me shoving my wheelie and knapsack off to one corner and quickly leaving the room.

I spotted Janis Joplin's leash hanging from the coatrack by the screen door the moment I returned to the kitchen. Thankfully, Tom had finished his merciless chopping and was now stirring a pot on the stove, sipping a glass of wine freshly poured from the bottle I'd brought. I beelined for the leash, not wanting to banter over the merits—or lack thereof—of the wine. (Tom was, I had already learned, a bit of connoisseur. I wasn't.) The moment I pulled the leash from the coatrack, Janis's whimpering turned into an all-out howl of impatience.

Tom turned from his stirring briefly. "There're some Baggies in the top drawer right there," he said, gesturing to a small pantry cabinet.

"Baggies?"

He raised an eyebrow. "For the poop?"

"Oh, right," I replied, suddenly remembering that my mission was not simply to escape Tom-in-a-Towel but to possibly provide a little relief for Janis, who was now tugging full throttle at the leash I'd snapped on her.

I opened the drawer, pulled at least three bags from the box I found (I wasn't taking any chances with a dog this size) and headed out the door.

Once I got to the top of the wooden walkway that led to the beach and saw the ocean rolling toward me in crashing white waves, I remembered the other reason Sage had managed to prod me into taking this share. I loved the beach. Had spent half my childhood on it, mostly with Sage and sometimes Nick, when Nick realized being the only guy among girls might be an asset. And later, with Myles, who grew up two towns away from me on Long Island, though we hadn't ever met until we both lived in New York City. That was another thing that had drawn me to Myles: He understood the angst of growing up in the shadow of Manhattan. The hollowness of claiming native New Yorker status when you knew no two islands could be more different than Long Island and the island of Manhattan. Myles had strolled along this very beach with me once....

Now, as I stepped on the sand, felt the breeze in my face, all I could remember was that walk along the beach with Myles. I even started to relish the memory a bit, and I might have enjoyed it even more if Janis didn't seem hell-bent on taking us straight into the tide.

"Whoa!" I yelled, tugging back on the leash. Whoa? That was a horse command. Despite all my recent experience with the dogs of the Washington Square Park dog run, I couldn't think of the command for stop. So I went for the obvious. "Stop!"

Surprisingly, Janis did stop. Though I wasn't sure it was my plea that did it as I watched her raise her face into the wind, then drop her nose to the sand, sniffing furiously for a moment. And just when I thought she was going to give me a reason to whip out those bags I'd stuffed in the pocket of my jeans, she took off at a dead run.

"Janis!" I yelled, pulling hard against the leash. Then I remembered the appropriate command. "Heel! Heel, Janis, heel!"

Not that it did me any good. Janis would not be heeled. So I started to run right along with her. I really didn't have a choice. Besides, the last thing I needed right now was to lose Maggie's beloved dog. Especially after the coriander fiasco.

Just as I was starting to get comfortable with the idea of a late-night jog—I did, after all, like to run, though usually in sweats and not jeans—I realized we were almost to Saltaire, the next town over. I didn't know how much stamina this dog had, but I wasn't going any farther than Kismet, I thought, as I eyed the lonely tuffs of dune grass we passed.

Spooky.

I kept my gaze on the beach in front of me and then was sorry for it when I caught sight of pale white skin in the tide. I quickly looked away, embarrassed. Oh, God, some happy couple was doing a little romantic *From Here to Eternity* roll in the tide. And if I didn't get Janis to heel, I was soon going to be right on top of them.

"Janis, heel!" I said. But Janis only ran faster, and just when I feared I was about to become an unwanted third to the twosome in the tide, I realized it wasn't a twosome. Just one person. A woman. And judging by the way her skin glowed pale against the darkness, she was naked.

What the hell…?

Suddenly the leash flew out of my grip, and I watched in horror as Janis became smaller and smaller, practically disappearing against the darkness. Shit! I started to run faster, though I wasn't sure I wanted to know what was happening in the tide.

I finally caught up, but only because Janis had come to a dead stop, letting out a howl that sent a shiver through me as I looked down on those sightless eyes, wide and blue, staring up at me.

Maggie.

Naked. Her hair matted with seaweed.

And, from the look of things…

Dead.

Maggie
It's all over but the shouting.

My funeral depressed me. Not because I was the main event, but precisely because I wasn't there. Not really. First there was the priest, who kept calling me Margaret. I guess that's what it said on my birth certificate, though no one has ever called me that except my mother, and I hadn't seen her for years. It was nice of her to come, though the way she stood huddled in the corner with two of my brothers, sobbing like an idiot, embarrassed me. But at least someone was crying. Outside of Zoe, which was pretty weird, since the girl barely even knew me. The other surprise was Sage, who I discovered was behind the big wreath of lilies by the coffin. Probably out of guilt.

Tom, of course, was the perfect host, though I hadn't seen him shed a tear yet. But that was Tom. Onward and upward. Life goes on, etc., etc. I know I made some mistakes in my life. Some pretty damn big ones, too. But watching Tom greet people, dry-eyed, accommodating, I wondered if perhaps the biggest mistake of them all had been marrying him.

He didn't even remember to put a rock ballad in the funeral program. I always loved a good rock ballad. Funerals are such dull affairs. I thought a little Queen might liven things up. Or even something more rousing, like Rod Stewart's "Maggie May." Tom played that one for me on our third date. He'd taken me back to his place, and after he'd cued up the track, he gave me that look guys always get when they're in the early throes of courtship—hungry, a bit gooey-eyed—and asked me if I was going to break his heart like Maggie May. Of course I fell for that type of doomed romantic talk—especially when it was set to music.

I should have realized then it would be Tom who'd break my heart first.

I guess after everything that happened between us, I shouldn't have expected my husband to remember my funeral request. After all, it had been ten years since I'd made it. We'd just been married and, filled with the kind of paralyzing fear that the great big bubble I'd stepped into when I'd entered Tom's world would burst, I had given him my last request. "You're crazy to even think that," he'd said, kissing my head, much like a father would a child. "You're only twenty-nine."

Well, now I've just barely cracked forty and I'm about to be buried. Who's the crazy one now?

I wasn't surprised when the police ruled my drowning accidental. What else was the medical examiner going to find beyond a woman who had had a little too much to drink and was skinny-dipping on a balmy June night? I knew I shouldn't have taken the Valium. Now they're blaming the whole thing on me.

I suppose I couldn't really complain about the funeral. If there was one thing I could always count on Tom for, it was to throw a good party. In fact, it was one of the things in our marriage we did best together. We put on a good show. Though I was a little surprised when he chose oak for my coffin. Oak? Have I ever liked oak? Ten years and two houses of furniture later, you'd think he'd know I was a solid mahogany girl. But it just goes to show you how many years you can live with a person and not pay attention. It bothered me though. If nothing else, I'm all about the details.

It wasn't that Tom and I didn't have a good marriage. In fact, some would call it fairy-tale. I know my friend Amanda did, but then I had gotten the fairy tale that *she* was hoping for. Others, mostly Tom's family and even some of the more snide in his circle, saw it as a classic case of Midlife Crisis Meets Gold Digger. Mostly because I was a decade younger than Tom. Those people really annoyed me. Gold Digger. I hadn't even been interested in marriage when I met Tom. I had just started working for WQXY radio. It was my first job in my field of choice, though I had studied communications in college with some vague idea of doing something a bit more glorious than working for the accounts payable department, I had discovered I was good at what I did. I had a good head for numbers and had one of those filing systems so organized some might attribute it to mental illness. I was happy enough though. I was young and, mostly due to Amanda, who was in PR, I got to go to my pick of parties. I could give a shit about all those things that seemed to fuel Amanda—like marrying well and before thirty. Thirty seemed like light years away and marriage like one of those things you did when you started thinking about IRAs and 401Ks. And since I was barely supporting my half of the two-bedroom apartment Amanda and I shared on the West Side, I was nowhere near that mindset. But according to Amanda, that was exactly when you met your proverbial Mr. Right. When you weren't looking.

I didn't even feel like going out the night I met Tom. But Amanda insisted. She had gotten invites to some kind of fundraiser. I had been dragged to enough of them by Amanda to know that they were boring as hell. Filled with the kind of people who identified themselves by what class they came out of Harvard or Yale. I usually went and entertained myself by making up identities as I went along. When I had too much to drink—and I drank at lot at these humdrum affairs—I was Maggie Germaine, reporter for *Rolling Stone.* Or Maggie Germaine, brain surgeon.

But the night I met Tom Landon, I didn't care about impressing anyone. I was simply Maggie Germaine, the fifth child of an otherwise unremarkable family living on the South Shore of Long Island. Usually I never admitted to South Shore, except to give some vaguish impression that I lived somewhere near Southampton, the more desirable part of the South Shore. But the truth was, I grew up in Shirley, later restyled Mastic Beach, though the real estate values never came up to par with the kind of name that suggested cocktails and cabanas. Mastic Beach was more Budweiser and monster truck shows. To Tom, the only son of a North Carolina manufacturing family, Long Island was the legendary home of Howard Stern and the Shoreham nuclear power plant. It was bizarrely exotic in the way a seven hundred pound cat on the cover of the *National Enquirer* is. Though you don't want to understand the forces that could bring such a thing into being, you can't look away.

It seemed Tom couldn't look away the night we met, and I don't think it had anything to do with the Long Island upbringing I'd tossed in his face. But when I forked over my phone number, it was with the kind of blasé indifference born of having had this kind of conversation one too many times already.

Of course, it was just the kind of indifference that works like a charm, at least according to Amanda.

He took me to La Grenouille on our first date. I figured he was trying to impress, but the truth was, dining at places like La Grenouille was a way of life for Tom. Not so for me. My typical culinary experience in Manhattan included the All You Could Eat Ribs Night at Dallas BBQ. Which was probably why, over four courses filled with foods I had never heard of, much less considered, my indifference morphed into insecurity. I was suddenly very aware of the cheap rayon cling of the dress I wore, embarrassed that I could barely choose a wine and a bit overwhelmed by the understated elegance of it all. "Old Money," was what Amanda had called Tom Landon. "Old man," was what I had thought at first. Not so once I was sitting across that pretty table from him, surrounded by lush flowers, soft candlelight and simpering waiters with French accents. Tom brimmed with the kind of confidence I had not experienced in men up to that point. Maybe that's what attracted me most to him. That and the fact that he opened up to me a world I had been shut out of for most of my life. He had everything a man could want. An Upper East Side palace, a garment industry empire. You might scoff at Tom, thinking he'd been handed that empire on a silver platter. It didn't hurt that his father was the man behind Landonwear, a moderate ladies' wear line that Thomas Landon Senior ran from the manufacturing hub in North Carolina. But Tom struck out on his own, moving to New York after getting an MBA at Harvard. By the time I met him, he had just made a name for himself with his own company, Luxe.

Amanda didn't understand why I came home that night scoffing at everything from the fingerbowls to the fancy French menu. She couldn't comprehend my resistance.

Not that I really resisted. I went out with him again. And again. A part of me secretly enjoyed the raised eyebrows and whispers that broke out at the sight of me, young, blond and wide-eyed on Tom's arm. I guess everyone assumed I was simply soothing whatever ills lingered after Tom's divorce from Gillian, his first wife and the mother of his daughter, Francesca. But that was just it. There were no wounds to heal. Tom accepted his lot as divorcé and weekend dad with the same pragmatism that guided his business deals. Out with the old and in with the new. And since I had all the glitter and good wine and food that went along with being "the new," I didn't allow myself to wonder at his apparent lack of feeling for the woman he had left not a year earlier, the child he traveled to see for a few short hours on the weekend. I simply accepted his devotion to me like a kind of amused spectator. I threw my past up into his face, my underachieving alcoholic father, my bipolar mother, my pack of redneck brothers. It was as if Tom didn't hear me. Or didn't care.

Which was why when he declared, on our fourth date, that he would one day make me his wife, I laughed mercilessly. But my insides clamored with a mixture of fear and maybe even longing. I hadn't heard this sort of confident declaration from a man since I was sixteen and Luke, my then-boyfriend, told me he would love me till the day he died. Which I suppose was true, since not two weeks after I dumped him he did die, in a drunk-driving accident. But I wondered what it was that made Tom so certain about me when I wasn't sure of anything. My life. My career prospects. I felt challenged by his faith in me, challenged to be the cool, confident woman he saw staring at him across that candlelit table. I suppose the fact that I succeeded can be measured by the gap between the hard-living rock-and-roll groupie I once aspired to be to the careful, perfect wife I became.

Tom always wanted the perfect wife. I just wish he could have loved her a little more.

I wish *I* could have loved her a little more.

6

Zoe
Is it hot in here or is it just me?

"She looks, um, good," I said to Sage once we were seated at the back of White's Funeral Home on East 71st.

Sage gave me a look, and I knew exactly why. I hate when people say that at wakes and funerals. Who looks good when they're dead? But the truth was, Maggie did look good. At least better than the last time I saw her. I couldn't get the image of her sightless eyes and pale skin out of my head. I guess that's what wakes were for, I thought, remembering the last one I'd been to for Myles's father. But that had been a whole different thing. One of those sprawling affairs on Long Island, sprawling mostly because Myles's father was not only a father of five and brother to six, but a Suffolk County cop, killed in the line of duty. You can imagine how big that wake was. It even made the papers. People came from miles around, in such numbers that they had to limit the viewing hours just so Myles and his family could have some time to grieve in peace. And grieve they did. I'd never seen Mrs. Callahan so broken up. And Myles's sisters. I had always been so close to them, especially Erica, the only one who was still single and close to my age. I didn't even know what to say to Erica—to any of them. Myles had been so sweet, so good, trying to stay strong, keep it all together while everyone else fell apart. I knew he was grieving, had held him tight when he finally did cry the night after they buried Mr. C.

Which was why this sophisticated and utterly dry-eyed event had me wondering. If it wasn't for Maggie's mother, sobbing silently in the corner with Maggie's brothers, I would have wondered if anyone here even cared that Maggie had been cut off in the prime of her life. I looked over at Tom, standing up front near the entrance, smiling and greeting people just as merrily as he had during the first dinner party on Memorial Day weekend. Only it was his wife's wake. I turned to Sage again. "Don't you think it's kinda strange how unfazed Tom seems to be?"

Sage flicked her gaze over to Tom. "People grieve in different ways," she said.

That was true, I thought, looking at Sage now and wondering what she was feeling. She knew Tom and Maggie better than I did. But she wasn't one to cry either. Her toughness was legendary. It was rumored that she'd barely shed a tear when her kid sister died. I hadn't known Sage at the time, having moved with my mother to Babylon in my sophomore year of high school, but I had heard the stories, from Nick mostly. Hope had been eleven when she died, and Sage was fourteen, which was pretty young to keep things so bottled up.

"The whole thing just seems weird to me," I said, remembering how calmly Tom had responded when I had gotten back to the house. Like he was following some guidebook: What To Do In The Event Of Your Wife's Death. I had run back to the house, and in one breathless burst told him about finding Maggie on the beach. I didn't say "dead." I couldn't. Tom had picked up the telephone and dialed 9-1-1. I think he might even have given the sauce a stir before he threw on a pair of shorts and a T-shirt and headed down to the beach. Of course, I hadn't seen his reaction to the sight of his wife. He had insisted I stay at the house and wait for the police to show up so that I could direct them. Though I felt like someone should go with him, I was glad not to be the one. I was spooked enough by the memory of Maggie's sightless eyes looking up at me, her pale white flesh glowing in the darkness. By the time I led the Marine Bureau cop who showed up down to the beach a short while later, Tom was still under control. *I* nearly lost it, especially later at the house, when the questioning by the homicide detective began. All of us had to talk to the police—Tom, Nick, Sage and me. I was a bit freaked out by it, especially when I was asked where I had been, what I had been doing. If I had seen anyone else on the beach. I guess Tom got the same questions, and I imagine he answered them with more aplomb than I had managed.

I was startled by the questions, mostly because I had thought of Maggie's death as an accident.

"They always ask those questions," Sage had said on the way back to the city early the next morning. "You've seen *Law and Order.*"

"Yeah, but that's because they're investigating murder on that show."

Then Sage calmly explained that accidental deaths or deaths that occur at home are always investigated by the police as a matter of course. I had to take her word for it, Sage was a bit of an authority on accidental death scenes, seeing as her sister's death had been an accident, too.

If all those questions opened up the doubts in my mind about Tom's behavior that night, damp from God-knows-what and chopping garlic with barely restrained fury, apparently the police hadn't been fazed. In fact, that was the thing. Nothing seemed to faze them, I thought, remembering the weary face of the homicide detective who had questioned me, jotting down notes as if I were giving him one of Maggie's famous recipes rather than filling in the blanks about how she might have wound up floating in the tide. Accidental death by drowning was what the medical examiner came back with. *I wish the medical examiner were here to witness this,* I thought, watching as a pretty brunette sidled up to Tom, latching herself to his arm.

"Who the hell is that?" I whispered to Sage, nudging her away from the program she had begun to read.

Sage looked up, her green eyes bland as she settled on the brunette in question, then withering once she turned to me. "That's Francesca, Tom's daughter."

"Oh." Okay, okay. So maybe I was being a bit overdramatic. But what was I supposed to think with Tom over there yucking it up with some woman who was half his age? Especially considering that Maggie was nearly half his age, too. Actually, I was surprised to learn from the dates on the coffin that she was closer to forty than my own thirty. She looked pretty damn good for her age, I thought, watching as Tom merrily greeted a tall blonde. But maybe not good enough, I thought next, as Tom leaned to kiss the blonde, his hands roaming over her back as he hugged her.

"Hey, whatever happened to Tom's first wife?" I asked.

Sage practically glared at me. "She's alive and well and living in Boca Raton."

"I'm just asking."

"I don't understand why you're so worked up about this. The woman drank too much and went for a swim."

My eyes widened, but I kept my mouth shut. Sage was my best friend, but sometimes she was a total mystery to me. She could be the most generous person in the world—witness that whopping cluster of lilies up at the front of the room that she'd purchased on our behalf. But when it came to things like Maggie's death, she just closed right up. After a harrowing night of recounting the night's activities for everyone from the Marine Bureau cop who answered the call, to a detective from the homicide squad at the Suffolk County Police Department, we had ridden the train back to Manhattan the next morning in near silence, Sage lost in her own thoughts and Nick dozing off, only waking periodically to clutch his cell phone in his lap with a look of alarm, as if he'd just missed an important call. Tom had stayed behind, of course, and though at first I assumed he was under arrest, I later learned he had gone back to the house to secure it before leaving the beach. And to pick up Janis Joplin, who likely had to be sedated if the state I'd seen her in last was any indication.

"Where's Nick?" I asked now.

"He had some sort of a business meeting," Sage said, finally looking me in the eye again. I knew that look. She was wondering, like I often did, how a man who barely earned a living managed to have so many "business meetings." "He's supposed to be here by now," she continued, her gaze moving to the door. "Holy shit."

I swung my head around, fully expecting to find Tom in a new tryst with some willing female—for a married man, he sure knew a lot of hot, young things judging by the crowd that had showed up—and I was surprised to see him enveloped in a hug with a man.

"Who's that?" I asked.

"Good question. He's fucking hot," Sage said. Then, running a hand over her tousled, blond-streaked hair, which she'd just barely tamed into a French twist, she said, "C'mon. Let's go see how Tom is doing."

If I had wondered about my best friend before, I was positively dumbstruck when I found myself standing next to her as she smiled up at Tom, who immediately wrapped one arm around her slender shoulders, pulling her close. "Sage, sweetie, how are you doing? You know Vince Trifelli, right? Our VP of manufacturing?"

I saw Sage's eyes widen. "*The* Vince Trifelli? I think we must have spoken on the phone a few times, but I don't think we've ever actually met."

"It was Vince here who convinced me to get into leather goods in the first place," Tom told us all with a smile. "And then leather outerwear. But I can't give him all the credit for being the brains behind Edge, because Sage here deserves some, too." Tom waggled his brows at Sage. "Funny you guys haven't met," he said with a frown. "But I guess Vince has been on the road a lot. Poor guy has been suffering over in Italy for the past few weeks—all for the sake of Edge."

"I spend most of my time in China, Tom," Vince said. "Let's not forget that. And you know China is no picnic."

"Hey, if I could give you Italy all year round, buddy, you know I would," Tom said. He turned to Sage. "Sage has been making her own kind of magic for Edge. She's my best sales rep." Tom gazed fondly down at her, pulling her in tighter. "I don't know what I'd do without her."

"Ah, Sage," Vince said, his dark eyes roaming over her appreciatively. "Yes, I do believe we have spoken a few times. A pleasure to finally meet you."

I couldn't figure out what was bothering me more—the way Tom was practically groping Sage, the way Sage was letting him or the way Vince was gazing speculatively at Sage. I'd already pegged Tom as a wacko, but Sage? Hello? I mean, yeah, Vince was hot—dark-eyed, dark-haired, with rough-hewn yet exotic Italian looks, but this wasn't some pickup spot in the meat-packing district. This was a fucking wake.

People grieve in different ways. If this was grieving, then maybe I should start attending more funerals. It wasn't like I had anything else to do with my Saturday nights these days.

I felt relieved at the sight of Nick loping through the door, but whether it was because this happy little threesome had forgotten I was there, or because I didn't exactly want to be remembered by them, I wasn't sure. I slipped away—not that any of them noticed—and intercepted Nick at the door.

"Hey," I said, looking up at him and noticing his dark brown hair looked a little more unkempt than usual, his eyes tired.

"Hey, Zoe. Did I miss anything?"

Oh brother. "Not much. I think there might be some supermodels left for you to hit on."

"Huh?"

"Never mind," I studied his dark eyes. "So how are you doing?" I knew at least Nick had experienced some of the shock I had, judging by the way he kept replaying his final conversation with Maggie about the ill-fated dinner plan. I understood what he was going through. I had played Maggie's last voice mails back at least six times, listening to her cheerfully rattle off the ingredients she needed and trying to grasp how a woman could go from a clawing need for coriander to floating in the tide in the space of one evening. I wasn't sure if it was guilt that drove me to it, or my own need to somehow grasp how she could be there one moment and gone the next.

"Not good," he said, blowing out a breath.

I reached out, taking his hand. "Tell me about it."

"Well, I just had a meeting with Lance—you know, my Web site developer? Anyway, it looks like he's going to bail on me due to lack of funding."

I dropped his hand, biting back a sigh. I guess life was made for the living. Clearly Nick had let go of whatever angst he had felt over Maggie's sudden death.

"I thought you said you'd found a big investor."

Nick dropped his eyes and nearly blushed. Actually, the tips of his ears turned red, which is what typically happened whenever he was embarrassed. Or angry. "Uh, she dropped out at the last minute."

"She?" I asked, remembering that Nick's forte was landing women, not investors. Like Bernadine, whom he still kept dangling on a thread. I wondered if maybe he'd pulled a little too hard on that thread and hit her up for a little funding. After all, she was reportedly a big shot out at a software firm in San Francisco now. "Anyone I know?"

His eyes widened, then he shook his head. "Uh, not really." He glanced around. "Where's Sage?"

"Over there applying for the role of wife number three," I said, waving one hand blandly at the intimate grouping of Sage, Tom and Vince. I saw her lean in to whisper something in Tom's ear, her gaze fastened on Vince as she did. Nah, not wife number three. If there was one thing I was sure about with Sage, marriage wasn't her goal. I had a feeling, judging by the way she was looking at Vince, that she had just found her latest prey. I suppose I couldn't blame her; he was good-looking. Though a bit older than she usually went for. Maybe things had gotten desperate even for Sage. I mean, here she was making flirt time at a wake for chrissakes.

Speaking of which… "So you want to go up and see Maggie?" I said.

Now Nick was grabbing my arm, looking around as if Maggie might step out from behind one of the tasteful drapes with a freshly baked Bundt cake in hand. "What?"

I rolled my eyes, gesturing with my chin toward the coffin at the front of the room, decked in flowers. As if he could miss it. "To pay your respects." Clearly Nick hadn't been to many wakes.

"Oh, right," he said, nodding his head as if this made some sort of sense to him, though he didn't let go of my arm.

"Come up with me?" he pleaded.

For the second time that evening, I found myself kneeling before Maggie Landon, Beloved Wife—as the flowery banner at the end of the coffin declared her. I glanced at Nick, who kneeled beside me, though he seemed to be looking at everything but the overly made-up face of Maggie. I couldn't blame him. Dead people freaked me out, too. And Maggie especially, considering I had seen her dead before the makeup job. I followed Nick's gaze, which now wandered over the line of flowers leading to the coffin, and took some heart. If the amount of money the local florists had collected on Maggie's behalf was any indication, she clearly was loved, despite the jolly ruckus her dear husband was creating in the back of the funeral home. "Those are the flowers Sage ordered from us," I said, pointing out the tall display of lilies, so huge it practically dwarfed the two baskets of mixed flowers it stood between.

Nick's eyes widened. "It looks expensive," he whispered and I knew the question of how much his share of the cost was going to be was floating through his mind. It had floated through my mind, too, as Sage pointed the flowers out when we arrived. I guess that's the way Sage grieved—expensively. I would have preferred to shed a few more tears. There was a good chance I wouldn't be eating next week after I forked over my share of the bill for that bouquet.

Oh, God, I was just as bad as the rest of them.

"We should probably say a prayer," I whispered, but whether I was reminding myself or Nick of why we were here, I wasn't sure.

I closed my eyes, only to open them again immediately. I never knew what to pray for in these situations. Eternal salvation? Yeah, I'd been raised a Catholic, but I wasn't sure what I believed in anymore. Now, as I looked at Maggie's dead face, the way her lips seemed pulled into the kind of smile I'd never seen on her face in real life—closed mouth, knowing and a bit too pink—I felt the same disturbing emotion as when I had found her on the beach. With a shiver, I looked up at the photos that had been placed in the casket. Maggie as a baby, with one too many ribbons in the short tuft of blond hair. Maggie standing next to Tom at some black-tie event, beaming at the camera. Maggie standing proudly before a berry tart. Maggie tossing a stick to Janis Joplin on the beach.

I closed my eyes again, expecting comfort to come, but instead a new reel of pictures flashed in my mind: Myles dressed in a dark suit standing stoically by his mother at his father's funeral, his eyes damp with tears he refused to shed. Another of his face across the pillow from me, his eyes fixed on mine. "I don't know what I would do without you in my life, Zoe," he had said, pulling me close.

Apparently he did. Because I was no longer in his life.

Now I felt, for the first time since this whole tragedy, a sob rolling up. But there was no relief in it. Only deeper sadness.

I wasn't crying for Maggie, I realized, once I opened my eyes and remembered where I was.

I was crying for myself.

"You done?" Nick asked, already beginning to stand.

"I guess I am," I said, getting up, knowing that I was at heart no better than the rest of them. Wondering if anyone really cared about anyone more than they did about themselves.

Myself included.

Sage
It's good to be the queen (again).

They say you can't take it with you.

It was the first thing I thought when I walked into the offices of Edge the day after the funeral, my eyes roaming over the pale gold that Maggie had chosen for the walls, the frilly little pillows she'd tossed about the couches in the lobby, the hideously senti-mental pastoral scene she'd hung above the reception desk.

I wish she could have at least taken that painting.

"Morning, Sage," Yaz greeted me from her perch behind the reception desk. I felt her dark eyes study my face as I glanced at the painting above her, and when I looked at her pretty, exotic features, punctuated by a tiny jewel in her nose, I had a feeling she knew exactly what I had been thinking. Yaz had, after all, witnessed the argument between me and Maggie over that painting, which didn't have the edge that I—or Yaz, for that matter—believed was the image Edge should try to project.

Not that Yaz brought it up. After all, it wouldn't have been… appropriate.

"So how are you doing?" she said instead, still searching my face.

"I'm fine," I replied a bit defensively.

One pierced eyebrow rose almost imperceptibly. "And Tom?"

Yaz hadn't gone to the funeral, mostly because Tom had refused to close the office and Yaz had quickly agreed to stay and answer the phones so everyone else could attend the services. She hadn't cared much for Maggie, and being a twenty-six-year-old Goth—if a woman as dark and exotic as Yaz was could be a Goth—she wasn't one to stand on ceremony.

"Tom's fine," I said finally. "But you know Tom," I said.

"Business as usual," Yaz replied, still staring at me, waiting for what—tears? Shrieks of happiness? Because the truth was, business was back to usual. As in back to the way things were before. Pre-Maggie.

"I'll be in my office," I said, needing an escape from the gleam in Yaz's eyes.

"Sure," Yaz said with a shrug. Then, "Oh, Sage?"

I stopped mid-escape.

"The samples for the fall line came back yesterday," she said, her gaze on me once more.

I gave her a quick nod. "Thanks," I said, then practically ran down the hall to my office.

Once I closed the door behind me, relief washed over me. As I took in my sleek black leather chair, the cool jewel tones I'd chosen for the walls, the way the sun slanted in across my massive desk, I felt, for the first time, a shot of sadness for my former manager.

Which was surprising, considering my office was the only bit of space at the offices of Edge that Maggie hadn't mutilated with her "flair for decorating."

Dropping my bag on the desk, I headed for the tall window, gazed out onto the streets, alive with the rush of people scurrying to their offices, clutching coffees and newspapers, already scattering Seventh Avenue with the debris of life.

Gone. She was really gone.

I shivered, remembering how I had, barely one month ago, during a rage over the changes Maggie had requested on my samples, declared to Yaz and anyone else in earshot, "That woman should be shot."

A knock sounded on my door.

I straightened. *Never let them see you sweat.* "Come in."

The door swung open on Shari Werner, my designer, who,

standing before me in a black Betsey Johnson dress, was either displaying her usual flair for fashion or was the only one of us who was still in deep mourning. Knowing Shari, whose hands fluttered nervously to her soft auburn locks, it was the latter.

"How are you doing?" she said, her gray eyes wide with sympathy and causing a sudden alarm to go off inside me. I'll admit, I'm not too good with emotion—mine or anyone else's.

"I'm fine," I insisted for the second time that morning.

"Have you spoken to Tom?" Shari asked, making me realize why all this concern was pouring out toward me. Tom and I were friends. Had been even before he'd hired me away from The Bomb. I guess people like Shari assumed that Maggie and I were friends, too. But that was Shari. Always assuming the best of people. She might have been the only employee at Edge who actually got along with Maggie.

"Poor Tom," she said now, her eyes welling up.

I reached for my coffee, carefully removing the lid and focusing on the fragrant black brew as Shari went on about "the tragedy" and "how young Maggie was, how much life she had ahead of her."

I swallowed a gulp of coffee, nodding in the appropriate places as I stepped behind my desk, fingering the fat file of orders I had let languish during my absence and even rearranging the pencils in my holder in order to avoid her gaze. When she finally paused in her eulogy, I looked up at her.

"So I understand the samples came back from production?"

Shari's brow furrowed, as if she suddenly remembered we were no longer at the funeral but back at work, where there were a million more things to do now that everything had nearly come to a standstill over the past few weeks. "Right," she said, nodding. Then, as if she couldn't let go of all that Maggie had left behind, she said, "Oh, these are the samples that Maggie redid the merchandising on."

"Yes they are," I said, studying her anew. It amazed me that Shari, who had spent months designing the fall/winter line only to have Maggie decide at the last minute to change the details on at least fifty percent of the bodies we had had cut, could feel such a generosity of spirit toward Maggie. But then, I guess one of Shari's biggest assets as a designer was that she followed orders well. After all, those bodies she had sketched were based on leather jackets and skirts and pants I had bought from the bigger designers and ordered her to knock off, adding, of course, the edge that made Edge unique. But I guess that was why I'd persuaded Tom to hire her. She was easily led. "Could you have Jamal hang them in the first showroom? I'd like to see how they turned out."

"Of course," Shari said, nodding fervently. Then she frowned. "Um, they're all still in the shipping boxes."

I sighed. "What has Jamal been doing?" Our stock boy was one of the few people who hadn't attended more than one night of Maggie's wake, due to claims of college workload and classes. And, as he said to Tom the one night he had shown up, someone had to tend to shipments while we were all gone. But Jamal had never been the most industrious of workers. Mostly because his idea of being in the fashion world was pretending to be P. Diddy. As in gold jewelry, glamorous lifestyle and nothing to do but be his hip-hop self.

Shari's eyes widened, and I knew her assumption was that Jamal had been properly mourning, just as she had been. "I'll get him right on it," she declared. "Shouldn't take him more than twenty minutes or so." Then she smiled. "That'll give you some time anyway. To adjust."

I raised an eyebrow at her. "Adjust?"

She blushed, making me feel more and more like a beast. "You know, to being back. After everything…"

"Right," I said, looking down at my file of sales orders. "A lot of catch-up," I said, nearly cringing as I did.

Shari had the good grace to make her exit, shutting the door firmly behind her.

I sank down in my chair, shoved the file away and put my face in my hands.

The truth was, I didn't feel like doing anything.

Fortunately, before I could fall into a heap of something that felt vaguely like pity—though I wasn't clear on what *I* had to feel sorry about—the phone rang. Assuming it was a client, I picked up, prepared to placate whoever hadn't received their order this week, and was surprised to find my mother on the other end.

But I shouldn't have been surprised, knowing my mother.

"Sage, I didn't think you'd be in today...."

"Why wouldn't I be in?"

"Well, wasn't the funeral yesterday?"

The operative word being *yesterday*. But my mother was of the school where mourning required at least a lifetime to be done properly. She'd been putting up memorials to Hope ever since my sister had died seventeen years ago. There was the annual "Keep Hope Alive" theater festival in my hometown to raise money for a children's theater fund in Hope's name. Though Hope had only been eleven when she died, she had shared my mother's love of acting. The "Keep Hope Alive" theater fund was a nice gesture, but my mother—and my father, who did lights for the show every year—should have been concentrating their efforts on keeping *themselves* alive. Between my mother's nonpaying gig at the repertory theater and my father's sporadic sales—he was a painter, the kind who made a meager living selling beach scenes in the local gifts shops—they were barely surviving. Which reminded me...

"Did you make that doctor's appointment?"

"Doctor's appointment?"

"To have those tests done?"

"Oh, right. Well, Sage, you'll never believe it, but the pain just went away. It was like a miracle."

What was really a miracle was that my mother had lived this long, considering she and my father had forsaken all the necessities of life—like health insurance—in the name of living the same life they had when they met in a commune in the sixties. They had left the commune shortly after I was born, even gave in to bourgeois life enough to marry some time after my second birthday and settle down—as much as two bohemians who still thought it was the sixties could settle down—in a small house in Babylon, Long Island. The house was the only thing that saved them, really. They'd bought it for a song when Babylon was more undesirable marina than valuable waterfront real estate.

I sighed, long and deep. "Mom, that doesn't mean you shouldn't have it checked out. I sent you a check over a month ago to pay for the exam."

"Oh, Sage, I really did appreciate your gift. We put that money to good use," she said happily. "We had the floors fixed in Charlie's apartment. After the laundry room flooded, they were all warped, and you know Charlie's got that bum leg...."

I wanted to argue that Charlie, their longtime tenant who lived in the basement, should perhaps pay for his own new floors, considering that he hadn't paid his rent in the three months since he lost his job. But it was pointless. My parents were of the belief that what goes around comes around. The problem was, it seemed there was often more going than coming.

As if she picked the thought out of my head, my mother continued, "Don't worry, Sage. We only paid for the materials. Charlie did the work himself. He's so handy that way. We're lucky to have him. Do you know he's going to repaint the living room for us with some of his friends? We're going to have a little paint party. Barbecue. You should come out for it."

No thanks. I generally avoided the frequent parties my parents threw, mostly because I found them stressful. The last time I had given in and attended, one of their hippie friends—after one too many bong hits—had gotten it into his head to start a bonfire in the yard and nearly set the tool shed on fire in the process. It was too much work to be around my parents and their friends because someone had to be the sane one, and in their circle of hippie artist (read: jobless) friends, somehow it always wound up being me.

"Oh, but you'll probably be out at Fire Island," she continued, her tone going pensive. The fact that I had, for the past three summers, foregone quality time with my parents in favor of a share with my friends at Fire Island was the only point of contention between me and my otherwise "live and let live" mother. Mostly because it made her "baby girl's" visits less frequent during the summer months, and since I was my parents' last remaining child, it was my duty to keep up the family front.

"Is your boss even going to open the house?" my mother asked now.

"I don't know what Tom's plans are," I said. She had voiced the question that had been sitting in the back of my mind all this time. I know it was wrong to wonder about such things in light of recent events, but the truth was, the beach was all I had to look forward to in the summer. And now, I thought, eyeing the stack of work that had built up during my absence, I wondered if I had anything to look forward to this weekend.

"Look, Mom, I've got to go," I said, knowing it was better at the moment to immerse myself in Edge rather than to ponder if I was going to have a life outside of it. "I'll call you next week. And please make that appointment. I'll send another check."

"No, Sage, not necessary. You've already done enough. We're fine."

Since I was in no mood to argue with my mother over her definition of fine, I said my goodbyes and hung up.

I felt the fight drain right out of me. In the wake of my conversation with my mother, the idea of tackling that folder of sales orders exhausted me. And come the end of the week, there was no hope of relief from it all. I sighed, turning on my computer. Well, maybe I wasn't missing much anyway, I consoled myself, remembering my ill-fated seduction of Chad. As the song says, you can't always get what you want. But now I was starting to wonder if I would even get what I clearly needed. Because in my book, there is nothing like a good piece of beach and a fine piece of booty to take my mind off more serious matters.

I clicked on my in-box and was about to murmur an expletive at the seventy-five e-mails that greeted me when my eye fell upon one with a subject heading that piqued my interest almost as much as the man himself had.

Re: Announcement—Manufacturing VP Vince Trifelli relocates to Bohemia offices

Well, well, well. Clicking on the e-mail, I opened it up and read.

After the successful management of our overseas manufacturing operations in China and Italy, Vince Trifelli is returning to New York to resume his duties overseeing production.

All inquiries and correspondence should be sent to Mr. Trifelli at his new office in Bohemia, New York. For further information, please contact Mr. Trifelli's assistant, Cindy Perkins, at 631-555-1400.

I smiled, suddenly realizing I did have something to look forward to, now that our hot manufacturing VP was back in the States and a mere train ride away.

In fact, it might be time for the head sales rep at Edge to get a personal tour of the production department, by the man in charge of making sure my skins were of the finest quality.

And maybe, while I was at it, I could get a little skin myself.

A knock sounded on my door, interrupting my thoughts. I clicked the e-mail closed, as if someone might guess, by a glance at its contents, that I had set my sights on Vince Trifelli. Office romance was generally frowned upon at Edge. Or at the very least, gossiped about. And if I hoped to take over Edge someday, the last thing I needed was to be accused of sleeping my way to the top. I could do it on my own. Especially now.

"Come in," I said.

The door opened, revealing Jamal, looking sullen in a do-rag, an oversized T-shirt and a pair of jeans hanging so low I thought they might hit the floor. "The new samples are in the first showroom," he said without any preamble, then disappeared.

"Nice to see you, too, Jamal," I said, biting back a smile as I got up from my desk and followed his ambling figure down the hall to the showroom.

Shari was already there, rearranging the six samples on the display hooks we had on the walls, as if by putting them in a certain order they might look better.

But nothing was going to help these samples, I thought, studying the details Maggie had added—a buckle on one model, shoulder lapels on another. And the most ridiculously gaudy buttons—ridiculous because these bodies had been designed for urban youth and those buttons looked more Madison Avenue Ladies Who Lunch—on the lot of them.

Details were everything in this business. Which was why I felt a flicker of irritation as I remembered how Maggie had insisted that very same thing, just as she added the very details that had nearly destroyed the look of these jackets.

I turned to Shari, who was regarding me anxiously now that she had finished her fiddling. "The buckle's not bad," she began.

Not bad? How could she even think that? I shook my head, wondering once again whether Shari was the right designer for Edge.

Then I remembered Maggie, stepping in and ordering up all these changes, though she was the last person to be making design decisions.

"Take them off," I said, with a wave of my hand. "Everything. The buckles, the lapels, those *buttons*—everything."

Shari nodded, her eyes wide, as if I had just somehow blasphemed Maggie by dismissing her last decision at Edge. What a joke. This wasn't a eulogy. It was business. And I knew this business, probably better than anyone at Edge.

Living or dead.

8

Nick
It's a sign from the universe. Well, Federal Express. Whatever.

I should have waked and baked. I wanted to from the minute I woke up this morning, even reached for my bong to fill it, until I remembered my roommate had borrowed it the night before. And since Doug was still shut inside his bedroom with my bong and his girlfriend, I dropped the idea. I didn't like to roll joints. It was wasteful. Plus, I figured I probably shouldn't smoke anyway considering it was a workday—I should make some effort, despite the fact that everything I was working for seemed to be slipping out of my grasp at every turn.

So I turned on my computer and checked my e-mail, which was my second mistake of the day. Nothing but bullshit seemed to arrive over the Internet these days. Today was no different. Sixteen spam messages, offering everything from Viagra to invitations to view college coeds uncensored. Then there was the e-mail from Lance, my Web developer, who informed me that if I couldn't come up with the first payment for the site by next week, he'd be forced to take on another project. He was sorry, he said. He had to eat, he said.

Fuck you, Lance. The truth is your ass could stand to lose a little weight.
Hell, his whole life could stand to lose a little weight. I'd warned

him when he agreed to work with me on the Web site for the label that the financing might be tricky. That there might be some belt tightening and that he needed to be prepared to face lean times until we got this thing up and running. "No problem, dude," he'd said. "I'm with you all the way, dude. Revelation Records is going to be a revelation." Now he was fucking bailing in the name of grocery money. Where was the integrity there?

And he wasn't the only one. The other non-spam e-mail I got was from Bernadine. I didn't even have to open it (I did anyway) to know what it said. She didn't want us to hurt each other anymore, she said. Trying to keep the relationship going long distance was tearing us apart, she said. She loved me, she said.

Yeah, love. If love means bailing out on your boyfriend the second you get a better offer, well, good riddance, Bern.

I almost deleted the message right off, except that I always liked Bern's e-mails. Even the breakup ones. I had a small collection of them—sixteen in total—that I kept in a little file on my hard drive. Clicking on my mouse, I added the latest one to the folder.

Till next time you get horny and call me at three in the morning, Bern. I'll have the Astroglide ready.

Not even the thought of phone sex with Bern made me feel any better.

I lay back on my bed, picking up the remote for my stereo— complete with fifty-disc changer, a parting gift from Bern—and hit CD #47, which I knew was Metallica since I had been playing it ever since I got back from the beach almost two weeks ago. Yeah, you could say it was an act of regression. I'm not a metalhead anymore. Hadn't been since I was a pimple-faced teen. Nowadays I despise metalheads in general for their drooling love for the kind of clashing guitar riffs any twelve-year-old could replicate on a six string with only mild manual dexterity and a lot of hair spray. But even I'll admit that every once in a while, a man needs a few pounding chords to get by. Besides, I thought, adjusting the volume higher as the song began, maybe I'd get my roommate out of bed and get my hands on my bong. Might as well smoke. Nothing else going on today. Or tomorrow, for that matter.

I was just rolling into the second guitar solo, even went as far as raising my hands to air-guitar to it, when I came out of my headbang long enough to realize Doug was standing in my doorway, dressed in a pair of boxer shorts and blinking sleep out of his eyes.

He looked pretty annoyed. Fuck him. If it wasn't for me, he wouldn't even have a place to live.

Though truth be told, if it wasn't for him, I wouldn't have been able to afford this place after Bern moved out.

"Dude, bring it down a notch."

"Sorry, man, were you sleeping?"

"Well, I was, but between you and the fucking door buzzer—"

"Door buzzer?"

"Yeah, dude, didn't you even hear it?"

"Well, who was it?"

"Fucking FedEx. And the worst part of it was, they had the wrong buzzer. Some sort of package for Revelation?"

"Dude!" I sat up, stared at him. "*I'm* Revelation."

Doug blinked at me. "What?"

"The label, man," I said, shrugging jeans over my boxers and sliding into my sneakers.

"I thought you were calling it Bootleg Records?"

Fucking burnout. That was my last record company. Not that he remembered that.

I ran past him for the door, hoping to catch the FedEx guy before he left. It was the third time they'd come by—I had gotten a couple of "sorry we missed you" notes stuck to the door. I wasn't sure if they would come again, but I damn sure didn't feel like having to haul my ass to FedEx to spend a half a morning in line waiting for a package that might not be anything than more contracts to sign for Lance. For a guy who was in this allegedly for his love of music, he sure did create a lot of paperwork. And since Lance was bailing, who fucking cared about his damn contract?

But it could also be something else. Maybe something from the executive I had met with at the Music Festival three weeks ago. I had given him the demo of one of the bands I was planning to sign, as well as an overview of the label. He had seemed interested.

I ran down the steps, all three flights, spotting the telltale blue uniform just before the front door shut behind Mr. FedEx.

I leaped onto the final landing. "Wait!"

He stopped, turned to look at me with a bored expression.

"The package for 3C—Revelation Records? I can take that."

He handed it over, along with a pen, and I signed the line for "receiver's signature," my eyes running over the address label as I did. "Thanks, man," I said, handing back the pen.

I could barely make out the tiny, flowery scrawl, but once I did, my heart nearly stopped at the name above the E. 64th Street address.

Maggie Landon.

A bong hit might have been good about now. I mean, come on. It's not every day a guy receives a letter from a dead woman.

More than a letter, I thought, noticing the envelope had some heft to it. I hesitated before opening it—I mean, I was seriously freaked out.

Curiosity got the better of me and I tore it open, sliding out a package of neatly typed pages, all clipped together and topped by a lavender piece of stationery, monogrammed at the top with a big *ML*.

The note was short, and in the same flowery script I'd seen on the address label.

It was dated June 9th. Three days before I'd tried to tell her who was in charge of Revelation.

Three days before she…

Dear Nick,
I jotted down a few notes for the business plan for Revelation. Let's talk about them this weekend at the beach. I can't tell you how excited I am about working on this project with you. I can't wait to get started!
Maggie

A few notes? I thought, flipping through the packet of pages and seeing that she had not only included song lists, but financial projections, graphs charting the label's development, publicity angles—you name it.

Jesus Christ. This woman was a piece of work.

Was being the operative word.

I shuddered, remembering how *gung ho* she had been about the label when I'd told her about it. Then how angry she'd seemed when I tried to tell her that I was the man with the business plan, not her. It was, after all, my label. I even said as much, which was probably a mistake, considering that Maggie's spirits had damp-ened a bit. If only she would have listened to reason.

I shuffled through the papers once more, peering inside the en-velope as if I expected to find a demo tape from Maggie herself (she had also told me that night that she had dreamed of being a singer once) and was amazed at what I did find floating down at the bottom of the cardboard mailer.

A check. For twenty-five thousand dollars.

Hell, if I knew Maggie had already forked over the cash, I would have done things differently that Saturday night. Appar-ently, she hadn't been planning to renege on her offer to put up a little money.

A little money. Fuck. This was more money than I'd ever had in my life. At least, all at one time.

The front door opened, letting in a waft of humid air and my neighbor from the fifth floor, some guy I barely knew—yet I still found myself stuffing everything back in the envelope.

"How's it going?" I said, nodding, a smile plastered on my face that I hoped might mask the unease pumping through my sys-tem.

"Hey," he replied, blowing past me with barely a glance and heading up the stairs.

Once he turned on the second landing to ascend the next flight, I followed suit, slowly climbing the steps as if my body were weighted down with the thoughts whirling through my head.

The first woman to believe in me. I mean really believe in me. To the tune of twenty-five large.

It was like a sick fucking joke. It was, in fact, the story of my life. The minute I finally get somewhere, the bottom falls out. Like my last start-up, which crashed about five minutes after I finally got some good people on board. Now I lose my first big investor on the brink of signing my first promising band.

Then I remembered that, in the envelope I clutched in one sweaty hand as I trudged up the steps, I still had the investment.

Yeah, I really had lost it. That check wasn't any good now, was it?

I reached my apartment door, sliding the envelope under one arm to somehow camouflage it, as I headed through the door.

Doug was now on the couch with Lou—short for Louise, though she looked more like a Lou, with a short, butch haircut and shoulders of a linebacker. Doug, who was about six-one and slender as a rail, liked his women large, and Lou was no exception. They made kind of a funny couple, especially right now, swaddled together within an afghan with a box of Pop-Tarts, watching TV. Doug looked up from where he'd been nuzzling Lou's neck. "Did you get your package?"

"Yeah, I got it," I said. *No thanks to you.* "Don't you guys have to go to work today?" Doug and Lou worked together in IT support and were usually nine-to-fivers, not that I begrudged Doug that. He always paid his rent on time. But right now, I needed to be alone.

"Nah, man. This weekend is the Fourth of July and Lou and I had a few floaters, so we figured we'd get an early start on the weekend."

Great, I thought heading straight for my room, filled with the reminder that not only did I have a check I couldn't cash, but I had blown a wad of cash on a beach house I wasn't even sure I was going to see again.

Once inside the privacy of my room, I nearly stumbled over a pair of shoes I had left lying in the middle of the floor as I reached for the remote on my stereo to shut out a refrain of Metallica's "Am I Evil?" before I had to give the question the first real consideration I'd given it since I was a teenaged metalhead.

I sat on the bed, dumping the contents of the envelope once more, letting the sheaf of papers flutter free from their clip and grabbing the check.

Twenty-five thousand dollars. I could do a lot with that money. Like sign my first band, get Lance back on board, finally get this show off the ground. Hell, I'd still have money left over for expenses.

It was almost too good to be true.

It *was* too good to be true. There was no way I could cash that check. I mean, it probably wasn't even good anymore now that Maggie was...

I studied the check, which was also dated June 9th. Two days before Maggie...

Which meant that it was probably still good. I mean, it's not like Kismet Market wouldn't be cashing her check for all the food she'd purchased that Friday night....

Okay, now that I was officially disgusted with myself, I got up, headed to the desk and, without even thinking, clicked on the e-mail from Bern, as if to ground myself. Skimming past the first paragraph, which went on about how we didn't have a future together (it was her usual refrain in letters of this type), I came to the part where she went on to wish me well. Because she always wished me well.

I never want to be the one to cast a shadow on your dreams. Your dreams, your intelligence, your integrity—it's these things that I love most about you. And in order not to destroy the memory of how good we were together once—how good you are and always will be—we need to make a clean break. I love you, Nick. I always have and I know I always will....

See? I'm not evil. Bern loves me. And Bern is good. So good. Do you know Bern used to volunteer for Big Sisters? God, I love that woman. She kills me with these letters. Kills me.

Maybe I'll call her later.

My eye fell on the e-mail from Lance, which I'd left in my in-box, hoping to take the time to prepare a properly scathing reply for bailing on me.

But he wouldn't bail on me if I cashed the check. I mean, I could just try it. See if it worked. I studied the check once more, noticing that only Maggie's name appeared on it and remembering how she had leaned into me, her eyes glistening, her breath warm on my ear as she whispered, "Let's just keep this between us, okay?" Which meant this was Maggie's own money she was investing. She was free to do what she wanted with it, I thought, my gaze falling on the massive business plan that still lay in a heap on my bed.

Reaching over, I picked up the first page, which was a Power Point presentation outlining the various steps, with special fonts and colors—the works. Clearly this woman needed to get a life.

Shit. I didn't mean that like it sounded.

I skimmed the page, which outlined her ideas for the first phase.

Not bad, not bad. Not that I hadn't thought about this stuff already.

I looked back at my screen at Lance's e-mail message, taunting me, beckoning me. Then nearly jumped out of my skin at the sound of the cheerful musical tone that alerted me I had a new message.

Sage, I thought, seeing the familiar sagedaniels@edgeleather.com address pop up in my in-box and feeling a prickle up my spine at the subject line: "Maggie's Dream."

Fucking weird, right?

I clicked on the message.

Hey, guys,
Looks like we're on for the beach this weekend. See below.
xoxo Sage

I scrolled down to find an e-mail she had forwarded to me and Zoe from Tom.

Sage,
Thanks for all your help holding the fort while I took care of things. I'm off to Chicago to deal with that buyer from Wentworth's, so we'll catch up at the beach this weekend. The weather is supposed to be fabulous! Just perfect for the annual Fourth of July bash.
Tom

Tom was opening the house. This weekend. Not only opening the house, but having a fucking party.

Clearly Maggie's husband had no qualms about living in Maggie's Dream now that his beloved wife was gone.

And I wondered why I should have any qualms about keeping Maggie's *other* dream alive.

After all, it was the least I could do for the poor woman, right?

Maggie
It's like a nightmare. Only, I won't be waking up.

That bastard. I can't believe he's opening the house. My house. Okay, he bought it, but he bought it for me. During the second year of our marriage. It was probably his last act of love.

Now it just seemed like a cruel joke.

Look at Sage in my kitchen. Already mixing up the pot lids and creating chaos in my recipe-filing system. Who the fuck does she think she is?

This is *my* house. Nothing can change that. Not even death.

Of course, that's going to be a little hard for me to enforce. Already I could see my marigolds, the sweet little plants I'd potted on the front deck only weeks ago, dying from neglect.

It was almost too much to bear. Who am I kidding? It *was* too much to bear.

Maggie's Dream was the only thing I'd ever called my own. Because the house on Fire Island was mine in a way that the apartment on E. 64th never was. The apartment was hers—Tom's first wife, Gillian. Oh, Tom let me repaint the living room and choose new area rugs for the bedrooms, but it was Gillian who had met with broker after broker looking for the perfect home for her life with Tom. If it were up to me, I would have gone for prewar elegance, rather than reconstructed modern grandeur. But a woman isn't supposed to complain about these things. What did I really have to complain about? In the space of a year, I had gone from a poorly heated, ramshackle two-bedroom in midtown to a triplex in one of the best neighborhoods in Manhattan.

Still, it was hard being second. I tried to explain this to Tom, but from his viewpoint, it would have been foolish to give up the apartment. He had bought it for a song back at a time when real estate values in New York weren't as astronomical as they are now. It just wasn't practical to sell the apartment and buy new, and Tom was, if nothing else, a practical man.

Then there was the decor. Antiques passed down through generations and deemed too precious to put away or sell off to strangers. It didn't matter that the chandelier in the living room didn't speak to *me*—it clearly was still having some cosmic conversation with Victoria Landon, Tom's long-deceased great-aunt. Then there was the Art Deco furniture that Gillian had salvaged at antique fairs from the Hamptons to Paris. We certainly couldn't get rid of that stuff, because, as Tom said, unique pieces such as those were hard to come by.

And Gillian, of course, no longer wanted the furniture. Why should she? She got a brand-new house in Boca Raton and an alimony settlement fat enough to allow her to move on to a whole new period of furniture.

But Maggie's Dream was mine. Had been from the start. Well, mine and Tom's anyway.

I remember the first time I saw the house. We had gone out late one afternoon on a Saturday when Dolores Vecchio, the broker who was working with us, called to say she had found exactly what we were looking for. I was a bit distrustful, since she had already ushered us through some less than spectacular homes in the neighboring town of Saltaire, which was Tom's first choice since he had friends with homes there. I wasn't fond of the houses—or Saltaire, for that matter. Too many rules. No barbecues or riding bikes at night. I mean, really, who ever heard of a beach house without barbecues or nighttime bike rides? This new place was in Kismet, and when I saw it, I felt like this house was fated to be mine.

It was so beautiful, hovering on stilts high above the ocean, as if that great swirling mass might swallow it whole. The beach had eroded a lot that year due to a hard winter, but somehow the precariousness of the house, which sat a bit too close to the crashing waves back in those days, only added to its majesty.

Of course, Tom resisted. "One good storm and that house will go right into the ocean." But I stood firm. The house would last. It had to. I could see myself spending my summers there.

It was one of the few battles in our marriage that I won.

Now, as I watched my house infested with the very shareholders I hadn't even wanted to take on, watched them lie about my sofas, sipping cocktails (and leaving rings on the furniture, mind you), I wondered if I had really won at all.

I felt a little like Mrs. Ramsay in *To the Lighthouse,* dying in parentheses.

Oh, who am I kidding? I'm no Mrs. Ramsay, despite the lovely view of the lighthouse from my house. No one would be writing books about me, least of all Virginia Woolf. No, there would be no books, no songs about Maggie Landon. Even the police had reduced me to a four-page report, which I wouldn't exactly call lyrical. Or even just, for that matter.

I wondered if anyone would even think of me now. Or ever. Well, I knew at least one person would. Out of fear, if nothing else.

Fear of getting caught.

10

Zoe
Just when you thought it was safe to go into the water again…

"Who's up for striper tonight?" Tom said, startling me from where I lay on the blanket, eyes closed. Not that I had been sleeping. More like closing my eyes against the brightness of the day. Or reality.

I sat up, blinking at the sight of Tom heading down the beach toward us, outfitted in long khaki shorts, a T-shirt and baseball cap and sporting two long fishing poles. Janis Joplin loped beside him, tongue lolling.

Ah, a man and his dog and his fishing rod. With that grin on his face, Tom looked like he was posing for an ad in *American Fisherman* magazine.

I hate sports. Especially sports that involve killing.

"Hey, Tom," Sage said, smiling up at him from where she sat in her beach chair, a copy of *Vogue* spread across her legs. "Finally decided to get out of the house, huh?"

"Yeah," he replied, stopping next to us, his gaze going pensive. "Too nice a day to stay inside."

Too nice a day to feel depressed about the fact that your wife died two weeks ago, I thought, watching as he tied up Janis a short distance away from us, underneath the umbrella Sage had set up earlier. Then he waved and grinned as he headed down to the shore to set up his fishing pole.

"Don't tell me you don't think that was weird," I said to Sage once I was sure he was out of earshot.

She looked up from her magazine, regarded me for a moment behind brown-tinted sunglasses. "What was weird?"

"Tom. Smiling. Soaking up the sun. Fishing!"

She turned back to her magazine. "We gotta eat, don't we?"

I stared at her until she finally looked at me again. "Okay, Zoe, tell me what's weird," she said, giving in.

"The fact that Tom hasn't so much as wrung out a tear since Maggie's death," I began. "The fact that he barely even reacted the night her body was found—"

"You don't know what was going on in his head."

"I *saw* him, Sage. I mean, I was the one who told him about… about Maggie. If you could have just seen how he acted. He was a little too cool about the whole thing. As if he somehow expected it. I felt like I was watching one of those videos they show you during safety week in high school, demonstrating how you should act in an emergency."

I saw her look up, running a hand through her sun-streaked waves while she watched Tom dig out a hole in the sand to stand his rod. "Tom was always good in an emergency. Very organized. You should have seen him during the blackout last summer. He had both floors of the office evacuated within fifteen minutes."

"But this wasn't a blackout, Sage. His wife had just drowned!"

She turned to me again, lifting up her glasses to look at me. "You better put some sunscreen on those shoulders, Zoe. You're starting to burn."

"Oh, never mind," I said, flipping onto my stomach and closing my eyes. I was able to ignore Sage for a full five minutes— until I felt the sun beginning to burn at the edges of the navy blue tankini I wore. I rolled over onto my back, feeling a sudden urge for fresh company, seeing as present company didn't seem to want to acknowledge my worries, much less my existence at this point, judging by the way Sage immediately focused on her magazine again. I guess I couldn't blame her. I had been harping on the subject from the minute we arrived at the house last night and I was faced with the lonely look of Maggie's Dream sans Maggie. Okay, maybe I was feeling guilty for being here. I had just turned in my final edits on the documentary to Adelaide, and I was, well, curious enough about Maggie's death to return to the scene of the crime. Now I was glad I had come. I don't think I would have believed it if I hadn't been here to see Tom arrive this morning, cheerful as can be, pulling a wagon loaded up with food for the big Fourth of July bash he was still planning, because, as he said, Maggie would have wanted it that way.

I had to wonder about that as I watched him tossing out the meal she'd worked so hard on the night she died, in order to make room for all the beer he'd bought. I went out for a run to cool my head, only to come back to find him bagging up Maggie's clothes in big black trash bags. "No point keeping this stuff around," he said, when he caught me gawking at him. I recovered enough to suggest that he might at least consider giving her clothes to charity. I guess it was a point in his favor that he seemed to be mulling over my suggestion. Except for the fact that he actually had the gall to ask me if I wanted to have a look through, to see if I wanted anything.

What I wanted was his head. I mean, could you blame me for wondering about the guy? Though, the strange thing was, I seemed to be the only one wondering. "When's Nick coming?" I asked.

"He said he'd be here before two," Sage replied, looking up at the sun as if she could tell the hour by its position. "Looks like he's already about a half hour late," she finished, proving that she could. I wasn't surprised. Sage was in touch with those sorts of things. Natural stuff, like figuring out north and south without a compass and what herbs you could eat without being poisoned. I used to think she was the kind of person you would want on your *Survivor* team, but now, as I watched her lift the magazine to smell a Calvin Klein fragrance ad, I wasn't so sure.

"What's he doing, anyway?" I asked. "He's missing half the weekend."

She shrugged, then looked at me as if I should talk, considering I had missed more than my share of beach time so far. What she said was, "Your thighs are getting red, too."

I looked down at my thighs, which looked fine to me. Still, I flipped over again, just to be safe. I wasn't so adept at sunscreen. I'd put some on earlier, but only succeeded in increasing the amount of sand sticking to my body.

Slipping my sunglasses on, I gazed up at the house, which stood high on the dune in front of me, trying to remember that this was the beach and I was supposed to be having fun, though fun seemed out of my grasp. I had a lot on my mind. I guess I always had a lot on my mind. Oh, to be young and carefree, I thought dryly, watching as a young and carefree-looking girl made her way down the wooden steps to the beach.

She was dressed in a soft cotton sundress that I might have called innocent if not for the fact that it was cut a bit shorter than most. I studied her face as she approached, a soft, confident smile freshly painted in pink, eyes shaded by black sunglasses, her shoulder-length dark brown hair smooth, as if she'd just had a professional blow-dry, her bangs perfectly trimmed. She looked familiar.

"Isn't that Tom's daughter?" I asked, finally recognizing her from the wake and funeral.

"Daddy!" she shouted, answering my question.

Sage looked up as the girl skipped gaily by—or she seemed to skip anyway—stopping once she reached Tom at the shore.

I watched as they embraced, then spoke animatedly for a few minutes.

"I wonder what she's doing here," Sage said.

At least she wondered about something, I thought irritably, studying father and daughter on the beach. I watched as Tom gestured to the house, as if he were giving instructions.

"Didn't you tell me she lived down in Florida with her mother?"

She nodded, her eyes on Tom and his daughter as they made their way back up the beach, toward us. "She goes to school down there, I think." I saw her gaze narrow behind her brown-tinted frames. "I guess school is out. Or maybe she even graduated. I think Tom may have mentioned she was graduating this year."

"Have you girls met my daughter?" Tom said, approaching us. "Francesca, meet Sage and Zoe. Your new housemates for the summer," he continued, his smile broadening. "Francesca has decided to spend the summer up here with us." He shrugged. "It's not like we don't have room."

I tried to contain my surprise at that little remark. Mostly for Sage's sake. Because I was starting not to care what our happy host thought. What the hell was wrong with this guy, anyway?

"I'm going to go get settled in, Daddy," Francesca said, beaming up at her father.

But Tom's gaze had already returned to his fishing rod. "Hey, looks like I got something! Must be my lucky day!" he announced, before jogging back toward the shore.

I watched as annoyance flashed across Francesca's face, before her creamy features moved back to her formerly cool expression. "Nice meeting you both," she said. Then, turning on her high-heeled flip-flops, she headed back toward the house.

I saw Sage frown. Finally, a reaction out of her.

"Good thing we came last night," she said. "Now we have a claim to the green room. I mean, I know she's his daughter, but I don't want to lose one of the best rooms in the house."

Fortunately, I had my sunglasses on, so she couldn't see me roll my eyes. God forbid anyone should encroach on our beloved room, which just so happened to be the second biggest after the master bedroom, complete with its own private bath and a lovely view of the lighthouse in the distance.

"I'm going for a walk," I said, jumping up and dusting the sand off me as I did.

"You better put sunscreen on those legs."

"I'll be fine," I muttered, sliding my shorts on, more for modesty than anything else.

With one last glance at Tom, who had just let out a whoop as he began to reel in his first catch of the day, I headed up the beach.

I had only gone about fifty yards when I realized where I was headed. And remembered…

Maggie's sightless eyes staring up at me with a look of surprise…or was it resignation?

It was neither of those things, I thought, chastising myself. The woman was dead. A dead woman couldn't feel anything.

And neither could her husband, apparently.

I shook off the thought, plowing on, trying not to notice how many of the blankets I passed contained cozy little couples. Trying not to remember that I might have been one of those cozy couples this summer.

When I came to a break in the line of houses near the end of Kismet, I knew I was in the right spot, recalling the loneliness of the dunes that night. I wondered, not for the first time, why this land didn't have a house on it, since it was prime oceanfront. Realized if there was a house here, maybe someone might have witnessed what had happened that night on the beach.

I looked out into the tide once I was standing right about where I had found Maggie. I think half of me expected to find her still there, rolling in the waves, forgotten.

Of course, she wasn't there. In fact, I was all too aware that there was nothing about this particular stretch of beach that might indicate a woman had died there two weeks before.

I stared out into the ocean, watching the waves rolling over one another in the distance, trying to imagine someone—well, Maggie—stepping into that inky darkness alone.

Unless she wasn't alone.

Stepping closer to the tide, I watched the waves crash in the distance, mesmerized by the constancy of it. A memory washed over me of my father, pulling me through the waves, hands braced under my armpits as I screamed, not trusting him not to let me go. I guess that first instinct had been right.

The tide washed over my feet and I jumped.

Fucking cold!

What sane woman would willingly jump into the Atlantic Ocean in June?

It had been hot that day, I thought, beginning to walk back along the shore, remembering how I had spent the unseasonably warm day in Adelaide Gibson's air-conditioned living room. I knew, too, that by evening the water would have been warmer, having been heated all day by the near ninety-degree temperature.

Okay, so it wasn't that cold. Maggie was simply walking along the beach on her way back from Fair Harbor and decided to take a little dip. Yes, the queen of the tasteful beach cover-up had decided to drop her drawers and take a dive, just for the hell of it.

Yeah, she'd been drinking, according to all reports, but I just wasn't buying it. It just didn't make sense that she would have gone into the ocean at night alone. Didn't she watch all those teen movies where people died doing the same thing? She seemed like such a reasonable person. In fact, almost *too* reasonable, from what I could see. She had to have been forced, I thought, remembering a damp and angry Tom chopping vegetables.

But even that was too much to fathom—Tom drowning his wife. Yet there was something about him that spooked me. Something in his indifference that made me wonder if he was capable of pushing his wife underwater. What kind of man faced his wife's death without so much as a tear? Opened the very beach house he'd named in her honor the week after her funeral and was planning his annual Fourth of July bash as if the fact that neither Maggie nor her esteemed potato salad were going to be around didn't faze him? I couldn't help but think of Scott Peterson, cheerfully making plans with his new girlfriend days after he had murdered his wife and unborn child.

What kind of men were these?

"Zoe? Is that you?"

I turned, shocked to hear my name being called in a town where I knew virtually no one, and found myself face-to-face with a man I once knew better than myself.

"Myles?"

"Hey," he said, jogging closer until he was standing before me, bare-chested, his sandy brown hair looking even sandier in the sun, his golden brown eyes on mine. Before I could sputter out my surprise, he was bussing my cheek with a kiss, as if we were old friends rather than a freshly severed couple. "So I see you decided to take that share after all," he said, as if my presence on the beach were the surprising thing.

"Of course," I said. "What are you doing here?"

He ducked his head shyly. "Well, some friends from law school had a house with an open share and, I dunno, at the last minute I figured, what the heck."

What the *heck?* my brain echoed. "Oh," was all I said.

"So how are you?"

As if he cared. "I'm fine. You?" Even as I asked, I found my eyes roaming over that hairless, perfectly carved chest. Yes, he was fine.

In fact, Myles had been born fine, I thought, feeling suddenly resentful of his naturally athletic build.

"I'm doing okay," he replied. "You know…"

I looked up into his eyes, saw the hesitation there, and realized that maybe things weren't so fine with Myles. "Everything all right at home? How's your mom? Your sisters?"

"Everyone's good, good," he said, bobbing his head a bit too merrily. "How about *your* mom?" he asked. "She okay?"

"She's fine," I said, suddenly feeling swamped by sadness. This was what we had come to. Polite questions and head nods. And separate summer shares. I wasn't sure whether I wanted to sob or smack him across the forehead for not caring enough to think of my feelings.

Maybe Myles sensed this—at least, I hoped he was somewhat aware of the grief his actions were causing me—because he said, "If I'd known you were going to be here, Zoe, I would have called. I just thought you'd given up on the whole idea. You said as much that night we…you know, decided to take a break."

We decided? And if this was a break, no one told me. In fact, if I remembered correctly, Myles said he didn't know if he was ready to take the next step. With me, anyway. I would have argued the point now, but something about his pensive gaze stopped me.

"Hey, if you're here, then you must have been here the night—God, Zoe, did you take that share in Tom Landon's house?" He reached out, taking my hand in his. "I'm so sorry about what happened."

I looked into his eyes and saw the first genuine sympathy I'd seen from anyone yet, and Myles didn't even know Maggie. "Yeah, me, too."

"How's the husband doing?"

"Fine," I said, with a shrug, dropping my eyes to the sand, studying Myles's feet, his long, even toes, already beginning to tan. "He's here, too," I said, looking up at Myles again. "This weekend." I paused. "He's out fishing as we speak."

He nodded, his eyes on mine, assessing. Then he blew out a sigh. "The whole thing was just freaky, if you ask me."

"I know," I replied, glad to find out at least someone agreed with me. "Were you out here that weekend?"

"No, but I heard about it. Made the Long Island newspapers, according to my mother."

"I saw her, Myles, I mean—I found her. On the beach."

"God, Zoe. How—"

"I was out walking Janis Joplin—the dog, that is. Maggie's dog. It was like the dog knew something, you know? She was going nuts—pulling me along on the leash, as if she were looking for her. And then we found her...."

When I saw the horror in his eyes, I felt fresh horror move through me.

His hand tightened around mine. "Hey, Zoe, if you ever need to talk..."

"Myles!" came a female voice in the distance. We both turned to see a blonde in a bright yellow bikini jogging down the beach toward us. She was thin, yet curvy, and when she stopped before us, breathless and smiling, I realized she was also beautiful.

"We're short a player! You in or not?" she exclaimed, one thumb gesturing over her slender shoulder at the volleyball net set up in the distance.

Myles dropped my hand as he turned toward the blonde, and my antennae went straight up. "Sure, just give me a minute, okay?" Then, as if he realized the blonde and I were sizing each other up and that some introduction might be necessary, he said, "Uh, Haley, this is my friend, Zoe. Zoe, Haley."

Haley nodded at me, a bit dismissively I thought, then turned her sunny little face up at Myles once more. "Five minutes?"

"Sure thing," he said, smiling back at her. She nodded and headed merrily back up the beach to her teammates.

"So we're friends, is that what we are?" I said, feeling less than friendly as I watched Haley's perfect little ass get smaller and smaller as she jogged away from us.

Myles looked at me, surprised, I suppose, at the anger in my tone. I couldn't blame him. *I* was surprised. I was usually a little more subtle than that. Still, I couldn't be stopped. "So if I'm a friend, what's Haley?"

"She's...a friend. I mean, she was in a few of my classes."

Which meant she was not only cute, but young. Everyone in Myles's classes was twenty-three or twenty-four, since Myles had worked for a not-for-profit foundation for a few years before re-turning to school to study law. The fact that he was in the class-room with so many young people had bugged him a bit. But apparently it didn't bug him anymore.

"It's her house I'm staying in. With six other people," he added quickly. "All friends. From law school."

"How nice you have so many friends out here," I said.

"Zoe—"

"Look, Myles, I have friends out here, too," I said. "And the truth is, I don't need any more. Especially you."

11

Nick
Somebody's been sleeping in my bed.

"Finally!" Sage said when I came through the door Saturday evening. "We were beginning to think you weren't going to show up."

"Have I ever been known to miss a party?" I said, leaning in to buss her cheek. "Whatcha making?" I glanced at the large mixing bowl she stirred.

"German potato salad."

"Whoa, Sage. I didn't know you were a German-potato-salad kind of girl," I said, sliding my knapsack off my back and moving in closer to inspect her creation. Mmm…looked good.

She looked somewhat offended. "I can cook. I've always been able to cook. It's just more fun when you have a real kitchen to do it in. And a real reason. I'm making this for the party tonight. I told you, it's potluck." She lowered her voice. "I didn't want Tom, you know, putting himself out with cooking after, you know, everything."

"Right," I said, nodding my head. "Where is Tom?"

"He's out on the back deck mutilating innocent aquatic creatures," came Zoe's voice from the sofa in the living room, where she was lying down. I assumed she was lying down anyway. All I could see were her feet.

"Hey, Zoe," I called out by way of greeting.

"He's cleaning fish," Sage explained. "He caught two stripers today, and he's going to grill them up for the party tonight."

"Cool," I said, patting my stomach. I loved grilled fish.

"So what did you bring?" Sage asked now, reaching for the pepper grinder and beginning to turn it over the bowl.

"Bring?" Shit, I knew I forgot something. "I figured I'd pick up some beers at the market," I hedged. "Actually, I think I might even have some left over from the last weekend we were here, since we didn't get to, uh, drink them."

"Nick, I did tell you everyone was making food, right?" Sage said, stopping midgrind to stare at me.

I looked at Zoe. Or rather, Zoe's feet. "What did Zoe make?"

"Apple pie," Zoe replied.

"Really?" I was impressed. Hell, maybe I had underestimated the women in my life. "I didn't know you baked, Zoe."

Her feet came down as she sat up. "I don't. Mrs. Smith does, though. I got it at the market."

"Whoa, Zoe, what happened to your face?" I said, once I saw her beet-red cheeks and nose.

She turned a shade redder, if that was possible, and slapped her hands over her cheeks with dismay. "Does it look terrible?"

It didn't exactly look good. But I knew enough about women not to say that. "It looks okay."

"Really? Everyone's not going to think I'm a freak, are they?"

"Nah," I said. "Anybody asks, just tell them you got that disease. What's it called again? The one where your face gets real red and your skin dries out?"

"Ohhhhhh!" She jumped up from the couch, running from the room on legs that were almost as red as her face. Except in stripes. Long red stripes. Ouch.

"Aloe vera's in my bag, Zoe," Sage yelled after her. "Just keep putting it on!"

She turned to me, pausing in her stirring. "What the hell did you have to go and say that for?"

"I don't know," I replied. "Wasn't thinking, I guess. Besides, she's not usually so sensitive. What's up with that?"

"She ran into Myles today," Sage replied, wiping the excess salad off the mixing spoon, then tossing the spoon in the sink.

"Oh, yeah? Does he have a share out here, too?"

"Apparently. Zoe's not happy about it, so…" Sage said, giving me a meaningful look. As if I needed a reminder not to bring up the "M" word. I don't know what Zoe was getting so uptight about. If Bern were here, I'd see it as an opportunity. A booty opportunity, that is. Of course, if Bern were here instead of San Francisco, we wouldn't be broken up or whatever we were. I hadn't heard from her since Dear Nick letter number 7,675. Not that I cared. I had better things to do now that I was a man with a plan. Or rather, a man with an investor. Uh, that is, an investment.

"So what took you so long to get out here? Zoe's scalding notwithstanding, you missed a nice beach day."

"Oh, I had some business to take care of," I said, my eye straying to the knapsack I had dropped on the floor, which contained my brand-spanking-new laptop, purchased today at Comp USA. It had taken me a little longer than expected—the crowds were chaotic—but it was worth it. This new machine kicked ass—and was fast as hell. Which was what I needed. With the new Web site for the record label, I'd need more speed and functionality. Besides, now that I had a little cash to play with, it was about time I updated my PC.

"What kind of business?" Sage covered the bowl with foil, then slid it into the fridge.

"You know, computer stuff," I answered vaguely, wondering if I should have brought the laptop out here with me. Not that I'd spent a lot of money, but I didn't want Sage to wonder about my sudden cash flow. I didn't think she was computer savvy enough to notice my new upgrade, but you never know.

I picked up my bag. "I'm gonna go put this stuff away," I said, making an exit before she could question anything else—like the brand-spanking-new knapsack I was carrying. I needed it, you know? It had a special insert to store the computer in, and I didn't want anything to happen to this baby.

I headed down the hall to the purple room, which was on the other side of the communal bathroom from Sage and Zoe's room. Aside from the fact that it looked like an Easter egg, it was the best room in the house, in my opinion, mostly because it had a private entrance that led out on to the back deck. Okay, the best room would be Tom and Maggie's—uh, that is, Tom's—since he had an ocean view and master bath. But since I had the purple room all to myself, that meant I could push the two twin beds together and make a double, whereas Sage and Zoe had to contend with trying to sleep on those twin beds without tumbling off. But then again, I'm a big guy—nearly six feet. Okay, five-eleven and a half, but still, a guy like me needs room. In fact, I should set up the bed right now, so I can just tumble right in after the party later, I thought, remembering the last time I had tumbled into bed here, too drunk to deal with pushing the beds together, and wound up on the floor in the middle of the night. Swinging the door open to the room, I was surprised to discover someone had beat me to it—in fact, not only had someone already pushed the beds together, but a female someone, if the pink thong on the floor was any indication. Wow, that was a tiny thong. Probably Sage's. What the heck was Sage doing in my bedroom? Maybe she hooked up last night and needed the privacy.

I began to slide my pack off my shoulders, when I saw a decidedly un-Sage-like item on the nightstand. A Britney Spears CD. God, no. If Sage did go for either of the two tarts who had taken over the teen world, she was more a Christina Aguilera girl than a Britney girl. And Zoe…Zoe was into that vagina rock. You know, like Sarah McLachlan, the fucking Cranberries. Besides, I couldn't see Zoe in that thong. She was cute and all, but that little scrap of pink…let's just say it wasn't her.

I put my pack down, dumbfounded, then headed back to the kitchen for some answers, but Sage had already left the kitchen and Zoe was probably still slathering on whatever remedy she could find for that burn of hers.

The sliding glass door to the back deck opened, allowing in the only other person who could possibly get her butt into that thong—and that CD into her player, God help her. I had no idea who she was, but as I watched her yawn, then stretch that lithe, tan, bikini-clad body, I knew that, music tastes notwithstanding, I wanted to know her better. A lot better.

"Is it time for cocktails yet?" she asked, blinking as she took in the room, her eyes falling on me with what looked like genuine interest.

"So you must be my new roommate," I said, raising an eyebrow. "Nick," I said, holding out a hand to her.

"Roommate?" she said, putting the smallest hand I had ever seen in mine, catlike blue eyes gazing up at me from beneath thick, dark bangs. God, she was young. She couldn't be more than eighteen, if that. Mmm, but she was nice. Maybe that's what I needed… a nice young babe. No neuroses yet. No hassles.

"Yeah, the purple room is where I usually sleep. Not that I mind sharing," I said, giving her my cockiest smile. Yeah, this was shaping up to be a helluva weekend. Good food in the making. Hot chick in waiting—

"Nick, you made it!" Tom said, stepping in behind the brunette babe, carrying a bloody, beheaded fish in his hands. Yuck.

"So I see you've met my daughter, Francie," Tom said, pausing briefly to acknowledge the girl before marching toward the kitchen.

Daughter? Uh-oh…

"Francesca," she corrected, her eyes still on mine. "A pleasure to meet you, Nick," she said, giving me the kind of smile that said she was very glad to meet me. Oh, man…Tom's daughter. It figured. Did I have the worst luck in the world or what?

"Daddy, you didn't tell me I was going to have a roommate," she said, her eyes moving over me in a way that made me feel uncomfortable with Tom standing right there.

Not that Tom noticed, I thought, watching as he laid that fish on the counter. "Roommate?" He laughed, then looked at me. "Francie decided to come out and keep her old dad company. But I guess I hadn't sorted out the sleeping arrangements."

"I can stay in Nick's room, Daddy. We can separate the beds." Then she smiled up at him. "I'm a big girl, after all."

"Oh, no, no," Tom said. "I don't think that would work.…"

Embarrassed, I looked at Francesca, then noticed her smile had deepened. As if she liked the way Tom was acting all overprotective and shit. Okay, let me revise my assessment. Young chicks are weird.

"After all, what would the neighbors think?" he continued with a hearty chuckle that turned Francesca's smile to a frown. Then he snapped his fingers. "Hey, I got it. You can sleep on the day bed in my room, Nick," he finished with satisfaction. "Sound good?"

"Uh, yeah. I'm easy," I replied, watching as Francesca waltzed past me and out the sliding glass door once more, a pout on her pretty face. Okay, so I didn't get to sleep with the weird hot chick, but I did just step up to an ocean-view room.

I'd say the weekend was turning out a-okay.

Sage
What's the Fourth of July without a little spark?

"Look at this place," Zoe said.

"I know," I replied, smiling as I gazed around. We were standing on the back deck of the house, which had been decorated with great diligence by Tom. Red, white and blue lanterns lined the railings that overlooked the ocean. Matching candles flickered on the patio table. Inside the house, the living room was strewn with candles and streamers and more lights in red, white and blue. "He did a great job," I continued, peering through the sliding glass door and spotting Tom, who was presiding over the small crowd that had begun to gather in the living room, "He always does."

I felt Zoe shift uneasily beside me. "That's not what I meant."

"I know what you meant," I said, more sharply than I'd intended. I knew Zoe wasn't in the best of moods tonight after her run-in with Myles, but I was tired of her chronic critique of Tom's postmortem behavior. He needed to move on. We all needed to move on. "Tom already explained to us why he's decided to hold his annual Fourth of July bash. He didn't want to disappoint anyone, least of all us. We're his first shareholders."

"Gee, what a guy."

"Zoe," I said, turning to face her. "Tom *is* a nice guy." Probably too nice, I thought, thinking about how he'd slaved all day, preparing for this party he felt we shouldn't do without. Not that I said that to Zoe. "Why don't you direct your anger where it belongs?"

"What's that's supposed to mean?"

"It means you've done nothing but whine about Tom ever since you ran into Myles this afternoon. Why not just admit to yourself that seeing Myles here was upsetting?"

"I'm not upset!" she cried, her sunburned face going a shade darker as she did.

"Hey," Nick said, stepping through the sliding glass doors, beer in hand. "Simmer down. Zoe, what's the matter?"

"Nothing is the mat—" she began.

"It's a party, lighten up," he continued, gently knocking his beer into her arm. "Let me get you a drink."

"I'm not thirsty," Zoe replied.

"As if that matters," Nick said, with a roll of his eyes. "Let me get you a beer."

"I'm not in the mood—I mean…no, thank you," Zoe said, her gaze seeking out the ocean view.

"Suit yourself," Nick said, taking a healthy swig out of his beer. "Sage?" he asked, looking at my half-empty tumbler of tequila on the rocks.

"I'm good, thanks," I replied, studying him and noticing for the first time that he'd taken the time to give his hair that gently gelled, tousled look. He'd even put on a nice shirt. A new shirt, I realized, noting that the baby blue cotton button-down he wore tonight was not the usual swag—a freebie T-shirt picked up from one of his cronies at the various record labels. Even the shorts—khaki and in the latest cargo style—seemed new. "You're looking spiffy," I said.

Nick raised his eyebrows, then smiled. "I'm feeling pretty spiffy." Then he chuckled, sipping his beer as he glanced inside the sliding glass doors.

I followed his gaze to Francesca, who was seated on the edge of the couch talking to one of Tom's friends and wearing the shortest miniskirt I had ever seen. "You'd better steer clear, Nick."

"What?" he replied, his eyes wide with innocence. "You're kidding me, right? I wouldn't touch that. She's practically jailbait."

I looked him in the eye, assessing. "She's twenty-one. Hardly jailbait."

"Twenty-one? Really?" he said hopefully. "Wow. She looks much younger than that."

"Nick, she's Tom's daughter."

"Sage, give me a little credit, would you?" he said, shaking his head and turning to Zoe for backup.

I could tell by the bemused frown on Zoe's face she wasn't going to be much help. She didn't disappoint.

"Nick, if something happened to Bernadine, would you be throwing a party two weeks later?"

"It's his annual bash," I argued.

Zoe held up a hand to silence me, which was really annoying.

Nick seemed startled by the question, his dark brows furrowing as he considered it.

Considered it a bit too long for Zoe's liking. "Well?" she said, brown eyes bulging.

"Okay, let me just ask, are me and Bernadine still, like, a couple?"

Zoe's eyes widened ever farther. "You're kidding me, right?"

"Well, if we've been broken up a while—"

"That's it?" she said. "The relationship just ends and you forget about her as a human being? You don't even care whether she lives or dies?"

"Zoe—" I began.

"This is not about Myles," Zoe insisted, though the tears glistening in her eyes said otherwise.

"Zoe, listen," I began again, softly this time.

But Zoe was in no mood to be coddled. "You know, maybe I'll have that drink after all," she said, then disappeared inside the sliding glass doors.

"Poor kid," Nick said, watching after her.

I sighed. "I know it was tough seeing him out here, but she needs to let it go. It's been three months."

"Look at me and Bern. Six months later, and we're still hanging on."

I looked at him. "I thought you said you'd broken up?"

He rolled his eyes. "Yeah, right. I wouldn't be surprised if I heard from her this weekend. The holidays always get her all emotional and shit."

"It's the Fourth of July, Nick. Not Christmas."

"Yeah, well, for girls it's all the same."

I raised an eyebrow at him.

"Most girls," he said with a wry smile. Then he looked at my glass, still half-empty. "C'mon, looks like you could use a refill. Or better yet, a shot."

I could use something, I thought, my eye falling over the small crowd as I followed him inside. But as I looked around at the mostly middle-aged and predominantly married crowd, I was pretty sure I wouldn't find it here.

Still, I accepted the shot Nick poured me once we got to the bar in the far corner of the living room.

"To a killer summer," Nick said, clinking his beer bottle into my shot glass.

"Yeah, killer," I said, looking around at the scattered crowd, hoping my prospects might get better.

My prospects didn't get better, but they did get more familiar. Some of the garmento crowd that flocked to Fire Island showed up. There weren't many of us out here, but we stuck together, and I was glad, too. At least I had some people I could relate to at this party. I was getting bored watching the marrieds flirt with spouses other than their own—inevitable, considering the amount of alcohol that was being consumed. It wasn't like I had my friends to talk to. Nick dove right in, chatting away with anyone who would listen to his schemes, male or female, and Zoe had virtually disappeared. I decided not to resort to my habitual worrying about her. She was a big girl.

As was I, I thought, indulging myself in another shot at the behest of Stan Sackowitz, one of Tom's big customers, who believed he might bring me back over to the retail side if he plied me with enough alcohol. "We could make beautiful music together, Sage," Stan was saying as he clinked his glass into mine. "And a lot of money, too!"

I smiled, downed my shot obediently. "You know I'm very loyal to Tom, Stan."

"Loyalty will get you nowhere!" he insisted, downing his own shot. "Think where you would have been had you stayed with The Bomb Boutique."

"That's right, Stan. That's why I'm never going back to retail," I said with a smile that I hoped ended this seemingly endless conversation. Not that I really minded. I had become a hot property in the leather business in a relatively short time. Mostly due to Tom's faith in me. But also because I was damn good at what I did. Zoe always said I could sell indulgences to monks. And though I was never sure if she meant that in a good way, I knew that she was right.

So I talked the talk with Stan, and later with Viv, a buyer from Bloomingdale's. The conversation inevitably turned to Maggie at some point, some whispered declaration about "the tragedy" and "poor Tom." I suppose that's what people say when deaths occur, but it all seemed so ridiculous somehow. As if their sympathetic murmurs tied them to the situation in some intimate way. Everyone wanted a piece of Maggie, it seemed, now that she was dead. "I worked with her to set up the billing for Bloomingdale's," said Viv. "Nice woman."

I practically snorted. The only reason Edge would be hanging in Bloomingdale's this fall was because I had convinced Viv that they needed a younger leather line on their racks. Maggie's chief talent was handling the books. She was more a numbers cruncher than the creative talent she imagined herself to be. Not that anyone else realized that, seeing as she was at the helm of Edge. I just hoped Tom remembered who the real head of Edge was, when it came time to choose a new one.

I wasn't sure what disturbed me more, those who gushed on about the tragedy, or those who openly speculated about the circumstances.

"They say she was drinking a lot that night," said Jenny Lewis, who I had shared a house with last summer over on Pine Walk. "She must have been. I mean, who would go in the ocean in June? And naked!"

I didn't even grace that one with a reply.

The worst of the bunch was Donnie Havens, the head of shipping for Edge, who owned a house with his wife, Amanda, a few doors down on West Lighthouse. Latching on to my arm and reeking of one too many beers, he nearly bawled when I asked him if he had any idea when our first shipments would be coming in for the fall collection.

"Oh, God, Sage, those were the jackets that Maggie was waiting on. What will we do without her?" he asked, his eyes practically tearing up in his tanned face.

I could think of a few things. What I said was, "We'll survive it, Donnie."

"Of course we'll survive it, Sage. But it won't be the same. Not without Maggie. God, I loved that woman." Then he did sob.

Oh, brother. This was the man we entrusted to get our livelihood to our retailers?

Then, as if he realized he might be going on too much to a woman who could have a say over whether or not he keeps his job, he said, "So, Sage, does this mean you'll be taking over the Sales Manager job in Maggie's stead?"

I stiffened, probably because Donnie was the first person to say out loud the ambition that had been thrumming through me from day one. "That's up to Tom, Donnie," I said coolly.

He smiled at me, even looked a little handsome despite that bad toupee he was sporting. "I'm sure that's what Maggie would have wanted. Besides," he said, his gaze roaming over me in a way I found vaguely discomforting, "I can't think of a better person for that job now. You're smart. Beautiful. Just like Maggie."

I looked at him, not sure what was bothering me more—the comparison to Maggie or the fact that Donnie seemed to be staring at my breasts. Fucking lech. "Listen, Donnie," I said, gesturing to his wife, who I noticed was watching us from her post on the couch in the living room. "Why don't you go and show your wife some appreciation while she's still alive and well?"

Donnie's eyes widened, but he got the hint, marching off in the direction of his wife, then detouring around her and heading for the back deck.

One shot later, I was able to shrug off Donnie's creepy perusal. I was even starting to enjoy myself. As was Tom, I noticed, eyeing him as he sucked down another in what was starting to seem like an endless line of martinis. I knew Tom wasn't a big drinker—

typically no more than a martini or two when the occasion called for it. So the fact that he had clearly put down more than his usual quota had me wondering if perhaps he was taking things harder than he made it seem. And who could blame him, really? I couldn't even fathom losing someone after spending a decade with them.

Which was probably why I didn't spend too much time with any one person, outside of Zoe and Nick. I shivered, realizing the three of us were well into our second decade ourselves. Fifteen years we'd been friends. And though most of the time I wanted to shoot both of them, I didn't know what I'd do without them. I felt a little bit like I was losing Zoe during the whole Myles phase. Not that I didn't love Myles, but Zoe got so sucked into that relationship, I barely saw her. Though it was nice having her back in my life more regularly, this Myles thing had hit her hard. Too hard. I guess that's what happens when you start thinking about forever. You're bound to get hurt. People change. And, I thought, watching as Tom laughed a bit too merrily at something one of his friends said, people die…

It just wasn't worth the risk.

For my part, I wasn't so sure marriage was everything it was cracked up to be. Being with someone for a lifetime—caring for someone for a lifetime—was a lot of work.

I ought to know, I thought, my gaze falling on Nick, who was now deep in conversation with none other than Francesca, despite my admonitions. I could tell by Nick's body language that he was flirting big-time. Probably bragging about his new label. I think he scored more booty than anything else out of the two labels he had started. Bernadine fell for him when he was starting up the last one. Even saw him through its demise. Now it looked like Nick was hoping Francesca might fall for the hype, too—and keep his ego and his bed warm.

Not if I had anything to do with it. This wasn't just any girl. This was Tom's daughter, and I didn't want Nick fouling the nest. Especially since it was the nest I hoped to rule some day.

I stepped into the living room, hoping to lure Nick away on some pretext, when the sight of a man stepping through the sliding glass door at the front of the house stopped me dead in my tracks.

Vince Trifelli. Looking like an angel of mercy in a white polo shirt that showed off his tan, and a pair of jeans that hugged his lean hips.

I glanced over at Nick. I'd deal with him later. There was still time yet. Yes, Nick was a fast worker, but Francesca, who stood with her arms folded, didn't seem like she was exactly falling all over him just yet.

I watched as Vince greeted Tom, pulling him into a hug, his hand moving soothingly over his back, and felt a curl of warmth inside. Affectionate, caring. What more could a girl want?

I decided that this girl was going to go and get it.

I wound my way over, stepping up to Tom and touching his arm. "Hey, good-looking. Can I get you anything?"

Tom, as expected, swung his arm around me, pulling me up beside him and practically leaning on me for support. If I got him anything, it would be a glass of water, that was for sure.

"Sage, you gotta meet this guy. This guy, he's like my brother," he said, pulling Vince in to his other side so that he was holding on to both of us.

I looked Vince in the eye. "I believe we've met."

He nodded his head, the slightest of smiles coming to that perfect mouth of his, but whether he remembered me or not I couldn't say.

"My brother, I tell you," Tom slurred on, putting his other arm around Vince's shoulders. "Do you know how long I've known this guy?"

"No, how long?" I said, still holding Vince's gaze.

"Seventeen goddamned years!"

Vince broke eye contact with me, smiling up at his friend. "Goddamned years, is it?" he said.

Tom ignored him. "We started our first business together. Hell, we had our first marriages together."

Alarm shot through me, and I glanced down at Vince's left hand, feeling relief when I saw it was bare.

Tom yanked me closer. "And Sage, Sage here is my right arm. My right arm, I tell you!"

"I believe she's your left at the moment," Vince said.

When I looked up again, Vince was smiling in full, a flash of white teeth against dark skin.

Mmm-hmm, this was some man. "I think we might be his whole support system at the moment." But the minute I said the words, Tom lifted away from both of us, lured off by someone shouting his name from the deck.

I smiled after him, watching as he weaved unsteadily through the crowd. Once he was through the sliding glass door, I turned to Vince. "So. I didn't know you were a Fire Island junkie, too."

His eyebrows drew together. "I wouldn't say 'junkie.' I have a place over on Seabay, but I don't get out as much as I should. And then there was all that time in China. And Italy…"

"Ah, Italy," I said with a sigh.

He treated me to another one of those smiles, and my insides started to warm in a way that I couldn't attribute to tequila.

"But now you're back," I said, studying his dark eyes as he gazed out through the sliding glass doors.

"Yes," he said distractedly, "now I'm back. And just in time, I see," he continued, his gaze narrowing on Tom as Tom leaned drunkenly against the sliding glass doors, talking to a petite blonde.

I followed his gaze. "He's lonely," I said, realizing for the first time that it was true, despite Tom's somewhat desperate attempt to carry on as normal.

"Yes," Vince said, his gaze still on Tom. "Tom needs someone to take care of him. He always did. He was lucky to have Maggie. And now…"

He looked at me, and I realized that he was, in fact, the first person to see through Tom's facade of cheer.

Another point for Vince. He was sensitive. And that was something you didn't often encounter in a man. Or at least the men I had known up until now. Maybe that came with age, I thought, studying the flecks of gray through his otherwise dark hair and wondering just how old he was.

Instead, I asked, "So you and Tom started a business together? I'm assuming it was garment industry, too—what line?"

Vince looked at me. "What line?" he said, his eyes widening. Then he chuckled. "I started up Luxe with him."

I raised an eyebrow. "Really? And all this time I thought Luxe was Tom's baby."

He frowned. "Well, it is now. But I was there at the beginning. Helping him set up. He was new to New York and I had the contacts, so..." He shrugged. "I've been in this industry since I could crawl. Even longer than Tom in some ways, since I started out running truck shipments as soon as I knew how to drive."

And now he was the VP of manufacturing. A self-made man. I liked that, too.

But just when I was going to ask him more, I saw his eyes narrow on someone outside. "Would you excuse me?" he said. And with a brief nod, he disappeared into the crowd. I spotted him once again talking to one of the vendors we worked with at Edge.

Clearly, Vince hadn't come here for pleasure, I thought, realizing that he hadn't so much as flirted with me, though he was talking quite animatedly with the vendor over there. Maybe that was another thing that came with age in a man. Vince might be more motivated by the head between his shoulders than the one between his legs.

And as I watched him work his charms, I realized that I might prefer that kind of man for a change.

I went in search of Zoe, who had been MIA since her emotional outburst on the deck. Though once I found her, I kind of wished she'd stayed hidden away.

"What are you doing?" I asked when I spotted her, coasting through the living room, video camera in hand.

"What does it look like?" she said, panning the room.

"The question is, why are you doing it?" I asked.

She shrugged, still not lowering the camera, only pausing as she came upon Tom and the cluster of women he stood among. "Figured Tom might want some footage of his annual bash."

"Zoe—"

"What?" she said, finally lowering the camera. "At last I'm getting into this whole Fourth of July thing and you're still complaining?"

I glared at her. "I wouldn't be complaining if the festivities were really your focus. I know what you're up to, Zoe. The only time you have that camera in hand is when you're gathering evidence."

"Well put. I never thought of it that way." Then she frowned.

"Now that you mention it, I did capture some pretty good footage on the back deck earlier." Then she gestured to the back deck. "Who is that guy, by the way?"

I turned to look and saw it was Donnie Havens, who had at least stopped his sobbing and was now leaning up against the railing, not a hair on his toupee out of place despite his recent blubbering, and smoking a cigar.

"Donnie Havens. He's the head of shipping for Edge. Works out of the Bohemia office. He has a house three doors down."

Zoe nodded, her eyes speculative. "Is that right? He seemed pretty broken up about Maggie's death a little while ago. I thought maybe he was a relative or something."

I smiled. "He's probably sad that Maggie won't be sharing any more hot tubs with him this summer. He's a bit of a lech, that one."

"Hot tubs?"

I narrowed my eyes at her. As much as I didn't like Donnie, I knew he was harmless. Of course, these days everyone was suspect in Zoe's mind. "Don't get any ideas. He has hot tub parties all the time. Tom goes, too."

"Well, just so you know, I'm not the only one with ideas."

"What are you talking about?"

"It seems I'm not the only one who thinks Maggie's drowning was a bit unusual. Apparently, some of the guests thought it very convenient that Maggie died. You see that woman over there?" she asked, gesturing with her chin. "Dolores Vecchio. She's the broker who worked with Tom and Maggie on the house. According to her, Tom was a smart cookie for taking out the mortgage insurance on Maggie's Dream. Do you know that the entire mortgage on this place gets paid off when one of the mortgage holders dies?"

"She told you that?"

"Well, not me. I was just checking out the view. But if you don't believe me, I probably have it here on tape. You'd be amazed what this mic picks up from a distance."

I shook my head in disbelief. Then, lowering my voice, I said, "Zoe, I know Tom. He wouldn't hurt a fly."

"Really? Would you swear to that in a court of law?" she asked, picking up the camera once more and pointing it directly at me.

"Zoe—"

"Hey, guys," Nick interrupted. "Someone's shooting off fireworks on the beach. Come down and check it out!" Then, without even waiting for us, he followed the flood of partygoers out the sliding glass door.

A smile tugged at Zoe's lips—the first one I'd seen all day. "Good thing I have my camera," she said, heading for the door. "Come on."

Of course I followed. And within moments, we had staked out a spot a short distance from the crowd, and I found myself seated on the beach between my two best friends, gazing up at a sky scattered with more stars than I'd seen in a long time.

"Look at that sky," I said, thinking wistfully of Vince, who I knew was standing somewhere in that crowd to the right of us and who I wished was right here beside me.

Apparently, Zoe was on a totally other wavelength. "You know that guy Tom's talking to?"

I bit back a sigh, following her gaze. Or rather, her camera, which she had pointed right at Tom and a tall, portly-looking fellow who was yucking it up with my boss. "I have no idea."

Zoe put the camera down. "That's the chief of security at Saltaire. Tom's alibi for the night of Maggie's death. Apparently Tom went over there for drinks that night. Or so he says."

"Alibi? Zoe—"

Nick laughed uneasily. "Zoe, c'mon man. I gotta sleep in the same room with the guy."

I rolled my eyes. "Don't listen to her, Nick."

She must have heard the sheer exhaustion in my voice. Either that or she knew better than to try my patience. Because Zoe did quiet down, turning her attention—and her camera, for that matter—to the fireworks that had begun to crackle across the sky.

"Ooohhh," Nick said, mimicking the crowd as a roman candle opened up in a burst of light above us. "Ahhhhhh," he mimicked again, as it showered down on the beach before us.

I looked at him, a smile pulling at my lips.

"What?" he said. "You gotta make the right noises. It's a tradition!"

"Ooohhh," Zoe said, peering at the next spiral of color through her camera.

"Ahhh," I chimed in, leaning playfully into Nick as I did.

I laughed, realizing that, for the first time since the party began, I was really enjoying myself. In fact, I could have ooohed and ahhhed all night—because it seemed like the fireworks were going to go on that long. Except I was startled out of my sky-gazing by a sound that wasn't so pleasant. Shouting, I realized, turning my head to discover it was Tom who was the cause of all the ruckus. He was on his back on the beach, waving away the small crowd that had begun to gather around him. I jumped up, Zoe and Nick following in my wake as I beelined for Tom, who was attempting to get up.

"I'm fine!" he insisted. But his face was mottled and his eyes fuzzy, I noticed once I got close.

"Ah, Sage," he said when he saw me. "Could you tell these people I'm all right?"

"He passed out cold," a short, squat blonde said.

"Daddy, let us help you," Francesca said, though she didn't move any closer, as if she was afraid of being puked on or something.

Janis Joplin started to howl, yanking on the post where her leash had been tied.

"Damn dog," Tom said, twisting in an attempt to see where Janis was.

"Let me help you up, Tom," I said, reaching out a hand.

He took it, pulling heavily on it as he eased to his feet.

"Here let me help."

I looked up to find Vince beside me, angling his shoulder under one of Tom's arms to support him. I smiled at him, then slid under Tom's other arm. Good thing, too, as Tom must have been walking on rubber legs, judging by the way he was leaning on me.

"I don't know what I'd do without you guys," Tom said. I felt Vince attempting to turn him toward the house and I moved in tandem, but Tom stopped, his glassy eyes gazing out on the ocean. "Oh God, oh God," he muttered.

Janis Joplin began to howl again.

The sound seemed to sober Tom up. Or I thought it did anyway. "Damn dog. I told Maggie to keep her at the house."

Vince and I both stopped stock-still and looked at each other.

"She never listened, that one. Not once. Ten years and she never heard a word I said." He fixed his gaze on the ocean once more, apparently mesmerized by the sight of the waves crashing. Then his eyes narrowed, his mouth firmed. "Maybe she's better off dead." Then he laughed, the sound sharp and high-pitched against the sudden silence.

"Yeah," he said, pulling suddenly, furiously, against the hold Vince and I had him in and breaking free. "Everyone thinks I got off easy. Well, she's the one. She's the one who got off easy!"

13

Maggie
The daughter I never would have

The beach house was the only place I ever found any peace. Fire Island has that effect on most everyone. Probably because there are no cars, no hassles and no worries except how to best spend the day. There weren't even that many people, mostly because the only way to gain access to most of the island is by ferry. Keeps out the riffraff. The day-trippers. Even kept out my family, in some ways. My mother never understood why Tom and I bought a home off the mainland. But then, my mother never really did understand anything beyond her own suburban existence. Which was probably why I rarely saw her or anyone in my family after I married Tom.

Even Tom loosened up at the beach, kicking back with his fishing rod, catching up with friends and cooking with me when we entertained there, which was often. It was as if the house brought us back to ourselves, who we were outside of our upscale Manhattan existence.

Sometimes I even imagined that house could save our marriage.

I remember the first time we brought Francesca there. She was fourteen at the time, and in the few years I had been married to Tom, I hadn't really had a chance to bond with her. I thought it was because she lived down in Florida with her mother, but when she came to the house during our first summer there, I learned otherwise.

The truth was, Francesca hated me, probably from the first time she met me, just months before I married Tom. I can only guess that she saw me as some kind of rival for her father's affections. To Francesca, I was the reason Tom's trips to Florida were so infrequent, though I was sure his lack of attentiveness happened way before I came along.

The irony of it all was that I understood Francesca's sorrow every time Tom withheld his affections. Understood why his financial generosity and benign indifference were not enough.

Still, I tried that weekend she came, not knowing it would be both the first and last time I shared our oceanfront home with her. I even painted one of the bedrooms purple, knowing it was her favorite color, stocked the house with her favorite foods and the CD player with her favorite music. We shared that in common, too—a love of music. And though our tastes were different, I knew her love of Madonna's rebelliousness was right in tune with my own rock and roll youth.

Of course, Francesca refused to see that she and I shared common ground, spending the weekend roaming the beach with the friend she had brought along, searching for adventures that didn't include me and Tom. I couldn't blame her. Hadn't I been the same way when I was her age? I guess part of me was surprised to find myself in the role of shunned parent. And a lot of me was hurt by the hatred I saw in her eyes.

Not that Tom noticed any of it. He kept to his routine of fishing, cooking and relaxing. Even taking off on an all-day offshore fishing boat tour right smack dab in the middle of the weekend his daughter was there.

She never came back again.

By the time we put her on a plane back home, I was relieved to see her go. But my relief was only momentary. When Tom and I came home that night to our New York apartment, I realized that I had been hoping to gain in Francesca and Tom the family I had alienated myself from.

And reminded me that I was more alone than ever.

That winter, I dreamed of having a child of my own. Of

course, that wasn't going to happen. I had agreed to Tom's no-more-children rule when I agreed to be his wife. I had thought I was sure at the time. Tom was so certain he'd even had a vasectomy a few years after Francesca was born. After spending that miserable weekend at the beach with her, I couldn't blame him.

Still, that didn't stop the longing in me.

Of course, Tom could have had his surgery reversed. But, as he reminded me whenever I brought the subject up, I had known what I was getting into.

I suppose I had, but everyone changes.

Not Tom. Tom had already figured out his life, what he wanted, who he was. I had left my own behind—my job, my family. I couldn't blame Tom for the fact that I had quit my dead-end career in radio. Or that I rarely went to see my family. Those were my choices, but when I made them, I was still figuring out what might make me happy.

In hindsight, I'm not sure a child *would* have made me happy. Maybe it was a passing fancy. I'll never really know. But I knew I needed something to soothe the ache of loneliness that filled my days.

Something more than what I had with Tom.

14

Zoe
You should see the other guy.

The minute my foot strikes the dusty trail toward Fair Harbor, I feel reborn. Running does that for me. Though this morning, I think I might have to run to the end of the island and back to shake the unease that's dogged me ever since Tom's drunken display the night before.

Maybe she's better off dead.

Somehow, with the sun shining down on my shoulders, the fresh breeze pumping through my lungs, I'm having a hard time believing that.

As I fly over the sandy path, I wonder if Maggie ever took this route. She was a runner, too. At least that's what she told me that first beach weekend, as I did my pre-run stretches on the deck. She'd even recommended a running path, a scenic six miles to the Jones Beach tower. I'm sure it would have been a lovely run.

But today I had more than running on my mind.

I blew out through my mouth, nodding briskly, as is the custom, at the jogger who passed me, trying to imagine what it might have been like to hurry down this trail on a moonless night.

In search of…coriander.

Okay, so maybe I don't understand this woman exactly. Yeah, I like to run, but I don't like to run for groceries.

"Morning," another passing jogger belted out.

I nodded. Who liked to talk during a jog?

Jogging was when I did all my thinking.

What I was wondering now was why Tom was convinced his wife was better off dead when it was clear to me that *he* was better off. An oceanfront house free and clear and—judging from the number of women who cozied up to him at the party last night—a range of choices for Mrs. Tom Landon Number Three.

If he wasn't a murderer, then I understood less about men than I realized. Which was why I decided pursue another trail. Maggie's…

The first thing I noticed about the Fair Harbor Market once I was standing before it, sweaty and heaving, was that it was a helluva lot bigger than Kismet Market. Big enough to carry a full wall of produce, a freezer case full of fish, meat and poultry and quite possibly…coriander.

I ducked inside and headed straight for the produce aisle, feeling in the know now that I have already purchased the herb—it was right by the produce in Gourmet Garage. But as my eyes roamed over rows of tomatoes, lettuce, bananas and apples, all I realized was that I was starving. I hadn't had breakfast yet, and I was way too hungry to be in a supermarket without a dollar to my name.

And covered in sweat, I realized, catching sight of myself in the security mirror at the end of the aisle.

"Can I help you?"

Startled, I looked up to find myself face-to-face with a tow-headed teenager who was eyeing me suspiciously. Probably because I had been staring way too long at the security mirror.

"Do you sell coriander?"

He frowned and I felt a momentary triumph. At least I'm not the only one who never heard of the herb until two weeks ago. But then I noticed the henna tattoo on the back of his hand and realized he was way too young to know anything yet. "Is that like…an herb or something?"

Or something. "Yeah. Exactly." Look at me. Educating the young. Who says there's no hope for me?

He nodded, then turned toward the condiment aisle, bypassing a line of mustard, ketchup and pickle relish, to a smallish section that I could see at a glance contained cayenne, garlic powder, salt....

Everything except coriander.

Now what? I thought once I stood outside the store again, blinking against the sunlight. So the store doesn't sell coriander. Doesn't prove that she didn't come there looking for it, as Tom claimed to me and, I can only assume, to the police.

You think she would have called and checked first. But I have no way of verifying whether she did or not.

Okay, so she comes up to Fair Harbor Market and, distraught over not finding her key ingredient, she decides to walk home along the beach.

God, maybe it was a suicide.

Who kills themselves over an herb?

I headed for the beach, figuring at the very least I could finish my run on a more scenic route. At best, I might be able to figure out what was going through Maggie's head.

As I climbed the wooden walkway to the beach, I wondered if she'd even come to the market that night. I'm not sure what time she died. Nick claimed she was still home when he left for The Inn at seven-thirty, which meant she must have headed to Fair Harbor some time after that.

Was the Fair Harbor market even open at 7:30 p.m.? I know Kismet market wasn't open that late. Not until the full season began. And full season didn't begin until July Fourth.

I turned around, jogged back to the market.

"What time does the market close?" I asked the cashier, a short, dark-haired girl who stood studying the split ends at the tips of her hair.

"Eight o'clock," she answered, not looking up from her inspection.

"What about before July Fourth? Like on a Saturday night?"

She looked up. "Seven," she answered, eyeing me as if I were a simpleton for not knowing that.

The big question was, had Maggie known it? Did she even go

to the market that night? And if so, what the hell was she doing during the two and a half hours between when Nick saw her at the house and the time I found her on the beach?

She wasn't just chopping vegetables, I thought, remembering that most of her meal was left unmade. Where did she go?

Not to the beach, I realized, once I climbed down the wooden steps to it. The sun didn't set until at least eight-thirty in June. In fact, it was just starting to go down when I left the city that night, around eight. I can only assume she wasn't inspired to strip down naked and dive in during daylight. It was hard to imagine Maggie skinny-dipping at all, much less doing it at a time when the whole world might catch a glimpse of her goods.

I headed for the shore, walking at a brisk pace.

Okay, so let's assume Maggie did go to the store and then realized belatedly it was closed. She then decided to walk home. Why not? She was in no hurry. Dinner was already ruined, I remembered, trying to shake off my own guilt for my part in that. Besides, walking along the beach was nice. Especially when the sun was going down.

Once I began to pass through Saltaire, I remembered that Tom was in Saltaire the night of the drowning—or so he said. At the chief of security's house. Maybe he walked home along the beach, ran into Maggie. A fight ensued. I mean, they had been fighting earlier that night, at least according to Nick. I wondered if Tom had mentioned that little detail to the police. I also wondered if the chief of security at Saltaire had hedged about the time Tom had left the house. God, did people do that? It seemed insane to imagine a man charged with law enforcement for his hamlet would do such a thing, but people stuck together on Fire Island. I suppose anything was possible. There was no one else to corroborate the story. No witnesses. It wasn't even the full season yet, so it was possible the beach was empty. It was never really full of people at night. There had been no one on it when I had taken my walk with Myles last summer. And there was no one on it when I took my ill-fated stroll with Janis.

But Maggie was naked. Did a woman fighting with her husband suddenly drop her drawers?

Unless the husband was playing apologetic. Maybe he'd even seduced her into the water.

Did married people seduce one another?

There was always the possibility that Maggie was with someone else. Like a lover. I thought of Donnie Havens and his hot-tub parties, then quickly shook off the thought, remembering his hairpiece. God, if Maggie *was* having an affair, I would hope she would choose better.

Then I remembered that she had been pretty cozy with Nick that first weekend. Not that I thought Nick could be responsible for taking another life. Hell, he could hardly keep his own together. Besides, he barely knew Maggie. Yeah, he was a fast operator when it came to women, but not only would he have had to have started an affair, it would also have had to spiral pretty far out of control for him to murder her.

Jesus, where was I going with this? Nick was my friend. I'd know if he was a murderer. Right?

Maybe I was trusting my gut too much, but my gut said Tom. Myles always said I relied a bit too hard on my instincts, which sometimes got me into trouble. It was one of the reasons I had a difficult time finding film work these days. I had become known as a bit of a maverick in the industry—that was the polite word for loose cannon—when I had exposed a manufacturing company for illegal dumping in the midst of making a corporate video for them. Yeah, I lost the gig—you didn't turn the camera against the company who was bankrolling you and expect them to be grateful. But at least the company had been slapped with a big enough fine to keep them from doing that again. Of course, the job offers hadn't exactly flowed in after that little incident.

I shook my head, trying to bring myself back to the present situation, wishing, as I did, that I had Myles to bounce ideas off of. He was always so level-headed, and I'll admit I needed that kind of sounding board when I was concocting my conspiracy theories.

Or in this case, murder theories.

Now, gazing around at the beachgoers as I entered the hamlet of Kismet, I wished I would run into Myles, despite my disheveled appearance. Just to talk this through. He'd always been such a good listener....

Then I remembered that Myles was likely discussing legal matters and God-knows-what-else with a certain blonde in a yellow bikini.

Jerk.

Still, I found myself combing the beach for him as I walked. I wasn't sure what I needed more, to see Myles and be reminded that he wasn't mine anymore, or to talk to him and remember that he should be. We were so good together....

My heart stopped when my gaze fell upon a golden-brown head, standing beside a small motorbike with four wheels—a quad, I think they're called—a hundred yards away. The face, even hidden behind silver aviator glasses, was familiar, but I realized right away it wasn't Myles. Though it could have been, had Myles followed in his cop father's footsteps like he'd once planned. This guy was in uniform, a Suffolk County police uniform, and looking a bit like Mr. Callahan probably did back in the day.

Then I remembered I had seen this cop before. He was the officer who had responded to the 9-1-1 call the night of the murder. I'm sorry, did I say murder? Drowning. Myles would say "innocent until proven guilty," which was probably why he was up for a job in the D.A.'s office, while I was lucky if I would eat next week.

Before I could think twice, I was hurrying over to the aforementioned officer, who was just about to get on his quad and drive off now that he'd finishing chastising a dog owner for allowing his golden retriever to frolic on the beach without a leash.

It's a wonder these guys weren't investigating Maggie's death a little more thoroughly. I mean, really—ticketing dog owners? Surely murder was more interesting.

"Excuse me?" I yelled, seeing as my only link to the non-case was just about to ride off down the beach without satisfying my now rampant curiosity. "Officer..." I tried to remember his name, then realized I didn't have to remember when I jumped in front of the quad he sat on, catching a glimpse of his nameplate as I did. "Officer Barnes?"

He stopped, turning his sunglassed gaze on me and making me very aware of my sweat-stained T-shirt and running shorts.

He lifted his aviators for a better look, and I thought I saw a flicker of interest in those baby blues he revealed.

No way. I certainly wasn't going to win any beauty pageants in this sweaty getup.

"Hi," I said, uncertainly. "You probably don't remember me...."

He dropped his glasses back on his nose. "I remember you," he replied coolly. Or maybe it just seemed cool. Everyone sounded cooler when speaking from behind aviator glasses. Beneath those aviators was a strong jaw, stubborn mouth, straight nose. Regulation cop. Where did they find this guy—central casting?

"You were at the house the night of the 10-32," he said.

"10-32?"

"Oh, sorry." His lips quirked ruefully. "The drowning incident."

Definitely central casting. He had the part down pat. Still, I answered politely. "Yes, I was. Good memory."

"I never forget a pretty face."

Holy cow. This guy *was* checking me out. The breeze blew, pressing my damp shirt against my breasts. Seduction by sweat. Hey, maybe some guys were into that sort of thing.

I had never used sex appeal to my advantage. In fact, I wasn't even sure I knew how. Still I was willing to take a crack at it. In the name of justice, of course.

Giving him what I hoped was my most winning smile, I said, "Zoe Keller, in case you're not as good at names." I held out a hand, which he looked at for a moment, then shook. Mmm, nice grip. "I guess that doesn't happen every day either?"

His expression was puzzled as he looked down at our linked hands.

"A 10-32," I prompted, dropping my hand.

"Oh, that. Actually, it happens more often than you think," he said, leaning back on his quad. "Do you know that last summer there were thirty-seven water-related accidents in Suffolk County alone?"

I felt my eyes bulge. Maybe I was making too much out of this. "Really?"

His chest seemed to visually puff up. "Well, not all of them resulted in a DB."

"A DB?"

He smiled. "Sorry. Dead body. But nine out of ten times, it's usually an alcohol-related incident. Victim has a few drinks and gets into the water. Kinda like your friend there."

I frowned. Why did this story seem so simple to everyone else? "How many people would you say skinny-dip by themselves?"

His eyebrows raised and I saw that smile tinge his lips once again. "You know, we don't have statistics on that. How about you?"

"Me? I don't have any statist—"

"No, skinny-dip. Ever do it?"

"Uh, no," I replied, feeling like a prude. Worse, a sweaty prude. I didn't care what this guy thought, I reminded myself.

Was he looking at my breasts?

Okay, maybe I did. "How about you?" I asked, even though this conversation was slowly becoming beside the point. "Ever skinny-dip?"

"Sure," he replied. Something about the way his mouth clenched made me think he was just boasting. I suddenly wished I could see his eyes.

As if he read my mind, he lifted his glasses. "Perhaps someone should show you what you've been missing," he said, his gaze intent on mine.

Uh, nope. He wasn't boasting.

I felt my body tighten, and as soon as it did, a wave of embarrassment followed. What was I doing panting after some cop on a motorbike? I wasn't… I wasn't that kind of girl. Besides, I was never too good around authority figures, witness the scar over my left eye, earned when a cop tried to stop me from plowing through a police barricade with my camera during an antiwar demonstration.

I dropped my gaze to his chest, noticed it was looking rather firm under his sexy little uniform.

Maybe I *was* that kind of girl.

Since I was too embarrassed to find out, I got back to the matter at hand. "Let me ask you something," I said, studying the Marine Bureau insignia on his chest, "is there any way to tell when a person drowns, how it happened? I mean, if the person was pulled under by a wave. Or, say…a person."

He dropped his glasses back down now that I had turned to less flirtatious subjects.

"Well, generally speaking, the first thing you look for is evidence of a struggle. Torn clothes. Marks on the body."

"And were any marks found on the body?"

"Well, I was the first officer on the scene, and I didn't see any," he said defensively. Then his lips firmed, as if he remembered something. "I really shouldn't even be talking about this case."

"Really? Why?"

"It wouldn't be ethical."

I bit my lip. Leave it to me to find a noble cop. But it didn't make sense. Last I checked, all civilians were entitled to information contained in police records due to the Freedom of Information Act. I knew that much. Hadn't I dug into files myself, while filming my doc on homelessness, when I needed information on one of my subjects who went missing three weeks before I was done? Yes, I could go the official route, but I knew it would take time. And if Maggie was murdered, I didn't have time.

I was going to have to appeal to Barnes's ego. And if the way his chest was all puffed up was any indication, this might have been his first big case. He couldn't have been any older than my own thirty. He probably hadn't handled many DBs, as he called them. "Well, maybe you can just speak generally about…about 10-32s. I just find this stuff fascinating, Officer Barnes."

"Jeff," he replied. Then he smiled. "You can call me that. Since we're speaking unofficially."

"Jeff," I repeated, smiling right back at him. "So if there is no evidence of a struggle, that would rule out someone pushing the victim under? What if the victim knew the person?"

He shook his head. "Doesn't matter if it was the victim's best friend pushing her under. If a person is being forced under water she—or he—is going to fight it. Kicking, scratching. Something always turns up—a DNA sample under the nails, for example."

He said this with such confidence, I was starting to believe that maybe I had been unduly suspicious. Then I thought of something. "How do you know the victim wasn't dead when she went into the water?"

"Well, that's easy enough. When a person drowns, they inhale water into the lungs. The medical examiner would be able to tell that due to the condition of the lungs, the presence of micro-organisms from the water in the person's system."

Micro-organisms? Yuck. Even if Maggie wasn't murdered, drowning didn't sound like the most pleasant of deaths.

"What if she—that is, the victim—was unconscious? Would she inhale water then?"

He stiffened. "Look, Zoe, I don't know what your interest is in this case, but I don't feel comfortable talking in too much detail...."

That was interesting. What had made him so uncomfortable? I switched tracks. "Oh, well. I guess I can go to the department to get my information. But it's too bad. That'll take time, and I was hoping to get my research down before I started filming."

"Filming?" he replied, his interest piqued.

Gotcha, I thought, trying not to smile. Worked like a charm every time. I knew from long experience that it was easy to get somebody to talk about a subject if they knew their words might one day be immortalized on film. "I'm a documentary filmmaker. I directed *Invisible People,* a piece on New York City's homeless. Maybe you've heard of it?"

He frowned. "No, I haven't."

So much for my ego.

Still, he seemed interested. "What are you working on now?"

"Oh, just something on water-related accidents. For PBS."

"Really?"

I nodded.

"Well, I can answer a few questions, I suppose."

Bingo. "So let me ask you, how can you tell if a person was conscious—in any sort of drowning, that is—before he or she hit the water? What if she was hit over the head? Or he," I added, quickly.

"Well, as I already mentioned, we would look for evidence of a struggle. If she had suffered a blow to the head rendering her unconscious, the autopsy would reveal that."

"So let me ask you, does the investigating officer go over the autopsy? You know, to compare his findings at the scene with the medical examiner's?"

"Well, not necessarily me. That is, not necessarily the first officer on the scene."

"Who would?"

"Drowning deaths are turned over to homicide, and they do the follow-up. Accidents like that always are followed up by them," he replied, a bit defensively I thought.

"Oh. So who has access to that information?"

"Whatever detective was on homicide that night." I saw him physically slump as he said this, as if he realized he was no longer my hero.

But I realized there was someone who *could* be my hero. Myles. Last summer he'd interned at the D.A.'s office for Suffolk County, thanks to his dad, who'd recommended him for the position. Hell, Myles might even know the homicide detective who was on that night. His father probably had.

I would have to talk to Myles. If he was still willing to talk to me.

15

Nick
Money doesn't grow on trees. But far be it from me not to plant a few seeds.

"Dude, I got you covered. That's what I'm trying to tell you."

This was a first for me. I'm sitting on the beach, gazing out into the ocean, plastic cup of beer in hand, making a deal. It's the kind of thing that can give a guy a woody, you know?

And I would have a woody if Les Wolf, aka Paranoid Lead Singer of Nose Dive, knew enough not to look a gift horse in the mouth. I'm offering this guy a chance to sign with Revelation, and he's hemming and hawing over money. "No worries," I told him last week when we started hammering out the deal, and he's still worrying.

"So you're going to put up ten thousand just for publicity. That's over and above the advance and recording costs," Les said.

I glanced over at Sage, who was still fast asleep on a blanket on the other side of the umbrella from me. Still, I lowered my voice. "I told you, dude. Money is not a problem here."

"And all the monies we discussed—for the advance, publicity, recording—those will be in the contract?"

I sighed. "My lawyer's working on it right now." Good thing my dad was my lawyer. I had just popped a payment of two grand in the mail to Lance to get him working on the site, and after I paid the monies I promised in this contract, I was going to be back where I started again. Nearly broke. But all that would change. Just as soon as we got our first CD distributed, the royalties would start rolling in.

"Listen, Les, I'd love to talk all day with you, man, but I got another client to call." Another client. Yeah right. Another beer maybe. Not that I'm a bullshitter. But when it comes to negotiating, you gotta treat the prospective client like you would the prospective lay. Always make them think there's someone you want more.

Smiling, I listened as Les promised to call as soon as he talked to the rest of the band. "No later than next week," he said.

"Later," I said, snapping the phone shut with a smile. Worked like a charm.

As if to prove my point, my cell rang again. I looked at the caller ID. Bernadine. Of course Bernadine was calling. Probably because I hadn't yet responded to her post breakup call. The one she always followed up the breakup letter with. I never understood why the call was necessary. I guess Bern wanted to make sure I understood all those heartfelt thoughts she put in her letters. Hell, if I didn't understand by now…

I hadn't responded at first because I was in a bit of a mad scramble before I got out to the beach.

And now…

Now I realized I had gotten the upper hand by not calling back. And I figured I'd hold on to it a bit.

As the call rolled over into voice mail, I sucked down the rest of my beer. If only they had waitress service out here on the beach. I could sure use another cold one.

With that thought in mind, I got up and headed up to the house. Maybe Zoe was back from her run. Though I appreciated the privacy while I conducted my business, I was getting a little bored watching the waves break with just that mutt staring at me. Sage had passed out the minute her head hit the beach blanket. I guess she'd had a lot of tequila last night.

Unfortunately, Zoe was not at the house. But Tom was. Cooking again. Geez, didn't this guy ever take a break?

"I see you decided to join the living," I commented as I walked past the counter where he was busily chopping away at something or other. Seemed to be a habit with him. Maggie, too, come to think of it.

Actually, I tried not to think of Maggie. It only made me feel guilty, especially after I filed her business plan away in my drawer file, under *U* for useless.

Tom looked up at me with a puzzled frown. "What's that?"

"You feeling any better?" I asked. He had been in pretty sorry shape the night before. I guess I should be grateful, seeing as I didn't have to put up with any late night chats with Tom once I crawled into bed myself. But the snoring! Jesus.

"I feel fine," he replied, same puzzled expression on his face.

"Okay, buddy. Just wondered. I mean, you had a lot to drink last night."

He shrugged. "Ah, that was nothing."

No, dude, it was something, I thought, remembering his little display after the fireworks. At least it kept Zoe occupied, concocting her crazy theories.

"Nick, will you do me a favor?" Tom said now. "Can you go up to the market and pick me up some dill?"

Dill? I never saw anything like dill in that market, and I was about to make that point when he continued, "And if they don't have any in the produce section, ask Bobby. They usually have a secret stash in the back for residents." He winked at me, as if he were somehow letting me in on the dill conspiracy.

Whoop-de-doo.

"I'll walk up there with you, Nick."

I looked up to see Francesca, leaning languidly against the sliding glass door, clad in a baby-blue bikini.

"You better put something on," Tom said. "You'll get a burn walking around like that."

That's not the only thing she'll get, I thought, watching as Francesca narrowed her eyes on him.

"You need anything else?" I asked. I was immediately sorry I did. Because I wasn't gonna ask for money—in fact, I would feel a little dumb doing that, seeing as he was probably cooking that meal for us. And though I was grateful to be served a home-cooked meal, I didn't feel like emptying my wallet in that overpriced market. I had bills to pay. The band. Lance. Comp USA.

Shit. I'd forgotten about the Comp USA. Man, I really was almost outta cash. I guess I didn't have to get that new iPod, too. Maybe I could get Les to come down in the advance a bit....

"Naw, that's it. Just dill. Thanks, Nick."

"No problem," I said, then stepped through the sliding glass door and on to the deck to wait for Francesca.

She came out moments later, having added the tiniest miniskirt to her bikini outfit. I was surprised she managed to get by Tom in that getup.

We started to walk down West Lighthouse toward the market. Of course, Francesca didn't say a word. But she hardly had a thing to say last night at the party, even after I told her about my label. Well, she did seem kinda interested. Her eyes lit up a bit when I mentioned I was in the music business. Which only made me more curious about her.

"So you down here for the summer, huh?" I asked now.

I felt her looking at me from behind her black sunglasses. Gucci, too. I bet they were real. "Here and Manhattan," she replied.

"Is that right? You live in the city?"

"Mmm-hmm."

"Whereabouts?"

"64th and Park. With my dad," she replied, as if the answer was obvious.

"Oh." I didn't think Tom's daughter lived with him. At least Sage hadn't said so. Maybe it was a temporary thing. "You go to school up here?"

She smiled, stopping to pull a pink flower off a bush in front of house we passed. "I'm done with school."

"Congratulations."

No reply as she tucked the pink flower behind one ear.

"So where'd you go?"

"Florida International University. In Miami."

"Nice. Beach all year round."

She shrugged. "It was my mother's choice, not mine. She's in Boca."

"Oh." Damn, this girl was a tough nut to crack. "So you got a boyfriend you left down in Florida?"

"Boyfriend?" She sputtered out a laugh. "I don't believe in boy-friends."

What the hell did that mean?

"I mean, really," she went on, "what is a boyfriend? A friend that's a boy?" She laughed again. "I don't play with boys."

"Oh yeah," I replied gamely. "What do you do with them?"

A mysterious smile curled her little pink mouth. "Wouldn't you like to know."

"Dill. You know? I think it's an herb…or something. Anyway, you got any?" I asked Bobby with no small amount of irritation. Not that it was Bobby's fault I was irritated, I thought, watching as Francesca leaned over the freezer case in that minuscule skirt.

I focused my attention on the ever-accommodating Bobby—at least, he was accommodating every time Sage came to the market with me—and saw that he was shaking his head at me.

"Nothing?" I replied. "Not even in the back?"

Now Bobby, who looked a little like John-Boy Walton, aged about twenty years and outfitted with a gut and graying goatee, was eyeing me somewhat suspiciously. "For Tom Landon. Lives over on West Lighthouse?" I added. Jesus, what was with this dude? It wasn't like I was asking if he was hoarding weapons of mass destruction or anything.

And if I was, apparently Tom's name was the magic word, because Bobby nodded, mumbled something about "having a look in the back," and disappeared, leaving me to contemplate Francesca, who had apparently made her selection—a cherry-red ice pop that she was currently performing fellatio on.

Hurry, Bobby, hurry. Or I was going to do something I might regret.

I swallowed that thought as I eyed her perfect breasts pouring out of that bikini top. I would never regret a taste of her. But good old Tom sure wouldn't appreciate it. Or Sage, for that matter.

"Mmmm…" Francesca said, popping the ice back in her mouth again. She wasn't looking at me, but I knew she was aware of me.

That's the kind of girl she was. Acting all innocent and shit, but she knew exactly what was going on. I knew the type.

"Maybe you ought to take that outside," I said.

That bright blue gaze focused on me.

"You're dripping on the floor," I explained. Not that it mattered. Within moments, a little squirt of a kid—couldn't have been more than ten—was suddenly beneath her, smiling up at her as he swabbed the floor with a paper towel. "No problem, miss!" he declared.

Yeah, I knew the type. Which is why I was glad I had decided to steer clear. Or Sage had decided. Whatever.

I watched as Francesca's eyes widened, and she ran off to a rack at the back, returning with some kind of snack I had never seen before. They looked like potato chips but they were multicolored. And the bag was black. "Oh, I love these!" she declared, her mouth now bright red from the pop. "Can we get these? Please?"

For a minute I felt like the parent trying to decide if I should appease all my kid's desires. But I wasn't a parent—and I didn't want to be, at least not to this chick—so I said, "You can get anything you want."

Which was the wrong thing to say, apparently. Because once we reached the register, I realized that even if I didn't want to play the parent, I was going to have to pay the piper. Little Francesca didn't have a dime on her. I should have guessed. I mean, where would she have put it? I thought, eyeing that little skirt, my gaze traveling over her flat little abs.

It was probably the thought of my tongue gliding over those abs that had me pulling out my debit card. I had to. Little Miss Thang over here had, in addition to the bag of chips, also plunked on the counter a container of nail polish remover, some nail files and a pack of Marlboro Reds. I had to bite my tongue against an antismoking comment, for fear I was becoming the daddy here. At least, the sugar daddy. "You better ring that up, too," I said to the girl behind the counter, gesturing to the pop Francesca waltzed out the front door with.

"That'll be $17.65," the cashier replied, without batting an eye. And why would she? Eighteen bucks was nothing in a place like this. Though it was something to me, that was for sure, feeling a stab of panic as the cashier slid my card through the machine.

Shit, I forgot I bought all those clothes, too. I was probably a few more grocery runs from flat-out broke.

Maybe Lance could wait for his next payment. Once he started building the site, he might be able to work on enthusiasm alone.

Pocketing my card and grabbing the bag, I stepped outside, watching as Francesca dumped her half-eaten ice pop in the trash, then turned and beamed a cherry-red smile at me.

"Ready?" she said.

"Yeah," I replied, gazing distractedly at her ass as she started down the road to the house.

We walked back in silence, mostly because I no longer felt like talking. Instead, I was worrying.

What made me think I could get by on twenty-five grand?

"Look!" Francesca said, stopping suddenly.

I looked up and found myself staring through the reeds at a deer. A doe, I guess it was, standing protectively over a smaller deer. The baby, I guess. What did they call those again? Whatever. They were all over Fire Island. Like giant, tick-infested rodents.

"So pretty!" Francesca sighed, grabbing my arm, pressing one of those perfect breasts into me as she did.

Oh, man. Pretty was an understatement.

"I wish I had my camera," she said wistfully.

I wished *I* had her camera. She'd pulled it out at the party the night before, and it was quite a camera. The latest in digital. It had to cost at least a grand.

Nothing's too good for Daddy's little girl.

Then another thought emerged. Maggie wasn't the only investor in this town. Or in my beach house. Maybe I didn't have to look any farther than my own backyard.

I looked down at Francesca's happy little face as she gazed at the deer in wonder.

What I was wondering was how much influence Francesca had over Daddy. And if maybe Daddy might want to buy his little girl a little stock in a music label.

Hey, why not make it a family business?

Oh, God, that was terrible. Maybe I was evil.

I looked down at Francesca, her mouth parted dreamily as she stared at the deer. It wouldn't be a bad thing for her to develop a few cultural interests. I could be her mentor. I glanced down at her cleavage. A mentor with…benefits.

"C'mon, let's go up to the house and get that camera before they go away," I said, gazing down at her.

"Okay!" she said, squeezing my arm with excitement as she smiled up at me.

And what a smile it was. I felt a warmth curl inside me, and I'm not just talking about the one that had already started in my groin.

She wasn't just hot. She was kinda…sweet, too.

I mean for a kid.

A rich kid, that is.

16

Sage
My love life is going to the dogs. So to speak.

I'm not a calculating person. Generally speaking, anyway. But I do believe that some matters—like men—should not be left up to chance.

I also knew that this thing with Vince was not going to happen unless I made it happen. He was elusive, that one, darting off just moments after we had gotten Tom into bed last night. I had been hoping for a little post-Tom-tuck-in nightcap. Apparently, Vince just wanted to go home and tuck himself in.

So I decided to use my resources. In this case, Janis Joplin, who was looking a little neglected anyway. I figured she could use a nice walk along the beach. It was a beautiful day. Everyone was at the beach. Everyone except Zoe, who had gone running, probably to avoid getting burns on top of her burns. Nick had been there for a little while. I heard him gabbing on with someone on his cell phone, before he took off to God knows where. Who brought a cell phone to the beach? Everyone who mattered to him was at the beach, though I was starting to think no one mattered to Nick more than Nick.

I had nothing to lose by taking my stroll. I was getting a little exercise, and that never hurt. Janis looked like she could use the companionship. As much as she looked anything. I wasn't much of a dog person, though I had grown up with a dog. Well, Hope's dog anyway. My parents had bought her a German shepherd puppy for her tenth birthday—she had been begging for a dog the entire summer before. But Hope was gone before Prince was barely housebroken. I had taught him to walk on a leash, mostly because my parents were too catatonic to remember they'd ever had a dog, much less another daughter. They never had him fixed, and he was gone by year's end, too. Ran off, I suspect, with the mongrel down the street.

I guess there was no accounting for taste.

Now as Janis led the way along the shore, I realized it felt good to have a leash in my hands again. I think Janis was enjoying it, too. Tom hadn't exactly been paying much attention to her anyway. I was starting to give some serious thought to dog ownership. I had been stopped by no less than three guys—two of them quite good-looking—on my way down the beach.

Not that I was interested. I seemed to have only one man on my mind. Vince.

Maybe it was the challenge. Zoe had accused me often enough of loving the chase more than anything else. Yes, it was true my interest had spiked the minute he outmaneuvered me at the party, but it wasn't just that this time. There was something about him. Something I had glimpsed in his eyes as we carried Tom back to the house together. A genuine caring.

I don't think I was imagining it either. After all, no one else— none of Tom's other pals—had rushed to help Tom the way Vince had.

But I guess they were best friends. Which was why I needed to be careful, too. I wasn't sure if Tom would approve of dating within the office. Then I remembered Yaz had dated a sales rep at Luxe, which was a full three blocks down Seventh Avenue from the showroom for Edge. And the office Vince worked from was all the way out on Long Island.

Still, I would have to be discreet. At least initially. Tom was paying me a pretty fat salary as head sales rep at Edge. But that didn't mean I had to lose an edge on getting next to Vince.

Now, where the hell was he?

My eyes scanned the beach as I got closer to Seabay Walk, the block where Vince mentioned his house was located. Chances are, he had set up camp on the beach close to Seabay, which was about five blocks east of West Lighthouse Walk, where Maggie's Dream was located. But as my gaze moved over the blankets and beach umbrellas that lined the sandy shoreline, I suddenly couldn't picture Vince out here. He seemed too worldly and sophisticated to be lying on a beach blanket. I could see him on a sailboat, dressed in whites. Sitting outside a beachfront café sipping a martini—not that we had any beachfront cafés in Kismet.

Maybe gazing into my eyes across a table in Rome…

Mmm. I always wanted to go to Italy.

I heard Janis gasp and realized she was choking as she tugged me along. Who taught this dog to walk on a leash? I wondered, realizing that it was probably Maggie and that Maggie had left off…midtraining. I think they'd only gotten Janis this past year. I pulled Janis to a halt and she sat, looked up at me, her brown eyes all innocence, her tongue flecked with foam.

Clearly I wasn't ready to pick up where Maggie left off with the dog. The poor thing was dying of thirst, and I hadn't even remembered to bring water for her. So much for my new life as a dog owner.

Then I felt my own throat grow dry at the sight of darkly tanned legs. My eyes roamed up to the darkly handsome man attached, who was sitting in a low beach chair, talking on a cell phone.

Okay, so maybe the cell phone on the beach was a guy thing.

The question was, did I wait for him to get off it before I moseyed by or…

Suddenly my choice was taken away from by none other than Janis, who leaped forward, barking wildly as she pulled me toward the water.

Oh, God. She was going to take me right into the tide.

Yes, I was wearing a bikini, but drowned rat wasn't the look I wanted for my next meeting with Vince.

"Janis, heel!" I yelled, and miraculously, she did, though I think it had less to do with my command than with the little girl who sat just at the tideline, laughing as Janis practically bowled her over in attempt to lick every inch of her face.

"Janis!" the girl squealed, reaching her arms around the dog's neck to embrace her as she did.

Janis? What, did everyone on the beach know Maggie's dog already?

Unless…

"Sophia!"

I turned to see Vince, now standing, cell phone abandoned as he called out, his face creased with what looked like the concern of a…of a parent. For his child.

Oh, God. I knew Vince came with baggage, as in the ex-wife variety, I just hadn't counted on a kid.

He walked down the beach, his eyes lighting with recognition when he saw me.

"Oh, it's you," he said.

So much for a hearty hello-good-to-see-you-again.

"Yes, I was just taking Janis for a walk," I hedged.

He smiled finally, relief evident in his features. "For a second, I thought Sophia was being attacked by a strange dog. So many labs on the beach. I guess I didn't recognize Janis."

So many girls, too. At least he recognized me.

"I like your bathing suit," the little girl said, startling me. I looked up to discover she was now standing by my side, studying me curiously as she fondled one of Janis's ears.

I felt an urge to pat the kid's head.

"Oh, I'm sorry, Sage, this is my daughter, Sophia," Vince said.

All the fight drained out of me, now that he had confirmed it. His daughter. I studied Vince as he smiled down at Sophia. He looked even more handsome, if that was possible, in a pair of cargo shorts and a white button-down rolled up at the sleeves. Sophia looked just like him, too. Same dark eyes and long lashes. Same exotic features.

A father. I guess it made sense. He had been married, and he had to be close to Tom's age. But still, it disturbed me. I had never dated a man with children. Hell, most of the men I dated *were* children.

"How's Tom feeling today?" he asked.

"He's okay. He slept in a little bit."

He nodded, as if this answer satisfied him.

"We gonna go in the water now, Daddy?" Sophia asked.

He sighed. "Not now, kiddo. We have to head back up to the house."

Sophia's face crumpled, and she looked ready to stamp one of her pretty little bare feet. I couldn't blame her. I wanted to stamp my foot, too. This guy was always running off somewhere.

"Daddy has to send a few e-mails," Vince replied. Then he looked at me. "You leave the office for a few days and chaos ensues."

"But the office is closed for the holiday weekend," I said.

He smiled ruefully. "They aren't celebrating the Fourth in China, unfortunately. In fact, it's almost Monday morning in Shanghai. And I need to get some information to my team at our factory there."

Well, I like an ambitious man. But now I knew why I never dated them—because they were never around to date.

"But I want to stay at the beach!" Sophia wailed.

I resisted an urge to clamp my hands over my ears. I wasn't so sure I liked children. Well, I liked them well enough. Just didn't want to deal with them.

Then I looked up at Vince, saw the struggle in his beautiful features and, before I could think twice about it, I said, "I could keep an eye on her."

Vince looked at me. "Are you sure?"

"Yeah, I'm sure." As sure as I'll ever be.

Just moments after Vince left and Sophia sat looking up at me expectantly, panic set in. I hadn't dealt with a kid since I was a kid, and then it had been my sister. What was I going to do with this one?

"Janis looks hot," she said, smiling fondly at the brown lab, who had crawled under the umbrella to cool off, yet still sat heaving in the heat. "Maybe we should go in the water?"

"No," I answered quickly. Not the water. "How about something to drink? You got anything to drink in the cooler for this poor old dog?"

Sophia giggled. "She's not old. I'm older than she is."

"How old are you?" I asked.

"Six. But I'm gonna be seven after Santa Claus comes."

Six. God, I couldn't remember being six. I remembered Hope being six, but I don't think I ever was.

I shook off the thought, stepping over to the small cooler and pulling off the lid. Three bottles of water and a few ice pops in an assortment of colors. I felt Sophia step up next to me. "Ice pops!" she squealed, grabbing one before I could stop her.

Well, I supposed a little sugar wouldn't hurt anything. Besides, it might keep her occupied for a bit, I thought, watching as she struggled with the plastic wrap.

"Here, I'll help you." I took the pop from her, tearing the wrapper off and handing it back. She looked at me as if I had solved world hunger, smiling happily as she popped the tip of the bright green ice in her mouth.

Grabbing a bottle of water, I opened it and took a good sip before turning to Janis, who sat, tongue lolling, as she gazed up at me.

How was I going to get this water in her?

"Here, use this," Sophia said, spotting my dilemma and reaching for a yellow bucket that sat abandoned on the beach blanket.

"Thanks," I replied, taking the bucket and filling it before I placed it before Janis, who perked up immediately, lapping up the water within moments.

Well, that took up at least four minutes. I looked at Sophia.

"Want some?" she said, holding out the pop to me as a gooey green line began to trail down her arms.

Yuck. "Uh, no thanks. I'm trying to quit."

She giggled. "Silly," she admonished. "Who would quit eating ice pops?"

Give it time, kid, you'll see.

Sitting down on the beach chair Vince had abandoned, I studied the horizon, the waves crashing on the beach.

"So how old are you?" Sophia asked.

"Thirty-one," I answered, surprised by her curiosity.

"Wow," she said. "That's almost as old as my daddy."

Hmm. Maybe I could turn this baby-sitting gig into an opportunity. A research opportunity. "How old is Daddy?"

"Forty-four. That's double digits," she said, licking a drip from the ice pop with satisfaction.

I smiled at her. Forty-four. Okay, older, but not as old as Tom, who was forty-eight if I remembered correctly.

"So do you live with Daddy?" I said.

She shook her head. "I live with Mommy."

Well, that was one hurdle down. I could deal with the whole kid thing better if the kid wasn't around all the time. "Where's Mommy today?"

"Home," she replied, maneuvering the ice pop to catch another drip.

"Where's home?"

"Brightwaters."

Just across the bay. A little too close for my comfort. "Where's Daddy live?" I asked, pumping the kid shamelessly.

She scrunched her nose. "In a condom."

I bit back a smile. "Condominium?"

Smiling brightly, she nodded her head.

"Where?"

"Brightwaters."

Uh-oh. That was a bit close to the ex. I wasn't sure I liked that.

But I supposed I would have to deal with it, if I really wanted this man. A vision filled my mind of Vince at the party the night before. Those broad shoulders. Dark eyes. Big, big hands.

Oh yeah, I wanted him. At least once. Maybe twice.

Okay, maybe I could do with a whole lot of him.

Besides, this kid business wasn't bad after all, I thought, sinking deeper into the chair. At least I was out in the sun. Relaxing…

"Ohhhhhh!"

I sat up, just in time to watch the rest of Sophia's ice pop slide off her stick and into the sand. Shit, now what? The kid looked like she was about to burst into tears. I could handle just about anything but tears.

"Sophie, honey, it's okay—"

The teary face dissolved, replaced by a frown. "It's Sophia."

The kid had moxie, I thought, looking at the way her dark brows pulled together over her perfect little nose. She had some cheekbones, too. Just like her daddy. "Sorry," I said finally.

She seemed to forgive me immediately, beaming me a thousand watt smile. "You want to help me make a sand castle?"

Actually, I had been thinking about taking a nap. Now I glanced at the assortment of buckets and shovels and wished I could shut my eyes and make it all go away. "Maybe later," I said noncommittally.

Sophia's face began to crumble again.

"Okay, okay!"

So that was how I wound up on my knees in the sand. After I had wiped off the green goo from Sophia's hands the best I could with a wet nap I found in Vince's beach bag, we set to work.

I remembered that I was quite the little castle-maker back in the day. Granted, I didn't have these fancy molds that Sophia had to make turrets, or a special shovel to carve out a moat. I was lucky my mother and father even remembered sunscreen when they took me to the beach. But as I dug up sand, molded corners, patted down the sides and carved out a few windows, a memory of me and Hope on the beach emerged. I shook it off, focusing on Sophia, her tongue between her teeth as she shoveled out the moat. It was one of the few jobs she could manage, and she had made a mess of herself in the process. Sand covered her everywhere—her knees, her chin and probably elsewhere, I realized, watching as she tugged at her bathing suit bottom.

"Can we go in the water now?" she said.

There was no way to avoid it any longer, I thought, looking at her flushed face and sandy arms and legs.

"Come on," I said reluctantly as I stood up.

"Yay!" Sophia yelled, jumping up and racing toward the tide.

"Sophia!" I said, running to catch up.

She stopped, turned around, a puzzled expression on her face.

"Wait for me," I said meekly.

She did, and within moments, we were both standing with our feet in the tide.

I stared out to the horizon, concentrating on the feel of the surf washing up against my legs....

And nearly fell over when I felt a small, wet hand clasp mine. I looked down with surprise and found a shivering Sophia smiling tremulously at me. As if she had given me her trust, then realized she wasn't sure if I could be trusted.

A wave rolled up, soaking my thighs and practically bowling Sophia over.

"Be careful," I said, clutching her hand tighter as she squealed.

I shivered, as an image filled my mind of rushing water, tugging at a listless body....

I couldn't save her. I couldn't....

I shut my eyes, but that didn't stop the images. And when I opened them again, I was surprised to feel them fill with tears.

But that was nothing compared to the fear that clutched at me when Sophia wrenched free of my hand.

"Sophia, no!" I shouted, the lump in my throat thickening to panic as I watched her narrowly escape a crashing wave.

"Sophia!" a male voice echoed, and I felt a wash of relief so strong tears did fall. I swiped at them quickly, before turning to see Vince heading down the beach toward us.

"Daddy! Sage and I are swimming!" Sophia yelled, running up the beach to meet him.

Giving me just enough time to swallow the rest of my tears. God, what was wrong with me? I thought I had this under control.

By the time Vince made his way down to the tide, Sophia now hoisted up on one lean hip, I had it under control.

Or so I thought.

"Is everything all right?" Vince asked, his gaze roaming over me speculatively.

"I'm fine. I just—" I looked around wildly, my eyes falling on Janis, who had stood, as if alerted to some trouble. "I need to get back."

Then, before I had to answer the questions I saw in his eyes, I jogged back up to the blanket, disentangling Janis's leash from the umbrella stand and heading quickly back toward the lighthouse and home.

17

Maggie
If I can't make it here, I can't make it anywhere.

Tom was the one who suggested I go back to work, which was ironic since he was the one who'd encouraged me to leave my job. Maybe he sensed my unhappiness. Not surprising, since I complained often enough. But if my lack of direction in life left me lethargic, it spurred Tom into action. First he suggested I come to work for him at Luxe, but the last thing I wanted to do was spend my days shuffling along in his shadow. I already did enough of that at home. He talked to friends in various industries, but the job offers were few and far between, and when they came, they were usually administrative, which made sense, since that was the only kind of job I had ever held during my not-very-glamorous and short-lived career in the music business. Then he started bringing home bulletins from the local colleges, believing a few courses might help me better define my dreams.

But as I flipped through course catalogs, I realized that I didn't have any dreams. Not anymore.

I also learned something about Tom during my malaise. And that was that he was at his happiest when he thought he could help. I started to understand all that passion he had shown me when we first met. Back then, I had been a glorified secretary on a meager salary and Tom was the white knight come to save me. He had been my hero then, and now, I realized, he was trying to be my hero again.

I loved him for trying. And hated myself a little more. I had never seen myself as a damsel in distress, but there I was, the disillusioned housewife with no more prospects and even less ambition than I'd had years ago.

Of course, it wasn't Tom's fault my life was nowhere. Though I sometimes wondered: If I hadn't been surrounded by the comfort and security he provided, might I have done something more than master the art of a making a respectable crème brûlée?

But it wasn't Tom who saved me this time around; it was Amanda.

Amanda had managed to finally get married, though Donnie Havens wasn't the prince she'd once looked for. When they first met, he hardly made enough to support himself, much less a wife and family. But he seemed to really love Amanda, so much so that he mortgaged the tiny house they bought on Long Island at least twice to give her everything he thought she needed. Still, she seemed happy enough—or at least around me she acted like she had it all. Maybe she did. Like me, she never had children, though she said it was because she was devoted to her career. I might have been jealous of her ambition, except that I sometimes wondered if she hung on to that job simply because Donnie couldn't afford to give her the lifestyle she desired on his own.

Still, I was grateful Amanda did keep her job. Especially since she helped me land a position with a client of hers, a small record label in need of a marketing assistant. And though it was hard, at age thirty-four, to find myself taking orders from a boss who was half my age, I did a good job at Global Records for the seven or so months I was there. At least *I* thought so. But my boss, Lewis, didn't seem to agree. Or he got tired of arguing with me over our differences about how to run the marketing department. Lewis said I was "out of it." But really, what did he know? Rock and roll was here to stay, not like that derivative mix of pop and dance music Global Records was trying to push.

There were other jobs, too. Mostly in promotions (it was the only thing of value on my résumé) or selling ad space. But the one thing that became clearer and clearer to me was that I was unfit for a workforce that catered to a demographic I had lost touch with.

So I gave up, believing I no longer had what it took. Not the courage. Or the will.

I was washed up by thirty-six. Not even my therapist could convince me otherwise. Nor all those self-help books I read.

No, there was only one thing, it seemed, that kept me from sinking completely into the black hole my life had become. And that was the much lauded serenity of Valium.

18

Zoe
Stalking and other stupid people tricks

Why wasn't he answering?

I looked up from where I sat on the bench, cell phone clamped to my ear, studying Adelaide Gibson as she stood chatting with three of her cronies in the Washington Square Park dog run.

Clearly, they weren't ready to start filming yet. I wondered if the rest of the people she had invited to the dog run today were even going to show up. I certainly hoped so, considering Adelaide's two pals here had only racked up five dogs between them. All King Charles spaniels, oddly enough. Maybe Adelaide should start a club. Didn't she know anybody who owned a mutt? Or even a good, old-fashioned beagle, for chrissakes?

My call rolled over into voice mail, as it had done the six other times I'd called. "Hi, this is Myles. Leave a message." *Beeeeeep.*

I hung up, just as I had done the last six times. Yes, I needed to speak to Myles, but I definitely didn't need to speak to his voice mail. I wasn't sure he would call me back, considering the way I'd treated him the last time I had seen him. I had tried to find him again on the beach, roaming up and down it no less than ten times before I left Fire Island on Monday. But I hadn't run into him. And even if I had known where his beach house was located, I certainly couldn't go there. Especially since Ms. Bikini U.S.A. was shacking up with him.

Now my only hope was to catch him on the phone, but even that was becoming hopeless. Maybe I would run into him. He did live near this park, as did I, which was probably why I'd agreed to meet with Adelaide at the run on such short notice. But right now I had more important things to worry about than Adelaide and her dog tribe. Besides, she was starting to become a bit obsessive about this documentary. I had given her what I had thought were the final edits last week only to receive a call from her yesterday— she felt we needed more footage of the dogs "frolicking," as she put it, in the dog run.

"Zoe, we're reeeaaadddy!" came the now familiar trill.

I looked up to see that two more women had joined them in the run. And three more dogs. All King Charles spaniels. So much for variety, I thought, studying the women as I approached, camera in hand. They all looked to be sixty or over, and they were kinda dressed alike in pastel sweater sets paired with skirts or, for the more daring of the set, capris. Maybe this was some kind of club.

Adelaide gave me a brittle smile as I stepped before the group. Not that she was mad at me. I've since learned it's the only smile Adelaide knows how to give. Could be the lipstick job—a soft pink that exceeded the lipstick line. Or the facelift. I could practically see the scars beneath that blue-gray salon coif of hers.

But she was all class, that Adelaide. Old money. The brownstone-on-the-park level of money. "Zoe, dear, it appears everyone is here now. We can begin," she said, her dark eyes gleaming at me, as if this news should excite me as much as it apparently did her.

She raised one sweater-clad arm gracefully, gesturing to the small crowd she had assembled. "Everyone, this is Zoe Keller." Then she went around the circle and introduced all her friends, as well as their dogs. I noticed one of the women—Beatrice, I think her name was—lift a worried hand to her cheek as she looked at me, her expression pained. I'd been getting that look for days, despite the fact that the burn had simmered down somewhat. I lifted the camera in front of my face, more to hide than anything else, as Adelaide instructed everyone to let their dogs off the leash and "act natural."

As I watched the women flutter about, snapping off leashes and cooing at their dogs and each other, I wondered if that was possible.

What a crowd. Whoo-hoo. Let's make a movie. I turned the camera on, but things didn't get any better on my viewing screen. We needed more dogs—like other kinds of dogs. This film almost seemed politically incorrect, in terms of equal opportunity for canines. No wonder Adelaide had wanted to come to the dog run in the middle of the day when no one else was there, dog Nazi that she is.

After about ten minutes, I knew I had enough footage of the dog run for about ten documentaries. Still, I kept filming, if only not to hear Adelaide complain.

Where was Adelaide anyway? I thought, realizing that all her friends stood clapping and cooing at their dogs in the run, but that Adelaide was somewhere off-camera.

I heard a muffled sob behind me and, lowering the camera, I turned around.

To find dear old Adelaide standing behind me, an embroidered handkerchief crushed to her mouth and tears rolling down her face.

"Adelaide?"

She waved a hand at me dismissively. "Have you got enough?"

"I think so." I stepped closer, reaching out to touch her arm, until I remembered what a tough old bird Adelaide was. But she didn't look so tough now.

"Adelaide, are you okay?"

"I'm fine," she said, despite the fresh tears that rolled down her softly wrinkled cheeks. "I just didn't expect this to be so hard. Seeing all these dogs, so much like my Fifi."

She muffled a sob and finally I did put an arm around her.

"It's just so hard letting go," she said into her handkerchief.

I gave her a comforting squeeze. Didn't I know it.

Much as I wanted to sit in the falafel shop all day, there was no way I could eat another falafel. I hadn't even been all that hungry for the first one, I'll admit. But the falafel here are so good, and I needed something comforting after my harrowing afternoon in the dog run with Adelaide.

Of course, I had finished my falafel a half hour ago and had now resorted to reading the specials posted on the wall. Okay, so maybe the only reason I was sitting for almost an hour in this tiny little restaurant on Thompson Street was because two stories above me was Myles's apartment.

He had to come down some time, right? Besides, he loved falafel. We ate enough of it together when we were at his place.

Maybe he had gotten a job. That would explain why he wasn't around on a Tuesday afternoon. But Myles was waiting on a job in the Manhattan D.A.'s. office, and that position wasn't due to open up until fall. He was a shoo-in for the job, considering he had graduated this past spring from NYU Law with high honors and had interned last summer in the Suffolk County D.A.'s office. When we broke up, he had been planning to take the summer off.

Of course, he'd also been planning to forgo a share at the beach. So what did I know?

With a sigh, I stood up, grabbing my knapsack and waving to the sole owner and falafel maker at the back of the store. "Take care, Ahmed."

"Goodbye, my friend," he said.

Well, at least Ahmed was still talking to me.

Once I stood out front of the restaurant, I slid my knapsack on my back and looked up, seeking out Myles's window on the third floor.

Was he even up there?

"Zoe?"

I startled, turning to find Myles standing next to me, looking tan and adorable in a T-shirt and jeans, and a bit surprised.

As was I, despite the fact that this was what I had been hoping for for days. "Myles!"

"What are you doing here?" he said, his golden brown eyes studying me.

"Getting falafel. What else? You know Ahmed's falafel. It's, uh, irresistible." Noticing he carried a knapsack, too, I asked, "Did you just get back from the beach?"

"Yeah. We decided to walk to the Sunken Forest yesterday. I didn't realize how far of a hike it was from Kismet. Took us all day. It was pretty cool, though. Have you been yet?"

"No, I haven't," I replied, fighting not to ask who was a part of the "we" that went on this little day trip. Instead, I studied his T-shirt, which I noticed had the logo for an environmental organization I once did a short film for. I had given it to him, since it was two sizes too large for me.

"Nice shirt," I said.

He smiled. "Some chick gave it to me."

"Some chick, huh?" I replied, a smile edging at my lips.

"Yeah, some crazy chick who doesn't want to be my friend anymore because I took a beach share on her island—"

"Myles, I'm sorry, I—"

He shook his head. "It's okay. I guess I should have spoken to you beforehand. It's just that I honestly didn't think you were going to go out there. You said as much."

I frowned. "I didn't think I was going to be out there. But Sage kinda thought it would be good for me. Now I'm not so sure."

His expression turned sympathetic. "I guess things must be pretty bleak over at your place."

I shook my head. "No, my house is pretty cheerful." I looked at him. "Except for the fact that I might be sharing it with a murderer."

His eyes widened. "What?"

Okay, maybe I was being a little melodramatic. So I explained. How I had found Tom at home that night, damp and angry in his kitchen. How he had responded to the drowning. How he had been acting ever since, especially the night of that strange Fourth of July party. How his only alibi happened to be the chief of security at Saltaire.

Whether or not Myles was as worried as I was, I wasn't sure. But he did invite me up to his place to talk. I took it as a good sign.

I took it as an even better sign that Myles's studio looked pretty much the same as it did the last time I had been in it, three months ago. Same Escher poster hanging over his bed. Same bookshelf, lined with volumes and volumes of law books. I was especially happy to see the spider plant I had given him was still alive and well and thriving on his windowsill.

"The place looks good," I said, after I dropped my knapsack on to the floor beside the couch and turned to Myles, who stood in the small galley kitchen, which sat just off the living room.

"Yeah," he said, gazing around the small space with what looked like dissatisfaction. "Want something to drink?"

"Water would be great," I said, watching as he turned to the refrigerator and pulled out two small bottles of purified water. The same brand I had recommended to him after explaining the horrors of the tap water he used to mindlessly imbibe. See what a good influence I was on his life?

Moments later, when I was seated across from him on his sofa, going over the minute details of the investigation I had begun— i.e., my trip to Fair Harbor—I wondered if water intake was about the only impact I had made on him.

"I don't know, Zoe, it's not much to go on. I mean, what motive would Tom have for killing his wife?"

"How about a mortgage free and clear on a million-dollar beach house?" I said.

His eyes widened. "Wow. He's got that house free and clear?"

"Now he does," I said, explaining the little insurance provision that paid off his mortgage just as soon as he filed Maggie's death certificate with the bank.

His gaze turned pensive. "Looks like a nice house, too," he said. "I bet you get a great view of the ocean from those windows in the front."

I tried to squelch the glimmer of happiness I felt at the idea that Myles might have roamed up the beach this weekend, hoping for a glimpse of my house—or better yet, me.

"Still," he continued, "I can't see it. Doesn't he own the company Sage works for? He's gotta be loaded."

I had already thought about that, long and hard, since returning from the beach. So I gave him the answer I had come up with. "The fact is, Tom *is* loaded. But he's also financially overburdened at the moment. Sage told me he went out on a limb last year when he decided to start up Edge. I mean, yeah, he did some leather accessories for Luxe, even a few jackets, but he was mostly in textiles. Leather outerwear is a whole new business. I bet he's up to his eyeballs in debt. Sage told me a few months ago that part of the reason he started Edge was that Luxe wasn't doing as well as it had in years past. I wouldn't be surprised if he was a little hard up for cash. I mean, think about it—he even took on shareholders in his beach house this year."

Myles chuckled. "C'mon, Zoe, he couldn't be bringing in that much cash through shareholders. He's only got the three of you, right?"

"And his daughter," I added, though I didn't think she was paying a dime. Not that I mentioned that. Though the fact that she moved right in on Maggie's turf bugged me, too. "But it does seem kind of odd that he opened his house after all these years of it being just him and Maggie. Now why do you think a man would do that?"

He shrugged. "I dunno. Maybe he likes the company."

"Or maybe he needed a buffer between him and Maggie," I said, thinking of my own roommate, who had used me as a buffer between her and her last boyfriend. But Corinne had been dating someone new for over a year, which was probably why I never saw her anymore. She was always at his place. Mostly because she wanted to be with Roland alone. As in, ninety percent of the time.

"Look, Zoe, don't you think the police investigated all these things?"

Now we were getting to the main reason I had come to see Myles. Okay, maybe it wasn't the only reason—I was enjoying being with him, after all. "That's what I'm wondering about. I have to be honest. I wasn't too impressed with the homicide detective who questioned us that night. He treated the whole thing as some routine incident."

Myles looked at me. "You should never treat any investigation as routine. What was his name?"

"Erickson, I think." I had managed to remember his name, probably because the guy irritated me so much with his bland questions. "Why, you know him?"

He shook his head. "Maybe my dad did."

I took my opening. "But you still know some people in the department, right? Friends of your dad's? Maybe someone who could do some poking around for me?"

"I haven't spoken to anyone there since my father's funeral," he replied, sounding a bit angry as he did, which was surprising. I knew Myles had some conflicted feelings about law enforcement ever since his dad died in the line of duty, but I didn't think he was holding it against the entire Suffolk County Police Department.

"But you'd talk to them for me, wouldn't you?"

He shook his head. "You're barking up the wrong tree, Zoe."

Now I was angry. "Well, excuse me for thinking a man who was going to work for the Manhattan D.A. might care a little bit about justice."

His next words came out so quietly, I wasn't even sure I heard them. "I'm not going to work for the D.A.'s office."

"Excuse me?"

"I said I'm not going to work for the D.A."

My eyes widened. "Oh, God, Myles—" I began, reaching out to touch his arm, which felt surprisingly cool under my hand. "I'm so sorry. I thought for sure you'd get the position—"

He looked at me then. "I've been offered the position, Zoe. I'm just not going to take it."

"But why?" I said, looking into his eyes. "You've wanted that job since forever. Well, at least since you worked for the Suffolk County D.A. I don't understand."

He shrugged, dropping his gaze. "I changed my mind."

A coldness clutched at me and I removed my hand from his arm. It didn't make sense. Working for the D.A. had been Myles's dream. During the past year, it seemed like getting that job was his whole life. "What are you going to do?"

He fiddled with the label on the water bottle in front of him. "I've had a few interviews at some corporate law firms. In fact, I just got a call for a second interview with one of them."

"Corporate law? Myles, that doesn't sound like you."

He looked at me. "Maybe I've changed."

I wanted to probe him further, but something about his expression told me to hold my tongue. "I guess you have," I said carefully.

Maybe it was the silence I lapsed into that had him sputtering out answers. "I would have made nothing at the D.A.'s office anyway, Zoe. Do you know what the starting salaries are for lawyers in the corporate sector? Sometimes as much as one hundred and twenty thousand a year. That's nothing to sneeze at."

I raised an eyebrow at him. "Neither is murder."

"Zoe, you don't know that for sure—"

I sat up. "That's just it. We don't know that *for sure.* Which is why I wish you could just make one call to the S.C.P.D. Just to get the facts on this case. You must still be talking to Paul Stover over there—you guys were good friends."

"I can't, Zoe."

I sat back hard on the couch, arms folded in front of me, probably looking a bit like a petulant child. But I didn't care what I looked like right now. I was angry.

Myles must have sensed this, because he leaned back, too, letting his head come to rest on the cushion, before turning to look at me. "Look, Zoe, did it ever occur to you that you're wrong about Tom?"

I didn't answer him. Instead, I stared straight ahead, at the spider plant on the window. Actually, I was thinking about taking it home with me. I wasn't sure I even trusted Myles with the care and feeding of that plant anymore.

"Not all men are like your father, Zoe," Myles said softly. "Not all men are bad."

That's when I felt my anger spike. But I kept hold of myself long enough to stand up, grabbing my knapsack from the floor as I did.

Hoisting my knapsack on my shoulder, I headed for the door, turning back to him only to take one last parting shot.

"Not all of them are good either."

19

Sage
The kingdom is at hand.

Being on Fire Island for the long holiday weekend had not only recharged my batteries but cleansed my soul. I felt in control again. In command. I *was* in command, now that Maggie was no longer around. In fact, when I came into the office on Wednesday morning, I was even starting to think about whether or not it was premature to talk to Tom about the sales manager job. I didn't want to offend him by broaching the subject too soon after Maggie's death.

On the other hand, I also didn't want to lose out on the job I had wanted ever since the day Tom hired me.

Which was why I felt a tremor of foreboding when Yaz informed me as I breezed past the reception desk, that Tom wanted to see me in his office.

I paused. "Did he say what it was about?"

She shrugged. "No. Only that you should head over there as soon as you got in."

I nodded, turning around and heading for the elevators once more. And as I walked the two blocks down Seventh Avenue that lay between the Edge showroom and Luxe's offices, I started to worry. Tom wasn't the type to call impromptu meetings. He was always so scheduled.

And superorganized, I thought, once I stood in Tom's office, which was so neat you could perform surgery in it.

"You wanted to see me, Tom?"

"Sage," Tom said, turning in his chair away from the computer screen he'd been staring at to face me. "Come on in. Have a seat."

I sat in one of the leather chairs that faced his desk.

"Listen, Shari came to see me yesterday about some samples you were sending back to production for changes."

A coldness moved through me. "She did, did she?"

He nodded. "She was concerned because, well, you know, the sales manager is the only one who can authorize such changes...."

That little bitch. How dare she go over my head and make me look bad? "Look, Tom, have you had a chance to see those samples?"

"I have, and I—"

"Surely then, you agree with me that the changes were necessary. The buttons were too heavy. And the shoulder flaps were an abomination—"

"I do agree with you, Sage. Shari was just concerned because up until now, she's been taking her orders from Maggie, and since Maggie's not around..."

Maybe it was the accusation behind his words, but I felt my anger suddenly spike. So much so, I broached the very subject that had been dancing through my mind these past few weeks. And not very delicately. "Listen, Tom, I know you loved Maggie and I know you thought she was the perfect person to run Edge, but the truth is, I was the one doing all the merchandising until Maggie came along—"

"I recognize that, Sage, and I—"

"Wait, let me finish. You probably don't realize this either, but I was the one who got the lion's share of the retailers on board for Edge. And I was the one who saved our asses with the Urban Lives account, because if it had been left to Maggie, they would have destroyed the samples we sent. I had to remerchandise everything, not to mention soothe egos so the buyer there would even consider looking at our goods again. That was me, Tom. Not Maggie. Me!"

Tom stared at me, dumbfounded, while I caught my breath. It

wasn't easy. My heart was racing in my chest, and from the way he was looking at me, I had the feeling that far from landing the job I wanted, I had lost the one I had.

Shaking his head, Tom said, "Sage, I'm not arguing with you. Look, you don't think I know how instrumental you've been since the start-up of Edge?" He stood, walking to the window. "Maggie didn't have any experience in the industry. I knew her weaknesses when I hired her, but I thought they'd be outweighed by her business sense. She always had a good head for numbers and I figured she'd be a whiz managing the budgets. And she was, to a certain degree." He sighed as he turned to face me once more. "I knew she was leaning on you when it came to many things, which is why you were the first person I thought of when the job opened up again."

"You did?" I said, letting out the breath I'd been holding.

"Of course. Sage, I know I probably should have given you the job to start with, except you didn't have the management experience—"

"But I managed The Bomb—"

He held up a hand. "At the time, it seemed like a huge leap that you could go from managing a retail store to managing a wholesale sales office. But I took a chance on you when I brought you over to Edge as a sales rep, and I'm going to take another one right now."

I felt the blood rushing to my head, heart thrumming.

"The job is yours, if you still want it."

"Oh, Tom, of course I want it!"

"But there are two conditions," Tom warned. "You'll help me hire a new sales rep. And you'll come to me with any questions. I know you, Sage. You like to handle everything yourself."

"I promise," I said, "I really do."

Then, before I could think better of it, I rounded the desk and threw my arms around him, enveloping him in a hug.

And when I leaned back to look at him, I was surprised to discover that we both had tears in our eyes.

"So he just gave you Maggie's job?" Zoe said, when I called her with my good news. Not exactly the reception I'd been expecting. In fact, I was hoping at least my best friend would be happy for me, especially after the conversation I'd just had with my mother when I called to tell my parents the news. Of course my mother was happy for me. For about two minutes. The remainder of the conversation was spent talking to me about her progress on the "Keep Hope Alive" theater festival she and my father were busily preparing for.

Sighing, I said, "I think the proper response, Zoe, is 'Congratulations.'" What was wrong with everybody?

"Hey, Sage, I'm sorry. I'm really happy for you. I'm just wondering about Tom. I mean, Maggie's barely cold in her grave, and he's giving away her clothes to the poor, her job to you—"

"Zoe, Tom is running a business. He can't let his company go to hell just because he lost someone. No matter who that person is. You might understand that better if you had a *real* job."

She was silent on the other end, and I suddenly realized that maybe I had gone too far. "I'm sorry, Zoe. I didn't mean that." I blew out a breath. "It's not that I don't care. It's just that somebody needs to do Maggie's job now that she's gone. And I happen to believe I'm the most qualified person."

"I know you are, Sage. I'm sorry. I am happy for you. But—"

"No buts, Zoe. Just let it be, okay?"

I could practically feel her squirming on the other end of the phone, until finally she said, "Maybe we should go out for drinks. Me, you and Nick. To celebrate."

I smiled. Now that was more like it. "Actually, Tom mentioned something about having a little dinner party at the beach house Saturday night."

"Another party? He just threw a party."

"Zoe—"

"Well, who's coming? Not all those people who were there last weekend."

I was tempted to taunt her by telling her that twice as many people were coming, but instead I said, "No, just us. And some other people from the company. Donnie Havens and his wife. Vince." At least I hoped he invited Vince. Because if he didn't, I would.

"Well, that sounds…nice," she said.

I rolled my eyes. "Look, Zoe, I have to go. My other line is ring-ing." I felt relief at the sight of another extension lighting up on my phoneset. I was hoping the new caller would give a more en-thusiastic reception to my news.

And once I hung up with Zoe and picked up the new call, I did find a very excited Nick on the other end of the line.

"Hey, Sage," he said breathlessly.

"Nick," I said, wondering at the jubilation in his tone. "I was just going to call you."

"Oh yeah? What's up?"

"I just got promoted to sales manager of Edge!"

"Hey, it looks like we got two things to celebrate then."

"What's that?"

"Well, I just lined up my first band for the label."

I frowned. "Wow, that was quick. How'd you manage that?"

"I have my ways."

"Nick, you didn't borrow money from your dad again, did you?"

"C'mon, Sage, what kind of man do you think I am?"

A poor man. "I was just wondering how you got a band under contract with no capital. Don't you have to pay them?"

"Hey, listen, Sage, that's my problem, not yours. The band will get paid in due time. I got it covered."

I bit my lip. I had heard that before. Only to learn Nick had hit up his father for a loan. I wondered if he'd even paid that one back yet. His parents were doing better than mine, but by no stretch of the imagination were they rich. Somehow I held back from saying anything more. Last time I'd tried to tell Nick how to run his life, he'd accused me of smothering his dreams. I guessed I had to watch him fall down all by himself, though I had watched him do it so many times, it was getting harder and harder.

"Hey, listen," he said now, "I'm calling cause I'm trying to round up some people for Nose Dive's first New York City show tomorrow night."

"Nose Dive? What kind of name is that?"

"I know—cool, right? Sort of a riff on the Led Zeppelin name. You know that story, right? How when Zeppelin was start-ing out, someone told them they were going to go down like a

Led Zeppelin? They took on the name right after that. Probably to tempt fate. Nose Dive is kinda doing the same thing."

It was easy to tempt fate when you were talented, and Led Zeppelin was a talented band. But Nose Dive I'd never heard of, and if they were anything like some of the other bands Nick had dragged me to see, I had to wonder. "Where are they playing?"

"Don Hill's. Show starts at 11:00 p.m. You in?"

The last thing I needed during my first week of my new job was to be going out late. "You know it's a school night, Nick."

"Come on, Sage. This is the band I'm hoping to launch Revelation with. I'd like to get a good crowd there, you know?"

Though I was just as worried about this latest venture as I had been about all the others, I had to show support. What were friends for, right? "I'll be there."

"Cool. Could you let Zoe know? And if you could e-mail your list, too, that would be awesome. See if you can scatter up a crowd."

"I'll see what I can do."

"You're the best, Sage. But you knew that already, right?"

"Yep," I answered, rolling my eyes.

"So I'll see you tomorrow night then, right?"

"Okay," I said.

"Excellent. Listen, I gotta bolt."

"Wait, Nick—"

"What's up?"

"You forgot to say congratulations."

"Hey, don't you worry about that, sweetie. We'll be celebrating tomorrow night."

"Whatever," I said, hanging up the phone.

I wasn't sure exactly what we would be celebrating, but at this point, I would take what I could get.

20

Nick
Yeah, I got a good band. I just hope I'm not the one singing the blues.

I was glad, at least, that Ray was covering the door, but that was all I was glad about tonight. The crowd was looking pretty thin for a Thursday, and Thursday was one of Don Hill's most happening nights, band-wise.

Not that I was worried. It was early yet. Nose Dive didn't go on until eleven, and it was—I looked at my watch. Shit, ten forty-five.

Okay, so I was worried.

Sage and Zoe weren't even here yet. I hoped they at least showed up. I didn't bust Ray's ass to get them comp admissions for nothing. He was a good guy, that Ray. He owed me anyway. I had packed this place enough times, back in the day.

I just hoped I could pack it tonight.

"Hey."

I looked up to find Les Wolf, lead singer of Nose Dive, at my side. He was looking good. For an ugly motherfucker. My eyes roamed over his freshly shaved head, demon-green eyes and bushy-as-hell brows. At least he had dressed okay, I thought, studying his black T-shirt, black leather pants and thick, black-soled boots. And he was a hell of a musician. Wrote all of Nose Dive's songs, with a few exceptions where he'd done some interesting collaborations with the band. Chicks dug him, too, despite his somewhat scary face. And though I hate to admit it, that matters.

I saw him glance uneasily around the half-filled space.

"Don't sweat it, Les. If you build it, they will come. I got some of my peeps coming. And after we get the CD out there and put our publicity plans in effect, you'll see bigger crowds."

"Yeah," he replied. He didn't look reassured. That was the thing about these artist types. They needed lots of reassurance.

"Hey, dude, you guys are the best new band out there. Remember what happened with Radiohead?" I said, naming one of my all-time favorite bands. "Yeah, they had a hit with *Pablo Honey*. But it wasn't until *OK Computer* that they really got the respect they deserve."

"I know, you're right," he said, looking up on the stage where his bass player was still setting up.

"You guys pretty much ready to rock and roll?"

"Pretty much," he answered, but I could see he was no longer listening to me. I followed his gaze.

Finally, I thought, watching Sage strut in wearing a pair of low-slung jeans and a midriff-baring sea-green tank top that showed off her flat, tan stomach and brought out the green of her eyes. Zoe was lagging along behind her, looking pretty cute herself. For Zoe anyway. Not that she wasn't cute, but she didn't, let's say, show off her assets. She's got a nice little body, Zoe, though you'd never know it. But tonight I could see the T-shirt was a bit tighter than usual. And she had some killer heels on with her jeans. I don't think I've ever seen Zoe in heels.

I don't think Zoe has ever *been* in heels. She looked pretty damn uncomfortable.

"Hey," I said, leaning in to kiss Sage and then Zoe. "Did Ray comp you at the door?"

"He did," Sage said, winking at me. Then I saw her look at Les. "Hi," she greeted him. Probably because he was gawking at her. Sage had that effect on men.

"Sage Daniels, Zoe Keller, meet Les Wolf, lead singer and the brains behind Nose Dive."

Sage beamed her usual fifty-watt smile, which I think might

have blinded Les, judging by the way he stood there, tongue tied. "Nice to meet you," Sage was saying. "Nick has been raving about you guys. I can't wait to hear you jam."

Good old Sage. Laying on the charm, as usual. I was glad, too, 'cause Les was still hemming and hawing over the contract. The more warm and friendly he felt toward me—and my friends, who are an extension of me, right?—the better.

Seeing that Les had finally recovered enough to hold up his end of the conversation Sage had engaged him in, I turned to Zoe.

"So how's it hanging, Zoe?"

"It doesn't hang, Nick, remember? At least not in these jeans, it doesn't."

"Yeah?" I said, leaning back to check her out. Wow. Those jeans were tight. Who knew Zoe had such a nice ass? Maybe I had underestimated her. "Well, you're looking pretty hot."

"Thanks," she said, her face a mixture of pleasure and embarrassment. "I think." She rolled her eyes. "I'm taking a page from Sage's book. Actually, I'm taking clothes from Sage's closet. I showed up at her apartment in shorts and sneakers and she threw a hissy fit. I just wanted to be comfortable, but she accused me of being depressed."

"Depressed? Why would she think that?"

She shook her head, gazed off at the stage. "I had a little run-in with Myles. Nothing major."

I put an arm around her. "Ah, Zoe."

"Don't 'Ah, Zoe' me. I'm fine. We just had a…a disagreement. It really wasn't anything."

I looked at her, noticing she had a touch of makeup on, too. "Don't worry about him. You could have any guy you want."

"Yeah," she said, looking away. "It's not him I'm worried about." Then her eyes narrowed. "Look at that girl—she's wearing shorts."

I turned and saw the tall blonde she was referring to. "Uh, those are hot pants. It's a little different." I looked at Zoe again. Actually, I leaned around to look at her ass. "So these are Sage's jeans? I can't believe you fit into them."

"Thanks a lot," she said.

Oops. Now she looked pissed at me. "I mean, you look good, Zoe. You should dress like this a little more often."

"Forget it," she said. "Do you know I had to lie down on the bed to get these pants zipped up? And the only reason I could fit my ass into Sage's jeans is because these are a little too big on her. And these shoes. Jesus. I thought women had evolved since the days of stilettos?"

I laughed. Zoe. She was funny when that femi-nazi side came out. Not that I ever called her a femi-nazi. Actually, I did once. She nearly clubbed me. "Hey, listen, I'm glad you came," I said. I meant it, you know? There were very few people you could count on nowadays and I was appreciative of Zoe and Sage's support. They were the two people in this world I knew I could rely on. Not like some of the other people I'd invited to this gig, I thought, glancing around.

"Hey, don't sweat it, Nick," Zoe said, as if reading my mind. "It's not always the crowd that counts. My first documentary got zip in terms of distribution, but I garnered a pretty nice critics award. Really bolstered video sales."

See, that's what I love about Zoe. The chick's got integrity. She knows firsthand what it's like to get behind what you love, even if the world isn't behind it initially.

Les sidled up to us. "Could you excuse us for a moment?" he said to Zoe.

"Sure," Zoe replied. "I'm gonna get a drink. Nick, you need anything?"

I pulled a twenty out of my pocket. "Get me a beer. A Stella Artois. And get yourself whatever you want."

Zoe looked at me with surprise. "Thanks, Nick."

See? I could be a good guy in times of plenty. Okay, semi-plenty. But I was working on that. I turned to Les. "Oh, dude, sorry man. You need anything from the bar?"

"Not from the bar, no," Les said, a gleam in his eye.

"Oh yeah? What can I do for you, buddy?"

"You gotta hook me up with that chick, dude. She's amazing."

I looked around again, trying to site out the object of his desire, but all I saw was Sage heading for the restroom. "Who, dude?"

He shook his head at me, as if it were obvious. "Sage. She's pretty fucking cool. Do you know she's a Nick Cave fan? I was weaned on fucking Nick Cave. And she's hot, man."

I must have been looking at him funny, because he said, "I mean, if you're not already hooked up with her, dude."

"Nah." I saw Les frown and realized he was wondering why I *wasn't* hooked up with Sage. "I mean, we had a minor…thing a long, long time ago," I hedged, hoping he didn't verify with Sage at some point. "But we're friends now, you know?"

"Cool. Then hook me up, dude. I'm counting on you."

"I'll see what I can do."

"Thanks. I better go. We're going on in a few minutes."

"Hey, break a leg, okay?"

He laughed. I mean a genuine laugh. I don't think I'd ever even seen Les smile before that.

"I don't need to, dude. I'm feeling inspired, if you know what I mean."

Then he took off, happy as a fucking clam. I watched him high-five Cliff Jackson, his bass player, and I nearly laughed myself. Shit, he had it bad.

Then I saw Sage returning from the bathroom, and I prayed she might have felt the same vibe for Les. I mean, he wasn't exactly her type, but you never know, right?

"Hey," Sage said. "Band going on soon?"

I nodded, studying her green eyes and wide mouth. Yeah, I could see why Les was hooked. Sage always had that look. Like she'd just climbed out of bed—or was looking to climb back in. I don't mean that in a bad way. She just had this sexy, unkempt look. Not that she was unkempt. If Sage was anything like Bern— or any of the other women I knew—she probably spent a good hour getting herself to look that tousled. "So what'd you think of Les?" I asked.

"He seemed like a nice guy," she said. Then she narrowed her eyes at me. "Why?"

"Nothing," I said innocently. I knew from long experience, you had to play these kind of things cool with Sage. "It's just that he thought you were pretty cool."

She smiled, then shrugged. "Not my type."

"What do you mean, not your type?"

She thought about this for a moment. "Too young."

That threw me. "Too young? Sage, he's thirty-three. That's two years older than you—and a heck of a lot older than most of the guys you date."

She shrugged again. "People change, Nick. Maybe I've changed."

She looked the same to me, I thought, watching as she sized up a leather-clad twenty-year-old who strolled by. But I didn't have time to argue. Mostly I didn't feel like it. This was my night, after all.

As if on cue, Zoe returned with beers for both of us.

"Nothing for me?" Sage said, as Zoe handed me my beer. "I thought we were supposed to have a toast for my promotion. Gonna be pretty hard, if I don't have a drink."

Shit. Now I'd fucked up. "Sorry, Sage. Look, let me get you something. The best tequila in the house for the new sales manager of Edge."

"Never mind," she said, taking off for the bar.

I looked at Zoe. "Oops."

"We'll do a toast, Nick. Don't sweat it. Besides, Tom is having a dinner party in her honor Saturday night at the beach."

"Oh yeah?" I replied. "That's cool." Still, I probably should get Sage a little toasted tonight. Not just because of her promotion, either. But because it was clear I was going to need to get her a little looped in order for her to show some interest in Les. Though I wasn't sure that would even work. She could be damn difficult, that Sage. Maybe Les would forget about her. I mean, there were other chicks out there, right? He'd get over it.

Sage returned with her usual tequila on the rocks. "Bartender bought me a drink. Pretty nice, right?"

Maybe there weren't many chicks out there like Sage. She was something, I thought, praying Les would get over it. He was a big boy. Besides, he had his career to think of now.

I looked around nervously, noticing that the crowd hadn't thickened very much. "Did you e-mail your list?" I said to Sage, with a bit more accusation than I intended.

She frowned at me. "Of course I did, Nick. I said I would. But it's not easy to get people to come out and see a band at eleven o'clock on a Thursday night. Most people have to work in the morning."

It was that kind of attitude that really pissed me off. "I don't get people. I mean, you can sleep when you're dead."

"Or when you're old," Zoe said with a chuckle.

"I'm not getting old," I replied with a smirk.

"We all get old," Sage said.

"Yeah, and we all die," Zoe said. Then she frowned. "Though some of us sooner than absolutely necessary, I think."

I saw Sage send her a look. I didn't blame her. Zoe was pretty wiggy ever since Maggie died. "Hey, let's move on to a better topic," I said, holding up my beer. "To Sage Daniels, the best fucking sales manager Edge Leather ever had."

Sage smiled. "I'll drink to that," she said, raising her glass to clink with ours.

But she had just barely taken a sip when I saw her eyes widen with anger, this time directed at me.

"What the fuck is *she* doing here?" she asked.

I followed Sage's gaze and saw Francesca waltzing through the crowd. Holy shit, she actually came. I felt a little excitement move through me. I wasn't sure if this was because of what she was wearing—black mini, stilettos and just about the tiniest tank top I'd ever seen—or simply because she'd shown up. All because I'd asked.

"Nick, what did I tell you about messing with Tom's daughter?" Sage began.

"I'm not messing with her!" I said. God, but I wanted to do something with her, I thought, watching as she raised her gaze above the onlookers she left in her wake—and there were a lot of them—before settling it on me. Okay, now I was excited. Would Sage be able to tell? Good thing these jeans weren't tight. "I only invited her 'cause she needs a little help with her musical taste. I mean, Britney Spears? C'mon…"

"Nick—" Sage began.

"Hey, at least she's getting something from Britney. Like fashion inspiration," Zoe said with a small smile. "I think she may even have more midriff showing than the goddess of exposure herself."

"Look," I said, ignoring Zoe's amused comments and focusing on Sage. "She's staying with Tom for the summer and she's got no friends in town. She's lonely."

"Yeah, she looks lonely," Sage said, gesturing with her chin.

I looked back at Francesca, who had just been waylaid by a giant thug of a guy. Shit.

"You better keep your eye on her, Nick," Sage said. "If anything happens to her while she's out with you, Tom is going to—"

"Okay, okay," I said, stomping off in Francesca's direction. A guy can't even do a nice thing in this world anymore without catching shit.

"Nick!" Francesca called out as I stepped up to her and the giant. Then she wrapped an arm around my neck, pulled me down to her mouth and planted a big one right on my lips. Whoa. Clearly I'd made some headway by inviting her here.

Then I looked up at the giant, saw the obvious surprise in his face and realized that maybe Francesca's intention had been to make headway with him.

"Hey, dude, no offense, but the lady is here as my guest."

"Is that right?" the giant replied, his surprise now turning to anger.

Damn. Did she have to start things up with a guy, like, twice the size of me?

I looked at Francesca, saw the wide-eyed look she gave me, and realized for the first time how very young she was. Almost innocent. If that were possible.

Possible or not, I felt a surge of something in that moment. Something that made me say to my giant friend, "Yeah, buddy, that's right. She's with me. You wanna make something of it?"

The minute I said the words, I was pretty freaked. I mean, this guy could fucking kill me with one good whack of that beefy fist. But the most amazing thing happened.

He didn't.

Instead, he held up both his hands, as if disavowing all claim to Francesca, and backed away.

Backed the fuck away.

Needless to say, I was feeling mighty pleased with myself when I walked up to Sage and Zoe with Francesca on my arm.

Though Sage was none too pleased with me, it was clear.

But she didn't have time to put in her two cents. Not only because Francesca was smiling in her usual queenly fashion at her, but because Nose Dive had just taken the stage.

"Is everybody ready to rock and roll?" Les barked into the mike. For a quiet guy, he sure did have stage presence. I gave him the thumbs-up, glancing around as I did. A handful of people had gathered before the stage. Okay, so we weren't going to take down the house, but it was their first show at Don Hill's, right?

Then the guitarist, Jess Gunther, laid into his Stratocaster, moving into the opening of "Like a River." I closed my eyes to savor the melody. It was an instant classic. God, these guys were even more awesome live.

I opened my eyes just as Les began the opening lyric, savoring the words. Genius. The guy was a fucking genius. I couldn't wait to hear the rest of the songs. Les said he had some new material he was going to try out tonight, which was cool, because I wanted to get these guys in the studio and get this CD recorded ASAP.

I turned to look at Zoe and Sage. "Pretty brilliant stuff, right?"

Sage looked at me, as if trying to come up with an appropriate response.

"Makes me want to slash my wrists," Zoe replied.

"Yeah, that's it. It's kinda depressing, Nick," Sage said.

Jesus. Were they paying attention? "Listen to that melody. It's genius."

Sage shrugged. What was I even bothering asking them for? Sage can't tolerate a song she can't shake her hips to, and Zoe is into that vagina rock. Talk about slashing your wrists. You had to have PMS to listen to the stuff Zoe listens to.

"Hey, at least somebody likes it, Nick," Sage said, gesturing with her chin toward the stage as the band rolled into the next song.

I looked up to see that Francesca had disappeared from my side and was standing before the stage, front and center, her eyes fixed on Les, mesmerized.

"Well, there you have it," I said, with no small satisfaction. "That's the demographic anyway, from a music business point of view."

"What's that supposed to mean?" Zoe asked.

"Not that I plan on catering to such things," I said, "but most of the music-buying public is young."

"And what are we, old?" Sage replied dryly.

"Well," I said, gesturing to Francesca, who had begun to sway in time to the music. "Older than her."

Now I'd managed to piss them both off. Hey, if you can't take it, don't dish it out. It wasn't like anyone was going out of their way to make me feel fucking cheery. This was the band that was gonna launch my label, for chrissakes. Show a little support, would you?

Still, I was relieved when the next song began. The tempo was faster, the lyrics more lively. I looked over and noticed that though Zoe stood stock-still—she wasn't much of a dancer anyway—Sage, at least, had begun to move those famous hips of hers.

And Francesca...

She was grinding her hips up there like she wanted to...

Fuck. I was going to have to keep an eye on her.

But it was going to be my pleasure. Oh, yeah.

I didn't care what Sage said. Francesca was of age, and if Tom had anything to say about it, he could talk to me directly. Besides, I thought Tom liked me. I had a way with the parents, you know? Bern's parents fucking love me.

And in Francesca's case, I was hoping for parental approval.

I started to dance myself. Well, kinda. I hadn't had enough beers yet to really get grooving. But I was feeling good. And when the band came to the end of the first set, and the crowd, though still meager, let out a heartfelt roar, I was feeling pretty fucking awesome.

Especially when a flush-faced Francesca rushed up to me just as soon as the last song ended, looking very much like she might want to take me into the restroom and get it on right now. And why shouldn't she? I showed her a good time tonight.

She stopped before me, barely catching her breath before she blurted out, "I want to meet the band. Well, not all of them. Just the singer. He's like, the hottest guy I've ever seen!"

Uh, right.

21

Zoe
It's a dog-eat-dog world. So don't forget your poop bag.

I was starting to understand why they said dogs were a man's best friend. Well, in this case, a woman's. It seemed like Janis was going to be my only ally in this investigation I was conducting. She was at least the only one who seemed to be showing the effects of grief. I could swear she looked downright depressed sometimes, but maybe she had always looked that way. Still, when she looked at me with those big brown eyes, I imagined that she was silently imploring me to carry on with this whole trail I'd started following since the night she and I found Maggie on the beach. Which was why I had leashed her up and taken her for a walk along the beach this fine Saturday morning.

No, I wasn't looking for Myles. I already knew he was going to be no help and I was still a bit bewildered by his attitude. I didn't even know him anymore. Or *he* didn't know *me*. He certainly didn't believe in me. Or my instincts. Which left my ego a little bruised, to say the least.

Now my little murder trail was starting to feel more like a trail of bread crumbs. But still I persevered—I had to. I couldn't ignore my gut, even though everyone else told me I should. So last week I had contacted the S.C.P.D. myself to order the police report on Maggie's death, only to learn it was going to take two weeks to receive it. And even then the police report wouldn't show all the avenues the cops had discarded before the death had been ruled accidental.

Which was why I had resorted to Operation Janis Joplin. But this time out, I was hoping to run into a certain square-jawed cop on a quad. He was my only resource at the moment. I wasn't sure what I would do when I found him—let Janis off the leash? That oughta get Jeff's attention, since he was clearly a strict enforcer of the leash law if nothing else. I was certain it wouldn't be my getup—long shorts and a long-sleeve cotton shirt. I wasn't taking any chances in this heat. I did want to make it at least to middle-age with some undamaged skin left on my body.

I was nearly at the end of Kismet when I spotted him, heading west on his quad, looking pretty cute as he sat high on the motorbike, shoulders straight, jaw firm.

But just when I was about to give him a sunny little wave, he blew on by, sending Janis into a barking frenzy.

Damn. "Janis!" I said, feeling the leash slide out of my grip.

I swear, I didn't do that on purpose. In fact, I started to even feel a shot of panic as I watched my four-legged friend dart down the beach.

Janis's escape did, however, achieve the desired effect. As Janis whizzed past him, Jeff stopped his bike, turned around to find the negligent dog owner and spotted me.

I raced up to him. "Could you—I'm sorry, Jeff. She kinda got away from me. Maybe you could, uh, ride after her?" I said, my gaze moving frantically to Janis, who was becoming smaller and smaller on the beach.

I shivered, remembering the last time she had gotten out of my grip.

But Jeff didn't sail off after her on his quad. Instead, he put two fingers in his mouth and let out a whistle that almost shattered my eardrums.

My jaw dropped as Janis stopped, then turned and loped back over to us.

"Thanks," I said, once I had her leash once more and Janis sat looking up at me as if to say, "What's all the fuss about?"

"No problem. Anything for a pretty lady." He smiled.

I smiled back. Okay, the pretty lady thing was a bit old-fashioned, but somehow, whenever I was with this guy, I did feel like I was in some kind of fifties-style western. Maybe it was the uniform. Gave him that alpha-male edge.

"So I see you made it back to the beach. Enjoying yourself?" he said.

"Yeah, got in late last night."

"Oh, yeah? Working late on your documentary?"

I nodded. That was true, but he didn't need to know it wasn't on my fictitious water-related accidents documentary. I had met up with Adelaide Gibson at her apartment last night for a new viewing of the re-edited dogsnatchers.com doc, complete with the added footage of the frolicking King Charles spaniels in the park. We even had dinner afterward, because I got the feeling after the viewing that Adelaide realized our time working together had come to an end, and she was a little lonely. "Yeah, things are coming along okay," I said. "I actually put a request in for the police report on Maggie Landon's death, but it's gonna take a while to get it. It's too bad, because I was hoping to use it for my film."

I saw Jeff frown, and for a moment, I thought he was considering moving things along in the police department process, until I saw him point at the ground. "I hope you've got some bags with you to clean that up."

I turned to find Janis hunched over, doing her doggie duty. Ah, crap.

Literally. I reached into the pocket of my shorts for a bag. "Yeah, I do." Then, maybe because I didn't want to start picking up dog turds in his presence, or I was hoping to get the conversation back on track, I said, "So, do you ever get out to the Yaphank office?" Yaphank was the headquarters for the Suffolk County P.D., where the homicide department was located.

"Well, my patrol is the beach. But when I check in, it's in Great River. That's where the Marine Bureau is based."

"Ah," I replied, not sure where this left me.

"So you like living in the city?"

I was startled at that, trying to remember if I had told him where I lived.

As if he read my mind, he said, "I was the first officer that night. I took your address and phone number, remember?"

Right. I had, after all, been questioned. Funny that he remembered where I lived. "Yeah, I like it." Then, as if hoping my Long Island roots might make him feel a little more kinship with me, I said, "I grew up on Long Island though."

"Oh yeah? Whereabouts?"

"Babylon. Well, for high school anyway. Before that I was in Huntington."

"Well, a Suffolk County girl." He smiled. "I'm from Bayshore. Born and bred."

Bingo. I smiled again, suddenly wishing I had on something a bit more flirtatious than this oversized shirt. Maybe I might get somewhere with this guy.

A moment later, I realized I *was* getting somewhere with this guy, though I wasn't sure it was where I wanted to go.

"So, Zoe, I was hoping to run into you. I'm coming into the city next week to help a friend do some work around his new apartment. I was wondering if maybe you wanted to hang out or something."

Or something. What the hell was "or something?" I started to panic, realizing that "or something" was a date and I hadn't gone on a date since Myles. "I, uh—"

"Maybe we can catch a little dinner. Talk."

Then I realized "or something" might very well be *something*. At the very least, I would have a chance to pick his brain a bit more about Maggie's death. "Sure, that would be fun."

"Great," he said, smiling at me. But that smile dropped off his face instantly, and his body went rigid as he sat up higher on his quad, his head turning slightly as he looked at some point beyond my head.

"I gotta go. I got an open container violation at three o'clock."

I turned, spotting a group of guys off in the distance, two of them holding beer bottles in their hands, which apparently was a no-no in Kismet.

I turned to Jeff, who had already kicked into gear, and with a nod of his head, he took off.

Leaving me with nothing.

I looked down at Janis, who smiled happily up at me, next to the little pile she'd just made.

Nothing but shit, that is.

And a date, I thought, studying Jeff's broad shoulders as he hunched over the motorbike. Not a date, I thought, shaking off the warmth that seemed to fill me at the sight. An interview, I reminded myself, trying not to stare at his ass as he stepped off the bike.

Of sorts.

"Next up on Oprah, *women who risk their lives for others. Tune in to see if you have what it takes!"*

I changed the channel, since I was pretty sure dating police officers didn't qualify. What had I been thinking when I accepted that date with Jeff?

Well, I knew what I had been thinking. But as I'd walked back along the beach with Janis, all I could think about was Myles. I probably wouldn't even have to go on this date if Myles hadn't abandoned me.

"You would never leave me, would you, Janis?" I said, ruffling the dog's ear as she sat beside the couch where I was reclining. She looked up at me, cracking a doggy smile. Of course, I couldn't be sure how genuine that love was, considering that Janis had bolted on me at the beach. She seemed pretty loyal right now, but that might be because of the mountain of dog treats I fed her when we got back to the house.

Now, as I scratched Maggie's dog behind the ear while staring at the paintings of beach scenes Maggie had so lovingly hung on the living room wall of her house, I realized I had to go on that date, even if the idea of sitting across a cozy little table from someone other than Myles was starting to depress me. I wondered just how far I would have to go for Maggie's sake.

"Anybody home?"

I sat up suddenly, startling Janis, who began to bark.

"It's just Myles," I said to Janis when I spotted him peering through the screen door.

Just Myles? I thought, standing up quickly and shutting off the TV, as if to make sure I hadn't somehow beamed him in here. "Come in," I said, once I realized the man standing at the door wasn't some phantom I'd conjured up but Myles in the flesh.

"Hi," I said, stopping at the kitchen island, all at once feeling wary. Janis began to whine, probably sensing my sudden discomfort.

Or not, I realized as Janis trotted over to Myles, tail wagging.

Traitor, I thought, watching as Janis nuzzled affectionately at his hand.

"You must be Janis Joplin," Myles said, giving her a good scratch behind the ears that had her tail moving so furiously her whole back end was getting into the action.

I understood all too well why Janis had succumbed so easily to his charms. He did look good. A little too good. In fact, he was dressed rather nicely for the beach, in a pair of cotton Dockers and a baby blue polo shirt.

"Nice place," he said, looking up at the wall of windows that opened on to the ocean view. "Very nice."

I decided not to bring up the fact that he could have had a share in this nice place and got to the more pressing question. "What are you doing here?"

That golden brown gaze finally focused on me. "I made a phone call yesterday. To my friend Paul, over at the Suffolk County P.D."

My insides felt warm. "Myles, thank you, I—"

He shook his head. "Don't worry about it." He looked around. "Are we alone?"

"Yeah, everyone is down at the beach—Tom, Nick, Sage— didn't you see them?"

"I walked along the streets to get here."

"Oh," I said, suddenly realizing he was wearing shoes. A pair of brown leather boat shoes that looked kind of new. "So where is your house, anyway?"

"On Pine Walk. Daydream Believer," he said, giving me the house name. "Ever seen it?" I shook my head. "It's nice. But not as nice as this." He gazed around. "Is that Tom?" he asked, pointing to a photograph of Tom holding a large fish on the end of a hook.

"Yep, that's him," I said, studying Myles's face for a reaction.

"He seems like an okay guy."

"Yeah, so did Ted Bundy," I replied. "Come in. Sit down. Can I get you something to drink?"

"I'm good. Look, Zoe, I can't stay long...."

I absorbed this information, wondering where he might be going in that nice little outfit he had on. And with whom. But I held my tongue, leading him into the living room.

Janis followed, lying down at the foot of the love seat Myles plopped down on. I sat on the sofa opposite him, watching as his gaze moved to the windows once more. "How much did you say he paid for this place?" Myles asked.

"I don't know for sure. But it's probably worth at least a million by now," I replied, wondering at his interest. Myles had never seemed to care about material things. But then, I'd never seen him in an Izod shirt either, I thought, noticing, for the first time, the little alligator on his blue polo. "So tell me what you found out."

He turned his gaze from the ocean view. "Why aren't you down at the beach?"

I shrugged. "Too hot," I said. "C'mon, Myles, tell me what you learned."

"Well, before you get too excited, Zoe, I didn't find out much. Yeah, it was Erickson who conducted the investigation, but from what Paul told me, there was very little suggestion of foul play. No hard evidence anyway. No signs of a struggle."

I frowned, staring at his hands as he fiddled with a coaster that had been left on the coffee table. "That's what Jeff said, too."

He stopped fiddling. "Who's Jeff?"

I looked up at him and saw something stir in his eyes. Jealousy. Myles was jealous! At least I hoped he was jealous. Maybe that was a good enough reason to go on this date. Still, I refrained from throwing it up in his face. Especially since he looked positively miffed. There was enough satisfaction in that, after all. "I'm sorry—Officer Barnes. He's with the Marine Bureau. He came to the house that night. We've been talking, you know. Since the incident."

Myles leaned back on the couch. "So why didn't you just ask him to order up your report?"

"He's with the Marine Bureau, not Homicide."

"But if he was first officer on the scene, then he would have access."

I shrugged. "Nah, Jeff's too much of a goody-goody." Then I remembered the proud thrust of his chin and the way he'd practically spoken in police codes for the first five minutes of our conversation. Maybe I was wasting my time by going on this date. "He'd never bypass the proper channels."

"Is that right?" Myles said, glaring at me now.

Oops. "Look, maybe he would have. But he's not as familiar with these types of cases as you are," I said, hoping to ameliorate the dig by some ego-soothing. "What does he do, really, except give out beer tickets and noise-disturbance warnings? Now you were in the D.A.'s. office—"

"*Were* being the operative word," he said.

"Myles—"

"Never mind," he said, waving a hand in the air dismissively, that glint of anger—or confusion, I couldn't tell—in his eyes once more. "The only other thing of interest was the toxicology results."

I looked at him.

"It was pretty standard stuff," he began. "Her blood alcohol level was high—nothing crazy, though. But Paul told me they took a few extra days to make the determination because they also discovered she had some Valium in her system."

"Valium? Isn't that dangerous—to take Valium and drink?"

He shrugged. "People do it all the time."

"But you're not supposed to, right?"

His golden gaze met mine. "People do things they're not supposed to all the time."

I knew by the sorrow rimming his eyes that he was thinking of his father, how he had gone into that abandoned house without calling for support like he should have. How he had been shot when a wild-eyed kid with a gun startled him from behind. I wanted to touch Myles's hand, do something—anything—to douse the sadness I saw in him.

I didn't, of course. I couldn't. And that made me even sadder.

"Look, Zoe, the Valium in her system could mean nothing— they followed up and found out she had a prescription."

"But?"

"Well, there was some concern about it, apparently, seeing as she had a lot of it in her system."

"So what does that mean?"

"Well, it could mean a lot of things. But in the final analysis, they ruled 'accidental.'"

I frowned. "Why would they do that?"

He ran a hand through his hair, as if he was just as uncomfortable with the conclusion as I was. "The thing is, it's hard to tell a lot with the toxicology results. Yeah, she had a lot in her system, but whether it was enough to put her out—well that's debatable."

"You mean she might have been unconscious before she even hit the water?"

"Anything's possible, Zoe." His gaze met mine. "I also did a little Internet search on Tom. It seems he was a big contributor to the Police Benevolence Society."

My eyes widened. "You don't think the police looked the other way because—"

"I'm not saying that, Zoe. I'm just telling you what I found out."

I studied his gaze, saw that he was questioning the ethics of this case, just as I had all along. "Come with me," I said, jumping up and heading for the master bedroom.

Once we were both inside Tom's private bathroom, I shut the door. Then opened the medicine cabinet, my eye roaming over the contents. Tylenol. Midol. Aftershave lotion. I reached out, grabbing the two prescription bottles I came across. Both for Valium. One Tom's. One Maggie's.

"Well, look at this—his and her tranquilizers," I said, studying the labels and realizing that Tom's prescription had about twice the number of milligrams as Maggie's did. I showed Myles.

"She could have taken his by accident," he said, but I could see the uncertainty in his eyes.

"Or Tom could have *given* her his. Hoping it would look like an accident."

"There's no way to prove that, Zoe."

"Which is what Tom was probably counting on."

I felt a sudden tension in Myles. "We probably should get out of here. In case he comes back."

I nodded, opening the door and heading back into the living room, stopping short of the sofa and turning to Myles. "So what do we do now?"

He sighed. "I'm not sure there's anything we can do, Zoe. It's all circumstantial. It doesn't necessarily mean—"

"I know, I know. But something doesn't feel right about this whole thing."

He smiled at me, though I noticed his eyes looked a little sad. "Always the renegade, Zoe. I mean, short of getting Tom to confess, what can you do?"

"I don't know," I said, realizing that despite the fact that Myles seemed to be tilting toward my side now, it might not do me any good. "Maybe I can get him drunk."

"Zoe," Myles said. "Don't do anything stupid."

I looked at him, taking heart at the concern in his eyes. "I won't." Well, maybe just a little stupid. I smiled at him. "Thanks for helping me out, Myles."

"Anytime," he said. "Really. I shouldn't have been so hasty the other day, it's just that I—"

"It's okay."

"Promise me you aren't going to try and confront him."

"Myles—"

"Promise," he said.

"Myles, I can't promise you that."

He shook his head. "Well, you could at least promise me that you'll call me first. To talk it out. You know you can be a bit of a hothead."

My insides warmed. "I will."

Suddenly a cell phone began to ring, the sound muffled. I whipped my head around, spotting my cell on the coffee table inside just as I realized that it wasn't my ring I was hearing. It was Myles's.

"You gonna get that?" I said.

"Nah," he said, dropping his eyes. The phone rang again, and he began to rattle the keys in his pocket. "Listen, Zoe, I have to go. I have dinner plans."

So that was what the spiffy little outfit was about. "Oh. Where? The Inn or The Out?" I said, trying to make light of it.

"Actually, I'm going to try out Le Dock tonight. In Fair Harbor?"

I knew Le Dock. Or I knew *of* Le Dock. Sage had told me about it. She'd gone there on a date once. Apparently it was very romantic. "Sounds very cozy," I said, hearing his cell phone beep as the call rolled into voice mail. "You better call her back or she might worry she doesn't have a date for tonight."

"Zoe, it's not like that," he began, then stopped, realizing he'd gone right where he didn't want to go.

"No?"

He started to shake his head, but something stopped him. Something in his eyes. I knew that look. Myles was incapable of lying. That's what I'd loved about him. But now I wished like anything he could be untruthful. I didn't want to know he had a new girlfriend.

"It's not anything serious anyway."

Because I was a glutton for punishment, I asked, "It's her, right? The girl in your beach house? Haley."

He didn't answer, which was as good as a yes in my mind. Then he sighed. "Look, Zoe, I'm trying to be a friend to you, but I just don't know how."

Neither did I, I thought, realizing that maybe I shouldn't be relying on this man I had relied on for almost two years.

And wondering if I had a choice.

22

Maggie
What to do in the event of an emotional emergency.

Maybe it was the haze of prescription happiness I was living in, or maybe it was just some old discontent within me that had never died, but I started to become paranoid about Tom.

Perhaps it was all those late nights at the office, but I began to wonder if my husband was sleeping with someone else.

He certainly had opportunities. He had his pick of the sales reps who worked for and worshipped him. The buyers—mostly female—from his nationwide customer base. The models he used in his advertising. I wasn't so worried about the models. Tom wasn't the model type. I knew Tom's type. Vulnerable, sweet-faced and a little bit lost. Kind of like I used to be, before he gave me up as a hopeless cause. You see, that was the thing about Tom. He only liked problems he could solve. And my problems, he had discovered, were beyond his reach.

I started looking for evidence—hotel receipts, lipstick stains. I started to suspect every little mouse of a girl who marched through his life. That's why when I came into the Luxe offices on one of my "surprise" visits and found him having a cozy little lunch in his office with his admin, I was certain I had found the one.

Danielle Winston was twenty-seven, living with her parents and pathologically addicted to the idea that she would never amount to anything. In other words, a train wreck waiting to happen.

But not if Tom could stop it. He must have thought I was blind to his desires, considering the fact that he would come home at night and tell me the latest trials in poor Dani's life. She didn't trust men (her stepfather had abused her when she was a child). She was up to her eyeballs in debt. She just needed a little boost to get by, and Tom, dear Tom, was giving up his lunch hours and staying late some nights just to give it to her. But I suspected pep talks weren't the only thing he was giving her.

I couldn't find any proof, and what I needed desperately was proof. So I started to follow her, and believe me, this was no easy pursuit. Danielle Winston lived a seedy little life for a girl from Queens. In fact, one day I followed her all the way to a tenement building in the Bronx, only to discover that Danielle's greatest passion wasn't Tom but crack cocaine.

At least I succeeded in getting her fired. Tom didn't care much for drug addicts.

But my quest was ultimately a failure. Because what I discovered during the long and weary nights I spent scouring Tom's desk for a hidden token of affection for someone else, smelling his clothes in search of a perfume that wasn't my own, was that I was looking for a reason to walk away from my marriage. Without accepting any blame.

Nick
I sold my soul to the devil. I just hope I get a return on my investment.

When it came down to it, I realized I would do just about anything possible to make this label happen.

The problem was, I couldn't convince Sage to do anything possible. "Look, Les, I did my best," I said into my cell phone, my eyes on the ocean before me. "You know chicks. They're fickle. She might change her mind. Maybe it's a good thing, right? You gotta finish writing those last few songs for the CD anyway."

With the financials I was working with, I was gonna need to see a return on my investment sooner rather than later. Which meant I needed to get the band into the studio as soon as possible. "So when do you think you'll be done with the writing? I wanna book some studio time."

"That's the problem, man. I haven't been able to write a word."

I sat up in my beach chair. "You're fucking kidding me, right?"

"You know I don't kid about stuff like this, Nick. I'm fucking blocked. I think Sage might be my muse."

Oh, man. I was going to kill Sage. Okay, she wasn't interested in Les, but did she have to shake her ass in front of him all night at the gig last week? I still didn't understand why she didn't like him. Les was a nice guy. But every time I brought up his name,

she glared at me. Then I heard her talking to Zoe about that
Vince character she was apparently into now. That old guy
from the party. And Sage said something about him having a
kid. A kid! Like that was attractive. In fact, I bet if I put Les
and Vince in a room together with Sage, she'd come to her
senses—quick.

Which gave me an idea.

"Hey, Les, you really want to hook up with Sage?"

"Of course, dude, what the hell have we been talking about
here?"

"Then come out to the beach tonight. We're having a dinner
party at the house for Sage."

"You serious, dude?"

"Yeah, I'm serious. It'll only take you a couple of hours to get
here." I gave him the Web site where he could get train and ferry
information and directions. "Just let me know what ferry you'll
be on and I'll meet you at the dock."

"Hey, I owe you one, Nick."

"Yeah, well, you can consider the debt paid in full once we get
those songs recorded."

"You got it, dude."

I snapped my phone shut with a smile. I'm still in the game, as
long as I keep the ball in play. I just hoped Vince would bring that
kid with him tonight—and she spit up all over Sage midmeal. Actually, I wasn't sure how old the kid was. Well, whatever. Sage
wasn't the guy-with-kid type. She was the hard-living, hard-
loving musician type. The Les type.

Yeah, I'm still in the game. Picking up my cup of beer, I gazed
down the beach, spotting Francesca, just as some lifeguard threw
her over his shoulder and starting running toward the water with
her as she laughed and squealed.

Jesus, somebody ought to put that girl on a leash. Like her father, I thought, looking up to find Tom squatting a few feet away
from me, pulling something out of a Tupperware container.
Mmm. Maybe it was lunch.

One look at the fleshy cluster in his hand and I knew it wasn't
lunch. Far from it, I thought, watching as he slid whatever it was
onto the hook he held.

"You know, I couldn't help overhearing," Tom began. "Sounds like you're having a little trouble with the new business?"

"No troubles," I replied. "Well, just a little management problem with a band I put under contract. Nothing I can't handle."

"Well, I know a thing or two about management, if you have any questions."

I nearly snorted. This guy who made ladies' skirts was gonna teach me about the music business? But then I remembered that Tom's interest shouldn't be sneered at. Especially now. And since I had clearly lost the interest of the daughter, maybe I should start working on the father. After all, I was going to need more money. I'd prefer not to launch this label with only one band. Especially a band with a lead singer who wasn't going to stick to the program.

"Here's the deal," I began. "I got this band under contract, but I was hoping to get them in the studio to record sooner rather than later. I'd like to get their CD pressed in a few months. But these creative types, you know? You give them limits, and they're always pushing."

"Oh, I know it," he said. "I've got a handful of designers working under me, and they don't even want to know me when I ask them to alter their perfect bodies to save production costs."

Whoa. Where was he going with this? "Alter their bodies?"

He laughed. "I mean their designs. But I know a thing or two about design myself. I wouldn't ask them to do something that would harm their work."

"I hear you."

He leaned back on his heels, still holding the mutilated flesh on the end of his hook. "The key, I think, is to get people to trust your instincts. Your leadership."

I nodded, studying the fleshy concoction. Didn't he have to, like, put that thing in the water?

"I used to send all my staff to management courses. Even the non-managers, so they could understand what their managers are up against. Good management is an intricate process. It requires a certain finesse. A strength of character."

I felt my eyes begin to droop. Man, that beer had hit me hard. I could use a nap.

"The most important thing, I think, is to be able to instill confidence in your employees. Let them know who's in charge."

Oh, man. This guy was worse than his wife with the advice. I was starting to think they were perfect for each other. I nearly smiled at the thought. Then I remembered I was supposed to be listening.

"Next thing you need is effective communication."

I nodded encouragingly, despite the fact that I'd heard enough. Out of the corner of my eye, I saw Francesca approaching. I guess her little stud had to go back on duty. Well, whatever. I was glad she was coming back. If nothing else, she always broke up the monotony. Man, look at those breasts.

"You can't hold an employee accountable for his actions," Tom continued, "if the employee doesn't understand what he's done wrong."

I don't even have to touch them. Just look, you know? See if those nipples are as perfect as I imagine them to be.

"Hi, Daddy," she said once she reached us.

Shit, I probably shouldn't be ogling the daughter in front of Daddy Dear. God, I practically had a woody.

Not that Tom noticed. My woody. Or his daughter, for that matter.

"That's why clear and concise communication is the key," he continued.

Francesca brushed past me without a word, settling down on her stomach on the far side of the blanket Tom had laid out earlier. What, I don't even get a hello? She's probably still pissed at me about the Les thing. I had introduced them that night, but I didn't have any control of who he did and didn't like. Now, as I watched her wiggle that perfect little body on the blanket, carving out some space for those breasts of hers, I was glad he wasn't interested.

I saw her first, after all.

Not that it was doing me any good, I thought, watching as she opened one eye briefly to glare at me before turning her face away. Maybe she was glaring at Tom. But why would she be glaring at her father?

I looked up at him, realizing he had stopped speaking and was staring at me. No, he wasn't staring at me, exactly. He was sort of staring with that weird, spacey look he gets sometimes. I raised my eyebrows, as if waiting attentively for his next words.

"You were saying, Tom?"

"Ah, never mind," he said. "I gotta go put this line in the water again."

Creepy. I wondered if Tom smoked a lot of dope when he was younger. He kinda reminded me of this guy Carl I went to college with, the way he shut on and off like that. Spacey. Or something. I turned to look at Francesca again, but she still had her face turned away from me.

Shit. I had definitely lost her. But I still had a shot at her father.

I stood up. "Hey, Tom, you got another rod, man? I'd love to learn how to fish."

After all, there was no better way to bond with a man than over sports. Too bad I wasn't much of a sportsman.

But I could be, if given enough reasons.

And I had one very good reason.

24

Sage
Every party needs a pooper. I think I got a two-fer.

"Sage, get out of this kitchen and get yourself a drink," Tom said, once he came out of the shower and saw that I had not only marinated the steaks and made the salad, but had a pot of mushroom risotto simmering on the stove. "If I'd known you were going to cook the whole meal, I would have come up from the beach sooner. This party is supposed to be in your honor."

I shrugged, then smiled up at him. "I like to cook," I told him, realizing as I said the words how true they were. I had enjoyed putting this meal together for everyone. This was exactly how I had imagined the summer to be. Good food, good friends.

Good man, I thought, as I saw Vince's broad-shouldered form shadow the screen door.

"Anyone home?"

"Vince! Come on in, buddy," Tom called out.

I watched as Vince greeted his friend. "For you," he said, holding up one of two bottles he carried.

"Whoa, nice, Vince, nice," Tom said, taking the bottle of red and studying the label.

"And this," he said, turning to me, "is for you."

I glanced at the bottle of champagne he held, noting the fancy

French label. Well, this was promising. "Thank you, Vince," I said, meeting his gaze. "That was very sweet of you."

"Well, it's not a celebration without some good champagne. And from what Tom tells me about you, it seems we have a lot to celebrate tonight."

My smile widened as I studied his handsome features. He looked different. More relaxed than the last time I had seen him, with his daughter. But then, so was I.

"Where's Sophia?" I asked.

"She's with her mother," he replied. Turning to Tom, he rolled his eyes. "Gabriella has a lot of rules when it comes to that kid. She's taking Sophia out to see family early tomorrow and she didn't want me bringing her back on the boat late at night."

A boat? Well, that was even more promising. A beach house, a beautiful man and a boat. He was getting better by the minute. "I didn't know you kept a boat, Vince."

"Of course." He smiled at me. "I love being out on the water."

And I'd love to be out on the water with him.

"Let me get you a drink, buddy," Tom said, leading Vince into the living room.

A moment later Zoe came in through the sliding glass door in running shorts and a T-shirt. "What's going on?" she asked, looking at the spread.

"What's going on is dinner, Zoe. I told you we were celebrating my promotion tonight. Where've you been?"

"I had a photo shoot," she said sarcastically, as she yanked on her sweaty T-shirt. "Where do you think I've been? Did a nice long run. All the way out to the Jones Beach Tower. Remember that thing we used to pass on the way to Jones Beach? We called it the giant penis, remember? Oh— Hi!" Zoe said, her face turning red when she spotted Vince, who had just returned to the kitchen, martini in hand, with Tom.

"Vince was at the Fourth of July party, but I'm not sure you two have had a chance to meet yet," I said, eager to introduce them. I had already told Zoe a little about Vince. Though she was surprised at my attraction for a man with a kid, she gave a somewhat tentative approval, seeing as I had at least set my sights on someone with a little stability in his life. "Zoe, this is Vince, Vince,

Zoe." Then I smiled. "I've probably known Zoe for about as long as you've known Tom, Vince. She's my oldest friend."

"After Nick, of course," Zoe said. "You've known Nick longer."

"Only by about six months. We all went to high school together."

"Now that's scary, huh, Vince?" Tom said. "We've got as many years of friendship between *us* and we've only known each other since the beginning of Luxe."

"Age is just a number," I said, smiling again at Vince.

"So, Sage tells me you have a daughter," Zoe said.

I watched Vince nod, his glance moving to me briefly. Did she have to make it so obvious that I had been chatting away about him? "Zoe, don't you think you ought to take a shower before we eat?"

Zoe caught my look, thank God. I feared she was going to go into her usual rapid-fire line of questioning. And the last thing I needed was for Vince to be uncomfortable. He was a guest at my party.

But he wasn't, I discovered, a short while later, the only single male guest. Because just moments after I had sat down on the back patio for some pre-dinner cocktails with Vince, Tom, a freshly-showered Zoe and an ultra-primped Francesca, Nick came home, with none other than Les Wolf in tow.

"Hey," Nick said, his smile broad as he slid open the door, allowing him and Les to step outside.

I narrowed my gaze at him. No wonder he had been so vague about the guest he'd told me he was bringing.

"Sage, you remember Les, right?"

"Hello, Les," I said, smiling tightly as Nick introduced Les around. I watched as Les mumbled "hello" at everyone. It didn't take me long to figure out just what Nick was up to, if the way Les kept glancing at me was any indication. I was going to kill Nick for trying to use my celebration to serve his stupid little schemes. He knew I wasn't interested in Les. In fact, the guy creeped me out, especially the way he stared at me all night at Don Hill's last week.

As it turned out, however, I didn't have to worry about Nick's scheme, because Francesca latched on to Les from the minute he sat down, leaving him to stare numbly at the considerable cleavage she was sporting tonight.

But Nick wasn't the only one trying to rain on my parade tonight. Because once Donnie and Amanda Havens arrived, Zoe took over.

"I'd like to propose a second toast," Zoe said, once we were seated around the dinner table and Tom had finished a lovely little speech in my honor. "To Maggie."

I nearly choked on the champagne I'd just sipped.

Not that anyone else noticed.

In fact, Donnie said, "Here, here. After all, it is the three week anniversary of her death. May she rest in peace."

"God, I still can't believe she's gone," Amanda said, her eyes beginning to tear up as she touched her glass to her lips.

"Did you know her well?" Zoe asked, standing to refill everyone's glasses.

"Maggie and Amanda grew up together," Tom said, his expression turning grim as he held out his glass to Zoe to fill.

"If it wasn't for Maggie," Donnie said, "I wouldn't even be working for Luxe, isn't that right, Tom?"

Tom smiled. "That's right. It was Maggie who brought us together."

"I don't think I knew that," Vince said.

"Oh, yes," Amanda chimed in, "Donnie was out of work, and Maggie talked to Tom, and the rest, as they say, is history. She was always so good to us."

"To Maggie, then," Vince said, raising his glass.

"To Maggie," everyone echoed, clinking glasses.

Of course, I toasted, too. I mean, I had something to be grateful to Maggie for, too—her job. Even so, I resented Zoe for turning the tide of my dinner party. Because turn the tide she did. Soon enough, Donnie and Amanda began reminiscing about Maggie, the dinner parties she threw, the generosity she showed to everyone around her. Even Vince went on a jag about how Maggie had cooked many a meal for both him and Tom when Vince came back from China and his wife surprised him with a divorce. "I don't know what I would have done without her and Tom to help me through that tough time," he said, his face pensive.

The only person who seemed to remember that I was not only

alive and well but the guest of honor at this fucking party was Les. Every time Francesca paused in her fawning over him, he turned that creepy stare on me.

"So, Sage," he said now, at what was probably his sixth attempt at starting a conversation. "I brought the new Nick Cave CD to listen to. I got an advance copy, and I figured since you're as big a fan as I am—"

"Not now, Les," I cut him off, staring at Donnie with menace as he launched into yet another Maggie story.

By the end of the meal, even Tom was starting to look bleary-eyed. I didn't blame him. The whole fucking evening was starting to feel morbid.

Which was why I was desperately glad when, shortly after dessert, Donnie and Amanda announced they were leaving.

"Got to get an early start tomorrow if we hope to land a big striper," Donnie said, winking at Tom.

"That's right," Tom said, getting up and beginning to carry the plates to the sink.

I took the opportunity to step onto the back deck with Vince, after giving Zoe a good kick under the table and suggesting that the least she could do was help Tom with the dishes. She got up and picked up a plate, though not without giving me a bewildered look. But that was nothing compared to the wounded expression on Les's face when I practically told him to fuck off when he tried to follow me and Vince outside. Well, not really. But I did practically close the sliding door on his leg, telling him that Vince and I needed to talk business. And I think he himself may have said something similar to Francesca before he ran off to God-knows-where, leaving Tom's daughter to sulk on the living room couch, her arms folded across her chest. Nick sat at the other end of the same couch, giving the appearance of watching TV, but I could see him stealing glances at Francesca.

Serves him right, I thought, settling myself comfortably across from Vince at the patio table, turning my gaze from the door as I resolved to ignore my so-called friends. Not so hard to do, I thought, studying Vince's profile as he stared out at the ocean.

Feeling my gaze on him, he turned to me and smiled. "You

know, when I look out at the ocean on a night like this, it almost reminds me of the Amalfi Coast."

I smiled back. "Do you miss Italy?"

He shook his head. "It's a beautiful country. But I'm glad to be home." He reached for the glass of wine he had brought out with him. "Ever been?" he asked, his dark gaze falling on me once more.

"Not yet," I said, meeting his eyes.

"Oh, you should go. Every young woman needs to see Italy. It's magnificent. Good food. Good people."

"Good romance," I said, my smile widening.

He nodded his head, as if he thought there might be some truth to that but wasn't willing to verify it.

"Maybe I'll get Tom to send me," I continued.

"That would make sense," he said, "seeing as you are now sales manager for the company's first leather division." He lifted his glass. "To you," he said.

I picked up my glass, savoring this toast even more in light of the way the evening had gone. Or maybe it was in light of the man making it, I thought, clinking my glass with his and studying his beautiful mouth as I raised my glass to my lips.

I got the feeling Vince might have been savoring the moment, too, when I saw the way he looked at me as he drank. Even more so when he said, "Maybe I'll travel with you. Give you a personalized tour."

"Sounds like a plan to me," I said, an image filling my mind of me and Vince on a beach in Italy. God, what I would give to be alone with this man right now.

Then he went on to talk a bit about the tanneries, and I saw a light come into those dark eyes I had not seen until now. I recognized it for what it was. Ambition.

Now that was a turn-on. I never realized how much until I saw the way it animated Vince's handsome features and sent his big hands into the air as he talked about the various skins he'd lined up for the fall collection, which were just going into production.

Maybe I still felt a need to prove myself. Or maybe I was hoping he would admire my own ambition, but I offered my opinions. After all, I hadn't gotten this promotion for nothing. I wanted to be sure everyone knew that after all the blood and sweat I'd put into the start-up of Edge, I had learned a little something about skin, too.

"I wouldn't put the 5012 model in the lamb," I said, when he suggested that we might upgrade the leather on one of our more youthful styles. "In fact, I probably wouldn't put it on the 5025 or the 5032, either," I said, naming two other styles. "Those styles are too rugged. They're spawned by hip-hop culture, you know? You don't want your leather so soft it can't take a tumble on the street." Then I smiled. "Or a bullet. Not that we're designing for gang fights or anything, but you get the idea. It's how this demographic likes to think of itself."

He smiled somewhat mysteriously, and I wondered if maybe my ambition might have turned him off completely. Because despite that flash of teeth, his eyes seemed annoyed. "I guess you would know better what the younger set wants than I would."

I laughed now, softening the blow, and, I hoped, closing the age gap he'd just opened up between us. "Hey, I'm about a decade older than that crowd, Vince."

His eyebrows raised. "How old *are* you, Sage?"

For the first time in my life, I wanted to lie. And lie up. Because I was suddenly getting the feeling that it might matter to Vince Trifelli that I was young enough to be his…kid sister. "I'm thirty-one," I said finally, deciding to go for honesty.

"Thirty-one." His dark eyes went ponderous, as if he were lost in some memory of what thirty-one felt like, and suddenly he did look younger to me, almost carefree. Not that it mattered. I liked him the way he was. Weathered. Older. Experienced.

Hot. What had I'd been thinking, chasing all those boys around for so long?

When he came back from wherever he had gone mentally and saw the way I was feasting on him, Vince's face seemed to harden. I wondered at that.

"So I assume it was you who suggested the remerchandising on those samples that came back?"

His tone was accusing. As if maybe he shared Shari's opinion that I had taken control of the reins before they'd been given to me. Hoping to put that thought quickly to rest, I met his gaze. "Yes, it was me. I couldn't, in good conscience, represent merchandise I wouldn't even consider wearing myself."

I saw his gaze flicker briefly over my tight tank top, my cargo skirt. "Is that right?"

"That's right. Those buttons were too heavy. And the shoulder flaps were an abomination. Those jackets looked like costumes for Sergeant Pepper's Lonely Hearts Club Band. And though I have nothing against returning to the sixties from a fashion point of view, I didn't think we should ever go there for that design. It was Maggie's idea—" I stopped, stumbling over her name. Even I couldn't avoid talking about the woman tonight. I wondered how long she was going to haunt me.

I saw him frown, and I feared he sensed some of my freshly stirred ire at my former boss. Though Tom hadn't seemed to blink an eye about giving me the position within weeks of his wife's death, I wasn't sure what Vince thought of the fact that I had, before she was even cold in the ground, not only taken over her job but undone all the changes she had made to the designs before you could utter, "May she rest in peace."

I guess you could say it was a little odd. And, yes, even cold.

I hoped he wouldn't notice.

He stared at me for a moment and then treated me to what seemed like genuine laughter. "That Maggie. She wasn't much for this sort of thing, was she? But she tried. Lord knows she tried." He sighed. "She was a good kid."

"The best," I said, though the words felt like rubber in my mouth.

"Well, Sage, I can see why Tom hired you. You know your skin."

I smiled, releasing that breath I hadn't even realized I'd been holding. I felt like I had passed some test I had no way to study for. With flying colors, too.

Because Vince Trifelli was looking at me with something that seemed like admiration.

And maybe, I thought, seeing that glint in his dark eyes, maybe even something more.

But I didn't get a chance to find out. Because suddenly there was a commotion on the front deck, and I saw Tom abandon Zoe at the sink as a woman I recognized from a neighboring house yanked open the sliding door. "Tom, come quick. There's a guy outside caught in the tide. I think he's in trouble!"

25

Nick
Occupational Hazards

"I've never seen anything like that," I said, shaking my head.

"You said that already," Sage reminded me, for the third time.

We were standing on the beach—me, Sage, Zoe and Francesca—watching as Tom leaned over Les, who was at least sitting up now, near the shoreline. JoBeth, the neighbor who had come running to the house when she spotted Les tumbling in the waves, stood beside them, arms folded, as if standing guard over the situation.

"I guess I'm in awe," I said now, still studying Tom as he put a hand on Les's shoulder while he spoke to him.

"I know *I* am," Zoe said. "Though I don't know if I'd call it awe so much as shock."

"Yeah, well, just chalk it up to that good instinct you have for people," Sage said, shooting a look at Zoe.

Up until five minutes ago, Sage had been pretty quiet. Now she seemed damned pissed. Maybe she was just as disgusted with Les as I was. Or maybe—and this was probably more likely—she was in a snit that her little tête-à-tête with Vince was disturbed by Les's shenanigans.

Speak of the devil, I thought, as Vince blew past us, carrying a blanket. I saw Sage's face visibly soften as he jogged to the shoreline and dropped the blanket around Les's shivering shoulders.

"I told you Tom was good in an emergency," Sage told Zoe.

"So the guy knows CPR," Zoe muttered, "that doesn't absolve him from everything." She didn't say this with much conviction, though she did have the good grace to cringe when she realized Francesca was out here with us. Not that it mattered. Francesca hadn't said a word since we'd run out here. Now she continued to remain quiet, not moving a muscle as she stood there, arms folded, staring at her father as he leaned over Les.

Francesca and Zoe aside, I was fucking impressed. "CPR? That was more than just CPR. You saw the way Tom ran into that water, cutting through it like a knife. Then he pulled Les out like Les was nothing more than a rag doll. It was like watching live fucking *Baywatch*."

Now Sage turned to look at me, an eyebrow raised. "Don't you think you ought to do something useful? Like go down there and see if your *friend* needs anything?"

"Tom told us to clear the area!" I protested. In truth, I didn't mind standing at a distance. This way, I didn't have to look at Les's pale, snot-nosed face. I'm telling you, that dude was a big disappointment. Wandering off by himself, then practically drowning in the ocean. If that was some lame-ass suicide attempt, I'm gonna kick his sorry butt. I just invested almost twenty grand in this guy, and he goes and gets himself all fucking worked up and depressed over a chick he's known for, like, five minutes? Hello?

JoBeth approached us, along with Vince, who was looking a bit shaken himself. Bunch of wimps. Now, Tom, he was the man. The man. The way he just took charge, dove in like that. It was something to see. I only wish Zoe had gotten it on camera, but I guess she had been just as surprised as the rest of us and too stunned to do anything.

"How is he?" Sage asked Vince.

"He seems to be okay. Tom's got it under control. I'm going to go up to the house, call Good Samaritan Hospital, see if we can get an ambulance to meet the ferry. Tom thinks Les should go to the hospital, just to get checked out, before he goes home."

"I'll go with you," Sage said, stepping up next to him as he headed toward the house once more.

I looked at JoBeth, her gaze roaming back and forth between me and Zoe and Francesca, her expression grim. Or maybe she always looked like that. I didn't know her well, despite the fact that she lived in the house across the way, but she seemed like one of those serious types, with the short hair and that permanent worry line between her brows. Or maybe that was an age line. She was probably in her forties or so, though she could have been sixty, for all I know.

"So, JoBeth, how did you know Les was staying at our house?" Zoe asked now.

JoBeth shrugged. "I didn't. But I did know that Tom was a life-guard for a couple of years down in North Carolina where he grew up. I think he told me once he saved something like ten lives."

"Seven," Francesca corrected, startling us all. "It was only seven." Then her eyes widened, as if she were surprised at the shock we were all exhibiting at her somewhat resentful tone. "What? I've only heard the stories, like, a million times." And with that, she pulled the throw she had wrapped around herself more tightly and stomped off toward the house.

Yep, I can call 'em. That chick's a psycho.

"Well," JoBeth said, "Tom seems to have everything under control, so I'm gonna head home. I'm beat!"

Zoe thanked her for coming, though I was having a harder time showing any gratitude. I was starting to think we should have left the fucking guy in the ocean. Come to think of it, I need to check with my dad to see if there's anything in Les's contract that covers us in the event of his death. Not to be insensitive or anything, but the guy's a fucking walking hazard.

It always amazes me how much better a bed and a pillow feel when you spend half an evening standing before the specter of death. Not that this was a usual night for me, but I've had my moments. Damn, I was tired. Almost tired enough to shrug off the guilt Sage heaped on me for not taking the ferry back with Les. Not that Les needed me. Tom was more than willing to go, which

I found surprising. He must have been on some adrenaline rush, because he came back to the house, packed Les up (I did help with that—I'm not that bad a guy) and shuffled him off to the ferry. Sage took me to task for that one, that was for sure. She was probably just pissed because Vince took off just as soon as Tom left with Les. I, of course, had to bear the brunt of Sage's misguided anger, since Zoe had departed for parts unknown, and Francesca—well, she was probably still in her bedroom, pouting over God knows what. If she could earn money with that pout, she'd be a fucking millionaire.

I blew out a breath, sinking down farther into the mattress as I did. God, this was nice. Breeze blowing in, ocean roaring in the background. Pretty awesome being in the master's suite. Especially without the master around. Nothing against Tom, but he snored like a chainsaw. In fact, I was hoping Tom didn't hurry back from his little paramedic duty there, because maybe I could get to sleep before he came back and started up the nasal symphony.

I heard a door shut. Shit. Just my luck.

But when I heard my own bedroom door creak open in the darkness, I looked up and found not Tom, but none other than Francesca.

"What are you do—" I stopped, mostly because I had my answer the minute Francesca's silky little robe hit the floor.

"Francesca—" I began, not sure if I was protesting or begging or what. Because if I thought Francesca was hot in those bikini tops and short little skirts, Francesca completely naked, with the moonlight spilling across her golden-tan skin, was astounding.

So astounding that whatever I was planning on saying to her never even got past my lips. Because suddenly she was on top of me, her sweet little mouth on mine as her hands went to my boxers, yanking them down. In fact, I thought she might rip them off, so I helped by kicking them off myself.

Then she was at me like a wildcat, her luscious chest pressed against mine, her teeth biting at me, practically devouring me whole as she pressed herself against my now impossibly huge erection. The minute I felt the warm heat of her slip over the tip of me, I came to my senses.

"Wait—Francesca, what are you doing?"

She sat back on her heels, a flash of annoyance on her face that I almost missed, so caught up was I in the sight of her smooth skin, her rosy brown nipples. "What the fuck do you think I'm doing?" she barked, then lifted her bottom up and proceeded to slide herself on me again.

The heat almost did me in. Almost. "Wait—don't you think we should, like, use a condom?"

She shook her head furiously. "My father's had me on the pill since I was, like, twelve." She slid farther down, and though stopping her now was pure torture, stop her I did. Because the mention of Daddy Dear reminded me of something else.

"We can't do it here. Your father could be back any minute!"

She looked at me then, eyes narrowing as a small smile creased her mouth. "Don't you think I know that?"

And then, before I could utter another protest, she slid down the rest of the way. Ahhhhhh… So tight…so fucking tight.

Okay, we'll make this a quick one.

That was probably the last sensible thought I had. Because everything else flew out of my head at the sight of Francesca, rising up and down above me, her round breasts jiggling, her pink lips parted and she let out the sweetest, softest little moans, her bangs falling gently over her eyes, which were shut. God, I would have given anything for her to open them just then, to look at me. But it seemed to me the closer Francesca got to that power-gasm she clearly was moving toward, the farther I felt from her.

Which I suppose if this were, like, a movie or something, I should have taken as foreshadowing.

Because the minute Francesca rattled out a groan that made clear she had peaked, I heard the shush of the sliding door. "I'm home!" came Tom's cheerful voice, and suddenly she was off me like a shot, grabbing up her robe and darting from the room, leaving me to come—probably out of shock more than anything else—all over myself.

But I suppose things could have been worse.

The door creaked open again, and I pulled the comforter over myself, trying not to visibly cringe as I felt it come into contact with the stickier parts of my stomach.

Tom popped his head in. "Oh, you're up."

Umm, not quite. At least not anymore. "Uh, yeah, I'm up. Sorta." I blinked, as if perhaps he had woken me from a dream rather than the fantasy I'd just been living in. "I think everyone's pretty much in bed. Asleep, that is. Except maybe Zoe. I think I heard her go out a little while ago."

He frowned. "That's strange. I thought I heard Francesca." Then he shrugged. "Well, Les is on his way to the hospital. I'm sure you'll sleep better tonight knowing your friend is all right." Then he smiled, his expression satisfied.

"Yeah, I'll be sleeping well tonight," I said quickly. Just as soon as I cleaned up the evidence.

God, I was gonna sleep like a baby. As long as I forgot about the fact that I had just boned Tom's baby, right in his fucking bedroom.

Hazardous. Jesus, I must be crazy.

Just as crazy as Francesca was, apparently.

26

Zoe
Inside I'm screaming. And not for ice cream, either.

I had found Myles's beach house easily enough, now that I had an address. But once I stood outside Daydream Believer, I wasn't sure what I was doing there. Or if he was even home yet from his dinner date. All I knew was that I needed to see him. In fact, I was just contemplating throwing a rock at his window—assuming I could figure out which window belonged to Myles—when Myles himself came out the front door, looking positively adorable in a khaki green T-shirt and dark blue surfer shorts.

God, I was glad to see him. Especially after the night I'd had. He had a stabilizing effect on me.

"Hey," I said, both relieved and embarrassed to be caught standing staring up at his window—yet again.

Still, he smiled anyway. "You stalking me now?"

"Yeah, that's it." I smiled. "So where're you going at this hour?"

"In search of Moose Tracks."

"I hate to break it to you, Myles, but there isn't a moose on the island. Deer maybe."

He shook his head. "No, silly," he said, grabbing the brim of my baseball cap and giving my head a playful shake. "The ice cream. You know, peanut butter cups and fudge in vanilla ice cream. Moose Tracks. You've never had it?"

"Can't say that I have," I replied, wondering who had turned him on to this new flavor. When we were together, it was Ben & Jerry's Chunky Monkey. "I hate to be the bearer of bad news," I said, "but it's almost midnight, Myles. The market is closed."

"They sell it at The Inn," he said. "Walk with me?"

I fell into step beside him, starting in immediately on the topic that weighed on my mind. "So I almost lost another housemate tonight to Mother Ocean."

"What?" Myles looked at me.

"Well, not exactly a housemate. This guy, Les—a friend of Nick's. He went out for a little walk on the beach by himself. Then a swim. Or who knows what? The next thing you know, he's swallowing a lungful."

"There seems to be a lot of that going around."

"Yeah, well, you'll never guess who came to Les's rescue."

"Who?"

"Tom Landon, of all people."

"Really?"

"You should have seen him, Myles. It kinda reminded me of that night—the night I found Maggie. The way Tom just snapped to attention. Like he was some kind of rescue robot. He knew exactly what to do. And he wasted no time doing it. Diving into that ocean—" I shivered, the memory coming back of watching Tom getting smaller and smaller against those dark waves. "Pulling Les out. Applying CPR. I could have filmed the whole thing and turned it into an instructional video."

"Wow. Who knew he had it in him?"

"Yeah." Then I laughed, but the sound was without humor. "Too bad he didn't get a chance to try that technique out on his wife."

I felt Myles looking at me. "I see someone has revised her opinion of Tom Landon."

I sighed. "Not exactly. I mean, yeah, he was a hero tonight, but there was something…I don't know. Something strange about it. Almost bloodless. It was as if, paradoxically, Tom was able to jump into that water because he didn't have any regard for human life.

His own at least. Getting Les out of that water was simply something that had to be done. Like cleaning the grill before the barbecue." I blew out a breath. "Yeah, that made a lot of sense. I don't know. Maybe I *am* blowing this out of proportion. I don't even make sense to myself anymore."

"No, I understand," Myles said. "I've often felt like that."

"You have?" I asked, turning to look at his solemn profile, noticing his clenched jaw.

"About my dad," he said finally, his voice quieter, his eyes on the cracked concrete in front of us. "You know, after he died."

But because I didn't know—couldn't know, since Myles had shut me out of his life so soon after that loss—I said, "Tell me."

I felt a hesitation in him, and I looked up, saw the way he kept his eyes focused on the dark road, as if he might burn a path for us. "I guess what I mostly felt was angry after what happened." He blew out a breath. "I mean, I know my dad was a fucking hero—"

I cringed, mostly because I rarely heard a curse word come out of Myles's mouth.

"But I couldn't help thinking sometimes that he cared more about his victims than he did about us. His family. Like that time he got stabbed on a domestic disturbance call. And then going into that house that night, without any backup. It was like he cared more about those hoodlums who were squatting in that house than he did about his own kids." He shook his head. "God, I know that sounds awful."

"It's okay," I said, stopping him, taking his hand in mine as I looked at him. "It's okay to be angry at him, Myles. You aren't perfect. And neither was he." But I could see by the swirl of emotions in Myles's eyes—anger, yes, but also sadness so deep I felt it widening the gap between us—that I couldn't reach him. How could I? Did I really understand what it meant to lose a parent that way? I mean, yeah, I had lost a parent, but my father was alive and well somewhere. His guilt was obvious. Whereas Myles's dad had died a hero. At least to the rest of the world. I thought of Francesca, her sullenness as her father ran to Les's rescue. Clearly she had some sort of resentment over Tom's hero antics. I wondered, briefly, if Maggie had resented Tom. Resented him enough to seek solace somewhere else.

I looked into Myles's eyes again and wished I could do something, anything, to take the sadness and anger away. But just as quickly as he'd opened up to me, I saw him close again, his golden brown eyes going vacant.

He resumed walking. "We'd better get moving. I'm not sure how late the kitchen is open at The Inn."

As it turned out, the kitchen was not only open but well-supplied with Moose Tracks. And take-out containers for ice cream, which surprised me. I guess I had strolled here under the impression that Myles and I might be sharing a table and a bowl of Moose Tracks. Who knew you could take out ice cream from a restaurant? I thought, watching as Myles accepted a bag filled with two pint-sized containers of the stuff. I didn't want to know who he was bringing all that ice cream back for. I guess, in light of everything, I was trying not to be selfish.

It wasn't easy.

"You gonna get some?" Myles asked.

For who? I thought, realizing everybody was likely asleep back at the house. Or doing their own thing. Suddenly I wished for that fantasy house that Sage imagined we'd have this summer, the three of us, drinking, laughing, having a good old time. What had gone so wrong?

I looked at Myles, wishing I could go home with him, curl up on the couch in his living room and share a bowl of ice cream and some laughs. But of course I couldn't. "I'm good," I said finally, and we headed for the door.

We walked in silence for a short while, or we did once we passed the rowdy crowd of revelers who stood outside The Inn, smoking and talking and laughing as if tomorrow might never come. Soon enough, we were alone on West Lighthouse, and when Myles didn't turn off on the road to his own house, I realized he was walking me home.

I sensed his mood was just as ponderous as mine, though I had no idea where his thoughts had gone until he stopped in front of a tall A-frame house that rose up prettily through the trees.

I looked at him as he studied the house, drank in his strong profile, the way his hair, which he'd let grow, now fell over his eyes. He turned to me, caught me staring and smiled. "Nice house," he said.

"It is," I replied, then dutifully turned to look at it.

"I could have a house like this," he said quietly. "Probably by next summer. I'm going on that second interview with Banks, Rutherford and Simms," he continued. "If I take the job, I'll be making a lot of money. Probably triple what I would make in the D.A.'s office."

I looked at him, wondering who he was trying to convince.

"It's not wrong to want things, Zoe," he said, his tone filled with accusation.

I opened my mouth to protest, but he cut me off.

"It's not wrong to want things for yourself. Or your family. That's what matters, Zoe. Taking care of yourself. Your family. Not running after bad guys and collecting citations."

Understanding expanded through me as I watched him struggle with his words. I wanted to touch him, to tell him that I understood, but I wasn't sure he would accept my affection, considering that he was looking at me as if…as if I were the enemy.

I swallowed hard, feeling a slight relief when we started walking again, if only because I didn't have to look at his eyes anymore, see the hurt, the anger—some of it, I sensed, directed at me.

Within moments, we were standing in front of Maggie's Dream, and I watched as Myles gazed up at the dark house. At least he didn't look so mad anymore. But it hurt, still. Hurt so much that he felt the only way he could have what he wanted was to walk away from me.

"I guess I better go before this melts," he said, turning to me and aimlessly waving the bag he held in the air.

"Yes, you better," I said.

Then I stood on the road, watching him walk away until he disappeared into the darkness.

Maggie
We all die alone. But some of us take hostages.

They say a parent lives on in his or her children. I don't think I truly understood this until my own father died. I was thirty-five when he passed. I hadn't seen him for six years, hadn't known him for even longer.

But I went to the funeral, of course. A child knows her obligations after all. Especially an only daughter.

It wasn't pretty. It's never pretty when a man dies of cirrhosis of the liver. I'm not talking about the body itself. My father looked as placid as he had looked in life. The mood at the funeral was ugly though. There really isn't anything nice to say about a man who lived his life for the drink. And died by it. He didn't suffer, at least not in a way anyone could see. Didn't lie in a hospital bed receiving get well wishes from loved ones.

Didn't even really have to die, at least according to Tom, who didn't believe in diseases of the spirit. Diseases of the body he could sympathize with, but a failure of will was something he simply couldn't buy.

I suppose I didn't buy it either, until I stood before my father's coffin, saw the shape of his mouth, so like my own, the line of cheekbone that marked me and my brothers as family. And understood what it meant to give up.

It lived in me, that desire, to chalk everything up to missed chances and dashed dreams. To take comfort in a solution that could destroy you.

I also realized that, although I hadn't had a father for years, I had been living all this time with the possibility of him. The hope that I could return home and find somebody there to care for me. Because as ill as he was, my father had taken care of us once. My mother's bipolar disorder made him the better parent by default. He hoisted us onto school buses, packed lunches for us—when there was lunch to pack. Helped us fill out college applications and outwit the financial aid departments.

And then, one day, he was gone.

"Everyone is responsible for their own happiness," Tom said as we drove home from the funeral.

I wasn't sure who he was referring to, my father or me.

Which was why, when my small inheritance arrived in the mail a few months later, compliments of the pension my father didn't live to collect, I took it as a sign. Imagined my father had died so that I could live a better life myself.

I knew twenty thousand dollars wasn't enough to escape my marriage. I had, after all, become accustomed to a certain kind of life. But as it turned out, during my seemingly pointless job in accounts payable for the radio station, I had discovered I had a good head for numbers. And though at the time I had been disappointed to realize my gift was for numbers and not music, now that I actually had some money of my own, I was going to put that gift to work for me.

After all, my happiness depended upon it.

28

Sage
I could use a ghost right about now.

After less than a week of walking in Maggie's shoes, I was starting to wonder if I really had what it took to fill them. Especially as I sat poring over the budget she had set up just weeks before she died, trying to make sense of it.

Not that Maggie wasn't organized. In fact, ever since I had moved into her office, I realized she might have been more zealous about her organizational systems than even Tom was. The problem was, though I knew just about everything when it came to the selling and merchandising of skin, I knew zip about budgets.

So much for my good head for business, I thought, running a hand through my hair again as I stared down at the mass of numbers in front of me. I had even resorted to calling Tom yesterday, but the only thing clear to me when I finally got him on the phone was that there was a reason why Tom had needed someone else to run Edge. He had his hands full with Luxe. His assistant interrupted our conversation so many times with various emergencies that I finally gave up. I didn't want to overburden him, after all. Or worse, make him realize I didn't have that head for numbers he'd once relied upon Maggie for.

I could practically hear her laughing at me from the grave.

Which was probably why I took that framed photo she had on her desk of her at the ribbon-cutting ceremony for the showroom and tossed it right in the trash.

Along with the fussy little stained glass flowers she had hanging on the windowsill and the pink mouse pad she kept by the computer.

This place was going to need a little redecorating, to say the least.

But I certainly couldn't tackle that today, I thought, looking at the clock and realizing it was close to noon. I wanted to get this budget business done before lunch.

Before Vince arrived anyway.

When I learned from Tom on Monday that Vince was coming to town, I immediately rang his office in Bohemia, hoping to get a lunch date. And though Vince wasn't sure he would even have time for lunch between his meeting with Tom and his appointments with various vendors around the city, he did say he would stop by.

I was looking forward to it. Especially after our cozy little chat on the deck was cut short by that character Nick dragged out to the beach. Of course, neither Nick nor Zoe could understand why I was so pissed off at them that night. And I was tired of explaining what should have been obvious to my two closest friends.

The intercom on my phone rang, and I grabbed the receiver. "Yes, Yaz?"

"Vince Trifelli is here to see you."

I smiled. Early. That was nice. "Send him down, Yaz."

Shutting the file of Excel spreadsheets I had been staring at for way too long, I stood up, catching a glance of my reflection in the mirror, the only useful personal item of Maggie's in the office. I gave my hair a quick tousle, then pulled my lipstick out of my handbag and dabbed it on.

That budget would have to wait. Right now, I had more urgent matters to attend to.

"Well, hello," Vince said, appearing in the doorway.

"Hey, Vince," I replied, smiling at him and stifling an urge to lean forward and kiss him. Mmm. He looked good. I didn't usually go for suits on a man, but Vince was no ordinary man, I thought, studying the way his linen suit fit his broad shoulders and highlighted his olive skin. "So does this mean I have a lunch date today?"

His brows furrowed. "Unfortunately not, Sage. One of my vendors needed to move his appointment up, so I don't have that much time."

I bit back on the disappointment that stabbed at me.

"But I'll make it up to you," he continued, his dark gaze meeting mine. "Dinner Friday night at the beach? Le Dock in Fair Harbor is pretty nice. Especially at sunset."

Well, well, well. I might have lost a lunch, but I had gained a dinner. Complete with sunset. "Sounds good to me," I said smiling at him. "Can I get you anything? Coffee?"

He shook his head. "I really can't stay long. I just wanted to see how you were doing. I see you moved into your new office," he said, his gaze roaming around the room.

"Yeah, well, it needs a little work, but I'll get to it." Then I realized what I'd said and stepped a little to my right, hoping I was blocking the trash can filled with Maggie's tchotchkes.

"I really enjoyed our talk the other night," he said, returning his gaze to mine. "I'm hoping we can talk some more. I'd love to hear some of your ideas for next year's styles."

Now style ideas I could handle, I thought. For a moment I contemplated asking Vince the questions I had about the budget, then realized I might look like a know-nothing. And that was the last impression I wanted to give him. "That sounds great. I've already got a few ideas about some styles we can do in lamb and goat," I said.

"That's what I like to hear, Sage. We need to do a few more styles in some good-quality skins. Not that I have anything against your bulletproof hip-hop styles," he added with a wink.

Clearly I had made an impression on him. At least he remembered some of the ideas I'd shared with him out on the deck last weekend.

"How's Les doing?" he asked now.

"Oh, he's fine," I said. "I think he may have had a little too much to drink that night."

He shook his head. "He's lucky to be alive."

"I know," I said, feeling pretty lucky to be alive myself. Especially with Vince standing before me, looking at me as if he might be finding me just as irresistible as I found him.

This was shaping up to be a pretty damn good day after all. Budgets notwithstanding.

He glanced at his watch. "I've got to run. So Friday then? Pick you up at the house around eight?"

"I'm looking forward to it, Vince."

"So am I," he said, giving me a look that said dinner wasn't the only thing he was looking forward to.

Yes, it was good to be alive.

I was feeling even more exuberant when, two hours later, I managed to make some headway on the budget. So much so that I even treated myself to a double-mocha-cino, delivered right to my office from the coffee shop downstairs.

And just as I was settling into my chair to drink it, the intercom rang.

"Yes, Yaz?"

"Hey, Sage, did Vince say where he was going this afternoon? I have a woman on the phone from the tanneries who's trying to get in touch with him."

I frowned. "I know he had a few appointments, but I'm not sure with whom. Why don't you put her through to me. Maybe I can help her."

"Sure," Yaz said, clicking off.

A few moments later, a woman's voice came over the line. "Hello, I'm looking for Vince Trifelli," she said in a husky Italian accent.

"Hi, this is Sage Daniels. I'm the sales manager for Edge. Vince isn't in the office just now. Maybe I can help you?"

"Oh, no, that's okay."

"Are you sure?" I asked.

"Well, if you see Vince again, just tell him to meet me at the hotel at six."

Meet him at the hotel? "Who shall I say is calling," I said, trying to keep the sudden tension I felt out of my voice.

"Just tell him it's Gianna. He'll know," she said. "Thank you. Ciao."

I'll give her ciao, I thought, dropping the receiver into the cradle. Who the fuck was she?

I dialed "O" for Yaz.

"Yeah, Sage?"

"The woman that just called—did she say which tannery she worked for?"

"Ummm, let's see, what did she say her name was… Oh, Lorenzo. Yeah, that's it. She said her name was Gianna Lorenzo. I'd assume she's from the Lorenzo tannery in Italy."

"Thanks, Yaz," I said, hanging up.

What was Gianna Lorenzo doing in New York?

And a better question was, why the hell was Vince meeting her at her hotel?

29

Zoe
Dating is murder. On the nerves, if nothing else.

As I stood before my closet, trying to decide between two equally unappealing shirts to wear to dinner tonight, I realized I was still just as clueless about dating as I'd ever been.

And when Jeff called me to confirm our plans for tonight, I discovered he was just as clueless about "da city," as he and his Long Island henchmen referred to Manhattan. On top of my current wardrobe dilemma, I even had to pick out the restaurant we were going to tonight. The whole thing was becoming pretty stressful.

It wasn't that I had never dated before. I just never went on dates. With Myles, it seemed we went right from our mythical meeting at a peace rally in Union Square to renting videos and eating takeout together at his place or mine. And before Myles, I always seemed to date someone from whatever film I was working on, but those were more like friendly drinks–after–work–turned–romantic sort of outings.

This, however, was starting to feel like an honest-to-God date.

And I knew I should probably try and think of it as a date, despite my attempts to see these plans as simply part of my big plan to get more info on Maggie's death. Though the idea of being with anyone other than Myles still pained me, I knew I had to move on. Myles clearly had.

I almost called Sage, then remembered that she was none too pleased with me these days. I guess I couldn't blame her. It had been a bit insensitive of me to raise the specter of Maggie during Sage's big celebration. I guess I just had Maggie on the brain. And sitting at that dinner table, with everyone who knew and allegedly loved her, watching Tom chow down his meal like he didn't have a care in the world, it seemed like the right thing to do at the time.

Of course, it wasn't. Which was why I had gone out and bought Sage a coffee mug that said "The Boss" in big gold letters. I wanted her to know I was happy for her, because I *was* happy for her. Just a little more unhappy for Maggie.

Sighing, I finally pulled a yellow tank top out of the closet and yanked it over my head. It was one of the few shirts I owned that didn't have some incendiary message on it. Besides, Myles always said I looked good in yellow.

Of course, I wasn't going out with Myles.

Now, as I stood before the full-length mirror on the back of my closet door, I realized I looked decent enough, if not desirable.

At the sound of my door buzzer, I took a deep breath. "Ready or not."

The first thing I noticed when I caught sight of Jeff's tall, lean form through the glass of my front door was that even when dressed in jeans and a button-down shirt, he still looked like a cop. Maybe it was the fresh-from-the-dry-cleaners look of his crisp button-down, or maybe it was the way he stood, broad shoulders thrown back, head erect, eyes alert.

"Hi," I said, stepping through the door.

"Hi," he replied, beaming a smile at me that went right to his pretty blue eyes.

I looked up at his square jaw, the dimple in his chin. I had forgotten how cute he was. My palms began to sweat.

"So where are we off to?" he said.

"Nice little restaurant," I replied, trying to surreptitiously wipe my palms on my jeans. I gave up, waving him along rather than taking his hand. "C'mon. It's just a few blocks west of here."

I had decided on Westville, a local haunt Sage and I had gone to once, mostly because it was in the neighborhood and because they served enough variety to accommodate vegetarians and car-nivores alike. I was pretty sure Jeff fell into the latter category. Most men did. Besides, the restaurant was kinda sweet. Casual, intimate without being over-the-top romantic or anything.

Now, as we walked down the tree-lined streets in silence, I found myself glancing at Jeff as he looked with interest at the storefronts and pretty little brownstones we passed. Even felt his discomfort when we came across two men holding hands. "Bet you don't see that on Long Island every day," I said, hoping to dis-pel the tension he clearly felt. Or maybe I was trying to keep him from making some homophobic comment. I had dated guys from the burbs before. I knew homophobia sometimes ran rampant in towns where everyone looked and acted the same.

"Yeah, well, to each his own," he said, chuckling nervously.

Whew. One disaster averted. Next obstacle to tackle: conver-sation. While I had plenty on my mind to talk about, I didn't want Jeff to think I was only after one thing. So to speak.

"How was your meeting with your friend?" I asked.

"Oh, it was fine," he replied. "Actually, he just got a place in the city and he needed a hand hanging up some shelving,"

"That was nice of you," I said. *Mental note: Jeff knows how to hang shelves.* This could come in handy in a boyfriend. Not that I was looking for a boyfriend, I reminded myself. Well, not really.

"Yeah, he's an old friend. We went to high school together, you know?"

"Yeah," I said, smiling. I remembered now what it was that I loved about Long Islanders. That strong sense of community. And though sometimes that meant difficulty letting outsiders in, once you were in, you were a lifer. If you needed a favor—an old fridge moved out to the garbage for special pickup or some shelves hung—there was always some friend a phone call away to lend a hand. I hadn't realized how much I'd missed that.

Maybe because I thought I had it with Sage and Nick. But I guess I let those ties languish when I was with Myles, believing he was the only backup I needed. That had been a mistake, I thought, feeling keenly the distance between me and Sage, especially in light of last weekend.

"This is it," I said once we stood before the tiny restaurant, then waited as Jeff held the door open for me. That was the other thing about Long Island guys—they didn't mind being the guy.

And, I realized, as I smiled up at him on my way through the door, I didn't mind either.

I waited until we got through our appetizer salads before I brought up the beach. Or more specifically, the most recent crisis at the beach. I figured it was an innocuous place to start.

"So I guess you heard about the near-drowning last weekend at Kismet?"

Jeff looked up from the cherry tomato he had been pushing around his plate. "Oh, yeah. That was crazy. I wasn't on that night, but my buddy Carl was. He told me about it. What was that guy doing out there, anyway?"

I shrugged, putting my fork down on my plate. "Attempting to drown his sorrows, I think."

"Really? Was it a suicide attempt? I hadn't heard that."

I shook my head. "I don't know what it was. All I know is it was a good thing Tom Landon was there." I looked at Jeff. "Kinda ironic, don't you think, that just a few weeks earlier, Tom's own wife was in the same situation, and despite all his lifeguarding skills, he wasn't there to save her."

Jeff met my gaze. "I guess there are no guarantees in life. I mean, just because I'm a cop, doesn't mean my wife or my child would never be a victim of crime. You can't always be there for your loved ones."

I dropped my gaze. Maybe it was the earnestness in his eyes when he spoke about having a wife and child. Or maybe it was the searing truth behind his simple statement. You couldn't protect those closest to you all the time, no matter how much you loved them.

But you *could* keep them from further injustice, I thought, remembering the issue that was burning at the back of my mind. "I know you don't like talking about the case, but I guess the way Maggie died still kinda bothers me, you know? I just can't imagine why any sane woman would go into the ocean alone, at night, after drinking." I withheld what I knew about the Valium as I was sure it would bother him that I'd been unofficially nosing in the official files. Not to mention who I had used to snoop for me.

"Let me ask you something." I smiled. "Just a general question?"

He smiled back. Maybe it was the beer he was drinking, but he seemed a little looser. "Go ahead," he said.

"How do the police rule out suicide in a drowning case?"

He shrugged, then leaned back to let the waiter clear away our salad plates and put down our entrées. Jeff, of course, had steak and mashed potatoes. What else would a red-blooded American boy like him eat? I thought, studying the way his blue eyes lit up at the sight of his meal.

I, myself, went with the only vegetarian entrée that appealed: the grilled veggie burger, which I noticed Jeff glanced at with something resembling distaste.

"Well," he began, returning his gaze to me. "There needs to be evidence to support it."

I thought about that for a moment. "Like what, a note?"

"Yeah, for one thing. Also, we interview family members and close friends to get a sense of the victim's state of mind."

I tried to keep from rolling my eyes at that. "That's it?" I pressed. Though I didn't think it was suicide myself—this based on my gut more than anything else—it didn't seem to me Officer Jeff and his pals were using much more than I was.

"Well, there's also the fact that she was naked."

I tried to stifle my surprise when Jeff went from the general to the specific. Maybe I should order him another round.

"That is," he continued, "it's not usual, that a person disrobes completely in a suicide."

"Is that right?" I replied, leaning back in my chair to consider this. I suppose it made sense. If I were navigating my own death, I would prefer to be found with my clothes on, though I might kick off the shoes before diving in, just to retain some sense of normalcy. I remembered how Les had been wearing his denim shorts. Maybe he had been trying to commit suicide. Or maybe he didn't know that denim was pretty uncomfortable as far as swimwear goes.

"So let me see if I have this straight," I continued, as Jeff cut into his steak. "The fact that she wasn't dressed and had not previously shown any suicidal tendencies allowed the police to rule out suicide?"

Jeff considered this carefully. Or maybe he was just waiting to swallow his steak. Probably the latter, because when he finally spoke, his tone was somewhat defensive. "There were other things, too. I mean, the stories of the witnesses we interviewed checked out—"

"What witnesses? Didn't you tell me there were no witnesses?"

"Well, not to the actual event, no. But you told us about her state of mind. Her intentions. As did her husband. And your stories checked out with the evidence we found. The dress we found on the beach, for example. She even folded it, like she wanted to keep it nice for when she got out—"

"Wait a second," I said, putting my fork down once more. "Did you say Maggie was wearing a dress?"

He blinked at me, and I could see a flush beginning in his face. Still, he answered, "Yeah, it was a dress."

I wondered at that. Maybe because I didn't imagine Maggie in a dress. Especially since she was cooking all night. And supposedly hiking all the way to Fair Harbor for coriander. "What kind of dress?"

His eyes widened. "What does that matter?"

I shrugged. "I'm a chick. We're interested in these things."

He shook his head, but I noticed he was smiling. "I don't know, some kind of pink girly thing."

Not very descriptive. "And what happened to the dress?"

"What do you mean, what happened to it? Nothing happened to it."

"I mean after the police were done with it. What do the police do with evidence? That is, once it's no longer considered evidence."

"We return it, of course," he replied. "To the next of kin. Probably her husband."

I looked at Jeff, who was staring at me as if he was fearful of the next words that might come out of my mouth, which I decided to keep shut on this little point. Mostly because that dress had me wondering if Maggie had dolled herself up that night to see someone. Someone other than Tom.

Of course, I wasn't about to share my latest insight with Jeff. Because if the police hadn't cared enough to wonder a little bit more about Maggie's motivations that night, then I was clearly going to have to follow up on this one on my own.

Besides, if that frown on his face was any indication, it was looking like I was in danger of not even getting a good-night kiss.

30

Sage
Men and other curiosities

"So I'm not understanding this," I said, once Zoe and I found seats on the upper deck of the ferry. "You liked Jeff or you didn't like him?"

"I do," Zoe replied, dropping her knapsack on to the floor in front of her. "I mean, I did, I guess. Until that kiss." She looked at me, her features flushed in the late afternoon sunlight that flooded the deck as the ferry pulled away from the dock. "I just wasn't feeling it, you know?"

"Well, he seems like your type."

"How would you know?"

I looked at her. "I answered a few questions for him the night Maggie died, too, you know."

"You remember him?" she asked, her expression incredulous. "I barely recognized him when I first saw him on the beach."

I shrugged. "Sure, I remember him. He was cute. In a boyish kind of way."

"Boyish is *my* type? I thought boyish was *your* type," she said, squinting at me.

I slipped on my sunglasses, just in time to hide my eyes rolling back in my head.

Zoe began to fish around in the oversized tote bag she'd placed on the seat between us. "I'm not sure what my type is anymore," she said, once she retrieved her sunglasses and slid them on to her face.

"I always thought you had a thing for guys in uniform. Look at Myles."

"Myles doesn't wear a uniform. He's a lawyer. Or at least he's going to be."

I shrugged. "Yeah, but he's got that cop attitude going on. Like his dad. And he's going to work for the D.A."

"Apparently not," Zoe clarified. "He's interviewing at some corporate firms. Suddenly he's hell-bent on making a fortune. Do you know he's even considering buying a house on Fire Island?"

"Really?" I turned to look at her. "Wait a second—I thought you weren't going to talk to Myles anymore."

"I can't *not* talk to Myles, Sage. That's like not breathing."

I frowned. "You just make things harder on yourself. It's no wonder you can't get into this new guy."

Zoe sighed. "Look, can we talk about something else? How's life at the office now that you're the big boss?"

I leaned back in my seat, smiling when I remembered the mug Zoe had given me today. "It's going great so far. Of course, there've been some challenges, but nothing I can't handle." I turned my face toward the sun. "What more is there to tell?"

"Are you nervous? I mean, about stepping into Maggie's shoes?"

A familiar anger stirred in me. "Why should I be? I was already doing the job before she stepped in. I didn't have the title, but I was the one working with the designer to develop the new styles. And it was me who did the merchandising, the selling in—"

"Okay, okay," Zoe said. "Sorry I asked."

Now I was sighing. "I'm sorry. I guess to me it feels like this promotion has been a long time coming, despite the fact that everyone seems to think I was born yesterday."

"I didn't say that. Who said that?"

I shook my head. "No one, I guess." Except me, I thought, remembering how I had nearly mastered the budget, only to realize I didn't understand how Maggie handled the shipping-and-receiving invoices. "But I do have some good news," I said, remembering my one triumph this week, though it was starting to feel like only a semi-victory. "Vince is taking me out to dinner tonight."

"He is?"

I nodded, though I was glad I had my sunglasses on. Zoe could read me like a book, and I didn't want her to see the uncertainty that still swirled through me. Yes, I was glad Vince was interested, but that Gianna Lorenzo thing had thrown me. Not completely, however. I could handle competition, if that was, in fact, what Gianna was. Especially competition that was usually an eight-hour plane ride away. I wasn't sure how she fit into the picture. But I planned to find out tonight.

"Where is he taking you to dinner?" Zoe asked now.

"Le Dock in Fair Harbor," I replied.

"Seems like the place to go for romance," Zoe said sarcastically.

"What's that supposed to mean?" I asked, looking up in surprise at her bitter tone.

Zoe shook her head. "Never mind." She shifted in her seat. "So just you and Vince are going?"

"Just me and Vince," I replied, a vision of us staring at one another across a candlelit table momentarily dispelling my doubts. "I guess it's nice to finally have a date with a man." Then I smiled. "If you know what I mean."

"Yeah, I do know," Zoe said. "The one thing that was different about Jeff was that he didn't even hesitate to pay the bill like other guys I've been out with. No warbling over the check, waiting for me to do 'the reach.' No acting like I owed him something afterward. He really was a perfect gentleman."

I looked at her. "So why not give him a chance?"

"I suppose," she said, her gaze moving to the trail of white foam the ferry left in its wake.

I smiled at her pensive expression. That was Zoe. Even a roll in the hay required major consideration. I wouldn't be surprised if she started to keep a video diary, if only to help her keep track of her ever-changing mind. But that's what I loved about her, too, despite all the craziness she caused herself—and me—sometimes.

"I'm glad you were able to come out on this ferry with me," I said now. "Do you realize this is the first ferry ride we've shared all summer?"

She sighed. "I'm sorry, Sage. I know I haven't exactly been fun lately."

I waved a hand dismissively. "No worries, Zoe." Then I smiled. "After all the summer has only just begun."

Nick
What am I running here? A psych ward?

"**Y**ou're where?" I asked. Though my reception was usually good out on the back deck of the house, I could have sworn Les just said he was in Milwaukee. As in Milwaukee fucking Wisconsin.

"Milwaukee, Nick. At my parents' house."

Jesus Christ. He did say Milwaukee. I sat up in the lounger, nearly upending my glass of beer. "What the hell are you doing there?"

"My mother thought it was a good idea. After what happened."

His mother thought it was a good idea? His *mother?* This is what I get for trying to give a kid a break. Fucking baby.

"I just got to get my head together, you know?"

I was about ready to tear his head off. "For how long?"

"Just for a couple of months."

"A couple of *months?* Les, we've got to get into the studio—"

"Dude, don't you think I know that? I'll try to come back sooner if I can."

"But you guys are playing next week at Plaid," I said, naming the club I had booked him in.

"The gig will have to wait, Nick. I can't perform now."

"Look, Les, I can't work on this kind of schedule. We're gonna have to rethink this contract."

"Dude, the deal's already signed. You can't just do that."

"I can do whatever I want!" I said, even though I wasn't too sure of that. I needed to check with my lawyer. That is, my dad.

"But we already cashed the advance check."

Shit. Could I make him cough the money back up? Since I didn't know, I said, "Are you gonna at least be able to write the rest of the songs while you're there?"

"I'll do my best, dude."

He'd do his best. I'd already seen his best, and I wasn't very fucking impressed. I leaned back in the lounger again, glancing back at the sliding door when I heard it open. Francesca. She was the last person I needed right now. Even she was stressing me out. "Look, Les, I have to go," I said, "but could you call me in a few days? I'm gonna need a progress report." And I wasn't talking about his mental health, either. I needed those songs written.

"I'll call you next week, dude."

"Do that," I said, clicking the phone shut and suppressing an urge to pitch it out into the dune grass that surrounded the deck.

"Sounds like someone could use some stress relief," Francesca said, stepping into my line of vision. She was wearing a pink bikini so bright my eyeballs started to ache at the sight of her.

"Yeah," I said wearily, tossing my cell phone on to the small table beside my lounger as Francesca sat down on the end. She reached for the drawstring on my suit.

"Francesca—"

She looked at me curiously, her fingers poised over the string.

"Your father's right inside."

She smiled, her hand moving over my shaft—already hard, despite my wishes—until her fingers grasped me through the material.

Damn, that felt good. But it always did. And I might have even gone for it, if not for the fact that I was tired, damn tired. Not of Francesca. But of having sex within earshot of Tom. I'd hopped into the shower earlier, hoping to cool off, except that Francesca had hopped in with me, with Tom right in the next room. Next there was the kitchen-counter encounter, which took place about two minutes before Tom returned from the market. Her indiscretion knew no bounds. Last Sunday she'd even given me a hand job right beneath the umbrella on the beach. I practically came, too, just as Tom was reeling in a motherfucker of a fish.

Not that he noticed. He never did. Which seemed to incite Francesca to ever more dangerous acts. Like right now, I thought, glancing over my shoulder at the sliding glass doors as she yanked down my suit and put her hot little mouth on me.

Oh, man, I just died and went to heaven.

Then I remembered Tom and realized I could actually die right now. And I wasn't so sure about making it to heaven.

"Francesca, stop," I said, sitting back and yanking up my suit, though it was painful, let me tell you. Painful. But I couldn't go on this way. *We* couldn't go on this way. It was too fucking weird. Not to mention stressful.

And I had enough on my mind at the moment.

Francesca looked up at me and I could swear I saw something that looked an awful lot like hurt in her eyes. "I'm sorry, baby," I said, reaching out a hand to touch her silky brown hair.

She sat up, turning her back to me. A bit childish, yeah, but sometimes—like when I had her hot and wet beneath me—I forgot how young she really was, you know?

"It's not that I don't want to," I began. "I just think maybe we should try something different." Bad choice of words. I wasn't sure what *different* might consist of for Francesca. Doing it on a float as we rode through Kismet? "What I mean is, I think maybe it should be more special."

She turned her head, her eyes narrowed suspiciously at me.

"Maybe we could have a little dinner first—"

Her eyebrows raised.

"At The Inn—"

Her eyebrows dropped.

"Or The Out," I finished. Not as cheap as The Inn, but at least it was cheaper than Le Dock, and I clearly needed to be on a budget from here on in. "Afterward we could take a little walk on the beach," I said, hoping to distract her from the other restaurant possibilities with the promise of romance. Girls liked that shit, right?

Of course, Francesca was no ordinary girl.

She seemed to consider it for a full moment, and just when I thought she might utter some inane protest, she stood up and said, "Okay." Then, with one toss of her shiny brown hair, she headed inside.

"You're both going out? Together?" Tom said, staring at me after I explained that Francesca and I were going out to dinner. A friendly little dinner, I described it as.

But no matter how I had sugarcoated it, Tom looked pretty pissed off. I was starting to worry that he might not be as oblivious to what was going on between me and Francesca as I thought.

"What am I going to do with this dinner I'm making?" he said, waving a hand at the meat defrosting on the counter. "I've got enough lamb chops here to feed an army!"

Nope. Still clueless.

"First Sage disappears," he continued. "Now you and Francesca—"

"Well, Zoe is around, isn't she?"

"Zoe's a vegetarian!" Tom said, slapping a hand on the counter in frustration.

"Ummm, she'll definitely go for the, uh, spinach. And the potatoes," I said, eyeing the produce he had taken out, too. I looked around, hoping Zoe might come out and save me somehow by converting back to a carnivore. But since she didn't, I asked, "Where *is* Zoe?"

"Oh, she's up in the attic," Tom said with a wave of his hand. "She's looking through Maggie's old clothes."

"Oh." I couldn't picture Zoe wearing Maggie's clothes—Maggie was a bit more upscale than Zoe could tolerate—but whatever.

"At least someone's interested," Tom said. "I'm having a heck of a time getting anyone from the Salvation Army to pick the stuff up. Or at least meet the freight ferry." He sighed. "I'm starting to think I ought to just throw it all out." Then his face brightened. "Or maybe I'll have a yard sale."

Oh, that was classy, Tom. Fortunately, I was saved from making a reply by the sight of Francesca, who stood in the entrance to the kitchen, finally ready to go.

Wow, I thought, studying the soft lavender dress she wore. It was worth the wait. I think she might have even put on makeup. She looked older. She looked hot. Well, hotter than usual.

I saw Tom looking at his daughter as she stood there, his gaze pensive. Shit, maybe he'd already figured out this little outing was not as casual as I had made it sound.

Then he snapped his fingers, a smile coming over his face as he looked at me once more. "I just remembered—I know a great recipe for lamb stew. I can use the leftovers and make us that for lunch tomorrow!"

Oh, brother. I looked at Francesca and saw, once again, what looked like genuine hurt in her eyes.

Damn. Francesca's m.o. suddenly became way too clear to me. All this time she'd been trying to get her father's attention. And, I thought, watching as Tom opened a cabinet and began pulling out ingredients, she clearly wasn't getting it.

Poor kid. I vowed to make it up to her. Now I was glad I'd suggested this little outing. Maybe that was what Francesca needed, you know? A little TLC.

That, I could do. Yeah, I thought, studying her as she stepped toward the sliding glass door, eyes lowered.

That, I could handle.

32

Zoe
For whom the dinner bell tolls

If Maggie Landon did live on, it was in her attic. After an hour of digging through the bags of clothing Tom had stored there, I was practically ill. Probably because all those sweatshirts, shorts, skirts and pants conjured up a woman—a life—that no longer was. Now I wondered why I had even bothered. What did I expect a dress to tell me anyway? I had learned all I needed to know from Nick. When I had asked him what Maggie was wearing the last time he saw her, he had said a shirt and jeans. Which made me wonder just why—or for who—she had changed into a dress. Still, the dress was a clue, and since it was the first real clue I had, I wanted to get my hands on it.

Not that I did.

By the time I climbed down again, sweaty and coated in dust, I felt vaguely nauseous. And completely demoralized.

"Find anything you like?" Tom greeted me once I stepped into the kitchen.

"Oh, uh, no. I mean, not really," I said, looking at the line of lamb chops on the cutting board before him.

There was a lot of meat there. Well, Sage wasn't here to enjoy them, and *I* certainly wouldn't enjoy them. I just hoped Nick and Francesca were hungry.

Then I realized how quiet the house was. "Where is everyone?"

"Well, as you know, Sage went out with Vince, and it looks like Nick and Francesca have followed suit."

"Nick took Francesca to Le Dock?" I said.

"Nah, I think they went to The Out for dinner," he said, raising the knife above the fatty end of one chop. "So it's just me and you for dinner." *Whack.*

I shivered, watching as he used the knife to slide the fat off to the side of the cutting board. Me and Tom for dinner? Yikes. "Uh, you know I don't eat meat, right?" I said, grabbing on to the first good excuse to run to The Out myself.

"Oh, I know," he said with a grimace as he lined up another chop to trim. *Whack.*

I stepped away from the counter, nearly falling over Janis Joplin, who was lying by the door. At least she was here to protect me. Then I remembered she hadn't exactly protected Maggie.

"I threw together a little red sauce for you. You do eat pasta, don't you?" *Whack.*

I looked at the stove and saw that there was, in fact, a pot with red sauce simmering. That was kind of nice of him.

Whack.

I swallowed hard. "Uh, you didn't have to do that, Tom."

He looked at me, eyes narrowed. "Oh, but you'll be glad I did." Dropping the knife, he turned to the stove, spooning up some sauce and turning to me. "Taste this."

I looked at him as he held out the spoon to me, his eyes coaxing.

Obediently, I leaned forward, looking into his eyes as I tentatively tasted from the spoon he held to my lips.

My eyes widened.

"Good, right?"

Good? I don't think I'd ever tasted a red sauce that good. Death by marinara. Was it possible? "It's fantastic, Tom." I mean, it was. "What's in that?" I said.

"Oh, that's my secret," Tom said with a wink that sent a shiver right to my toes.

★ ★ ★

As it turned out, I didn't die that night. In fact, two glasses of wine and a plate of pasta later, I thought I was in love. Just kidding. But I was feeling some sort of strange kinship with Tom, especially when he told me that before he followed his father's footsteps and went to work in the garment industry, he dreamed about joining the coast guard.

Maybe Sage was right. Maybe I did have a thing for guys in uniform.

"I told you I was a lifeguard when I was young?"

I nodded, despite the fact that I had heard the story second-hand.

"Saved seven lives," he said. "Eight now, if you count Les," he continued, pouring himself a glass of wine from the second bottle he'd cracked open once we'd settled in the living room. "More wine?"

I held my hand over my glass. Clearly I needed to keep my wits about me tonight.

"So I guess Sage should be coming back soon," I said, if only to remind him that someone else would be joining the house shortly.

He frowned. "I guess." Then he chuckled. "So you think maybe there's a little romance going on between those two?"

I shrugged, not sure if Sage would want to divulge to one boss that she was hankering for the other. "I don't know."

He sighed. "Well, I guess that's all right. Though I don't know about Vince."

"What do you mean?"

Shrugging, he picked up his glass. "Don't get me wrong, I love Vince. But I get the feeling Sage might need someone a little more established in life."

I raised an eyebrow. "He seems pretty established to me, Tom. Isn't he a VP in your company?"

"Oh, yeah. But I didn't mean it that way. I meant more settled, I guess. With his life. Right now he's still living in the same small condo he bought after the divorce."

"He has the beach house, though."

Tom chuckled. "He wishes. Nah, that house belongs to his ex-wife. Her family has had it for years. But they don't come out here much anymore, so Gabriella lets him stay there. It's a sweet deal. And it's nice for Vince to have a place to take Sophia once in a while."

That was interesting. I wondered how Sage would feel if she knew that. From the way she talked about Vince, I thought it likely his glamorous lifestyle was a big part of his appeal for her. It certainly wasn't the whole "kid" thing.

But just as I was considering the state of Sage's romance, Tom stood up to change the CD in the player. A soft romantic ballad filled the room.

Oh, dear. Was it too early to make a dash for my bedroom? Because suddenly it was looking like I was in a whole different kind of trouble.

Even more so when Tom straightened, looking at me with eyes clouded by all the wine he'd consumed. "Dance with me?"

"Oh, Tom, I'm really not much of a dancer—"

"Come on, Zoe, be a sport," he said.

"I really can't—"

"Sure you can," he said, grabbing my hand and pulling me off the couch.

I stiffened once he put his arms around me.

"Relax," he said, beginning to move gently against me.

Which only made me step on his foot.

"Easy, easy. Feel the music," he said, placing a firm hand at my back to guide me.

All I could feel was scared. Not of death. Actually, at the moment, death might have been the easier option.

"Maggie never liked to dance, either," he said.

I held my breath at the mention of Maggie's name.

"Well, she liked to dance, but that crazy freestyle dancing." He laughed, the sound rumbling through me as well.

"You must miss her, though," I said, trying to keep her memory between us.

He paused, but only momentarily. "Of course I miss her."

I was heartened by his words, even though I realized they were just that: words. I couldn't know what he was really feeling. Or hiding. "Do you ever think about that night?" I asked. "The night it happened?"

He didn't answer, though I felt his own body stiffen. Okay, I was getting into dangerous territory. But my need to know more overrode the fear that shimmered through me.

"I mean, it was kind of odd, wasn't it," I continued, "that she would go in the water like that? Alone?"

"I try not to think about it," he said easily, despite the tension I felt in him.

I wished I could look up at him, but realized I'd only get a bull's-eye view of his chin. What I wanted to see was his eyes.

Then suddenly he dropped his arms away from me, and I did look up, only to find a baffled expression on his face. "You really can't dance, can you?" he said, shaking his head at me.

My stomach plunged. I wasn't sure whether it was because he'd avoided my question or because I felt…insulted.

The only feeling I was sure of was the relief that washed over me once Tom disappeared into the bathroom. I headed immediately for the sink to wash dishes. Actually, what I did was load them into the dishwasher. I probably should have hidden in my room at that point, but Tom's avoidance of the topic of Maggie only made me more curious. Besides, cleaning up was the least I could do. He did cook for me tonight, I thought, rinsing off the last plate and sliding it into the crowded washer. I opened the top rack and was just trying to figure out a way to jam the two wineglasses in, when Tom came back.

"Those need to be washed by hand," he said.

"Oh," I replied, smiling tentatively at him as I closed the dishwasher and turned to the sink to soap up the first glass.

I felt him watching me as I hurriedly rinsed off the glass, placing it on the counter to dry.

But then I realized he had only been waiting for the glass when he picked it up and proceeded to polish it dry with the towel.

I almost laughed. That was Tom. Ever efficient. I had, at least, learned that about him in the past few weeks, I thought, placing the second glass on the counter when I was done and watching as he snatched it up and started polishing away.

Once he was satisfied with his handiwork, he grabbed both glasses and headed to the living room to put them away in the bar.

I was just drying my hands and contemplating how I could

safely return the conversation to the night of Maggie's death when I heard the sound of shattering glass.

"Goddammit!" he yelled.

Janis lifted her head and let out a little whine.

I stepped into the living room to see Tom stooped over, picking up the pieces of the glass he had dropped. "I'll help you with that," I said, dashing back to the kitchen and retrieving the dustpan and brush from under the sink.

I handed him the items, and without even so much as a glance at me, he grabbed them out of my hands, his movements brisk as he brushed the remaining pieces on to the dustpan, then stood to dump them in the garbage pail in the kitchen.

Uh-oh. He seemed pretty pissed off.

Which was why I was shocked when he finished his task and turned to me with tears—tears!—glittering in his eyes.

"Tom? Are you—"

"I'm fine," he said, leaning over to put the dustpan and brush away. Once he stood again, I watched as he swiped at his eyes with the back of his hand.

He wasn't fine. Far from it, I realized when he let out a sob so deep I felt an answering ache in my throat.

Even Janis began to howl.

Tom didn't seem to notice, his shoulders shaking as he fought the sudden wave of emotion now clearly moving through him.

"Tom," I said, reaching out tentatively to touch him, then pulling my hand back. I didn't know what to do. So I turned to Janis. "Shhhhh," I soothed, though I felt far from soothing at the moment. Janis must have sensed my alarm, because she immediately settled down, her head going to rest on her paws, her eyes on Tom.

I turned to Tom once more. "Maybe you ought to sit down," I said. Then I did take his hand, leading him to the sofa to sit.

My actions seemed to settle him a bit more, though the tears still streamed down his cheeks. I made a quick dash to the bathroom, grabbed a box of tissues, and returned.

"Here," I said, holding out the box to him.

He reached for a tissue, dabbing at his eyes and then blowing his nose. When he looked up again, I saw his tears had abated, his eyes filled with something close to embarrassment. "I'm sorry, I—"

"It's okay," I said, sitting down beside him.

He shook his head. "I don't know what came over me." He let out a shuddery sigh, his gaze moving to the row of wineglasses lining the bar. "Maggie and I got those glasses as a wedding gift," he said softly. "I told her I didn't want to keep them here. They're so fragile." He shuddered again.

"I'm sorry, Tom," I said, mostly because I didn't know what else to say. I was still bowled over by his sudden display of emotion.

"We already broke two of them last year," he said, still staring at the glasses. Then he turned to me, fresh tears moving into his eyes. "Now there's hardly anything left. Of us."

Then I did hug him, my hand moving soothingly over his back as he unleashed a fresh wave of sorrow. I was surprised when I felt tears sting my own eyes, realizing they were tears of sympathy. For Tom.

I made an even bigger discovery after I helped a bleary-eyed and unusually docile Tom into bed. Just as I was about to shut the lights and make my exit, I noticed the closet door hung open.

Glancing back at Tom, I realized he had probably conked out the minute his head hit the pillow. He was already starting to snore.

I didn't blame him, after the night he'd had. In fact, I wasn't sure I could blame him for anything anymore.

But since I was certain someone was to blame for Maggie's death, I turned to the closet, opening the door the rest of the way and studying the contents.

I needed to find that dress. I wasn't sure what it would tell me—still, it had to be more than I already knew. But after rifling through Tom's lonely little collection of trousers and shirts, I discovered it wasn't there. Frustrated, I closed the door, taking another quick glance at Tom, who let out a snort that nearly made me jump out of my skin. I walked over to the chest of drawers on the other side of the bed and slid open the top one. Socks and underwear. Tom's underwear. I closed it quickly, as if I had just walked in on Tom in his underwear. I moved to the next one—more T-shirts and polo shirts. Then the fourth, which was empty. Not empty, I realized when I slid it open farther and saw a clear plastic bag, which not only contained something that looked rather pink and girly, but was still tagged by none other than the S.C.P.D.

Bingo!

I glanced back at Tom, who was still sound asleep, wondering briefly why he hadn't thrown this up in the attic with the rest of her things, then realized he had probably gotten it after he did his closet clean-out.

But why save it? I wondered, holding the bag before me and realizing there was a gold watch, a pink wallet and a cell phone in there, too. Maybe he hadn't even opened it. Maybe he'd just tossed it in there, knowing he'd have to deal with it at some point. Whatever, I was glad he did.

I slid the drawer closed, then took my find back to my bedroom for a closer look.

Once I had dumped the contents out on my bed, I realized I had hit the jackpot. I held up the dress, which was pink and girly, yes, but also a little on the sexy side. Not over-the-top sexy, but then, from what I knew of Maggie, neither was she. If she was having an affair, surely there would be some evidence of that in her wallet or cell phone, right? At least, that's the way it was on all those detective shows I had seen. But her wallet held only a couple of receipts from gourmet markets near her apartment on the Upper East Side, a collection of credit cards and a photo of Janis Joplin as a puppy.

Pretty cute. But who carried a photo of their dog in their wallet?

I picked up the cell phone next, pressing the on button, feeling relief when the screen lit up and a brief melody played. At least it still worked.

Clicking on to voice mail, I was relieved when I was connected right away. I guess Tom hadn't gotten around to shutting her service off.

"One old message," the mechanized voice informed me, causing me to suck in a breath. Then I blew that breath right out when I heard my own voice echoing back to me. "Hi, umm, Maggie. I just wanted to tell you that I got the coriander, but I, uh, missed the ferry…"

I almost hung up on myself, embarrassed anew at my pathetic

excuses, but I waited through my whole weary explanation for the time-and-date stamp. "June 12th, 7:37 p.m.," the mechanized voice informed me.

I hung up. That sounded about right. I had just gotten back from the market and was on my way to Penn Station to catch the next train.

Clicking on the call history, I was given a choice of "outgoing calls" and "incoming calls." I hit incoming calls and got a neat little list of names, none of which I recognized except for the two listings for Edge and one for Tom's Long Island office, which I only knew because it was listed as *Landon, LI office,* followed by my own number. I began checking times and dates, starting with *Landon, LI office.*

June 12th, 5:06 p.m.

Why was someone calling Maggie from the Long Island office on a Saturday?

I checked the two listings before, both to the Luxe office. One was made Thursday, the other Wednesday. That made sense, since it was during the business week. Probably Tom.

I clicked on outgoing calls, located my own number, which was followed by a listing for a number with a 631 area code. The one after that said *Donnie and Amanda—beach.*

Now *that* was interesting. Area code 631 was Suffolk County, which could mean Fire Island. And Donnie and Amanda were definitely Fire Island.

But who was this 631 number? Clearly it wasn't in her address book, since it didn't have a name listed beside it.

I clicked on it and was about to dial it, until I realized it probably wasn't a good idea to be making calls from a dead woman's cell phone.

Grabbing my own cell phone from the nightstand, I dialed the number, prefaced by ★67. In case this was my murderer, I certainly didn't want him to have my number.

After about four rings, a machine picked up. "You have reached Fair Harbor Market. The market is now closed...."

Well, that proved one theory. Maggie had called the market. I checked the time of the call. June 12th, 7:20 p.m. The market had been closed by then, which meant she never had any intention of going there, despite what she'd told Tom.

My eye fell upon the listing for Donnie and Amanda—beach and I clicked on it to get the date and time. June 12th, 7:24 p.m.

It seemed Donnie and Amanda were the last people Maggie called that night. And if my guess was right, I was betting it was Donnie she wanted to speak to. He might even have been Maggie's last incoming call, since he worked from the Long Island office.

My eye fell upon the soft pink dress and the back of my neck prickled. Son of a bitch.

I think I just found Maggie's lover.

33

Maggie
No woman is an island unto herself.

My friend Amanda used to joke that you could take the girl out of Long Island, but you couldn't take Long Island out of the girl. We laughed about it often enough, boning up on our accents to great hilarity in the privacy of the two-bedroom we shared when we first moved to Manhattan, or over drinks at the bars we frequented when we were young.

But when I married Tom, a subtle shift occurred between Amanda and me, making the laughter a little less easy to share. Maybe it was because I had ascended to the throne Amanda coveted. Not that Amanda wanted Tom, but she wanted what he represented. Money, yes, but that wasn't all of it. Mostly, I think, it was that Tom came from a world far from the barren strip malls Amanda and I roamed restlessly through as teenagers. Tom's world of country clubs and private schooling was what Amanda aspired to. Which was why I found it strange that when Amanda did finally marry, she chose a man from the very world she and I had long tried to leave behind.

Donnie Havens had grown up two towns away from us on Long Island, though we didn't know him then. In fact, Amanda didn't meet Donnie until a couple years after I had married Tom.

She was still living in Manhattan, sharing that same two-bedroom with new roommate after new roommate. She still frequented the bars we used to go to, despite the fact that her mother warned her she would never meet anyone nice in a bar. And she met Donnie in a bar. A little dive up by Penn Station that she went to with some co-workers for happy hour one night. Donnie was in town for some sort of trade show at Madison Square Garden for a line of electronic components he was selling back then. With his thinning hair and blue-collar bravado, Donnie was the kind of man Amanda and I usually avoided. We knew his kind. He looked like the fathers who lurked in the backyards of our childhood, running lawnmowers and shooting the breeze over the hedges about what new car or boat they would buy, if not for the burden of mortgage payments and insurance premiums. The sons who bellied up to the bar, slamming down shots and trading barbs, believing they would never fall prey to the lassitude they saw in their fathers' lives.

But Amanda didn't avoid Donnie that night. In fact, she sat at that bar with him until closing. He made her laugh, she told me over the phone the next day, confiding with something that bordered on embarrassment that she had brought Donnie home with her the night before. And when I met Donnie two months later, after Amanda finally gave in to the fact that he was her boyfriend, I understood right away what she saw in him. It wasn't just that he was familiar to us, with his accent and his ready smile. Donnie was a good talker. And attentive to boot. I think he won Amanda over by virtue of the sheer persistence with which he pursued her.

I had to admit that, after two years of living with Tom, turning down the corners on a bed that had already gone cool and sharing silences that I wouldn't quite call companionable, I was jealous.

Not that I let Amanda know it. In fact, I wasn't even sure I knew it. Instead I invited them out to the house at Kismet time and time again, even more so after Donnie came to work for Tom at Luxe, believing all the while I was doing Amanda a favor by sharing my oceanfront home with her when really I was the one who was aching for the company. As well as for the attention, the compliments, that Donnie heaped on me unabashedly. I enjoyed the way he leaned in close to talk to me, as if I were the only person in the room. How he shared his grand schemes with me about all his future plans. Like me, Donnie was a dreamer. The difference was, Donnie still believed that his dreams might come true, despite the fact that he had failed at them over and over. Still, I started to feel a kinship with him that I had never felt with Tom, and for a while, I even believed it went beyond the similar backgrounds we shared.

But it wasn't until the year my father died that the urge to return to what was familiar took root in me. To find comfort in the arms of a man I could understand on a more basic level than I had ever understood Tom.

It was too bad that man happened to be my best friend's husband.

34

Sage
Enough with the appetizers. I'm ready for the main course.

There was something about the sun setting over the Great South Bay that always moved me. But watching the sky spread into a spectrum of brilliant pinks and purples and reds while sharing a bottle of wine with the most beautiful man I had ever laid eyes on thus far was something else altogether.

I think Vince felt that same sense of wonder, too.

"It's amazing that something so spectacular happens every night and most people don't even take the time to notice," he said, once the sun had sunk into the horizon completely and the waiter came by to light the candle at our table.

It was true, I realized, thinking of Zoe and how much time she spent fretting over the state of the world that she barely took time to appreciate it. Or Nick, so hell-bent on proving himself that he rarely saw beyond his own nose.

A memory of my mother, playing in the yard with me and Hope when we were kids, filled my mind. I smiled, the words she recited that day bubbling up inside of me. "'We'll talk of sunshine and of song, and summer days when we were young. Sweet childish days that were as long as twenty days are now.'"

When I saw Vince's speculative gaze, heat pooled in my stomach. "Wordsworth," I explained. "My mother was forever reciting poems to me and my sister when we were kids," I continued, suddenly feeling silly for spouting poetry when Vince had done nothing, outside of pausing before this sunset, to suggest that romance was on his mind. But I couldn't help myself. He seemed to bring it out in me. "It's funny the things you remember," I said, feeling shy. And I never felt shy with men.

He smiled slightly. "That's a beautiful thing to remember," he said, looking at me as if for the first time. "I don't think I'll forget it myself."

I'm embarrassed to admit how jubilant I felt hearing that I had somehow managed to strike a chord somewhere in Vince. The feeling, I discovered, was addictive. For throughout dinner, I found myself looking for opportunities to see that look in his eyes again, even though doubts still flickered in my mind about Gianna. I hadn't figured out a way to bring up the topic without seeming like some jealous fool. I wasn't jealous exactly. I just wanted to know what I was up against.

But by the end of the meal, my confidence was at an all-time high. Especially when the conversation turned to my favorite subject—Edge. Even more so when I discovered Vince and I shared a lot of the same views about how, exactly, Edge should be run. With some differences. Nothing we couldn't handle, however.

"I keep telling Tom, again and again, that he's still got to keep quality in mind, even with this younger customer," Vince said, as he poured the last of the wine into our glasses. "That's why I'm always advocating making bodies in the better leathers. It's a question of branding. Yes, we want Edge to be the leading name in young, urban outerwear, but we don't want it to become synonymous with trendy junk. He's always ready to downgrade to a lesser skin, usually from one of our Chinese tanneries. But there is nothing like Italian leather."

At the mention of the tanneries, I saw the opening I had been looking for all night. Choosing my words carefully, I said, "That's true. But mass-producing in Italian leather can get expensive. In fact, I understand the Lorenzo tannery has just upped their prices."

He raised an eyebrow. "So you're keeping up on the pricing now, too, are you?"

"I have to in order to understand what we're up against in terms of production costs." I hesitated for a moment, then plunged in. "In fact, I understand someone from the Lorenzo tannery was in town last week. Gianna, I think? I hope you had a chance to meet with her. Maybe work a little of your charm to help keep prices down." The moment the words were out of my mouth, I held my breath, hoping he wasn't charming her right into bed.

He smiled. "Don't worry about the Lorenzos. They're old friends of mine. Good people. Very fair."

Fair? As in the fairest of them all? Needing more, I said, "So I guess you did have a chance to meet with Gianna here?"

"Of course," he said, looking at me in a way that made me wonder if I was being too obvious.

But if he suspected the jealousy that I had, against my will, felt moving through me, he certainly managed to beat down the green monster with his next words. "It was nice to see Gianna. I spent some time with her family when I was in Italy. She's like a sister to me."

I slowly let out my breath. Sister, I could handle. "Well, let's hope sister Gianna remembers who her family is when it comes time to negotiate prices next year. Otherwise, we may have to stick to Chinese tanneries."

"I think we'll be fine. If not, we'll just mark up the price to the customer," he said with a wink.

"Yeah, and make my job selling it hell."

"Remember, you're not a sales rep anymore."

Smiling I said, "But now I have to take the hit if my reps can't move the stuff. I've got volume projections I'm accountable for. Besides, there's more to being a sales rep than getting buyers to leave the showroom with a big order for your goods. I'd say seventy-five percent of the battle is knowing what the buyer wants—and having it ready to show him—before he even enters the showroom. When I was managing The Bomb, I made it my business to make sure everything we put on those racks anticipated the latest trends." I smiled. "Tom probably told you, I used to drive him kinda crazy with the goods we carried from Luxe. I was forever asking him to remerchandise." My smile deepened. "But I think he respected me for that."

Vince returned the smile. "Clearly he did." And I could see that by the time the dessert course came, Vince's respect was growing for me.

By the time we headed back toward Kismet, I was feeling a little more than respect for Vince, which was why I suggested we walk home along the beach. Not only was I looking for a little romance, I was hoping Vince might open up a bit. We had spent so much time talking business, I had learned very little about the man himself.

And I wanted to know more. A lot more.

Once we hit the cool sand, I kicked off my sandals, and Vince followed suit. Breathing deeply, I gazed up at the sky glittering with stars and a pale slice of moon hovering over the crashing waves. Now this was something worth appreciating. And I felt glad, very glad, to finally have someone to appreciate it with.

"So tell me about you," I said, once we began to walk side by side along the shore.

"What do you want to know?"

I shrugged. "Oh, I don't know. What it was like in the beginning. When you met Tom and started up Luxe."

"Not a very interesting story," Vince said. "I was in textiles at the time—running a small shipping operation out of New York. But I was looking to branch out. I had been doing a little business with Tom. One day we started talking, and before you know it, we were making plans. Soon enough, we were business partners." He smiled. "Now we're practically family. He was the best man at my wedding."

I absorbed this information. "And you were married for how long?" I asked, hoping I wasn't prying too much. Yes, I was attracted to this man, but I needed to do a baggage check, didn't I? Most of the men I dated had barely gotten over their first heartbreak, never mind their first wife.

"Six years," he replied. "I gave that woman six years and a beautiful little girl, and she walked away."

"What happened? That is—if you don't mind my asking."

He shrugged. "There's not much to tell. I went to China to set up manufacturing for Luxe, and Gabriella couldn't hack it there. She packed her bags and left after two years. Said she missed her family. I was under the impression that *I* was her family. We had just had Sophia together, but she said Sophia was the reason she was going home. She didn't want our daughter raised in that environment. But Sophia was only a baby. She wouldn't have known the difference. I planned to get us back before she started school."

I frowned. "You didn't consider going back with them?"

He paused, but only for a fraction of second. "It wasn't so simple. I had signed a contract to work there—"

"But surely Tom would have understood."

His mouth firmed, and I saw a flash of something close to anger in his eyes. "Whether or not Tom understood was not the issue. Gabriella should have stuck by me. I was working hard to build my family a future. When she left with Sophia, it felt like a betrayal. I got angry. And when I get angry, I get stubborn. It's the Sicilian in me, I guess."

I smiled. I liked the Sicilian in him. That sense of loyalty. Though I worried about it, too. He had, after all, chosen loyalty to his work over his wife and child. Though I was sure he didn't see it that way.

"I stayed on another two years," he continued. "By the time I came home for good, the rift between us was too great. I don't believe in divorce. Never did. But that was the only option she gave me."

I thought about that, realizing that on this point we were in agreement. I didn't believe in divorce either, which was probably what kept me from making the leap to marriage. I didn't believe it worked for everyone. And I wasn't sure I could make that kind of commitment.

Then Vince stopped, his gaze moving out to the ocean, before he turned to look at me, his eyes filled with weariness and something else I couldn't fathom. "I guess you never really know someone, do you?"

I licked my lips, feeling, for the first time in my life, afraid. Because I realized in that moment that I now wanted to know someone well enough to take that leap. Wanted to believe...

I'm not sure who started it, but suddenly we were kissing, and I nearly groaned with relief. God, he tasted just as good as I'd imagined, I thought, pressing myself against him as the wind came off the ocean. Wondering, as I did, if the rest of him tasted as good.

And just as I was thinking I might get that taste, Vince broke off the kiss.

"I better get you home," he said, "before I do something we both might regret."

I smiled, knowing I would never regret a minute in this man's arms.

I looked at him. "What do you say we go to your home?"

His eyes searched mine, glittering in the darkness. "Are you sure, Sage?"

"Very."

I couldn't tell you whether Vince lived in an A-frame or a ranch. Okay, maybe I did get a vague impression of a low-lying structure as we flew up the wooden walkway together, hands clasped. And I might even have spotted a Ficus tree looming in the moonlight that spilled through the windows in his living room. But the moment he shut the front door behind us, pressing my back against it, I saw nothing but Vince's gaze, searing into my eyes as his mouth moved hungrily against mine. Felt nothing but the rasp of his beard against my face, his hands moving restlessly over my body.

"Come with me," he said, pulling back, before he grabbed my hand and practically yanked me toward the bedroom.

Within moments, I was on my back on the softest mattress I had ever felt, breathing hard as he pushed my tank and bra down in one shot, his hands moving a bit roughly on my breasts, a groan rumbling through him as his mouth met mine.

I heard an answering groan come up through my throat as I pulled at his shirt, sliding my hand beneath it until my hand made contact with that delicious place where his hip met his hard lower ab.

I needed more. I needed to see him. And apparently Vince needed to see me just as bad, because he leaned away from me, pulling my tank back up again until he succeeded in getting it over my head.

I helped him out on the bra, which was still wrenched beneath my breasts.

"Sage," he practically hissed at me, before he locked his gaze on mine, his tongue moving hotly over my breast.

I almost came right then. I wasn't even sure if it was his mouth on me, or the look that came into his eyes. Like he wanted to devour me whole.

Moving restlessly beneath him, I yanked at his shirt again until he got the message, standing up briefly to pull it over his head before pressing that hard chest into mine once more.

Then he gave me that look again, sliding both hands up my skirt until it was up around my waist, and slipping a finger inside my thong.

Not that he needed to know whether I was ready or not. He knew. I could tell by the way he smiled at me, just moments before his fingers made contact.

I moaned, and in answer he slid down my thong, then stood to drop his trousers and briefs, kicking them to the side.

Within moments, he was on me again. Not only on me, but in me, I realized, feeling the hot tip of him slip inside.

"Vince," I said, not sure what I was asking for, that's how insane I was. Then he slid in farther, and I remembered the question, shifting my body so that he slipped out once more. I looked at his glittering eyes, and prayed he had a good answer.

"You wouldn't happen to have a condom anywhere, would you?"

"Ah, Sage," he said, and I knew by the shadow that came into his eyes, that he didn't.

"My purse," I said, feeling suddenly glad I always carried my own condoms—and more than a little pleased that he didn't. "I think I may have dropped it somewhere in the living room."

He leaped up, moving through the shadowy room like a shot, and returned moments later with my bag in hand.

I almost felt a little sad about covering that beautiful erection of his in latex, but cover it I did, first with my mouth, then with the condom, once I located the packet in my bag.

And then he was in me, completely in me, his eyes on mine as he moved slowly, torturously, touching his mouth to mine in a series of soft kisses that made me ache all the way to my toes.

He started moving faster, those dark eyes on mine and an almost animal sound coming from his mouth.

This was how I had imagined it to be. No, I thought, looking into his eyes, this was better. Better than I could have possibly imagined. So good, in fact, I felt a clutch of possessiveness move through me as my body began to throb beneath his.

I cried out and he pressed his mouth to mine, his body shuddering against me as he let go, his hand moving to my hip to pull me closer.

I snuggled against him as he lifted his head, smiling gently down at me as his eyes roamed over my face, his eyes taking me, as if he couldn't get enough of me.

I knew the feeling, I thought, studying his dark eyes and long lashes, the gentle hook of his nose and stubbly slope of his cheek as I pulled him more tightly against me and, for the first time in my life, prayed I would never have to let go.

35

Nick
Love is the drug. But a little dope doesn't hurt, either.

A bottle of wine, two steaks and eighty-five dollars later, I realized that Francesca might be more than I could handle. Hefty price tag aside, dinner wouldn't have been so bad if maybe she had done more than sit sulkily in her chair, picking at her food. I guess I never realized how quiet she was. I even ordered us some after-dinner drinks in the hopes of getting some life into her, but she only sipped at her cocktail sullenly. Like she was depressed. Or something.

Maybe she had always been like this. Maybe I'd been so focused on that hot body of hers that I hadn't noticed the head wasn't screwed on too tight. I mean, yeah, I guess I thought she was psycho to begin with. But weren't most chicks psycho anyway, on some level? Especially once you got into their pants. Analyzing every little word you said. Making all sorts of demands and shit.

But this was different. Francesca wasn't making demands. Or analyses, for that matter. In fact, it was as if she was uninterested in everything. She barely even touched the expensive steak she'd ordered. Hardly batted an eye at the amazing sunset that shimmered across the bay as we sat over our meals.

It was making me a little crazy, to be honest. I was on edge the whole time we were at the restaurant, wondering what was going on in that head of hers. Talking way too much about myself, about my business, even going as far as mentioning the Les conundrum, but that only earned me a look of disdain.

By the time we were done and walking back to the house in the darkness, I was damn frustrated. Even more so when I looked down at her as she walked beside me, looking so fucking pretty in that dress, her hair falling over her soft cheeks....

"What are you doing?" she cried.

I wasn't even sure. All I knew was one minute I was wondering and worrying about her, and then the next, I had picked her up and flipped her over my shoulder.

"Kidnapping you," I replied, spotting the wooden walkway to the beach in the distance and heading straight for it.

"Put me down," she said, her hands beginning to pummel at my back. But she was laughing.

I never thought I'd be so glad to hear that happy sound.

Once we were on the beach, I did put her down, easing her gently to the cool sand, then plopping myself beside her.

"I've got something to cheer you up," I said, then reached into my pocket for my bag of weed. I hadn't been smoking much out at the house—at least not in the presence of Tom. Mostly because I sensed Tom might not approve. But Francesca looked like she did.

"Where'd you get that?" she said, her eyes lighting up.

"I have my resources," I replied, pulling out my one hit pipe and filling it.

I handed it to her, then held the lighter over the bowl, watching as she toked on the end of the pipe. "Atta girl," I said, which only earned me a puff of smoke in the face and a glare.

"I've smoked pot before," she said, snatching the lighter from me and taking another hit.

I watched as she inhaled, closing her eyes as she did, then opening them again as she blew out. "That tastes good," she said, looking at me with surprise.

"Of course it's good," I said, taking the pipe from her and re-filling it. "I don't fool around when it comes to my dope." I took a hit, then leaned over and placed my mouth against hers, blowing the smoke in. When I pulled my mouth away, she blew it back out, giggling as she did.

"Let me try," she said, taking the pipe from me and lighting it. Once she filled her mouth with smoke, I opened my mouth over hers to receive it, leaning back and looking into her eyes as I slowly let the smoke out.

"You have pretty eyes, Francesca."

She giggled again and I leaned in again, this time to kiss her.

Maybe it was the weed, but her mouth seemed a bit more tender beneath mine.

Nice, I thought, leaning back to look at her face. This was nice.

She smiled, looking almost shy. Then she giggled again. "The first time I got high was on the beach. Spring break in Fort Lauderdale, freshman year. That was a crazy night."

"Oh yeah?" I said, dumping out my pipe and pocketing it along with my weed. "I heard about those spring breaks down in Fort Lauderdale. Wet T-shirt contests and shit."

She laughed again. "It wasn't like that."

"Yeah, well, if you did enter a wet T-shirt contest, I bet you would win."

She looked at me in a way that made me wonder if she had.

"You miss school?" I asked, glad she was at least talking now. Maybe I might even learn something about her.

"Not yet," she said, her eyes going wide. "I just graduated, silly."

"So what are you going to do with the rest of your life?"

Her gaze became pensive, and she started fiddling with the tie on the front of her dress. "Daddy wants me to work with him at Luxe."

"And you don't want to?"

"Not really," she said, looking up at me again. "I want to do something a little more fun. More exciting."

"The music business is pretty exciting," I said. "In fact, once we get the CD pressed, I might need some help with publicity. You know, hanging up posters around the city. Handing out promotional materials."

She frowned. "I want to do more with my life than hang up posters, Nick."

"Hey, you gotta start somewhere, right?"

She glanced at me, a playful look lighting up her eyes as she wrestled me to the ground, the skirt of her dress floating around her as she sat astride me. "Well, I want to start at the top," she said, eyes gleaming.

"Is that right?" I said, tackling her until I rolled her easily beneath me.

She laughed, then pressed her mouth against me, immediately taking the advantage.

Yeah, this was nice, I thought, breaking off the kiss to lean my forehead against hers, gazing into her eyes.

She giggled. "You know you have three eyes."

"And two heads," I replied, pressing my erection into her.

Her gaze turned serious. "Make love to me, Nick."

She didn't have to ask me twice. In fact, it occurred to me, as I slid my hand beneath her dress, she never usually asked at all.

Not that it mattered, I thought, once my hands came into contact with her soft, soft skin.

I knew, even before I got her panties off, that she would be warm and wet.

That was another thing I liked about Francesca. She was always ready. I unbuttoned my jeans, glancing around at the dark and empty beach, taking a moment to relish the sound of the ocean, roaring in the background. And the fact that we were alone. Really alone. For the first time.

I slid out of my jeans and boxers, then into her, moving slowly, so slowly, it was torture.

The best kind of torture, I thought, watching the way her lips parted around her breaths, her eyes shuttered closed.

"Look at me," I said. The words came out harsher than I intended, but I realized, once her blue gaze was on mine, that she never really did look at me when we made love. Or had sex. Whatever.

I began to move faster, staring into her eyes, searching for something—I don't know what—exactly. Something beyond all the coolness in her blue gaze. But all I saw was her pupils widening like a cat's and something else, I thought, leaning in closer, and realizing it was only my own reflection.

"Oh, man. Oh, Francesca," I ground out moments later as I felt my climax shake through both of us as her eyes shuttered closed again, shutting me out once more. Burying my face against her neck, I savored the coolness of her body against my own heated skin. And when I finally had the courage to look up at her, she was smiling at me.

Kind of tender, you know?

And I felt something—I wasn't sure what. Something that made me believe I could have it all.

Have it all with her.

Zoe
Water, water everywhere and I'm about to sink.

By the time morning came, I had convinced myself that Donnie was the murderer I was looking for, even felt a desire to run my latest theory by Sage, if only to prove to her this trail I'd been following since Maggie died wasn't just some attempt to annoy her. But when I opened my eyes to the sight of Sage's bed still made—not to mention littered with every scrap of clothing she had brought with her this weekend—I realized my best friend hadn't come home last night.

I just hoped she'd remembered to use a condom.

When I didn't find Donnie on the beach, I headed to his house, which was just two doors down from Tom's. The house wasn't as lavish as Maggie's Dream, but Donnie clearly wasn't doing too badly as the head of Tom's shipping department, I thought, eyeing the squarish modern structure that rose up out of the reeds. It was still pretty early, but since the front door of the house was open, I assumed it was okay to knock.

After all, I had decided that my new documentary would be kind of a Maggie Landon tribute, and since Donnie seemed to be full of stories about Maggie's life last weekend, I figured he would be more than eager to make a statement for the cameras.

Stepping up to the screen door, I rapped on the wooden frame twice, wielding my brightest smile when Amanda Havens appeared.

"Zoe, hi, this is a pleasant surprise. Come on in."

I stepped through the door she held open, and was immediately taken aback by the decor. Though the house was smaller than Tom's, the layout was similar, with an airy kitchen and dining area that opened on to a living room and a sliding glass door that led to the deck beyond. Except the house I stood in now had none of the warm, sunny beach appeal of Maggie's Dream. In fact, I might have called the Havens' home a bit cold. The skylights over the kitchen area were nice, but the walls were a hideous too-green turquoise, and the furniture was black lacquer, topped by a rather grotesquely modern-looking chandelier that overwhelmed the dining area. I looked at Amanda's round, pleasant face and the checkered apron that covered her short, plump body, and realized she seemed misplaced in this house. Like a fifties housewife trapped in a tacky futuristic world.

Still, I said, "Nice place."

She smiled. "What can I do for you?"

"Actually I was looking for Donnie. Is he around?"

"No, he's down at the dock, cleaning his boat. Maybe I can help?"

I held up my camera. "I'm doing a little Maggie tribute—just something for Tom to have—and I thought Donnie might want to get one of those Maggie stories he told last week at dinner on film."

"Oh, that's a wonderful idea," she said. Then a wounded look moved into her eyes. "Actually, I wouldn't mind contributing a story myself. I mean, Maggie was my best friend."

Oops. I knew I should have had a cup of coffee before I left the house. What the hell was I thinking? "Of course," I said. "I meant the both of you. Well, separately. It would be nice to have a story from each of you." *Good, Zoe, real good. You're batting a thousand this morning.*

Fortunately, I only needed a curve ball to score with Amanda. "God, there's so many great stories I could tell about Maggie."

Oh, dear. I think I might have hit a home run. Except I didn't feel like taking the time to run all the bases. "Well, you can take time to think about it and I can come back."

She shook her head. "You know what, I don't even need to think about it. There's clearly only one story that would be appropriate. That would be the first time we took the car and went to the beach on our own. Without our parents, I mean. We were seventeen, and Maggie had just gotten her license. What a ball we had! I think it would be a perfect story—especially since Maggie and I spent practically our whole lives at the beach."

"This beach?"

She shook her head. "No, we grew up in Mastic. We went out to Smith's Point that day. Oh, this is going to be such fun! Let me just run and fix myself up a bit," she said, whipping off the apron and darting out of the room before I could stop her.

Now what had I gotten myself into?

What I'd gotten myself into, I realized, once Amanda returned, her hair newly combed and fresh lipstick on her lips, was a shipwreck. Of the emotional variety. And as I turned the camera on Amanda and listened to her recount her day at the beach with Maggie, I was wondering if I might not become one of the casualties. Because as she spoke about how she and Maggie had gotten up early one Saturday morning, filling up a cooler with lunch and drinks and setting off on their first solo ride down the highway that took them to the beach, I couldn't help but remember me and Sage doing pretty much the very same thing. At probably the very same age.

"Oh, Maggie," Amanda continued, addressing the camera as if her dead friend might actually be viewing this tribute herself someday, "you remember those guys we met? I forget what their names were—Sam or Joe—whatever, it doesn't matter now. One of them was so cute—you remember him? Dark hair? Lots of muscles. He was so into you. But you always got the pick of the litter, Maggie," she said, laughing, her eyes bright with the memory.

So had Sage, I thought, as I watched Amanda through the viewfinder. She always got the cutest guy, too, I remembered with a smile. She wouldn't have settled for less than the most beautiful man on the beach, whereas I went for the more introspective—okay, nerdy—type.

"Then they tried so hard to get a ride home with us, you remember, Maggie? But you stood strong. You were having none of that nonsense in your new car. Well, it wasn't so new, but it was nice enough, right?" She sniffed, blinking quickly. "And then it was just me and you, riding home against the sunset, laughing at those silly boys. God, we had so much to laugh about in those days, didn't we, Maggie? Didn't we?" she pleaded to the camera. "We always had each other. That was all we ever needed," she finished, tears suddenly springing from her eyes and rolling down her cheeks.

And when I lowered the camera from my eyes, I realized she wasn't the only one.

This had to be the worst scheme I'd ever come up with, I thought, swiping at my eyes and gaining control of myself once again. Enough control at least to ask the question I had planned to ask Donnie. I figured I had gone this far with Amanda—might as well get all the facts while I was here.

"Amanda, are you—" I began.

"Oh, I'm fine," she said waving a hand at me, then snatching a napkin from the counter to dab at her eyes. "It's just hard sometimes, you know? Losing a friend like that."

I could only imagine. Shaking off the thought, I said, "Can I just ask you one last question?"

"Sure," she said, looking at me once more, a tremulous smile on her tear-stained face.

"Were you here that night at the beach? You know, the night Maggie—"

"Oh, no," she said, shaking her head firmly. "I was out of town that weekend on business. At a promotional event for one of my clients. I'm in public relations," she said.

How convenient for Donnie and Maggie. "Was Donnie here?" I asked next.

"Donnie? Well, no—at least not that night. He had a boat show over in Sayville."

Or so he said. "Well, you're probably better off. It wasn't a good night in Kismet."

"No," she said, sadness filling her eyes once again. "It wasn't."

By the time I got down to the dock, I had worked myself into a lather. Though I wasn't sure who pissed me off more. Maggie,

for betraying her best friend, or Donnie, for betraying his wife with
her best friend. But when I spotted Donnie, standing on the deck
of his boat and looking pretty damned pleased with himself as he
polished the leather seats wearing nothing but a pair of navy blue
shorts and dark, wraparound sunglasses, his toupee looking like it
was about to take off with the next good wind, I decided it was
him I hated the most. Now I tried to get a grip on my anger, studying him for a moment as he rubbed a soft cloth over the seat in
front of the steering wheel, trying to figure out what his appeal
might have been for Maggie. I guess he did have a good build,
though he was a little on the short side. And he was younger than
Tom. It was possible Maggie could have climbed into the sack with
this guy. He had a certain, slick Long-Island-Guy-With-Cool-
Boat thing going on. If you went for that sort of thing.

"Hey, Donnie," I called out in the most cheerful voice I could
muster.

"Hey, Zoe," Donnie said, turning to look up at me as I stood
on the dock. "Gorgeous day out today, huh?"

"The best," I said, my gaze roaming over his boat, which had
Happy Havens painted in black on the side. Yeah, happy. I'd give
him happy. "Nice boat."

"She's a beauty," he said, smiling even wider.

Were those capped teeth? Oh yuck, Maggie. What were you
thinking?

"So, Donnie," I said, holding up my camera. "I decided to put
together a tribute video on Maggie. Something for Tom to keep.
Amanda just contributed a story. I wondered if you might want
to as well."

"For Maggie? Gosh, I'd be happy to. You know, I loved that
woman."

I bet, I thought, pulling the camera from my bag and raising it
before my eyes.

"Hang on a sec," Donnie said, smoothing a hand over his toupee. Not that it helped much, but at least it was no longer flap-
ping in the wind.

"So what should I do? Sit on the chair? Stand?"

"Whatever you feel comfortable with, Donnie." *This is your moment after all, you bastard.*

He remained standing, though he took a good few minutes trying to decide which side of the boat to stand on.

Then, because I couldn't bear another sobfest—especially since I suspected Donnie's wouldn't be as authentic as his wife's—I said, "I'm going to ask you a few questions, Donnie, and all you have to do is answer, okay?"

He shrugged. "Sure."

"Okay. So, Donnie, how long had you known Maggie Landon?"

He chuckled. "Well, that's easy. I knew Maggie almost as long as I've known my wife. Those two were like bread and butter, you know? As soon as I started dating Amanda, it was like I was dating Maggie, too. And Tom, of course. They were already married by then."

"Of course," I said, giving him a closed-mouth smile, so he wouldn't notice my clenched teeth. "So, about eight or nine years then?"

"Eight and a half," he replied.

"So the four of you were pretty tight, huh?"

"Oh yeah," Donnie said, one hand going to his toupee, which was starting to flap in the wind again.

"Spent a lot of time together at the beach?"

"Sure did. Well, Amanda and I have only had our house about three years. But before that we used to come out to see Tom and Maggie all the time."

"Good times, huh, Donnie?"

"The best," he replied with another hearty chuckle.

"So, Donnie, let me ask you. Were you here in Kismet the night Maggie died?"

He frowned, considering this for a moment. "No, actually, I wasn't."

"Where were you?"

I saw his jaw clench briefly, before he broke into another chuckle, this one not quite so hearty. "Hey, Zoe, what kind of film are you making anyway? What does it matter where I was?"

I lowered the camera. "Well, I was hoping to include some footage. Kinda like where were you the night Kennedy was shot. But with Maggie, of course."

"Oh," he said, looking a bit uneasy when I raised the camera again. I saw him think for a moment. Then he said, "I was playing poker with my buddies."

Jesus Christ. Could this guy even get his story straight? He told his wife he went to a boat show. "Are you sure that's where you were?"

Now he frowned. "Of course I'm fucking sure."

Oops. Losing the subject. "Okay, no problem. Just that it was a pretty nice night. I thought maybe you might have come here after the boat show. 'Cause your wife said you went to a boat show. So what time did this poker game happen? Before or after the boat show?"

Now he really looked flustered. "Can you shut that thing off? You're starting to give me a fucking headache."

I lowered the camera once more, which was probably a good idea. Because the minute Donnie thought I was no longer filming— I figured he was too stupid to realize I could leave the camera on and pick up everything with the mic—he let loose on his anger.

"What the fuck you asking me where I was that night if you already asked my wife?"

I shrugged. "I don't know. Just trying to get my facts straight for the film. I thought I saw your boat at the dock that night. When I came off the ferry. Around nine-thirty, ten."

"Well, you musta been high, 'cause I wasn't anywhere near this island that night," he said, his hands balling into fists.

"Okay, if you say so." Before he was tempted to use those fists on me, I said, "Thanks for the info, Donnie. I'll let you know when I've finished the tribute." Then I took off down the dock before he could say another word.

Because I realized, as I filmed Donnie standing like a peacock on his prized boat, that I didn't need to listen to his lies anymore.

There was someone else who could likely tell me whether or not Donnie had docked that night.

And that person was none other than Sage's abandoned paramour.

Good ol' Chad. The dock boy.

Fortunately, I remembered what he looked like, since Sage had pointed him out enough times that first weekend, when she'd set her sights on him. Though finding him was another matter. When I learned from one of his fellow dock boys that Chad was working the four-to-twelve shift tonight, I went back to the house to wait.

Of course, no one was there. Stepping onto the deck, I spotted Tom, Nick and Francesca lounging at the shore. But no Sage. Or Vince, for that matter. Jesus, she must have had a good time last night. Or was still having a good time, I thought, wondering if they were going to spend the whole day in bed. Still, I checked my cell phone, just to make sure she hadn't left any messages that might indicate when she might be home. I only found one message. From Jeff. And though it was a sweet little message about what a nice time he'd had last week, I opted not to call him back. Not yet. I wasn't sure whether it was because I no longer trusted anyone in law enforcement to help me get to the truth about what happened that night, or because I no longer believed Jeff to be more than a passing fancy, someone to bridge a small gap between Myles…and whoever came next.

Now that was a depressing thought. And since I didn't have time to be depressed, I fixed myself an egg-salad sandwich, then killed an afternoon reviewing my footage of the Fourth of July party, finally seeing Tom's drunken display for what I now suspected it was: the beginnings of grief. And I saw Donnie's endless sobs on the back deck as the pathetic attempts of a man whose ass I hoped to nail to the wall in a few short hours.

I was already seated on a bench just before the dock as the four o'clock sun rose into the sky, and I spotted Chad immediately at the other end, securing a boat into one of the slips.

"Hi," I said, approaching him as he pulled the rope tight and stood to study his handiwork.

He looked up, startled. Then a smile touched his golden-tan features as he slid his sunglasses to the top of his head. He was even cuter close up. No wonder Sage had been so put out when Chad wouldn't put out.

"Can I help you?" he asked.

"I'm hoping you can. Name's Zoe Keller," I said, holding out a hand.

As he shook it, I briefly considered telling him I was a friend of Sage's, but I wasn't sure what kind of reaction I'd get with that, considering what had happened—or not happened—between them that night. "What can I do for you?" he asked.

"I'm thinking about getting a boat, and I'm wondering if you could tell me how the docks work here. Do I have to sign up for a slip or—"

"Oh, yeah," he said. "Quite a little waiting list, too, if you want a private slip. We're talking at least a year."

"Is that right?" I replied. "So what would I do in the meantime, if I wanted to dock here for the weekend?"

"Well, we do have weekend rentals. Also nightly rentals, for customers of The Inn or The Out. That would be the slips right in front of the market there," he said, pointing to the dock where Donnie's boat sat. "Private slips are over on the other side of the dock. By the hotel," he said, gesturing to the hotel at the far end of the dock.

So Big Shot didn't have his own private slip yet. I was hoping that would work in my favor. "You wouldn't happen to keep track of who docks there on the weekends, would you?"

"Sure do. Everyone who docks here needs to show registration to sign up for a slip." Then he smiled. "And pay the fees, of course."

I smiled back. "You wouldn't be able to show me the sign-in records, would you?"

He frowned. "What would you need to see those for?"

"I'm just trying to get a sense of availability. See, if I get a boat, I want to be sure I'll be able to dock it. I plan on spending a lot of time out here."

"Well, I can tell you. We got one hundred slips and we tend to fill them up on Friday and Saturday nights. Especially during full season. But not always. Best to get here early."

"What about, say, a Saturday night in June?"

He shrugged. "Probably about a sixty percent occupancy rate."

"You wouldn't mind if I had a look at June, would you?"

"Well, I just told you—"

"I know, I'm just nervous, you know? I'm thinking about renting a boat for the month of June next year, but I don't want to invest if I won't be able to dock on a regular basis."

He glanced around. "I'm not really allowed to show the records, ma'am."

I ignored the fact that he'd just "ma'amed" me—I wasn't that much older than him after all—and said, "Just one little look." Then I beamed him another smile. "I won't tell anyone."

His expression turned uneasy. "I'd need to talk to my boss. And he's not here this weekend."

Sage had been right about Chad. Definitely a Rules boy. Then, spurred by the thought of Sage, I said, "Even if I was a good friend of someone you know?" Then I pulled out my ace. "Sage Daniels? You remember her, don't you? Pretty girl, with streaky brown hair and green eyes."

His eyes widened and suddenly his golden-tan features flushed bright red.

Oh, he remembered Sage all right. And clearly the memory made him uncomfortable. Of course, I knew why. Sage had told me every gory detail of her ill-fated night with Chad. Right down to the "I have a girlfriend" routine he'd pulled on her. And though I felt a little guilty using it against him—he did, after all, seem like a sweet kid—I was desperate.

"I know Sage remembers you," I continued, "in fact, she pointed you out to me just a couple of weeks ago. I think you were playing Frisbee with your girlfriend at the beach."

I saw him swallow hard.

"I don't suppose your girlfriend knows about Sage, does she? And she'd probably be pretty unhappy if someone happened to tell her about the little tumble you took with Sage that night, right?"

Yanking his sunglasses off the top of his head, he quickly slid them back over his eyes. "Come with me."

I followed Chad to a small wooden structure, which looked a bit like a shack, near the ferry dock, waiting just outside the door while he fished around inside, since the shack didn't look big enough to accommodate the both of us.

He came out moments later, handing me a clipboard thick with papers. "That's July on top. June is right beneath it," he said.

"Thanks," I said, watching as he folded his arms across his chest and glanced around nervously.

After I located the page for June, I quickly scanned the list of names and registrations until I came to Saturday, June 12th.

Running my finger down the line of boat owners who docked that night, I nearly bit through my tongue in frustration when I discovered Donnie Havens's name wasn't there. I even scanned the week prior to June 12th, only to learn that Donnie had docked the Friday night before. And left on the Sunday before.

"Can I see the list of private slip owners?" I asked, handing back the clipboard. Though I was quickly losing hope, I figured there was no harm in looking.

He scowled. "What do you need to see those for? I thought you said—"

"Chad, can I see it please?" I said, smiling sweetly. "I'd hate to think you'd lose such a great girlfriend. Especially after all you've sacrificed to keep her."

He stepped into the shack again, returning moments later with a separate list, which wasn't quite as long.

I quickly ran my finger down the list, my stomach plummeting to my feet when I discovered Donnie's name wasn't there, either. Dammit.

The only thing clear to me now was that Donnie more than likely had lied to his wife about his whereabouts that night, but apparently he hadn't lied to me. He hadn't been on Fire Island that night.

Which left me right back where I had started. With nothing.

Sage
What are friends for? Don't ask me. I haven't a clue.

"So Donnie Havens didn't murder Maggie. I don't understand why you're so depressed about it, Zoe."

"I'm not depressed," she said, slumping even lower on her bar stool.

We were at The Inn, where we were supposed to be seeing a band that was due to come on at ten, though it was edging on ten-fifteen and they were still setting up. Which was good news for Nick, who for some reason or another wasn't here yet. But bad news for me, since I'd been sitting here listening to Zoe's half-baked theories for the past twenty minutes. The only thing I had to be grateful for was that she had absolved Tom, though I was surprised to learn Tom had finally let loose the tight rein he'd been keeping on his emotions. And with Zoe, of all people.

"I don't understand why you can't accept the fact that the woman just drowned, plain and simple," I said now.

Zoe shook her head. "I'm sorry, Sage, but it just doesn't add up."

"What, exactly, doesn't add up?"

She sat up straight on the bar stool again. "For one thing, she had an awful lot of Valium in her system."

"Trust me, the woman needed Valium. I worked for her, remember?"

"Well, she also told Tom she was going to Fair Harbor Market that night, and the market was closed."

"So? She made a mistake and came home."

"I don't think she even went, Sage. For one thing, her cell phone records indicate that she called the market, so she probably knew it was closed. For another, Nick told me she was wearing jeans and a T-shirt when he left the house at seven-thirty. But a dress had been found on the beach with her body. She wouldn't change into a dress to hike all the way to Fair Harbor Market."

"Maybe she stopped at a friend's for drinks—"

Zoe shook her head. "No one saw her that night. At least no one who will admit it. She had to have had a lover. I thought that lover was Donnie Havens—and he might very well have been. I mean, he could have taken the ferry, though that seems like a stretch, considering how puffed up he is about that boat of his. And even if he did take the ferry, I have no way of proving it. They don't keep records of ferry riders."

I took another healthy sip from my drink. "I still can't believe what you said to Chad," I said, feeling a flash of fresh annoyance. Zoe had been surprised to learn that I hadn't appreciated her using the personal details of my life to manipulate Chad. Clearly she still didn't get it, if the way she was looking at me right now was any indication.

"Sage, you're not, like, still into him, are you?"

"No!" That was even more irritating. I sometimes think my best friend doesn't understand me at all. Or doesn't listen to me. "I told you about my date with Vince last night. What would I want with that little boy if I could have a man like Vince?"

Zoe smiled. "You really like Vince, don't you?"

I looked at her, feeling my insides warm just at the thought of Vince. "I do. I mean, I really do." I sighed. "Do you know that for the first time ever, I actually thought about being married?"

Zoe's eyes widened. "Okay, who are you and what have you done with my best friend?"

"Shut up," I said, laughing as I did, my gaze moving to the door. "I just hope he stops by." When I had learned Tom, Vince and Stan Sackowitz were going to The Out tonight to talk business, I felt a little pissed off that I hadn't been invited. After all, I was the one who had brought Stan in as a customer to Edge. I almost said something to Tom, but I got the feeling that the boys wanted a night out on their own to shoot the breeze, and though I found that annoying, too, I supposed I was going to have to live with it. At least I had had the gumption to tell Vince, when he swung by the house to pick up Tom, about the band that was playing here tonight. We had spent practically the whole day together in bed, but when I asked him to stop in for a drink after dinner, he seemed just as intrigued by the prospect as I was. I just hope he does come by, I thought, my gaze moving to the door once more.

"Where's Nick?" Zoe said.

"Who knows? He said he was coming tonight, but then he disappeared." As did Francesca, which caused me no small amount of worry, especially when I learned Nick had taken her to dinner last night. He was up to something. I just hoped it wasn't his usual stupid boy tricks.

But all thoughts of Nick dissipated when I saw Vince come through the door.

I smiled, waving him over.

"Hey," I said, feeling pleasure move through me when he leaned in and kissed me, as if I were the girlfriend, rather than simply the girl from the night before.

"You remember Zoe," I said, turning to Zoe.

"Of course. How could I forget your oldest friend?" Vince said, smiling at Zoe.

"Speaking of which, where is your old friend Tom?" I asked. "And Stan for that matter?"

"Tom and Stan looked about ready to fall asleep over dessert. They both went home."

"That's what you get for hanging with the old guys at The Out," I said.

"Oh yeah? As opposed to the hot young things at The Inn?" Vince replied with a wink.

I smiled. In fact, I was smiling so much since he walked through the door, my cheeks were starting to hurt. "Let me get you a drink," I said.

"Well, I can't really stay long."

The ache moved down to my throat. "Why not?"

"I've got to head out early tomorrow morning to pick up Sophia. Gabriella's going out of town for a couple of days and she's got an early flight. Which means I've got to be in Brightwaters by about 6:00 a.m."

"Do they even have ferries that early?" Zoe asked.

Vince smiled. "Oh, I don't take the ferry. I have a boat."

I saw Zoe sit up in her chair. "Is that right?"

"I'm going to get the bartender," I said. "Sure you can't have one little drink?"

Vince shook his head at me, though that smile was still on his face. "Okay, one drink. But only a little one."

I signaled Danny, just as I heard Zoe say, "So you work out of the Long Island office, too?"

"That's right," Vince said.

"That must be convenient," Zoe continued. "I bet you could take the boat straight from the office right to Fire Island on the weekends."

"Well, not exactly," Vince replied. "My office is in Bohemia. My boat is docked over in Brightwaters. Across the bay."

"Vince, what do you want?" I asked, once Danny stood before me. I threw a glance at Zoe, wondering at her interest.

"Dewars on the rocks," Vince said.

"I understand you were in Italy this year," Zoe said.

"Well, China for most of the year, but I did get to spend a lot of the spring in Italy."

Zoe nodded. "So when did you get back?"

"To the States?" Vince asked, picking up the drink Danny had placed on the bar in front of him.

Zoe nodded and I looked at her. Where was she going with this?

"June."

"When in June?" Zoe persisted.

Vince frowned, and suddenly I saw exactly where Zoe was going with this line of questioning. "What difference does it make, Zoe?" I asked, sending her a look.

"I'm just curious," Zoe said, keeping her gaze on Vince. "You were back for Maggie's wake. Just wondered if you happened to be here the night she died."

Vince's brow furrowed. "Here on Fire Island? God, no. I'd just gotten back from Italy that day."

"What time?"

"Zoe—" I began, glancing uneasily at Vince. What the hell was she doing?

"Oh, I don't remember—one, two o'clock."

"And you didn't come here?"

"I should think not. I was a bit jet-lagged," he said, his gaze narrowing on Zoe, as if he was suddenly wondering where this little inquisition was going. I didn't blame him.

"Zoe, can you come to the bathroom for a minute. I need to talk—"

But Zoe ignored me. "Did you go to the office that day?"

"I believe I did go for a few hours."

"So you were too tired to go to Fire Island, but not too tired to go to the office?"

He frowned. "I had business to take care of after my trip. If I came to Fire Island after that, I sure as heck don't remember."

"You don't remember? It was the day Maggie died. Where were you when Tom called you? I'm sure he must have called you. I mean, you two are close, right?"

"Vince, you don't have to answer her," I said, glaring at Zoe.

Vince glanced at me. Then he shrugged. "I don't mind answering. I was home. In Brightwaters."

"Just across the bay," Zoe said.

"That's right," Vince said, raising his glass to his mouth to drink, his gaze still on Zoe.

I was about ready to club Zoe. But since I couldn't, I said, "Hey, Vince, you up for a quick game of pool?"

Now they both ignored me. "So you could have easily come to Fire Island that night," Zoe pressed on. "You know, the night Maggie died."

"Zoe—"

Vince put his drink down on the bar and finally looked at me. "Is there something I should know about here?"

Before Zoe could stop me, I blurted out, "Zoe has this stupid theory that Maggie's death wasn't an accident."

"Sage—" Zoe began.

Now Vince's eyes went wide. "You're not implying that I—"

Zoe looked at him. "I'm not implying anything. Just asking."

He shook his head. "Tom is my best friend. And Maggie was like a sister to me," he said. "I can't believe you'd even suggest such a thing."

"Vince, I apologize on behalf of my *friend,*" I said, shooting a look at Zoe.

Vince sighed, smiling slightly at me. "That's fine, Sage." Then he looked at Zoe. "The truth is, Zoe, if you really think something like that happened, you probably should go to the police with your findings."

"I probably should," Zoe said. "I wonder, though, what they might make of the fact that Maggie received a phone call from the Long Island office on the Saturday she died. Especially in light of the fact that you might have been one of the few people at the office that day."

Vince stared at Zoe for a minute, then he chuckled, shaking his head. "So that's what this is all about?" Then he narrowed his gaze at her. "I think I already explained that phone call to the detective who called to follow up. He seemed satisfied with the fact that I had called Maggie on a business matter, if you must know. In addition to being friends, Zoe, Maggie and I did work together."

"Vince, I'm sorry about—" I began.

He sighed, looking at me. "It's fine. Look, it was a crazy night. I can't blame anyone for getting worked up about it. I was pretty worked up myself."

I took his hand between mine. "Maybe you and I should get out of here. Take a nice walk along the beach. Alone," I said, throwing a glance at Zoe.

He smiled, his gaze moving to the clock above the bar, before coming to rest on me. "You know, Sage, that sounds wonderful, but it's pretty late. I still have to pack, close up the house. I probably should go."

He put his drink down on the bar, reaching into his pocket and throwing a twenty-dollar bill down beside it. "I'll talk to you next week, Sage." Then he turned to Zoe and smiled. "Good to see you again, Zoe."

And with that, he left.

Leaving me with Zoe, who I turned on as soon as I saw Vince disappear through the door. "That was the last straw, Zoe."

"What? Sage, you can't blame me for—"

I stood up, slamming my glass on the bar as I did. "Oh, I can blame you, all right. And if you just fucked up this thing with Vince, you better believe I will."

38

Maggie
The other woman in Tom's life was not who I expected.

I suppose the worst thing I could say about Sage Daniels was that she saw only what she wanted to see. I guess I can't really blame her for that. I've been guilty of the same.

But blame her I did. How else could I defend myself against the way she looked at me, spoke to me, the way she despised me from the moment I took over the helm at Edge? She saw only a wife who slipped into a ready-made space in her husband's empire. Not a woman who'd finally found a place to dream.

Yes, it could be argued that I came to Edge driven more by a dream than a solid employment history. I didn't know much about the garment industry, except for what my husband brought home with him. And though Tom's work at Luxe often kept him long hours at the office, I accepted it. His ambition was one of the few things I really loved about him. If I didn't find myself inspired by ladies' wear for the middle-aged set, I was inspired by Tom's passion for his business. And on those occasions when he came home buoyant with the triumph of bringing in a new retailer or the successful sell-in of a new design, I remembered what I loved about him when we first met. Though Luxe was well under way by the time I entered Tom's life, I sometimes saw glimpses of the younger man, the one who had come to New York in search of a dream outside the shadow of his successful father. The man who had built an empire from the ground up. A passionate man.

I guess I hadn't counted on that being his only passion. After all, there was a time when he'd felt just as inspired by me.

When Edge was born, you could say it changed everything. Edge was the fashion of the street, spawned by music and hip-hop culture. We even had an early success when Missy Elliot sported one of our samples on a music video. And though I had never seen myself as a part of this business, I felt some sense of destiny when Edge came into being. The feeling all my dreams were right in my own backyard. If I wasn't a rock star, I felt like one when I took the reins of Edge.

Ironically, you could say that, in some ways, Edge gave new life to my marriage just as much as it destroyed it. Tom and I shared a common passion to make Edge a success. Now our nights were filled with strategies about how to take this younger market by storm. Champagne toasts at each success and whispered confidences about how to make it all happen.

Of course, my days at Edge only made me aware of how little I really knew about the industry. Sage never failed to remind me of that deficit. For every idea I had, she had a better one. For every retailer I brought in using Tom's connections, Sage was the one who sealed the deal.

It hurt to see Tom take Sage's side time and time again, whenever the heat rose up between us and we turned to him as a mediator. Hurt to realize that outside of my solid budgeting sense, I had little to offer in terms of creative inspiration. But I tried, Lord knows I tried. Which only earned me Sage's animosity.

But what Sage didn't know was that there wouldn't have even been an Edge if it hadn't been for me. Edge was my baby. My first child with the man I loved.

39

Nick
Who says I don't have a conscience? I just hope I don't have to live with it.

There's nothing like waking up to the feel of the ocean breeze in your face. Breathing deep, I opened my eyes. And nearly swallowed my tongue.

"Maggie?"

I sat up, glancing quickly at Tom's bed, which looked like it hadn't even been slept in, then turned my gaze once more to the apparition in my doorway.

I needed to lay off the dope, I thought, shutting my eyes. Only to open them again and see Maggie still standing there. Wearing a blue silk robe and a smile that could only mean one thing.

"Uh, Maggie, what are you—"

She laughed as she approached the bed. "Thought you were rid of me, did you?"

I shrank back against the headboard. "No! I mean, that is—well, yeah. You're supposed to be dead."

"Thought you were going to run that label all on your own, did you? Squandering my money—"

"I didn't squander your money. It was Les, I swear. He's a fuckup."

"Shhhh," she said, sitting on the bed next to me, one hand going to my face.

God, she felt real. I looked at her eyes, which seemed bluer than I remembered. Even her hair looked longer, almost wild. And her mouth...

Before I knew what was happening, that mouth was on mine, her tongue moving so hotly against mine, I would swear to it that Maggie was very much alive. I mean, a ghost couldn't give me a woody like the one I was growing right now.

"Make love to me, Nick," she said, sliding out of her robe.

My eyes went from her breasts, small but firm—not bad—to her face, then to the door, which stood half-open. "What about Tom?"

She laughed, pushing me down on the bed and pulling down the sheet to stare at my erection. "I see you've been waiting for me."

I looked down, surprised to discover that I was naked. I never slept in Tom's room naked. Not if I could help it, anyway.

Then all my thoughts flowed south as she climbed on top of me and began to move. And to moan. God, I loved a screamer. Who would have thought Maggie was a screamer?

But when she leaned in close, her breath hot against my ear, I realized that wasn't a moan I was hearing.

"You're gonna pay," she ground out, over and over again.

Suddenly the door flew open and I pulled away from her, just in time to see Tom standing over me. With what looked like a giant...fish hook?

"Ahhhhhhhhhhhh!"

"Nick!" came Francesca's voice, practically in my ear. Oh, Francesca. Only she could save me, I thought, opening my eyes to find myself staring into her sleepy blue eyes. I blinked at her as she smiled at me. "You must have been having a nightmare."

Jesus. What a nightmare. "I guess so," I muttered, dropping my head back to the pillow with relief and staring up at the purple ceiling fan, which must have been the cause of that "ocean breeze" I'd been feeling.

Purple ceiling fan? Shit, I had spent the night in Francesca's room.

I sat up, spotted Francesca's bra and panties on the floor. "I gotta get outta here," I said, scrambling from the bed.

She grabbed my arm. "Relax. It's only ten-thirty at night. We must have fallen asleep after that marathon fuck session." She bit my shoulder. "You were amazing, by the way."

A memory floated through my brain of me and Francesca, clinging to one another between the sheets as a Britney Spears song belted out from the CD player.

Holy fuck. The nightmare clearly wasn't over. I think I might have had the biggest orgasm in my life. To the tune of "Oops… I Did It Again."

"We gotta get outta here," I said, leaping up from the bed and reaching for my jeans.

"What for? I don't think my dad's even home yet."

Then I remembered where I was supposed to be tonight. Watching a band at The Inn with Sage and Zoe. And though I wasn't sure what kind of band The Inn had to offer, it had to be better than Britney Spears.

Mother of God, what was happening to me?

"C'mon, Francesca, get dressed. We need to get to The Inn right away."

Before I lost my mind. Because between my nightmare and the nightmare that was Britney Spears, I had to be losing it.

Besides, knowing Sage, she'd probably kill me if I didn't show up.

40

Zoe
I need a life preserver for my heart.

"Myles, it's me," I said into my cell phone.

"Hey, Zoe, where are you?"

"Out in front of your house."

A shadow moved past the windows, and then Myles appeared at the front door.

"What are you doing out there?" he asked, looking at me through the screen.

"Cracking up."

He opened the door, closing his cell phone and pocketing it as he stepped outside.

Concern filled his eyes once he stood before me. "Jesus, Zoe, what's wrong? You look like you just lost your best friend."

"I think I may have done just that."

"What happened?"

I blew out a sigh. Then told him everything. How I came to believe that Maggie's killer was her lover, not her husband. How I had first zeroed in on Donnie Havens, only to learn that Donnie wasn't even on Fire Island that night. How I had then practically accused the man Sage was half in love with of murdering his best friend's wife.

"I wouldn't be surprised if Sage never speaks to me again," I said. "She was pretty pissed off. Accused me of wrecking her relationship with Vince and then stormed out of The Inn as if the place was on fire."

"Well, if Vince is guilty, it sounds like you might have done her a favor."

I looked at him. "That's the worst of it. As soon as Sage left, I ran back down to the dock to see Chad. He practically threw the dock registration papers at me when I saw him." I gave Myles a halfhearted smile. "I think he was afraid of me since I threatened him earlier today. But when I checked the records for both the private slips and the public slips, I realized Vince's name wasn't on either one."

"That doesn't mean Vince wasn't here that night. He could have taken the ferry."

"Donnie could have, too, for that matter. But I can't prove it." I dropped my gaze. "Now I'm back just where I started. With nothing."

Myles grabbed my chin, lifting my face to look up at him once more. "Not with nothing. You found enough to figure out that Maggie didn't go to the market that night. That she possibly went to see someone. I mean, you've managed to convince me that something was up. I'm starting to wonder, too, if what happened that night was really an accident."

I studied his eyes, feeling warmed by the idea that someone at least was starting to trust my instincts. And Myles, of all people. But the feeling was only momentary. I sighed. "Still, all the evidence is starting to seem like just what it is—a whole lot of nothing. Nothing but some stupid nagging feeling about that night that won't go away."

Myles smiled at me, his eyes soft with understanding. "You know what you need?"

"A Valium?" I asked, not even able to crack a smile at my own humorless joke.

He shook his head. "You need to return to the scene of the crime."

★ ★ ★

"I don't know what we're doing here," I said, once we stepped onto the cool sand and I saw the ocean rolling out in foamy waves before us.

"Like I said, returning to the scene of the crime," Myles replied, grabbing my hand and leading me down the beach.

"I don't see the point," I said, pulling back on his hand until he released his grip.

He stopped, turning to look at me. "The point is to try and re-assemble what happened that night. It's an investigation technique. My dad used to do it all the time."

Despite the glimmer of hopefulness I saw in his eyes, I couldn't seem to rouse myself. "Aren't your housemates going to wonder where you went?" I asked. "I mean, surely Haley will wonder."

He shrugged, his gaze moving to the ocean. "She went out. They all went out. To do the bar scene over in Ocean Beach."

I studied his face. "Why didn't you go?"

He turned to look at me again. "You know me, Zoe. I'm not into that whole bar scene."

I smiled in the darkness. Yes, I did know him. He was just like me. A homebody.

So why weren't we home together?

You're together now. Be happy for a change, an inner voice chided. But it occurred to me that I didn't know the first thing about being happy. Probably because I was too busy thinking about what made people unhappy. Homelessness. Stolen dogs. Premature death.

Still, I walked beside him until we reached that lonely stretch of beach where this whole nightmare began. Turning to the horizon, I saw the moon hovering high above the crashing waves, felt the breeze upon my face, and found that, for the first time all summer, I wasn't thinking of Maggie at all.

"Pretty romantic," I said, then wished I could take back the words. I didn't want Myles to think I was pining for him or anything.

But even if he wondered where my mind had gone, he kept his own on the matter at hand. "Now you're on the right track. I bet the night Maggie died wasn't so different from tonight. Perfect for a stroll on the beach with someone she cared about. It was pretty hot that night, if I'm remembering it right."

I nodded. "It was."

"So put yourself in Maggie's place."

I shivered, watching the tide move up the shore where her body once lay. "I don't think I want to do that."

Myles smiled. "I mean *before* she died. Tell me what you think happened that night."

I looked at him. "Well, I can't be one hundred percent sure, but I think she went to see her lover. Whoever that was."

"Okay, what did she do? Go to his house first? Meet him at the beach?"

"Well, she made a phone call to Donnie Havens at close to seven-thirty, but she could have called him from anywhere."

"Assume for a minute that she was still home at that point, maybe getting ready to meet her lover—whoever he was. She's all excited to see him. Puts on a nice dress. Spends like an hour on her hair, her makeup."

I smiled. "This is the beach, Myles. No one spends that much time on their hair and makeup at the beach. In fact, I never do."

"Okay, so she pulls it all together in a half hour. Then what does she do?"

"Well, she certainly didn't finish her sauce. It was still half-made on the stove by the time Tom got home." I frowned. "That's another thing—why did she run out like that?"

"Maybe he came to her and they left quickly, afraid that Tom might come home."

I turned to look at Maggie's Dream, easily spotting the lights twinkling at the far end of the beach. "All right, so he comes to see her and they go for a walk on the beach. That would probably be about sunset. Maybe after."

"Let's assume it was after. Now what happened?"

I smiled. "Well, they probably kissed a little bit. I'm guessing the mood was playful. Or something. Why else would they have gone skinny-dipping?"

"So they take off their clothes and go in," Myles said. "What happened next?"

I sighed. "That's exactly the problem. I don't know what happened next. How Maggie went from skinny-dipping to floating in the tide."

"Maybe it was an accident," Myles offered.

"That's possible. Maybe she got caught in the tide and he couldn't save her." I looked at him. "But wouldn't he go for help?"

"Not if he didn't want to be found out by Tom."

I shook my head. "I'm sorry, but I'm having a hard time believing anyone would leave someone they loved to…to die."

"What if he had a lot to lose? I mean, if it was Vince or Donnie, they might have risked their jobs."

"Still, Myles, I can't believe—"

"Okay, okay. Let's backtrack for a minute. Maybe they were fighting before they got in the water. Maybe he tried to break it off and she got angry."

"But then why would she go skinny-dipping with him?" I said, throwing my hands in the air. "See, I knew there was no point to this. There's no way we'll ever know what really happened that night. What was going on in Maggie's head—or his, for that matter."

"There's only one way we can possibly find out," Myles said, yanking his T-shirt over his head and tossing it on the beach.

"What are you doing?" I said, alarm ringing through me as he reached for the fly on his shorts.

"Returning to the scene of the crime," he reminded me, sliding down his shorts and kicking them to the side. "C'mon, what are you waiting for? Get undressed."

My eyes widened. "I'm not going in there," I said, glancing nervously at the ocean, vast and dark, as it rolled toward us.

"Why not?" he said, his hand moving to the waist of his boxers.

"It's cold?" I said weakly, watching as the boxers came down. I bit my lip, trying not to stare. Not that I had time to stare, because Myles was suddenly off like a shot, racing toward the water, his tanned skin pale in the moonlight.

"Last one in is a rotten egg!" he yelled, diving into the tide and disappearing under the dark water.

"Dammit, Myles," I said, racing to the tide line in a panic and then coming to a dead stop when Myles popped up again, a smile on his face. "C'mon in, Zoe, the water's beautiful."

"I don't want to."

"It's not cold. I swear."

A foamy warmth washed over my feet, verifying the truth of his words. Not that that made me want to go in. "I'm scared of the ocean," I said, feeling like the big baby I was the moment the words left my mouth.

"Scared? C'mon, Zoe," Myles said, rising up out of the water to flex his muscles at me. "I'll protect you," he said in a deep voice. Then he laughed. "Just come in. You're missing all the fun."

It was those words, more than anything else, that had me pulling off my T-shirt. I was so tired of being the one pulling the plug on every game.

I slid down my shorts, tossing them behind me with my shirt. But when I reached for the clasp on my bra, I felt a touch of worry again.

And I knew it wasn't so much being in the water that scared me now but being in the water with Myles. Naked.

I hadn't been naked with Myles in a long time.

Too long, I thought, whipping off my bra and sliding down my panties before I could change my mind.

I stepped into the water, splashing past the crashing waves before they toppled me over. Then I dunked down, probably out of modesty more than anything else.

"You're right," I said, swimming closer to him. "The water is beautiful."

"Would I lie to you?" he asked, looking at me across the bobbing waves.

"No," I said, studying his wet, spiky eyelashes, those eyes I knew so well. "You wouldn't."

His gaze softened. "Come here," he said, reaching for me.

I hesitated, studying his face. Until suddenly I wasn't seeing his face at all, but scrambling madly as a wave crashed over me.

Darkness engulfed me and water filled my mouth as I struggled back to the top, panicking as the ocean pulled at me, until I felt Myles's arms close around me as we popped back to the surface.

"I got you," he said, pulling me close.

He certainly did, I thought, breathing hard as his chest made contact with mine.

"Come on," he said, gently guiding me out farther.

"Myles, I don't want to go—"

"Just a little farther. We need to get past the breaking point."

I might be close to that point already, I thought, feeling his body slide against mine in the water.

Finally he stopped moving, his arms circling me.

"So," he said softly, his gaze on mine. "You're in the water. With the man you love. Love so much, in fact, you threw off all your clothes and dived in after him," he continued, a smile touching his lips. "What happens now?"

I felt suddenly shy. "I think I would kiss him."

He raised an eyebrow. "You think or you would?"

I met his gaze. "I would."

"What if he kisses you first?" he said, touching his mouth to mine.

His lips were salty, but soft, familiar. Not so familiar, I realized when he took my lip between his teeth, biting gently, his hands moving restlessly down my back as he pulled me hard against him. No, it felt different this time. Hungrier, more alive than it ever had been between us. Myles must have sensed it, too, because he broke off the kiss, his eyes searching mine. For what?

I didn't know. I didn't know anything, I thought, looking into that golden brown gaze and seeing both the man I loved and someone else. Someone ravaged by past loss, uncertain what the future held.

Some of that uncertainty began to fill me. Because really, what did I know about him anymore? This man who I once knew better than myself. So much had changed between us. So much had been left unsaid.

I tightened my arms around him, suddenly afraid he might let me go, kissing his face, the hard planes of his cheekbones. His mouth.

God, I loved him. Probably too much for my own good, I thought, burying my face in his neck and curling deeper into his arms, relishing the feel of his heartbeat against my chest.

I wasn't sure how long we stayed that way, linked in the ocean, rising and falling with the waves. Long enough for our heartbeats to slow.

Well, my heartbeat slowed. The sound emanating from Myles's chest was getting louder, if anything.

Until I realized that whap, whap, whap I was hearing wasn't coming from Myles.

"What the hell is going on?" Myles asked, looking up at the sky.

I followed his startled gaze to the helicopter hovering over the bay side of the island. I could just make out the lettering on the fuselage: S.C.P.D. As in, Suffolk County Police Department.

41

Sage
A friend in deed.

"Sage, you sure you don't want to try just one?"

"No thanks, Jenny. I'm fine with my tequila," I said, watching as my former housemate started pumping the handle on the keg of beer with everything she had. I was starting to wonder why I had stopped by the house I'd stayed in last summer. I guess I had been hoping to find some friends to hang out with, especially after realizing Zoe wasn't as much of a friend as I thought she was.

These friends weren't any better, I thought, looking around at the small crowd on the deck, who surrounded Jenny as she held a funnel of beer over her next victim.

I mean, funnels? Come on. What, are we in college still?

Downing the rest of my drink, I was just about to make my way out of there when I was practically mowed over by a three-hundred pound beast of a guy wearing a Bud Lite T-shirt.

"Hey," he said, loud enough to rouse the crowd from their drinking game. "The cops are crawling all over the dock. Some dude took a header off one of the boats. I think he's fucking dead, man."

Within moments, I found myself swept along by the crowd, which stampeded toward the walkway to the street. Not exactly swept. I was running right along with them, with something close to fear nipping at my heels.

By the time I got to the dock, saw the crowds swarming in front of The Inn and The Out and littering the bay front, my fear had turned into all-out panic.

I pushed into the crowd, fighting my way through as far as I could, until I came to a dead stop behind a huge hulk of a guy who blocked me from going any farther.

Turning to the woman standing next to me, I asked, "What happened?"

Her eyes were wide behind her rimless glasses. "They found a body floating in the water."

"Do they know who it was?"

"I'm not sure, but I think it was the guy who works the docks? Thad?"

Oh, dear God. Not Chad.

Not…dead.

I was sitting alone in the darkness of the living room, having my fourth tequila drink of the night, when Zoe practically barreled through the sliding glass door.

"Sage?" she yelled breathlessly, heading for the bedroom.

"I'm in here," I answered quietly.

"What are you doing sitting in the dark?" she asked, stepping back toward the living room and flicking on the light.

"Oh, God, Zoe, shut that off," I said, shielding my eyes against the sudden brightness.

Ignoring me, she moved in closer, stopping just before the couch where I sat, and looked at me. "I guess you heard what happened."

"What do you think?" I said, looking up at her. "Why are you wet?"

"I, uh, I went for a swim. How are you doing?"

Raising the glass to my lips, I said, "How do you think?"

She frowned. "Why are you here all alone? You shouldn't be alone. Where is everyone?"

I shrugged. "God knows where Nick is. Probably down at the dock with the rest of the gawkers. Tom's sleeping."

"He doesn't know?"

I looked at her. "What, I was supposed to wake him up to tell him somebody else fucking died?" Emotion clogged my throat, nearly overwhelming me, but I held fast.

Not that fast. "Oh, Sage, you must feel awful—"

"Like you care how I feel."

Anger flashed in Zoe's eyes. "Of course I care about you. I'm sorry about what happened tonight. I mean earlier. I made a mistake."

"We all do, I suppose," I said, turning to look out the sliding glass door.

"A big mistake, apparently," she said.

Hearing the pain in her voice, I looked up at her again.

"I can't help but think I'm somehow responsible. I mean, I spoke to Chad tonight. If somebody tried to kill him, it was because they thought he knew something. Something the killer thought he might tell me. Or the police."

"Look, Zoe, I know you have murder on the brain, but Chad wasn't murdered. I heard he hit his head on one of the masts on a boat he was working on and fell in."

She shook her head. "That's not what happened, Sage."

I sighed. "Zoe, I'm in no mood for your theories tonight."

"It's not my theory. The police came up with this one all on their own."

"What are you talking about?"

She blew out a breath. "I saw Jeff down at the dock. You know, that cop I went out with? Of course, he wouldn't tell me anything. Especially not with Myles standing there."

"Myles?"

She blushed. "That's who I was, um, swimming with."

I picked up my glass again, took a healthy slug. "I'm glad someone had a nice time tonight."

"Sage, listen to me for a minute, would you? Jeff didn't say much, but he did say it was no accident."

I looked at her. "How does he know that?"

Zoe plopped down on the love seat across from me. "I have no idea. Maybe he has some evidence, but he certainly wasn't sharing it with me."

I studied her face, saw the mix of sorrow and confusion in her features. "Look, Zoe, this has nothing to do with you. You're not responsible."

"I feel responsible, that's for sure. I just can't figure it out though. Who would kill that poor innocent kid?"

A lump thickened in my throat, but I swallowed it down, along with the rest of my drink. "Your guess is as good as mine."

"I want to pin it on Donnie—he might have seen me talking to Chad, but what does Donnie have to hide if Donnie wasn't even here the night Maggie died?"

"Why not pin it on Vince?" I said, feeling fresh anger flare through me.

She lowered her gaze. "I…I already checked on Vince. He wasn't on Fire Island that night, either."

"Well, la-di-da."

"Sage, this is serious."

"Don't you think I know that?" I replied, folding my arms beneath my chest to keep me from striking out. Not at Zoe. But at the world. It was too fucked up to even contemplate.

But contemplate it, Zoe did. "I just can't see who else would have a motive. Unless Chad was a witness to what happened that night on the beach. But Chad was with you the night Maggie was murdered."

I looked up at her, saw something move through her eyes. And though it was only a brief flash, I knew exactly what it was. Blame. I stiffened. "You don't think that I—"

"No, Sage, no," she protested, her eyes going wide. "I would never think that."

But I knew she was lying. I had practically seen the thought cross her mind.

And that was enough for me.

I did the only thing I could do. I ran. Out the door, then over the cracked concrete and sandy paths of Kismet. The strange thing was, it wasn't the thought of Chad that haunted me, but the memory of Hope.

I couldn't save her. I couldn't….

The words rang through me, over and over, like the mantra they had been to me these past fifteen years. But they didn't soothe me.

They never really did. Never really erased the accusation I saw in the eyes of everyone the day they pulled Hope from the river.

Now that day came back to me with full force. My mother pleading with me that morning to pick up Hope after school, though baby-sitting my sister was the last thing I wanted to do. Walking in the rain to get her, because I did give in to my mother—I always gave in. Splashing through the stream with Hope on the way back. Once the rain let up, we had turned the fact that we were both soaked to the skin into a game, stepping into the swollen stream and leaping from rock to rock as we made our way home.

I remembered Hope's scream as she slipped from the rock, her body sliding effortlessly into the water, which was rushing more than usual due to the heavy rainfall. Remembered diving in after her, frantically following her listless body until she disappeared completely under water.

When I got to the end of the stream, some fifty feet down, and saw the way the sewer pipe sucked the water through, it was all I could do to stop myself from being pulled from that dark place I was certain had taken my sister.

They said I never shed a tear, but I cried long and hard into my pillow many nights when I was sure no one could hear.

Almost as hard as I was crying now.

Swiping at my tears, I came to a stop in front of Vince's house. And as I caught my breath, I realized that Zoe was right about one thing at least. I shouldn't be alone right now.

But when I looked up and saw the quiet darkness of the house, the front door shut against the night, I came to my senses.

I couldn't possibly barge in there like this, an emotional wreck. I didn't know Vince well enough for that. I certainly couldn't call him a boyfriend yet. I wasn't even sure if I could call him a friend.

That thought made me feel lonely.

Lonelier than I've ever been.

Zoe
Dog Day Afternoon

"Zoe, it's Adelaide. Adelaide Gibson?"

The minute I heard Adelaide's raspy chirp, I was sorry I had picked up the phone. I had been hoping for Sage, who I had called so many times this week, at home, at the office, I was really starting to feel like a stalker again. But what else could I do? She never picked up. And she never called back, no matter what kind of message I left—and I left plenty.

"Hi, Adelaide," I said, bracing myself to hear about the latest changes she wanted on the film.

"You're never going to believe what's happened, Zoe."

You'd be surprised, Adelaide. "What's up?"

"Fifi is home. My Fifi—she's come back to me."

I sat up on the sofa, where I'd been slouching. "How?"

"Well, I've been showing our little film all over town. At my garden club. My book club. I even had a viewing at the Jefferson Market Library."

Huh. *Invisible People,* notwithstanding, this might be one of my biggest distributions yet. "And somebody found Fifi?"

"You guessed it! Two days ago I received a phone call from Beatrice Simpson—she's in my book club. I think you met her in the park that day."

I was thinking Beatrice was part of the dog club, but whatever. "Go on."

"As it turns out, Beatrice had gotten a call from another friend of hers, who had a woman in her building with a King Charles spaniel that looked just like my Fifi!"

I frowned. "How could she tell? Don't they all look alike?"

Adelaide sucked in a breath, clearly offended. "Of course not. My Fifi had an unusual brown marking on her left ear. And a pink freckle on her nose."

I was going to have to take her word on that.

"Oh, Zoe, it's a good thing we kept that extra home footage of Fifi in, otherwise, how would this woman have spotted her?"

I decided to let that comment slide. "So what happened?"

Then she explained how the woman had received the dog as a gift from her fifteen-year-old grandson, who thought his granny was lonely and decided to pick her up a cute little pet.

"You're going to press charges, aren't you?"

"I don't know, Zoe. I feel kind of sorry for the woman. Not only was she clearly lonely, but she has a thief for a grandson! I'm going to have one of my friends at the Police Benevolence Society give that young man a talking to. But I just had to tell you the good news. And thank you for helping me bring home my Fifi!"

When I hung up the phone a few minutes later, I wasn't feeling any better, despite Adelaide's happy reunion with Fifi. Though I did have the thought that maybe I should get a dog. I certainly didn't have many friends left. I just wished I could talk to Sage. See how she was doing. But I had one recourse left: the beach. And though Kismet was the last place I wanted to be this fine Friday, I was going, if only to see Sage.

With that thought in mind, I looked up, saw that it was nearly four and began halfheartedly packing a bag. While I was hemming and hawing over whether to pack an extra pair of shorts to go with the six T-shirts and seven pairs of underwear I'd already stuffed into my knapsack, the phone rang.

I leaped for the receiver. "Hello?"

"Zoe, it's Sage."

"Sage, I've been trying to reach you all week."

"I know you have. I didn't want to talk to you."

I heard a rushing sound in the background. "Where are you?"

"On the ferry. Listen, I have something to tell you about Maggie."

My ears perked up. "What about Maggie?"

"Well, I was at work today, and I came across a folder that was crammed in the back of the drawer. Like it was hidden. In fact, I probably wouldn't even have found it if I hadn't decided to move my furniture around this afternoon."

"What kind of folder?"

"A folder filled with all these invoices for some high-end jackets we had made for the fall collection."

"Is that unusual? I mean, don't you keep all that info at the N.Y. office?"

"Well, no, which was why I was curious, especially since the invoices seemed to be hidden. So I start looking through them, and I noticed that some of the numbers looked kind of high. I might not have noticed that, except that we just got an early shipment in for some styles we did in lamb and goat. I know because I get a copy of the shipping invoice sent to me as the orders come in to the warehouse, and I remembered we didn't have as many pieces as the numbers on the payment order seemed to indicate. So I pulled out the shipping invoice and I realized I was right—the number on the payment order was higher than the number of actual goods received."

"Speak English, Sage."

"Meaning that payment was made for double the amount of skin needed for the number of jackets recorded as being received by the warehouse."

"So what does that mean?"

"It means that somebody was making off with all those extra jackets, and if my guess is correct, making a shitload of money with them on the black market."

My scalp prickled. "Well, who do you think it was?"

"Who else? Donnie Havens, the fucking slimeball. His signature is all over the shipping invoice."

I sucked in a breath. "So do you think Maggie found out and Donnie killed her?"

"That's what it looks like."

Something didn't feel right. "Do you think they were lovers?"

"I wouldn't put it past either one of them. Maybe she was in cahoots with him. Why else would she be hiding all these payment orders in her office? Maybe Donnie wanted to break it off and Maggie threatened to go to Tom."

"But Donnie wasn't on the beach that night. At least not according to the dock records."

"Maybe Donnie paid off Chad to change the records. Then, when you started asking questions, Donnie got scared his little bribe wouldn't keep Chad's mouth shut."

I suddenly felt ill. "Oh, God, Sage, then that means I was responsible for Chad's death."

"Zoe, look, you didn't know what you were dealing with. You thought it was a simple little affair. This is the big time—grand larceny. We're talking a lot of money here. I started looking through the rest of the payment invoices and realized some of the orders there looked a bit high, too. In some cases, as many as two hundred extra pieces, which could earn as much as sixty thousand dollars on the black market. And that's not counting the shipments that haven't come in yet. Who knows how long Donnie was planning on carrying on this scheme of his? I mean, he recently bought himself a new boat, and I know he and Amanda are up to their eyeballs in debt—they just bought a new house near the water in Bayshore."

I swallowed hard, remembering the opulence of the Havens' beach house. Tacky, yes, but opulent nonetheless.

"I'm getting on the next train out, Sage. I'll meet you at the house."

"No, you won't."

I sighed. "No, I mean it. I'm packing my bag right now."

"No, I mean I won't be at the house. Vince is cooking me dinner at his place."

"Sage, don't go over to Vince's until I get there."

"Excuse me, Zoe, but I think we just eliminated Vince as a suspect, did we not?"

I hesitated, then said, "Look, Sage, we can't be sure how high up this thing goes. Vince could be in on it, too."

"Need I remind you that Vince spent most of the past year in China? And then Italy. Why don't you trust my instincts for a change?"

"Okay, okay," I said, hearing the anger in her voice. "But promise me you won't talk to him about it?"

"Zoe—"

"Just promise me," I insisted. "At least until after we talk to Tom about what's going on. And I think we should do that together, Sage."

She sighed. "All right. I'll wait for you. I have the invoices with me but I'm not sure what time Tom is getting to the beach tonight. I guess we can talk to him in the morning."

"Okay, I'll see you out there, then."

"See you at the beach."

Nick
Busted

"What ferry did you say your dad was coming on?"

Francesca narrowed her eyes at me, as she braced herself on the bathroom vanity. "I didn't. But he's not here now. So why don't we stop talking and start fucking."

I smiled down at her. "You got some mouth on you, little girl."

"And you love it," she said, pulling my hips until my erection had nowhere to go. Except in her, of course.

Ahhhh. Oh, man, this was good, I thought, looking up into the mirrors that surrounded us, gazing at Francesca's hair falling over her back, her sweet little ass sliding backward on the counter as I pounded her. Clearly Sage and Zoe had gotten the better bedroom out of this deal. Who knew their bathroom had such possibilities?

"Harder," Francesca cried out, sinking her teeth into my nipple.

Oh, fuck. That hurt. Not in a bad way.

I pounded harder. So hard, in fact, I thought I might slam her into the mirror. That's all I needed was to break the damn thing. Reaching around, I slid my hands over her ass to brace her, knocking over the water glass on the sink in the process.

Crash!

"Shit!"

"Nick?"

I looked down, though I was fairly certain that wasn't Francesca calling out my name.

"Is that you in there?"

Sage. I froze, staring at Francesca's flushed face. Oh, fuck. Sage must have gotten an early ferry. She was right outside the door!

Something told me that might even be worse than having Tom out there.

I held my finger up to my lips in a shushing motion as I disentangled myself from Francesca's limbs. She smiled up at me, ready to jump off the counter and right out that door, until I stopped her. *Wait here,* I mouthed to her, grabbing a towel and wrapping it around my waist.

I slipped out the door, quickly closing it behind me. "Sage, you're here bright and early," I said, smiling at her.

She folded her arms. "What were you doing in there?"

"Using your shower?"

She narrowed her eyes at me. "I don't hear any water running."

"I was, uh, just finishing up—"

Suddenly the door swung open, and out popped Francesca, wearing only a bath towel and a smug little smile on her face.

"I can't believe you, Nick," Sage said, once Francesca had paraded herself past us and out the bedroom door.

"I can explain," I replied, pulling the towel around my waist tighter, as if it might somehow protect me from the rage I saw in Sage's eyes.

"Oh really?" she replied. "Then what I want to know first is, why you are carrying on your sordid little affair in my bathroom!"

I gave her a sheepish smile. "You've got some awesome mirrors in there."

She shook her head in disbelief. "Nick, this is not funny. The only thing I asked you to do this summer was to steer clear of Tom's daughter—"

"Oh, was that the only thing?" I challenged her, suddenly feeling pretty mad myself. "What about the request that I refrain from talking up my label to your friends? Schmoozing, I think you called it. Or the unspoken request that I disappear into thin air whenever you ran off with one of your boy toys—"

"Maybe you haven't noticed, but I haven't been with any of my so-called boy toys all summer."

"No, you haven't," I agreed. "Except for Chad."

I watched as her face turned bright red. Oops. Bad example. Still, she didn't run my life. "Look, Sage, I'm entitled to a little fun, too, you know. Isn't that the reason you dragged me and Zoe out here? At least I thought that was the reason. But ever since the summer began, it's like we're all living on your fucking planet. And we can't have any fun on Sage's planet. Nooooo. We can only have fun when you want us to have fun, laugh when you want us to laugh—"

"That is so not true."

"Well, it certainly feels like that. Sometimes I think the only reason you keep me and Zoe around is for props on the set of your latest adventure. Hey, folks, tune in as Sage Daniels and Friends Do Fire Island! Hey, don't worry about us friends—we're just walk-ons in the set of Sage's life!"

"Is that what you think? That I don't care about you? That I only invited you out here to make *me* happy?"

Her voice cracked, and I thought I saw tears filling her eyes. Oh, shit.

"I thought I was doing this for all of us!" she cried. "Ever since Bern left town, you seemed so down in the dumps, Nick. And Zoe—" She swiped at the tears that began to run down her face. "Forgive me for giving a shit about you!"

Now I felt like an ass. Especially when Sage sat down on the bed and really started crying.

I sat down next to her. "Sage, I'm sorry."

She looked up at me, her eyes so red *I* felt like fucking crying. When did she get so sensitive and shit? Maybe it was that time of the month.

"I didn't mean that the way it sounded," I began.

"Well, how did you mean it, exactly?"

I sighed. There was no getting out of this conversation. "It's just that's what it feels like sometimes. Like I'm living in the shadow of your happy little life. Everything just seems to come so easy for you."

"Everything comes easy for me?" she said, her eyes going wide. "Goddammit, Nick, how could you say a thing like that?"

Shit. I might as well salt up my foot, because I was bound to put it in my mouth again. Now she was crying even harder. Crying like I hadn't seen her cry in a long time. Come to think of it, I wasn't entirely sure I'd ever seen Sage cry. Not even at her sister's funeral.

Oh, yeah. I guess she hadn't had it so easy.

I reached out, putting my arms around her. "I'm sorry, Sage. I really, really am."

She leaned back to look at me.

"I don't even know what I'm saying half the time," I continued. "Maybe it's because I've had a rough time of things lately, you know? Seems like everything I touch turns to shit. The label—"

"I thought you said things were going well."

"Yeah, they were," I said. "I finally got a little money together. Not too much," I added quickly. "Then I sink most of that money into a band I believe in, only to find out the singer is a fucking head case."

"I'm sorry about Les—"

"It's not your fault." I shook my head. "Anyway, I'm sorting it out, making some new plans. I think it will be okay, but it's hard to trust that, you know?"

"Don't I know it," she said, a smile touching her lips.

Damn, I never felt so glad to see Sage smile.

I smiled right back at her. "So can you blame a guy for taking a little stress relief?"

She looked at me. "Is that all Francesca is to you? Stress relief?"

I thought about that a moment. "Nah, she's a good kid."

"But she's Tom's kid, Nick. And you don't have the greatest track record with women."

"What? I was with Bern for, like, two years."

She raised an eyebrow. "All told. But you guys, like, broke up at least sixteen times. And that was before she even left New York."

"This is different, Sage."

"I hope so. Because if you break Francesca's heart, Tom's going to suffer the consequences. And he's suffered enough this year."

I shook my head. "Don't worry about Tom. To be perfectly honest, I don't think he gives a shit when it comes to Francesca."

"That's not true. He just doesn't know how to show it—"

"I'm telling you, Sage, he practically caught us in the act and seemed just as clueless as ever about his daughter. I think it kinda hurts Francesca, you know?"

"You really like her, don't you?"

I smiled. The gig was up. "Yeah, I guess I kinda do, you know?"

Sage smiled, wrapping her arms around me and giving me the kind of squeeze she used to give me when we were kids.

"Then go be with her," she said, leaning back to look at me. "With my blessing."

"Okay, Mother Sage," I said, and ruffled her hair until she was laughing like I hadn't heard in a long time. Probably all summer long.

44

Sage
I'll take the beach house and the beautiful man (hold the wife and kid).

I was standing on Vince's front porch for only two minutes when it became clear he wasn't there.

Pulling my cell phone out of my bag, I looked at the clock. It was almost six-fifteen. We had plans for six.

With a sigh, I shuffled through my bag, found the e-mail he had sent me with his phone number on it, and dialed.

"Hi," I said, when he answered on the second ring.

"Sage, where are you?"

"I'm at your house. Where are you?"

"I'm sorry. I'm actually glad you called. I got held up. Gabriella was supposed to pick up Sophia earlier, but of course my ex is on her own schedule." He sighed. "I really am sorry. I would have called sooner, but your number was in my car and I was at the house with Sophia."

I bit back on my disappointment. After all, this was what I signed up for when I set my sights on a man with an ex-wife and a kid. "That's fine. I guess I'll just head back to my house."

"No, no. Go inside. The key is hidden on top of the window ledge. I'm right across the water. I just need to throw a few things in a bag and I'm there. Shouldn't be more than forty-five minutes. An hour tops."

"Are you sure?"

"Of course. Make yourself a drink. Sit on the deck and relax." He paused, then added softly, "Besides, I like the idea of you waiting at home for me."

Mmm. So did I. "Then I'll be there waiting."

"Looking forward to seeing you," he said in a husky whisper that sent a warm shiver right down to my toes.

Getting into the house was easy enough. Being in it was another matter. Once I flicked on the lights, flooding the shadowy living area with light, I was very aware of the fact that I was here alone. I hadn't paid much attention to the decor last time I was here—unless, of course, you count the sheets in the bedroom. And without the distraction of Vince, everything suddenly seemed so unfamiliar.

Now, as I dropped my bag down on the plush sofa and glided through the quiet empty rooms, I was all too aware of how little I really knew about Vince.

And reminded of what I did know, I thought, as my eye fell upon a large framed picture hanging on the living room wall. A photograph of a mother and child.

Gabriella and Sophia, I realized, once I'd stepped up to it, studying the dark-haired, attractive woman who sat on a swing chair in a lush garden, a smile touching her lips as she looked down at Sophia, who was curled up in her lap, asleep.

Okay, it was his child, but couldn't he find another picture of Sophia to keep at his house? Like one that didn't feature his ex-wife?

She was the mother of his child, I reminded myself, turning away from the photo, my gaze roaming over the soft pastel sofa, the wicker easy chair, the hand-painted fan that dominated one wall. And apparently, the decorator of this house. The decor was decidedly female. I guess that made sense. They'd probably bought the house together.

Still, it only reminded me how much a part of Vince's life Gabriella was.

I headed to the bedroom, smiling at the memory of me and Vince lying on those cozy white sheets last Saturday, even picking up a pillow to breathe in his scent.

I smiled wider, suddenly feeling like I belonged here.

Deciding to make myself at home, I headed back into the living room and fixed myself a drink at the small bar in the corner.

As it turned out, Vince not only had tequila but good tequila.

Now that's my kind of man, I thought, shaking the ice around in my drink then raising it to my lips to sip.

Now that's my kind of drink, I thought, feeling the burn move down my throat and settle warmly in my stomach.

Opening the sliding glass door, I stepped out onto the deck, studying the wrought-iron patio furniture, which seemed innocuous enough. I pulled the recliner around so that it faced the sun, which was just beginning to set, and settled in.

Not bad, I thought, putting my drink on the deck beside me as I listened to the reeds surrounding me blow in the wind. Not an ocean view, but this cozy little deck had its own merits. Like privacy, I thought, pulling off my tank top to get the full effect of the sun's last rays on my skin.

Mmm. I could get used to this. I *was* used to this, I thought with a smile. The beach was the only place I had ever found peace. And now, I thought, as a vision of me and Vince in an intimate tangle on this very recliner filled my mind, perhaps I would find more.

Of course, just as soon as I got comfortable, my cell phone rang. I thought about letting it go, then gave in to it, jumping up and heading to the living room to retrieve it from my bag.

My mother, I thought, once I looked at the caller ID.

"Hi," I said, suddenly remembering that I should have called her. The Keep Hope Alive festival began last night. How had I forgotten that?

"Sage, how are you, honey?"

"I'm good, how are you?" I said, returning to the deck and the recliner. "How's the festival going? Things get off to a good start?"

"A wonderful start. We did *Cat on a Hot Tin Roof* last night. You should have seen Janice Woodrow in the role of Maggie. She was *stunning*. I wish you could have been there to see it."

"I'm sorry." I hesitated. "I would have if I didn't have so much going on."

"Where are you now?"

"I'm at the beach."

"Oh," she replied. Then she added, "Well, you work so hard. You need your downtime, right?"

"Right," I said, wondering if she even believed the excuses I gave for why I rarely came out to the house anymore. I remembered the avalanche of feeling I had suffered last week, the relief I had felt in the tears that had flowed when I had allowed myself to remember my sister. And I had thought about Hope a lot this week. More than I had in years.

"So what's next on the agenda for the festival?" I asked.

"Well, tomorrow night we're doing a series of ten-minute plays. And Sunday night we're doing *Peter Pan* for the kids. Your father did all the set designs. And you'll never guess who's playing Peter Pan—Charlie!"

I rolled my eyes, trying to imagine Charlie, who was fifty if he was a day, donning green tights to play Peter Pan. But I guess he was tiny. And in my parents' world, there was a role for everyone. Even me, I realized, thinking of how many years I had tried to play caretaker to my parents. Always worrying about how they were going to eat, how they were going to live. Maybe for a change, I could just be me.

Which was why I probably found myself saying, "Hey, maybe I can take an early ferry on Sunday and catch the last show."

"Oh, Sage, that would be wonderful! You know how much we'd love to see you."

I did know, which was why her words sent a stab of guilt through me. But I shook it off. "I'm looking forward to seeing you, too."

And I realized, for the first time in a long time, I was.

Maybe it was the comfort I took from my conversation with my mother. Or maybe it was the tequila, but I found myself drifting off to sleep in Vince's cozy little recliner. I didn't fight it. After all, these were the lazy days of summer, right?

I was awakened abruptly by the sound of the sliding glass door opening behind me.

Lynda Curnyn

Blinking, I smiled when I saw Vince standing above me, looking at me rather hungrily.

But then, I was topless.

"Well, hello stranger," I said, my body tightening with anticipation.

45

Maggie
Be careful who you lust for.

When a woman thinks of having an affair, she's not looking for a man with a pension plan or a fat 401K. She's looking for a man who will love her like no other. Who would die at the thought of losing her and would risk everything to be with her.

Maybe I'd listened to one too many rock ballads, but I had been looking for that kind of man all my life. It didn't take me long to figure out that Donnie Havens was not him. Donnie was more "Paradise by the Dashboard Light," which was why I never fell prey to him. I was looking for a man who was more "Baby, I'm Amazed."

And I found that man in Vince Trifelli.

Before I met Vince, all I knew was the myth Tom fed me. Of the man who had befriended Tom when he was first starting out in New York. Of the partner who risked everything to help bring Luxe into being. Of the pioneer who traveled to China with a young wife, even started a family there, as he set up Tom's manufacturing overseas.

Vince Trifelli had become almost a legend in my mind. Imagine my surprise to discover, when I finally met him, just how very human he was.

Vince returned home from China an exile. His wife greeted

him with a divorce, his child hardly knew him. I guess I understood how abandoned he felt. Tom hadn't left me, but he had abandoned me in every way that really mattered. I felt as alone in the world as Vince seemed when he first came to the apartment on E. 64th Street. Which was probably why I befriended him, invited him over time and time again, fed him meals and listened late into the night while he told me of the pain of losing Gabriella and Sophia. Ironically enough, I fell in love with the way he loved his wife and child. In love with the shadow of pain in his eyes that mirrored the pain I felt.

Maybe this was what bound us together. Or maybe it was the fact that I discovered, during all those late-night talks we shared long after Tom had turned in, that Vince and I had a lot in common. Like me, he had grown up poor. Like me, he had spent his youth living in the shadow of the city, though his was more of a hard-knock life on the streets of Brooklyn. Like me, he had married into money. Apparently Gabriella D'Ambrosio was the one who held the keys to the kingdom in their relationship. But when Vince told me how he had made his way in New York, starting out in shipping and moving up to start his own exporting business, I understood why Gabriella had fallen in love with him. It was clear to me that Vince was not the type to hang on to anyone else's coattails. He had his pride, almost too much of it, I sometimes thought. But I suppose I even loved that about him, too.

Which was why, when he told Tom he wanted to introduce some leather products into the Luxe lineup, I encouraged the idea. Vince had developed relationships with a few tanneries and was eager to expand Luxe's offerings. Tom was hesitant at first. Luxe had suffered a lean season, and he was wary about growing the business at that point. But when he agreed to allow Vince to develop a few accessories for Luxe—some handbags, belts and even a few jacket styles, it was I who opened the champagne the night Vince came over, triumphant that he had just put through his first contract with the tanneries. Tom wasn't home yet, so Vince and I toasted together, again and again, until we found ourselves settled together in the living room, drunk on the promise of future success. I remember that night as clearly as the night I died—how Vince looked at me, his eyes growing sad as he said he had hoped to realize this dream with Gabriella by his side. "I guess you never really know someone, do you?" he said.

Ironic that those were the words he uttered just moments before he kissed me for the first time. He obviously knew me well enough to understand that such tragic romantic talk was the kind of thing I lived for. Of course, nothing happened that night. Nothing except for a few heart-wrenching statements from Vince about how he couldn't do this to Tom, how he had to let me go before it was too late.

And then he was gone. Off to Italy to pursue his new dream. Leaving me with a longing so deep I could barely live with my illusions about my marriage anymore.

By the time Vince came back, two years later, I was putty in his hands. When he told me how much he had thought about me while he was gone, I believed him. When I watched him struggle with the idea of betraying Tom, I killed all his arguments with a kiss.

Thus began the affair that consumed me for the better part of a year. And it wasn't just stolen afternoons that we shared, but also dreams. Vince wanted to grow the leather portion of the business and began talking about a new urban line of outerwear. Spurred on by the glow of ambition in his eyes, I echoed his vision to Tom. Tom didn't need much encouragement. The leather goods Vince had already developed had taken off, and Tom had himself been thinking along the lines of expansion.

When Edge was born, I had the joy of participating in the dream. The sorrow of realizing that that dream would take Vince away from me. Of course, he promised to come back for me, once he successfully got the manufacturing under way. So I was content to wait, even taking a job at Edge just after the first successful trade show with some idea my work there might keep me closer to the man I loved.

But that's the thing about romance with a capital *R*. You can't get too close to it. Otherwise, you'll find it to be as fleeting as your last orgasm.

46

Zoe
Last stop: Kismet

Myles was waiting for me at the dock. I gave myself about thirty seconds to relish that fact, along with the glow of concern in his golden brown eyes. But of course, he was only waiting there because I'd called him in a panic from the train and let him in on all the latest developments.

"Hey," I greeted him, feeling an almost Pavlovian urge to kiss him. Isn't that what one did when one met a loved one at the dock?

"Hey," he said, leaning forward to grab my backpack.

Okay, that was chivalrous. I'll take what I can get.

"What the hell do you have in this thing?" he said, holding it up.

"Stuff," I said. "Never mind that. We have to hurry."

He put the pack on the ground. "Hurry where, exactly?"

I looked at him. "To Donnie Havens's house."

Myles's eyes widened. "Zoe, we can't just go over there and starting shooting off accusations. That guy could be dangerous."

I smiled. "That's what you're here for. You do still practice karate, right? Or did you give that up, too?"

"Zoe, it won't matter what I practice if Donnie has a gun. I think we should call the police."

I rolled my eyes. "A fat lot of good that'll do us. They're still working on the Who Killed Chad mystery. They don't even realize this is bigger than Chad. Besides, Donnie Havens doesn't have a gun."

"There's no way you could know that, Zoe."

"He's a coward, Myles. I'll put money on it that if we put a little pressure on him, he'll crack."

"Zoe, let's just call the police—"

"For what? So they can tell me I'm imagining things? We can't let this guy get away with—"

"And I can't let you risk our lives just because you feel a need to play the hero."

Now I was angry. This had nothing to do with heroics and everything to do with justice. Two innocent people were dead. I looked him in the eye. "Fine. If you won't come with me, I'm going it alone." Picking up my bag, I strode off ahead of him.

I made it to the Kismet sign before he caught up with me. "I'm not letting you go alone, Zoe."

I fought to keep from collapsing under the weight of the relief I felt. The last thing I wanted to do was face Donnie Havens alone. I started walking again.

"Wait," Myles said.

I turned to look at him.

"Are you planning on clubbing him with this bag, or can we drop it off somewhere?"

"Oh, right." I thought about this a moment. We could drop it off at the house, but I didn't really want to get involved with Tom or Nick or anyone else who might be there. Besides, Donnie might go out for the evening, and I didn't want to miss him.

I turned to look at The Inn, which was already starting to fill up with early evening diners coming to watch the sunset. "Follow me," I said, marching off to the bar.

"Hey, Danny," I greeted the bartender as I approached. Leaning over the bar, I gave him a smile. "Do you think you could do me a favor?"

"Anything for you, gorgeous."

I liked Danny. "Do you think you could stash this bag behind the bar? I'll come back for it later."

"Sure thing," he said.

I turned to Myles, who handed the bag over the top of the bar, practically glaring at Danny while he did.

Oh, wow. Was he jealous, or what?

"Thanks, Danny," I said. Then I headed out of the bar, Myles at my heels.

"You were flirting with that guy," Myles said once we were outside again.

"Was I?" I asked, genuinely curious. Maybe I did know how to flirt after all.

"Yeah, you were, all right."

I glanced at him as we passed the market. He was jealous!

Okay, so I felt a little glad about that.

As we passed the dock, I spotted Donnie's boat. "Well, he's on the island. Let's just hope he's home," I said, my eye roaming down the line of boats and falling on the *Sweet Sophia,* which was parked in the second to last slip, near the hotel.

I thought of Vince's daughter, Sophia, and wondered if this might be his boat. Then I realized it couldn't be. This was a private ship, and I hadn't seen Vince's name on the list of private shipowners. Well, whatever. I could only assume Sage's ship had come in tonight. And if she was enjoying her evening with Vince, I was glad. Not only because I wanted Sage to be happy—and it was clear she thought Vince would make her happy—but it might keep her out of my hair while I sorted this whole thing out.

"Let's boogie," I said, picking up speed as we headed down West Lighthouse Walk.

"Nice spread," Myles said as we approached Donnie's house.

"Yeah. I guess this is what blood money buys you," I replied. "Wait till you see the inside. Tacky as hell."

"Zoe," he said, grabbing my arm before I could make my way up the wooden walkway. "We're not going inside."

"Okay, okay," I said, yanking my arm out of his grip and raising it to knock on the outside door.

And knock. And knock. No one answered, despite the fact that the front door was wide open. Before Myles could stop me, I swung the door open, stepping inside, leaving him to do nothing but follow me, muttering something about my stupidity.

Music wafted in from the back deck. Damn, what if he wasn't alone? I'll make him come to the front of the house with me, I decided, heading for the sliding glass door.

I stepped through the door, Myles at my back, and discovered that Donnie wasn't alone. Far from it. He was in the hot tub with a brunette who looked vaguely familiar.

And I knew it wasn't Donnie's wife.

Dolores Vecchio, I realized, finally placing her. The broker who sold Tom and Maggie their house. I'd seen her at Tom's Fourth of July party.

"Who let you in here?" Donnie said, standing up in the tub.

I was relieved to discover he at least had a bathing suit on. "Door was wide open, Donnie. You'd think you'd be a little more discreet." My gaze flicked to Dolores. "Under the circumstances."

"You get outta here before I call the police."

"You probably don't want to do that, Mr. Havens," Myles said.

Mr. Havens. That was Myles. Always so polite. "Look, Donnie, we need to talk. I'd prefer not to do it in front of your mistress. I, at least, still have some respect for your wife."

Dolores narrowed her eyes.

But Donnie hopped out of the tub, toweling himself off as he stepped past us through the sliding glass doors.

I followed, and though I knew Myles wasn't happy about it, he did, too.

"Now what's this about?" he barked once we stood in his living room.

"It's about Maggie Landon."

He narrowed his eyes. "What about her?"

"I want to know exactly where you were the night she died."

He rolled his eyes. "I told you already. I was playing poker with my buddies."

"We have a witness who saw you at the Kismet dock the night she died," I said, hoping he would take the bait. "And it wasn't Chad."

"Chad? Who the fuck is Chad?"

"The dock boy who died last week."

His eyes widened. "I had nothing to do with that. I was at a block party over on Pine. Ask anybody who was there."

"And what about the night Maggie died? You weren't on the dock that night?"

"Not the Kismet dock, no."

"Oh, but you were at one of the docks on Fire Island. Maybe Saltaire? I understand Dolores has a nice little house in Saltaire. Maybe you parked your boat in her slip? So to speak."

His face turned beet-red as he realized his error. "Look, I may have been on Fire Island that night," he said, glancing back at the deck, "but I had nothing to do with what happened to Maggie. I loved Maggie."

"Did you love her enough to forgive her for going to Tom about your affair? Or the fact that you were skimming profits out of his business?"

"What the hell are you talking about?"

"Donnie, don't bullshit me," I said, feeling very glad Myles was beside me. "We know about the jackets you were pulling off all those shipments."

"Jackets? I have no idea what you're—"

"Look, you animal, don't play innocent. We have evidence. Shipping invoices with jackets ordered that are nowhere near the number of skins paid for. And the invoices all have your signature on them."

He shook his head. "Now you're talking crazy. I don't fill out the invoice, and if I alter it, I need to get a signature from my boss to do so. If receivable is showing less coats than the purchase order indicates I should have, then that's someone in manufacturing. Only they can alter the invoice before the shipment. Not me."

"Manufacturing?" I asked now.

"Yeah, the factory—where they make the coats," he said, looking at me as if I were some sort of a dimwit. "Whatever happens in China, I have nothing to do with."

"China?"

"Yeah, that's where the factories are. And that's where the shipments come from. Only someone in manufacturing has the authority to change an invoice."

I looked at Myles and I knew with a glance he was thinking the same thing I was.

Vince Trifelli.

47

Nick
Busted, part two. And this time I think I'm going down.

It had to be a nightmare. There was no other explanation for the fear that crept over me at the sound of Tom's voice, shouting my name.

Dammit. I squeezed my eyes shut, rolling over in the bed and making contact with a soft, warm body. Francesca, I realized, opening my eyes and remembering where I was. In the purple room. Francesca's room. We'd come here for round two and I must have fallen asleep.

"Nick, where the hell are you?"

Oh, shit. This was no nightmare. I sat up, jostling Francesca awake as I did, not sure whether to run for my boxers or for cover.

I didn't get a chance to do either.

The door popped open. "Francesca, have you seen—" Tom began, then stopped, his eyes widening. "What the hell is going on here?"

"Daddy!" Francesca squealed. I glanced at her. For all her past shenanigans, she looked as scared as I felt. I suppose there was some comfort in that.

But not much.

"Get your ass out of that bed. Now!"

I wasn't sure who he was talking to at that point, but at least I had the sense to grab on to the top blanket when Francesca leaped off the bed, taking the sheet with her.

"Francesca, go to your room!" Tom shouted, his face turning a shade redder when he remembered she *was* in her room. With me.

He shook his head. "Never mind. You stay here. And you," he said, turning his gaze on me, which I swear, was like a fucking madman's, "come with me!"

He had barely slammed out of the room before I pulled on my shorts, hurrying for the door as I did. I glanced back at Francesca, whose eyes were wide with the first emotion I had seen out of her. And it was genuine fear.

A curl of protectiveness wound through me. "Don't worry, baby. I'll get us out of this."

If I survive this, I thought the minute I stepped into the kitchen and saw Tom standing by the kitchen island, shaking with fury.

But Tom wasn't looking at me. He was rifling through a briefcase he had laid on the counter.

For a moment, I swear to God, I thought about making a run for it. I'd seen enough Bond movies to know that briefcases were the perfect hiding places for guns. But Tom didn't pull out a gun, just a single slip of paper, which he proceeded to wave furiously in my face.

"What the hell is this?"

I leaned in as close as I dared, squinting to make out the writing on what looked like a check. A canceled check. I couldn't make out the payee, but I didn't have to. I knew exactly what it was. And who it was from.

"I can explain—" I began.

"Oh really?" Tom replied, a sickly smile crossing his face. "Then why don't you start with a damn good reason why my wife gave you a check for twenty-five thousand dollars not three days before she died!"

I sucked in a breath, suddenly realizing what this looked like. And it wasn't good.

The phone began to ring and I stared at it, praying whoever was on the other end might somehow save my sorry ass.

"Um, don't you think you should get that?" I asked, when I realized Tom wasn't even making a move for it.

"Never mind that. Now start talking."

I stared at his angry eyes as the phone rang and rang, like some kind of death toll. Tom must've turned off the answering machine.

And then it stopped.

Swallowing hard, I began to babble. "Look, Tom, I know how this looks and all, what with Maggie's murder and everything—"

Tom's eyes narrowed. "Murder? Who said anything about murder?"

Shit. Now I'd really fucked up. "It was just a crazy theory of Zoe's. This thing between Maggie and me had nothing to do with that. She was interested in my label and wanted to put up a little money so—"

"Wait!" Tom demanded, holding up a hand. "Back up a second. Zoe thinks my wife was murdered?"

I blew out a breath. Now I'd really done it. "Like I said, it was just a theory. And I want you to know, I never thought for a minute—not one minute—that you did it—"

"Me? What the hell are you talking about?"

Oh shit, oh shit, oh shit.

Now my phone began to ring, vibrating in the pocket of my shorts. "Um, do you mind?" I said, whipping it out and snapping it open before Tom could stop me.

"Hello?"

"Nick!" came Zoe's breathless voice over the line. "Where's Tom? I need to talk to him."

I looked at Tom.

"Hang up that phone this instant!" he barked.

"He's, uh, busy at the moment." I turned away slightly. "Maybe you should come home."

"Nick, I haven't got time for that. Now give me Tom!"

"Zoe, I think he's going to kill me," I whispered, glancing back at Tom.

"What? Nick, please just put him on the damn phone!"

I turned back toward Tom, holding out the phone. "It's for you."

He looked about ready to smack the phone out of my hand.

"It's Zoe," I said, hoping maybe she'd explain this whole mess to him better than I possibly could.

He snatched the phone out of my hand.

"Zoe, what's this business about—" He paused. "What's that? Slow down, I can't understand you." He frowned. "Vince? He lives over on Seabay. Sixth house from the beach. Why? What's that? Yes, his wife's family owns the house. I already told you that." He shook his head. "Yes, the dock slip, too. Now what's this about?" He paused. "The police? Why should I call—"

He froze, his eyes narrowing as he listened. "Why would he hurt Sage?"

He listened for a few more moments. Then realization dawned in his eyes. "How do you know that?" He shook his head again, his face turning redder. "Son of a bitch!" He paused to listen again. "I'll meet you there."

Then, he disconnected and quickly dialed again, a coolness coming over his face. "I need a police officer right away," he began, then rattled off an address on Seabay. "It's an emergency. A woman's life is in danger."

My eyes widened as he explained that he had strong reason to believe that Sage—my Sage—was in the hands of a criminal.

"I'm coming with you," I said, once he hung up the phone.

"Please, stay here with my daughter," he said. Then, before I could answer, he raced down the hall to his bedroom.

And when he returned, he had a gun in his hand.

48

Maggie
Dying is easy. It's living that's hard.

Vince once told me that he had waited his whole life to meet a woman like me. Naturally I believed him. Hadn't I waited my whole life for a man like him?

The night I died I went to Vince's house wanting desperately to believe that man still existed. That the deception I had uncovered the day before was just some meaningless human error rather than the act of a man desperate for revenge.

I wouldn't even have discovered Vince's treachery if I hadn't been so bent on being the loving, supportive woman to him that I had previously been to Tom. When Yaz called me that Friday to say she had our production manager from China on the line, I took the call, knowing Vince was in transit. I had, after all, been anticipating his arrival all week, feeling keenly all the months I'd lived without him.

Henry's English wasn't great, but I managed to make out that he needed to verify the number of units he was to produce on a style in Italian lamb. According to the payment order for the skin, which he'd looked up in Vince's absence, he was expecting twice the amount of skin he had anticipated and was frantic that he wouldn't be able to fulfill the order in time. Of course I looked into things at my end and discovered that the payment order was wrong, and the number of units Henry was to produce hadn't changed. Which relieved his mind and inflamed my own curiosity.

Thinking back on that day, I almost wished I hadn't asked Henry to fax me the payment orders on future shipments. But once I had them in my hand, I couldn't deny the truth. I wanted to, oh God, I wanted to. Even shoved those invoices in a folder in the back of the drawer when I couldn't get hold of Vince. I guess I still hoped he might have some explanation for the discrepancies I'd found. Something that might help me to believe I was not some pawn in his plot against my husband, but the woman he loved too much to betray.

I went to the beach as planned, though not even my sanctuary at the shore could ease my state of mind. No one knew the dread I was living in while I waited to hear back from Vince. I had already learned to hide behind the facade of the perfect wife, and that weekend I was in rare form. Maybe I was trying to hold on to my sanity, some piece of myself I still recognized, but suddenly I was like a mad housewife, scrubbing down the kitchen as soon as I arrived, fussing over my plants. On Saturday, when I still hadn't heard from Vince, I even began hatching plans for a big dinner party, believing I might somehow block out all my uneasiness by submerging myself in my familiar role as the consummate hostess.

By the time Vince did call, I had even managed to convince myself that my life was the same. That everything would be okay. Which was probably why I accepted his hurried excuses. He said he would explain everything when he saw me. And maybe it was because of the way he huskily suggested we take a suite together at the Palace Hotel the following week that I didn't argue. Didn't even feel miffed when he said he was going to Gabriella's that night to take care of Sophia, who had come down with a virus. Not that I had anything against his daughter, except for those times she kept me from being with him.

Then my big dinner plan fell apart, and I nearly fell to pieces. I think I managed to alienate everyone that night. Sage, who I'd blasted for jumping ship on me. Tom, who was disappointed to come home and find his wife standing frozen with indecision over a half-made meal. Only Nick seemed to have any sympathy for me, offering me an ear when I sobbed out all my misguided anger at my husband, and then suggesting that perhaps he and I have a nice dinner together at The Inn.

I was heartened by Nick's invitation, because really, that record label he had told me about weeks earlier was the only dream I had left, now that I feared the future I had hoped for with Vince was over. I could start anew, I thought, putting my sauce aside to finish once Zoe arrived with the coriander. After taking a quick shower, I felt better. So much better, I even threw on a dress. It was, after all, Saturday night. And I was still young enough to enjoy it.

But not strong enough, I realized when I walked to The Inn and saw Vince's boat at the dock.

All I could see was the lie. He was supposed to be with his daughter that night. I wondered how many lies he had told me. By the time I got to his house, I had convinced myself that he was there with Gabriella. That this was all a plot to earn enough money to win back his wife and child. He had told me often enough, after his divorce, how bitter he was that his wife deserted him when he was at his worst.

But if he was surprised to see me, I was even more surprised to discover he was alone, looking just as handsome as the day I met him and a bit bewildered by my attitude. I was so relieved to see him alone, I was ready to accept anything he told me, within limits. Of *course* the error had come from the tannery. It made perfect sense once Vince explained it all to me over a glass of wine. But when Vince suggested we keep this indiscretion from Tom, something in me rebelled. Vince claimed he wanted to protect his relationship with the tannery, which spurred in me an opposing desire to protect my husband. Maybe it was the pang of jealousy I felt when Vince emphasized his close ties to the Lorenzo family. After all, could those ties be greater than those he felt for the woman he professed to love?

Or maybe it was my realization that as much as I loved Vince, I couldn't betray Tom in the one area of his life that mattered most to him. My husband's business was everything to him. Compromising that could destroy him. And as much as I wanted something for myself, my urge to protect Tom in that moment was greater.

I insisted that he tell Tom everything. And I'll admit that I saw something flicker in Vince's eyes when he saw my allegiance to Tom. "Don't you trust me?" he had asked. "Of course," I had replied carefully, feeling that trust already begin to fade. But any doubts I felt were dispelled when Vince promised to talk to Tom in the morning.

I should have realized then that I wouldn't live to see the next morning. But I was too far gone at that point. Hopped up on one too many Valiums I'd taken to soothe my state of mind, and positively pliant by the time we finished that bottle of wine in Vince's living room. He looked so precious to me in that moment, gazing into my eyes with what I thought was love.

"I guess I should take you home," he said, and even looked sad at the idea. We had just stepped out onto the beach to make our way back, and as I looked up at the waves crashing on the shore, the moon high in the sky, I realized I didn't want to go home to my husband. I wanted to spend this night with Vince. Maybe some part of me understood that something between us had ended that night. Maybe I wanted to hold on to what I thought was still left.

We kissed for a long time, standing there as if neither of us wanted to let go. But then Vince did let go, a smile lighting his eyes as he yanked his shirt over his head. I was scared immediately—and I wish now that I had trusted that instinct. We had always been so discreet, and though the idea of making love on that beach pulled at me, it was too dangerous.

But Vince didn't want to make love. Instead, he dared me into the water with him. I laughed at him at first, feeling shy. I wasn't, after all, the kind of woman who would do something so spontaneous, so free, as to strip down to nothing and plunge into the ocean.

But I was once, I remembered. Before I became Maggie Landon, trophy wife, I was that kind of girl.

The water was so cold I swam into Vince's arms, seeking warmth. Then shivered when I saw the light in his eyes was gone, leaving only hate.

I guess Vince was right. You never really do know someone, do you?

I should have fought him. Maybe it was the Valium and the wine, but I wasn't thinking about survival in that moment.

I was thinking about the fact that I was about to be reduced to a statistic.

That no one would think any more of my death than they did of my life.

That I would never inspire a song, never really fall in love.

Which only made me wonder if I had ever really been in love. I had loved Vince mostly because of the way he loved me.

And now I didn't even have that.

49

Sage
Not your everyday skin flick.

If I felt like the wanton mistress when Vince came home and ravaged me right there on the back deck, I was starting to feel like
the little wife as I stood in the kitchen, draped in his button-down
shirt, watching him slice garlic for the sauce he was making. He
even looked like the handsome husband in a T-shirt and jeans, his
dark hair tousled and his face shadowed and sexy with stubble.

Correction: the *hot* husband. Which, really, was the only husband I wanted, if any.

Now, as he made us dinner, he even shared tidbits of his day.

Which meant his day at the office, thank God. I didn't really need
to hear any more about the wife and kid. Not tonight anyway.

But I liked listening to him talk about Edge. It felt like we were
sharing a dream.

"So the short of it is," he continued, sliding the freshly sliced
garlic into a sauté pan, "it looks like we'll have the styles we did
in crocodile finished in time for the fall launch."

I smiled. "That's a relief. I would hate to go out into the market half-assed."

He raised an eyebrow at me. "Well, we'd hardly be going in half-
assed, but I'm glad to be able to provide the variety. It'll be a nice

boost for the brand. Besides, I think we already used one of the crocodile jackets in our advertising."

"That's right," I replied, popping a freshly washed cherry tomato into my mouth. "I'd like to have the inventory on hand once the orders start rolling in." I tossed the remaining tomatoes into the salad I had prepared, my mind moving to the other inventory problem I had discovered earlier today. Yes, I had promised Zoe I would wait to talk to Tom, but now that I was with Vince, wrapped in the intimacy I felt whenever I was in his presence, I realized that Zoe's worries were just that: worries. There was no reason why I shouldn't find answers to the questions that had scratched at my mind ever since I'd found those invoices. And since Vince was the VP of manufacturing, I was sure he could at least shed some light on the situation. "Vince, I wanted to ask you about something strange I noticed in some of the invoices for Edge."

"What invoices?" he asked, turning to tend to the garlic in the pan, which had already begun to perfume the room with its heavenly scent.

"Receivables. You know, for jackets received by the warehouse," I said. "We just started to get some of our shipments in for fall, and I found some discrepancies between them and some payment orders I came across."

I saw his shoulders stiffen momentarily, his head rising slightly before he resumed his sautéing. "Oh, that kind of thing happens all the time. Sometimes we lose skins due to quality control."

I laughed. "Quality control? That's an awful lot of skin to lose to quality control. One of those payment orders was for double the amount of skin needed for the jackets we received. Then I looked at the purchase orders for our future ships and realized some of those skin orders looked pretty high, too. Anyway, I was going to talk to Tom about it tomorrow, but I wondered—"

Vince shook his head. "Don't worry yourself about it, Sage. Or Tom for that matter. He's got enough to think about. I can talk directly to the tannery. I think I told you I'm on good terms with the Lorenzo family. I'll give Gianna a call on Monday, see what's what."

Now I was the one who stiffened. And not just because he brought up "Miss-Tell-Vince-I'll-Meet-Him-at-the-Hotel," but because I hadn't even told him which tannery was concerned. Mostly because I had assumed shipping was to blame. It hadn't occurred to me that the errors had come from the tannery end. But now that I thought about it, most of those payment orders had come from one tannery.

"What makes you so sure it was the Lorenzo tannery?" I asked lightly, watching his face as he turned to the island again and began to slice mushrooms.

He shrugged, turning to slide the mushrooms into the pan. "Just a guess. We do most of our high-end business with them."

"With Gianna, you mean."

He glanced back at me, as if sensing my sudden tension. "I deal mostly with her, but it's her family's tannery." His gaze moved to my drink. "Looks like you're empty. Can I make you another?"

"No, that's fine. I'll get it," I said, swiping up my glass. "How about you? Another drink?"

"I'm fine, thanks," he said, turning to the stove once more.

I walked to the bar. Filling my glass with ice, I tried to sort the thoughts spinning through my head. If the Lorenzo tannery was putting through payment orders for more skin, then where was all that skin going?

As I poured the tequila, I wondered if maybe Vince's little pal Gianna was ripping us off.

"So, Vince," I said, stepping into the kitchen again. "You know I'm still a neophyte in this business," I continued, leaning up on the counter beside him so I could see his profile as he stood at the stove. "I'm just wondering how it all works. How do you decide how much skin to order for a particular style?"

He raised an eyebrow at me. "The amount of skin ordered is based on the number of units the sales manager gives me for the style." He smiled. "I would have thought you would know that, Sage, seeing as you'll be the one making those unit projections in the future."

And Maggie was the one making those projections in the past. Maybe my first assumption had been right. Maybe Maggie had been ripping off her husband. But something didn't make sense.

"Does she—that is, the sales manager—consult with the tannery about the skins, or does the tannery advise on how much skin is required for a style?"

He shook his head. "Boy, you really *are* a neophyte. Manufacturing puts through all the skin orders."

The back of my neck began to prickle. "You mean *you* do it?"

He nodded. "That's right. Me."

"So I guess you would know if the tannery was inflating the order, right?"

He shook his head. "Really, Sage, you shouldn't worry yourself about this. I told you I would call the tannery on Monday. It's probably a simple mistake."

"A pretty big mistake, don't you think? I mean, if the Lorenzo factory is overcharging us, shouldn't we let Tom know about it?" I asked, wondering if Vince already knew about those inflated orders and wondering why he hadn't done anything about it. Unless he was in tighter with Gianna than I realized, I thought, a sudden vision of Vince and Gianna in an intimate tangle filling my mind.

Vince looked at me. "Look, Sage, it's not a big deal. I'll give the tannery a call on Monday. Like I said, I have a good relationship with them."

I met his gaze. "I'm well aware of your relationship with the Lorenzo tannery," I said, feeling my temperature rise as the truth sank in.

"Sage, if you know what's best for you, you'll stay out of this."

But I was already in so deep, I couldn't help the anger thrumming through me at the thought of Vince sharing not only pillow talk with Gianna, but profits. "You cocky son of a bitch. What kind of fool do you take me for? Did you really think you could skim money out of Tom's business and no one would notice?"

The moment I said the words, I realized someone *had* noticed. Maggie.

Oh, God.

Vince must have seen the realization on my face. Not that he seemed ruffled by it. On the contrary. He smiled, a coldness moving into his eyes.

"Well, Sage, I've got to give you credit. It took Maggie a lot longer to figure it out. But then again, I already had Maggie's loyalty," he said, his gaze steady on mine. "And her heart."

A pain so sharp moved through me I thought I might crumble under the weight of it. Dammit, was that what all this wining and dining was about? Was he trying to make me a player on his team? But then I remembered the team I *was* on, and fresh anger filled me. "How could you do that to Tom? He was your best friend...."

"Tom." He laughed bitterly. "If it wasn't for me, Tom would be nowhere. Who do you think set him up in this business?"

"Tom didn't need you. He was born into this business."

"Yeah, well, he's got you snowed just like he's snowed everyone else. Tom Landon would have been nothing without Daddy Landon to give him a leg up. But Tom wanted to prove himself when he came to New York. He was Mr. Big Shot boasting about starting up his own company. But he was nobody in New York—nobody. Not until I hooked him up with all my contacts. He *owes* me."

"Owes you? What, being a VP in his company wasn't enough for you, Vince?"

"Not when I was a principal once. I sank a lot of money into Luxe, Sage. Borrowed money. But as soon as Tom got back into Daddy Landon's heart, he cut me out of the picture. After I gave him everything, he cut me off."

"Cut you off? He gave you the Chinese operation to run."

"He didn't give that to me. He only shipped me off there when he realized that someone had to pay for the deal we had made with the Locusio family."

My eyes widened. Tom dealing with the mob? "I don't believe you."

"Well, believe it, Sage. I may have been the one who took the loan, but somebody had to come up with the other half of the money to get Luxe off the ground. Tom was too proud to go to his father. So I used my contacts, made a little deal, and sank the cash into Luxe. But the business took longer than expected to show a profit, and Joey Locusio is not a patient man. Suddenly, I got the mob on my ass and no one to turn to but Tom. Of course, Tom acted all high-and-mighty. Like he didn't know where I got all that money from. But he's not as innocent as he looks. He knew. You think he gave me China out of friendship? No, Sage, that was guilt. After he tucked his tail between his legs and hit up Daddy Landon for the cash, he bought me out. Then he acts like the big hero, shipping me off to China, like he was doing me a fucking favor. Some favor. I lost everything when I went there. My family—"

"You lost your wife because you're a criminal, Vince." I shivered, remembering Maggie. "And now you're a murderer."

It was the wrong thing to say. And perhaps if I had been thinking about it, I might not have said it at all. But I wasn't thinking. I was so blinded by anger and hurt—for Tom, for Maggie, for Chad, that poor innocent kid—that I didn't even realize the danger I had put myself in until Vince was suddenly up close and personal, his hands wrapped around my neck.

I struggled against him, my knee going up to his groin. But Vince was quicker, blocking my attempt, his hands tightening on me.

Even as I fought, I felt myself sinking under the weight of him, my eyes moving to his dark gaze as I gasped for air. Still, I moved restlessly beneath him, my hands reaching for his face, his eyes....

For the briefest moment, I believed I might even win this battle, so energized was I by the hatred I glimpsed in his gaze.

Until my head hit the ground.

And darkness closed in on me.

50

Zoe
I don't need to save the whole world. Just my world.

"If anything happens to Sage, I swear I'll never forgive myself," I muttered breathlessly, picking up speed once we hit Seabay—Vince's block.

"Nothing is going to happen to her, Zoe," Myles said, his voice full of conviction, though he was running just as hard as I was.

I was trying not to imagine the worst. Trying not to think about the fact that Vince had brutally murdered Maggie for discovering what was likely the same scheme Sage had stumbled upon today.

I also tried not to think about what Vince might do to Sage if she even hinted at what she knew.

And there was no way I could bear the thought of Chad, who surely had lost his life simply because he had had the misfortune of being the only witness to Vince's arrival on Fire Island the night of Maggie's murder.

I bit back hard on the realization that Vince's arrogance knew no bounds. He had barely even covered his tracks after doing Chad in.

Which left me with at least one truth I couldn't deny: Vince was clearly capable of anything at this point.

Dear God, please don't let him hurt Sage.

Within moments, we were in front of the house. And just as I began to dart toward the lights that beckoned through the reeds, Myles grabbed my arm, practically wrenching it out of the socket. "Zoe, let me go first."

I pulled free, ignoring his words as I bolted up the wooden ramp to the front door.

It only took one glance through the screen to realize whose body was pinned beneath Vince's on the living room floor.

I flew through the door, grabbing the first object large enough to do damage—a vase propped up on a pedestal.

Heart pounding, I drew up quietly behind Vince, nearly biting off my own tongue as I smashed the vase against his head.

He fell to the side immediately. In fact, the effectiveness of my blow surprised me so much I blinked in confusion. But once the fog cleared, I found myself staring down at Sage, who was pale-faced, motionless....

"Oh, God. Sage!" I cried, dropping to my knees and grabbing her arms. I nearly sobbed with relief when her eyes fluttered open.

"Zoe," she whispered hoarsely, her eyes filling with tears as I cradled her in my arms. I heard Myles behind me and vaguely registered the sound of his voice barking out the address to the police, then slamming down the phone.

But I couldn't miss the warning he yelled out next. "Look out!"

I swung around, just in time to see Vince struggling to his feet.

Just in time to hear a blast shatter through the room, sending Vince sprawling backward, blood spreading quickly across his chest.

But that was nothing compared to the sight of Tom in the doorway, a gun in his hand, his face ashen as he gazed on the man he'd once called his best friend.

Epilogue

Zoe
Summer's over—not a moment too soon.

"Are you guys coming or what? Dinner is on the table!"

I stepped into the kitchen, zipping up the sweatshirt I had slipped on. It was a pretty cold night for October. But then, it was always a little cooler by the shore.

"Coming, Mother," I said, smiling at the sight of Sage, who stood hovering over the feast she had laid out on the dining room table, an exasperated look on her face.

"Where's Nick?" she said, ignoring my jab.

"Still on the phone," I replied, taking the seat opposite her and reaching for the bottle of wine to pour myself a glass. "I think I might have even heard him giggling. Do guys giggle?"

Sage shook her head, but I could see she was fighting a smile. "Only when they're besotted," she said, leaning over to stir the serving bowl of pasta she'd placed at the center of the table. "Everything is getting cold," she continued with a sigh, dropping the spoon and heading over to the kitchen island. I watched as she opened a drawer and reached for the aluminum foil. Then she changed tracks, slamming the drawer shut and stomping out of the kitchen. "Nick, you'd better get your sorry little ass in here!"

I laughed out loud. Which wasn't an uncommon event for me these days.

My gaze moved to the large windows overlooking the living room, and I shivered as the rain lashed against the glass.

It occurred to me that this was the first weekend it had rained at Kismet since we'd been coming out here.

I guess, in some respects anyway, it wasn't such a bad summer after all.

Of course, we hadn't, technically, been out here since that harrowing night at Vince's house. Mostly because Sage hadn't been able to bring herself to return to Kismet after all that had happened. I couldn't blame her. In fact, none of us had come back. Because really, what was the beach without our favorite beach bum and best friend, Sage?

Which was why Nick and I agreed to come immediately when Sage called to say that she wanted to close the house down for Tom. The good news was that Tom's business was back on track and the charges against him in the shooting death of Vince Trifelli had been ruled justifiable homicide. The bad news was that now that the dust had settled, the loss of his wife was hitting Tom pretty hard. In fact, he had gone down to North Carolina with Francesca to visit his family for a couple of weeks, which was why Sage had offered to come to Kismet and shut down Maggie's Dream for the season.

At least that's why she claimed she had come out here. But I had a feeling Sage wanted to put a few demons to rest. And maybe finally even get that fun weekend-at-the-beach with friends she'd been hoping for ever since she had dragged us into this house share.

Okay, so it was October and it was raining. At least I wouldn't get a sunburn.

"Admit it, Nick. You're whipped," Sage said, returning to the kitchen with a somewhat sullen Nick in tow.

"I'm not whipped," Nick protested. "Francesca and I had business to talk about."

I saw Sage smile as she plopped herself down in her chair at the head of the table. "Really? Since when do you call your business partner 'Pookey'?"

Now I was smiling as I watched Nick blush. Pookey? Jesus, I didn't think he had it in him.

But I guess love can do that to you.

"Hey, Sage, I'll call Francesca whatever she wants as long as she secures us that review in *Mojo.*"

Yeah, Nick had it pretty bad for Francesca. Not that he'll ever admit it. At least, not to us. Especially now that Francesca was officially an employee of Revelation. A little condition Tom had made when he agreed to continue to bankroll Nick's label. I had a feeling Tom wasn't just trying to secure his upstart daughter a job, but hoping to remain true to his wife's last wishes. I think he might have even made Nick use some of the ideas from Maggie's business plan for Revelation.

It amazed me how Nick always managed to land on his feet. Not only had he gotten financial backing, but his sex-kitten-turned-publicity-manager actually had a talent for twisting arms and getting people to pay attention to Nose Dive's debut CD.

Not that that was so hard to do, now that the single the band had produced from the CD had hit the airwaves.

It was eerie how "Deeper than the Ocean" had taken off like it had, especially in light of the lyrics, which freaked me out. If I hadn't seen Les pulled from the ocean that night, I would have sworn Maggie had written that song. All those metaphors about dying for love. Then there was that other song he'd penned about a man who kills his wife's lover. If I didn't know better, I would swear Maggie was orchestrating the whole song list from the grave.

Not that I believed in that sort of thing.

"When does the review come out?" Sage asked now.

"Two weeks," Nick said, smiling. "My distributor thinks we'll sell a minimum of thirty thousand copies. And that's only a conservative estimate."

Yep, it was pretty amazing how Nick had pulled out of this one.

"I guess we should have a toast then," Sage said, lifting her glass. "To Nick's first successful CD—"

"Whoa, whoa, whoa!" Nick said. "Let's not get ahead of ourselves. I mean, yeah, it looks like Revelation has a hit on its hands, but I don't want to jinx things by celebrating too soon." He picked up his glass anyway. "Besides, we have something else to toast."

"Oh?" I said, glancing at Nick as I picked up my glass.

He smiled, holding his glass up high. "To being at the beach with my best buds," he said.

Sage laughed as she clinked her glass into ours. "Nick, I didn't know you cared."

Oh, he cared, all right, I thought, smiling as I drank deep. I think I spent more time trying to calm Nick's nerves after he realized how close we had come to losing Sage. But that may have been because Sage wouldn't let anyone coddle her, not even her best friends.

In fact, up until last week, when Sage had called to ask us if we would join her at the beach this weekend, she had been pretty reticent about what had gone down the last time we were in Kismet. "I think it will be good for me to be out there. You know, after everything," she had said on the phone.

I couldn't agree more. In fact, I realized she looked more relaxed tonight than I had seen her in the past few months. Her face had lost that guarded look.

And I knew I wasn't imagining it when, after we had all heaped our plates with food, she finally brought up the "V" word. Well, sort of.

"So Tom finally hired a new VP of manufacturing," she said, her gaze on her fork as she fiddled with the food on her plate.

"Is that right?" I said, studying her expression.

She nodded.

"So are you happy with Tom's choice?" Nick asked, his eyes on her.

Her gaze flicked up over both of us, then she dropped her fork on her plate with a clatter. "Okay, cut the bullshit."

Nick and I exchanged a look. "Umm, what bullshit would that be, Sage?" Nick asked.

She sighed. "You guys have to stop treating me like some kind of fragile little doll every time we even come near the subject of… of Vince."

"We do not!" Nick and I chorused.

"Oh yes, you do," Sage insisted. "Not that I've really let you guys bring up the subject," she relented. She blew out a breath. "Listen, I'm okay. Really. It's not the first time I've fallen for the wrong guy." Then she smiled thinly. "Of course, I usually manage to steer clear of sociopaths."

"Sage, there was no way you could have known—" I began.

"I know. I know, Zoe. Trust me. I haven't spent six weeks talking to a shrink without finally understanding that I'm not to blame for nearly getting myself killed."

My eyes widened and I glanced at Nick, realizing that Sage's having sought professional help was news to him, too.

For a moment, I'll admit, I felt sad knowing that Sage needed more than even her best friends could give her. But I was relieved, at least, that she was getting help.

Now she reached out, grabbing my hand and Nick's in each of hers. "Thanks for coming out this weekend," she said, looking at us before her gaze moved over the living room, pausing on the large windows that practically let the overcast sky and windswept beach into the room. "I was a little afraid he might have ruined Kismet for me." She smiled. "But I'm glad to be back."

Then, before we could descend completely into sappiness, she released our hands. "C'mon, eat. I didn't slave all night over a hot stove to watch my efforts congeal on your plates."

I chuckled when I saw Nick obediently shovel another piece of meat into his mouth and I followed suit with a forkful of pasta.

Sage, however, ignored her own directive, her gaze growing pensive. "I don't know what bothers me more. The fact that Vince actually believed I might turn a blind eye to his betrayal simply because I was sleeping with him. Or the fact that I nearly fell for all that romantic bullshit he laid on me."

"There's no way you could have known what was really going on in that head of his. Maggie hadn't known," I said. "I mean, even I liked him at first."

"Well, you know *I* never liked that guy," Nick said a little too smugly.

I saw Sage struggling not to club Nick over that comment. But at least she was smiling. "I suppose you're going to tell us now that you knew Zoe and Myles would get back together, too."

"Hey, I always liked Myles," Nick said, winking at me. Then he frowned. "How come he didn't come out this weekend?"

"Are you kidding me?" I replied. "He's been swamped with

work. I think he's spending the weekend reviewing his new case-load. Not that he isn't enjoying every minute of it." I smiled as I did whenever I thought of Myles, who had finally realized what was good for him. Like that job he had taken with the Manhattan D.A.'s office.

And me, of course.

I looked at Sage. "Besides, this weekend at the beach was just for us, anyway."

Sage smiled wider, raising her glass once more. "Then perhaps we should have another toast."

Nick and I raised our glasses.

"To friendship," Sage said, her eyes growing a bit misty. "I don't know what I'd do without you guys."

I smiled, feeling a little misty-eyed myself.

Because the truth was, I *didn't* know what I'd do without my best buds.

And I hoped I never had to find out.

"I love you guys," I said, "you know that, right?"

"Love you, too," Sage said.

Even Nick had to confess that we were "okay for a couple of broads."

And the truth was we were okay.

In fact, we were more than okay.

And there was no better feeling on earth.

★ ★ ★ ★ ★

In her new novel, Jody Gehrman, author of *Summer in the Land of Skin,* explores what it means to live a *tart* life.

Claudia Bloom aims to lead a tart life. Meaning she wants everything she does to have that sharpness, that edge of almost-too-out-there to be tasty, but not quite.

After stealing her ex's VW bus, which promptly explodes on the drive from Austin to Santa Cruz, Claudia meets and falls hard for Clay, whose never-mentioned estranged wife is her colleague and whose mother is her boss. Looks like she is on her way....

Available wherever trade paperbacks are sold.

What happens when your cat makes it
to off-Broadway before you do?

Miss Bubbles
Steals the Show
by Melanie Murray

Stella (actress-in-waiting) wasn't home when the
"big break" fairy knocked. But her roommate and cat were.
Her roommate is up for a role on *All My Children* and her
beloved cat (Miss Bubbles) is starring in a prestigious
off-Broadway play with the man of Stella's dreams.
Is it time for Stella to hang up her head shot for good?

**Available wherever
trade paperbacks
are sold.**

From Lauren Baratz-Logsted, author of
The Thin Pink Line and *Crossing the Line*,
comes the most unusual make-under story.

A Little Change of Face

Scarlett Jane Stein has it all—great body, pretty face
and incredible breasts. So when her best friend makes
a comment that Scarlett has gotten everything because
of her good looks Scarlett undergoes a make-under to
become the dowdier, schlumpier Lettie Shaw. But will she
find someone who loves her for who she is inside?
Or will it turn out to be one big mistake?

**Available wherever
trade paperbacks
are sold.**

RED DRESS INK

Meet Sophie Katz

...she's divorced, addicted to caffeine, very protective of her eggs (from ever being fertilized) and doing whatever it takes to survive in San Francisco—especially now that a madman is on the loose and after her.

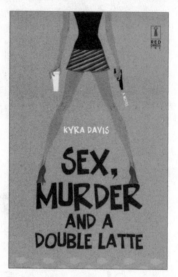

Sex, Murder and a Double Latte
by Kyra Davis

The perfect way to kick off your summer reading.

Available in May wherever hardcovers are sold.

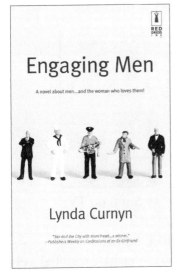
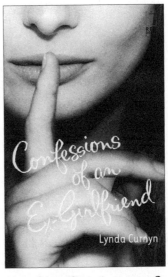

Are you getting it at least twice a month?

Here's how: Try RED DRESS INK books on for size & receive two FREE gifts!

Bombshell
by Lynda Curnyn

As Seen on TV
by Sarah Mlynowski

YES! Send my two FREE books.
There's no risk and no purchase required—ever!

Name (PLEASE PRINT)

Address   Apt. #

City   State/Prov.   Zip/Postal Code

Want to try another series? Call 1-800-873-8635 or order online at www.TryRDI.com/free.